THE MASTER OF STRATHBURN

HIGHLAND ROGUE
BOOK ONE

AMY ROSE BENNETT

DEDICATION

For the love of my life, Richard.
And for my family for always believing in me. I couldn't do any of this
without you xx

PROLOGUE

Lochrose Castle, Strathspey, Scotland
April 16, 1746

"You've got a bloody nerve, Robert."

"Aye, I do." Robert Grant, Viscount Lochrose—also known as the Master of Strathburn and lately "Traitor to the Crown"—squinted through the dark spots clustering his field of vision, trying in vain to focus on his sneering half-brother Simon. The hours-old bayonet wound across his shoulder blade throbbed with such thought-stealing intensity, it was all he could do to stay seated upon his trembling, sweating horse. There was no way he would be able to dismount unassisted. He'd end up with his face firmly planted in the gravel of the forecourt of Lochrose Castle. "But for the love of God, Simon..." Robert continued, his voice no more than a hoarse rasp. "Just help me down. I'm...I'm wounded, for Christ's sake."

He barely recalled the moment the English soldier's blade had sliced across his back. The horror of everything else that had taken place only hours before on Drumossie Moor flooded his mind. Made the nausea rise in his gullet anew.

Simon snorted. "You must've had a blow to the head then, or else

"

you would've remembered that Father forbade you to come back." He glanced past Robert, down the gravel drive toward Lochrose's wrought-iron gates. "You've killed them all, haven't you? It was a rout, just like Father said it would be, wasn't it?" His gray gaze, flint-hard with accusation and long-held resentment, returned to Robert. "He will never forgive you for this."

No doubt. Six-and-thirty Clan Grant men, dead. And I was the arrogant young cock who led them all out like lambs to the slaughter.

Robert swallowed down both the bile and bitter self-acrimony burning his throat. "I know," he croaked. "But please...I just need to hide until I can move on...tomorrow. I'll leave, I promise."

Even though he'd flagrantly disobeyed their father and led out the clan at Culloden, Robert prayed that he would be shown a modicum of compassion. That the earl would at least grant his eldest son and heir sanctuary for a single night before he fled Scotland to spend a life in exile in some far-flung place. Robert didn't want to put his family at risk for harboring a fugitive, but he just couldn't go on any farther.

Simon smiled, the sentiment not quite reaching his glittering eyes. "Of course, dear brother. I shall have a room prepared for you. Anything for family." He gripped Robert's forearm with one hand at the same moment he slapped the blood-soaked plaid sticking to his wounded shoulder.

Bastard.

Agonizing, white-hot pain instantly knifed through Robert. Even as black oblivion at last rose to claim him, he didn't fail to notice that Simon was still smiling.

～

The flickering of a torch in the near pitch-black darkness, the insistent throb of his shoulder, and a cold stone floor beneath him were all that Robert could discern when consciousness eventually returned. All that, and his deep and crushing despair.

Reluctantly cracking open an eye, he grimly absorbed the sight before him. There was to be no mercy for him after all, given that he'd been chained up like a dog in what used to be Lochrose's dungeons, but was now the wine cellar. He had no idea how long he'd been passed out down here, or whether it was day or night. But there was no doubt in his mind that Simon would have already sent for the English dragoons, or at the very least, the local Black Watch regiment by now. It wouldn't be long before he was carted off to be charged with treason.

All thanks to his half-brother.

Unless Father intervened... But at this particular moment, that possibility seemed as unlikely as being granted salvation by the devil himself.

You don't deserve anything, Robert Grant. You should have died on the field like the rest of your Jacobite brothers...

With what felt like a herculean effort, Robert pushed himself to a sitting position, the chain manacled to his left ankle rattling against the unforgiving flagstones, his shoulder screaming in protest. As dizziness and another surge of nausea took hold, he threw out his right arm to catch himself, striking and jarring his elbow. Glass clinked.

Despite his dark mood, his mouth curved into a parody of a grin. Perhaps he could drink himself to death before the soldiers came. He reached for a bottle, pulled out the cork, and took a slug.

Ah whisky, his favorite.

Robert was perhaps halfway through the bottle when the metallic scrape of a key turning in the lock of the cellar door echoed off the grim walls. He looked upward, eyes narrowed against the sudden flare of a lantern. In the doorway, at the top of the stairs, loomed the silhouette of a large man.

"Och weel, it's verra easy to see that ye're definitely yer father's son if ye dinna mind my sayin' so, milord."

MacTaggart. Robert would know the man's voice anywhere. One of his father's most trusted clansmen and a serving Black Watchman, Robert had known the man all his life. Indeed, MacTaggart had taught him to wield his very first sword and shoot his first musket.

Except that might count for nothing right now...

His guts tensed with wariness, Robert watched the burly Highlander descend the stone stairs. He was alone, thank God. No red-coated dragoons or other Watchmen appeared to be lurking in the shadows of the still open doorway. Robert took this as a slightly encouraging sign that he wouldn't be taken away. At least not yet...

He raised the bottle of whisky in a mock toast to his former master-at-arms. "Care to join me in a wee dram, for old time's sake?"

MacTaggart smiled crookedly. "I dinna mind if I do. Only a wee one mind, as I'll need a steady hand to fix yer shoulder." He placed the lantern and a large leather satchel on a nearby wine cask. After rooting around in one of the satchel's pockets for a moment, he turned back to Robert and grinned. In his hand was a wicked looking needle, long and curved. "Mrs. MacMillan has lent me her best roast trussing hook. She says it'll stitch yer shoulder up good as new. Ye're a lucky man."

Robert shrugged and offered the whisky bottle to MacTaggart. "There's no sense in mucking up Mrs. MacMillan's needle for this mere scratch. My head will sit just as well on the executioner's block, nicely trussed shoulder or not."

MacTaggart's craggy brow descended into a deep frown. Squatting down, he mercifully gripped Robert's good shoulder with one of his large, calloused hands and looked him in the eye. "Now we'll have none of that kind of talk, milord. Those bloody Redcoats willna get you. Yer father has instructed me to get ye away from here as fast as I can before dawn. And young Tobias Shaw has offered to go with ye to serve as yer squire. If I can get ye sewn up and out of here in the next hour, ye can both ride for the coast. There'll be a fishing boat ye can slip onto, just past Nairn. Lord Strathburn...well, he says what ye do after that will be up to you. There's coin and new identity papers in that satchel there. How does Robert Burnley sound for a new name? If ye can stand the notion o' pretending to be a Sassenach from now on..."

Robert would pretend to be a walrus if it meant he'd avoid capture and execution. He was glad of the uncertain light cast by the lantern when tears suddenly rose to sting his eyes. Despite everything he'd done, his father had not completely forsaken him. It was more than he deserved.

He took another slug of whisky before pulling off his torn and bloody plaid and shirt to expose the long bayonet slash across the expanse of his back. "I'd prefer herringbone stitch if you don't mind, MacTaggart."

CHAPTER I

Kingston, Jamaica
Ten years later, August 1756

"**A**re you sure you're not a Jacobite, Mr. Burnley? I hear there are quite a few skulking around the Caribbean."

Stifling a curse, Robert forced himself to give his most charming smile to the well-endowed and considerably inebriated Dowager Countess Ogilvy, or Eliza, as she repeatedly insisted on being called *sotto voce*. He moved his forearm slightly so the Scottish noblewoman would refrain from resting her ample bosom upon it, as she tended to do whenever she leaned forward to breathe huskily in his ear.

Although he'd been a dinner guest of the Governor of Jamaica, George Haldane, on several occasions over the last few years, Robert had never yet had the misfortune of being seated beside such a trying guest. He generally ignored the attentions of wealthy, upper-class widows, preferring instead to engage a mistress whenever he felt the need for feminine company. Given the Caribbean could never be a true home to him, he had no desire to take a wife or become entangled with a needy aristocrat like the dowager countess. He preferred simple, uncomplicated relationships.

Keeping his expression carefully neutral, Robert replied in a perfect imitation of an English gentleman's drawl, "As romantic as it might sound having a Jacobite to dinner, Lady Ogilvy, I'm afraid I'm about as Scottish as the spotted dick and custard we just had for pudding."

Lady Ogilvy giggled. Out of the corner of his eye, Robert noticed Governor Haldane turn his attention their way. He knew for a fact that the governor had served as a brigadier general in King George's army and had been present at Culloden. While the Rebellion against the British had ended ten years ago, Jacobites would definitely *not* be this man's cup of tea.

Ignoring the coil of tension in his gut, Robert calmly met the man's interested gaze, and raised his glass in a silent toast, watching for Haldane's reaction. Even though Robert had been residing in the British colony on and off for nearly four years, and he was confident his bona fides would hold up even under the most careful scrutiny, it was his natural instinct to be cautious.

Thankfully, Haldane simply smiled back at him, then winked. *Blast the man.* He obviously knew what a trial the Ogilvy woman could be and was merely amused by her behavior.

The dowager countess squeezed Robert's thigh under the table in a rather forward attempt to reclaim his attention. "Oh, you are wicked, Mr. Burnley," she simpered. "It's a shame you're not Scottish, though. I think I'd rather fancy seeing you in a kilt. Although now the King has had them banned, it's quite possible I'll never see a good pair of bare male legs again."

Across the table, Robert's good friend Captain Kenneth Drummond started to laugh from behind his glass of claret.

"I think perhaps I'm sometimes mistaken for a Scotsman because of the dubious company I keep," Robert said with a deliberately rakish grin. "Take the captain of my merchant vessel, the *Phoenix*." He gestured toward his friend. "He's a Highland rogue if ever I saw one, don't you agree?"

The dowager countess turned her slightly cross-eyed gaze toward Drummond, who was barrel chested, florid faced, and shaggily bearded. Robert had always thought his friend bore a remarkable resemblance to a Highland bullock.

"Hmmm," she murmured, clearly unimpressed before fixing her attention back on Robert. "You, my dear Mr. Burnley, are decidedly more handsome." She looked thoughtful for a moment. "In fact, I know who you remind me of—and what a handsome devil of a Scotsman he was back in his day. William Grant, the Earl of Strathburn."

Blazing, bloody hell!

Again Robert strove to keep his face devoid of any kind of reaction. How damned unlucky could he be, to be seated next to someone who'd actually known his father? He really couldn't wait for the governor to announce it was time for the ladies to depart so the gentlemen could indulge in pipe-smoking and port. Fortunately, Haldane was deep in conversation this time and had not noticed the countess's latest inopportune pronouncement. Though he noticed Drummond was still listening.

Despite the fact his gut had twisted with tension, Robert took a leisurely sip of wine. "Strathspey, you say, my lady?" It wouldn't hurt to be deliberately obtuse.

"Strathburn," corrected the dowager countess. "Honestly, the resemblance is astonishing."

"Strathburn, my apologies... And no, I'm not familiar with that particular noble family," Robert drawled in a low voice as he skimmed his gaze over the woman's décolletage in an attempt to distract her.

Lady Ogilvy smiled crookedly. Leaning forward so her nose was only inches away from his, she gazed deeply into his eyes. "You have Lord Strathburn's eyes, I think... Such a remarkable shade of dark blue." Sighing, she sat back and took a sizable swig from her wine glass. "I was in love with William once, you know. Every girl debuting my year was. But then he went and married that dreadful woman, Caroline Hamilton. And when you consider all the rest he's had to endure!" She touched the pearls at her throat. "My heart weeps for him."

"Whatever do you mean?" asked Robert affecting an air of bored nonchalance as he eyed the dowager countess over the rim of his glass.

"Och, it's such a tragic tale." The countess leaned forward again and whispered dramatically, "His eldest son, a Jacobite, disappeared after Culloden and now his rogue of a younger son, Simon, is proclaiming himself the sole heir." She snorted. "Now *there's* a pretender for you.

He's even styled himself as the Master of Strathburn even though Lord Strathburn hasn't yet had his oldest son legally declared dead. When I was last in Edinburgh for Hogmanay, it was common knowledge that Simon had gambled away half his family's fortune. And of course, none of the eligible young women will touch him with a ten-foot barge pole, despite his handsome looks—"

At that moment, the governor's wife stood to announce that the ladies would withdraw.

Robert cursed inwardly again. Although he was glad to be rid of the dowager's cloying company, he really wanted to hear more about how his father and the clan had been faring. The breadcrumbs of intelligence he'd managed to garner every now and again over the years had been scant to say the least.

As he and Drummond stood with the rest of the gentlemen, he exchanged a meaningful look with his friend. They needed to talk.

As soon as it seemed polite enough to disengage themselves from the rest of the assembled party, they armed themselves with port glasses and retreated to the wide balcony that overlooked Kingston Harbor.

"Ye ken, it's yer own fault you were cornered by Lady Ogilvy, being such a bloody handsome devil and all." Drummond laughed as he looked his friend up and down.

Robert ignored the jibe and shrugged. He was used to his friend's teasing about the attention he received from women. This evening he'd adopted his usual "polite society" guise—that of a wealthy English merchant. He was kitted out in snug-fitting black satin breeches and a finely tailored, midnight blue velvet frock coat with an abundance of frothy white lace at wrist and throat. Although he eschewed wearing a powdered wig. He really couldn't abide them at the best of times, and certainly not in these tropical climes. Instead, he wore his dark hair neatly clubbed at the nape with a black velvet ribbon. He certainly didn't clothe himself in the expensive attire of a gentleman and assume this debonair persona to attract the fairer sex. It was simply a way to blend into the upper echelons of Jamaican Society at affairs such as this.

Robert slid Drummond a sideways look. "What if I did go home? To Lochrose?" he said quietly.

His captain grimaced. "Hard to say what might happen after so many years. I could carry on 'trading' with yer French friend in Saint-Domingue and keep that side o' things afloat if ye decide to leave. But as for all yer other activities..." He shrugged a beefy shoulder. "I dinna have big enough ballocks to captain yer other vessel."

Other activities... Little did any of the "powers that be" in Jamaica know that for the last four years, Robert had been secretly working against the British government and their vile regime of pillaging and exploitation. As he flitted between Jamaica and Britain playing the part of "successful rakish merchant," Mr. Robert Burnley was actually collecting intelligence to ferry to a French privateer operating out of the colony of Saint-Domingue on the nearby island of Hispaniola. Said intelligence included the routes of other British merchant ships that the privateer would then target, and a percentage of the proceeds derived from the physical "booty" went to Robert and Drummond.

It was a venture which had proved both highly profitable and fulfilling. Pretending to be an upstanding merchant also gave Robert the freedom to do what he really wanted...

Aside from the *Phoenix* he also owned another vessel, the *Griffon,* which he docked in Saint-Domingue. However, the *Griffon* wasn't a merchant ship. It was essentially a "corsair" vessel and Robert took great joy captaining it. In fact, his current mission in life—his *raison d'être*— was to seize British slave trading ships enroute from Africa to the Caribbean and Americas to liberate the poor captured souls on board. Dutch, Portuguese, Spanish, and French slave trading vessels were fair game too. *Anyone* involved in the dark and evil practice of enslaving was beyond the protection of the law, in his eyes.

So far, Robert hadn't been caught. Of course, he employed extra measures to disguise his appearance, such as sporting a light beard and wearing a mask during attacks. And strikes were often staged under the cover of darkness.

He always seemed to have the devil's own luck when it came to dodging any sort of consequences. He just prayed that after a decade on the run and dicing with danger, his luck wouldn't run out...

Robert gripped his friend's shoulder. "I don't think anyone would question the size of your ballocks, my friend." Then he sighed. "Do you think Lady Ogilvy's information is reliable? I'm not sure what to make of it." Truth be told, the dowager countess's gossip about his family made Robert feel like a landlubber without his sea legs... He was more than a wee bit thrown.

Drummond's heavy brow descended into a frown. "'Tis hard to say, although there may verra well be a grain of truth in it. That last letter from yer squire's cousin, young Annie Shaw, hinted that there were troubles at Lochrose. Perhaps it's time ye returned to find out for yerself, my friend."

Robert took a sip of his port, considering Drummond's advice. Tobias Shaw, Robert's devoted squire, had a cousin who worked as a scullery maid in Lochrose's kitchens. Since Robert had acquired a townhouse in Kingston, Tobias had started up a somewhat surreptitious correspondence with the lass so he could glean tidbits of information about his own family back home. Of course, Tobias hadn't disclosed who his employer really was, only that he worked for a merchant in Jamaica. And Robert, for his part, was keen to hear anything at all about life at Lochrose.

Lochrose Castle. My true home. Robert sighed. Even after all these years, the pull to return to the Highlands, the need to find out how his father and the clan really fared, was as inexorable as the tug of the moon on the sea before him. It was in Robert's blood. He may go by the name of Burnley, but he was a Grant to his very bones.

Needless to say, there'd been countless times when he'd been tempted to return, to beg his father for forgiveness. Make amends. Reclaim his position. But it had been easier to ignore his innermost desire when he'd thought the clan was better off without him.

Apparently it wasn't. Simon had always been lazy and self-indulgent. And cruel. Robert had once stopped him from flogging a horse to ribbons after the poor beast had accidentally thrown him. On another occasion, Simon had shot one of their father's dogs for disobedience. Even at the age of seventeen, his half-brother had developed an appetite for debauchery, often drinking to excess, gaming, and frequenting brothels.

As for Lady Strathburn, Robert's stepmother... During his youth, Robert was aware of her extravagant tastes and wasteful nature. It had been a source of constant conflict between Caroline and his father over the years...especially when it was discovered that *she* was the one funding Simon's wild ways.

Now duty called to Robert as surely as the summons of the bagpipes or a *crann-tara,* a Highland clan's fiery cross. While he was a successful "merchant" and had built a life here in the Caribbean, it was abundantly clear that his father and clan needed him. Despite the risks —almost certain rejection by his father and the danger of arrest and execution—he had to try.

Robert ran a hand down his face. "You're right, Drummond. It seems the time has come to set sail for home." His mouth suddenly quirked into a wry grin. "Damned inconvenient that I probably still have a price on my head though."

Drummond slapped him on the shoulder. "Och, ye've faced worse. Take Lady Ogilvy for instance. It doesna get more frightening than that."

CHAPTER 2

Lochrose Castle, Strathspey, Scotland
October 1756

Jessie Munroe reined in her exhausted horse, Blaeberry, on the crest of a brae overlooking what was to be her new place of residence—Lochrose Castle.

She hesitated to call it home yet; that would depend upon whether her father's new employer, the Earl of Strathburn made them feel welcome.

The loch before the castle reflected the last of the evening light, the silver-gray waters shimmering as a light breeze ruffled the surface. The shade reminded Jessie of the heraldic pewter targe that had once graced the Great Hall of Dunraven, their former home. It was but one of the many priceless family heirlooms of their clan, Munroe of Dunraven, which they'd been forced to hand over to the bank when it had reclaimed the Jacobean manor house, and indeed the entire estate of the profligate Laird of Dunraven, her uncle.

Jessie pushed a lock of her incessantly unruly red hair out of her eyes and glanced over to her father. Alasdair Munroe, younger brother of the ruined Laird of Dunraven, was now the new factor of the Strathburn estate. Her father's pride had suffered a mighty blow with this fall in their fortunes within the last year. It hurt her heart to see him brought so low, not just in spirit, but also physically. Not only did he stoop in his saddle as if the weight of the world were on his shoulders, but his face was now more deeply lined, his red hair turning gray. She silently prayed that this new situation would restore some of his old vitality and return the spark to his brown eyes.

As if sensing her gaze, her father turned and his mouth twitched with a ghost of a smile. "Weel, Jessie lass, what do ye think of Lochrose?"

Jessie cast her gaze back to the sprawling turreted castle of pale honey-hued stone. Its mullioned windows winked at her in the fading light as she considered his question. Lochrose was impressive, much grander than the somewhat ramshackle Dunraven. Without a doubt, it was a very large estate and her father would be busier than he'd ever been for her uncle.

Not for the first time, doubts about her own future prickled through her mind. What would she do with her days after she'd finished assisting her father with the ledgers? How would she be received by the earl and his family, not to mention the other staff at Lochrose? The long-held frustration that she'd always had, even at Dunraven—that she was an outsider caught on the shadowy landing between the lower gentry and the upper servants—flared inside her.

But she wouldn't burden her father with her own disquiet. Instead, Jessie summoned what she hoped was a bright smile and answered his seemingly simple question. "It's beautiful, Da. Verra grand."

"Aye, indeed it is, lassie. I just hope that this time, I dinna fail in my duties managin' such a large estate."

Jessie reached over and squeezed her father's gloved hand. "We'll be fine, Da. I know it. Just ye wait and see."

Alasdair nodded and sighed. "It'll be a different life, Jessie. No' the one I'd hoped for you." As he patted her hand in return, a wistful expression filled his eyes. "If only Duncan Ross had offered ye his hand in marriage. Ye would be happily handfasted with a braw future, full o' wee bairns ahead of you."

Perhaps. Jessie was not averse to marriage, one day, but it would be to someone who truly cared for *her*, not just the contents of her bridal tocher. That someone was evidently *not* Duncan Ross. As soon as the Munroe's fortunes had dried up—and her bridal portion with it—so had the young laird's attentions. Deep down, Duncan's rejection still smarted a little, but she certainly wasn't going to show it, even in front of her father.

Jessie tossed her wind-blown curls out of her eyes again. "That's bletherin' haver, Da. Ye know as well as I do, that Duncan Ross turned out to be—and ye must excuse my coarse expression—a horse's behind." Her father's bark of laughter was such a reward to her ears, Jessie couldn't help but grin back. "I'm only three-and-twenty, Da. Please dinna fret about whether or no' I'll make a good marriage. Let's do our best to make a good first impression with Lord and Lady Strathburn, and their son."

"The son, Simon Grant, the Master of Strathburn, isna in possession of a wife, ye ken," her father replied with a conspiratorial glint in his eye. "I checked."

Jessie rolled her eyes as she flicked Blaeberry's reins. "Well, let's just hope he isna a horse's arse as well."

Three weeks later, Jessie cursed inwardly on finding herself in an extremely vulnerable position, in more ways than one. Perched on a ladder, reaching for an ancient and dusty volume on the topmost shelf of one of the many bookcases in Lochrose Castle's library, she was far from impressed when the son of her father's employer, the Master of Strathburn—and resident horse's arse—slid his hand about her ankle.

"You're certain you can reach it, Miss Munroe?" Simon Grant's voice dripped with contrived concern as his hand continued its upward journey under her wren-brown wool skirt to her stocking-clad calf. "Here, let me steady you."

As Jessie grasped the unwieldy copy of Homer's *Iliad*, she was suddenly possessed by the overwhelming urge to "accidentally" drop the epic work onto the slimy toad's periwigged head—but considering Lord

Strathburn himself had requested the volume, she refrained from giving into the impulse.

Besides, she was sure it would not go down well with the earl if she knocked his son unconscious. Or worse...

"I am verra steady, sir." Jessie forced the relatively polite reply through tightly clenched teeth. "But perhaps ye might take the book from me?"

She passed down the heavy tome so Simon was forced to grasp it with both hands. As swiftly as she could, she then descended the ladder and stepped away from the odious man. She wasn't daft; she would not give him the opportunity to trap her body up against the bookcase. Although she'd been living at Lochrose for less than a month, she was already wise to most of Simon's insidious methods of gaining close and unwelcome proximity to her.

"It's always a pleasure assisting you, Miss Munroe," Simon said in a silken tone. He traversed the richly woven Turkish rug to a mahogany desk and made a brief pretense of studying the book's pages. "An interesting choice of reading for a young lady like you, if you don't mind my saying so."

Looking up, his gaze slid over her body with such deliberate slowness, Jessie was unable to suppress a shiver. Displeasure and disgust tangled her insides into tight knots. Some might consider Simon Grant's gray eyes and patrician features handsome, but not Jessie. She was rapidly learning from experience that there was nothing attractive about this man whatsoever. The refined air he affected—from the top of his perfectly powdered periwig to the tips of his high-heeled, silver buckled shoes—it was all a facade.

The Master of Strathburn was no gentleman.

"Yer father asked me to locate the book," Jessie said as docilely as she could whilst undergoing the horrid man's continued scrutiny. Her father had begged her to control her sharp tongue around the earl and his family...which was easier said than done when she was in the presence of Simon Grant. "As yer mother is otherwise engaged with her seamstress this afternoon, she asked me to spend some time reading to his lordship while he takes tea. This book was his choice."

The Master of Horse's Arses smirked. "I see," he remarked dryly, turning his attention back to the volume.

Wonderful. Now he was going to read the cursed book. Under the cover of her skirts, Jessie began to tap her foot.

Within a few days of their arrival and her father's commencement as factor, the imperious Lady Strathburn had declared that Jessie was to serve as her companion. The countess's winter-gray eyes had regarded her with a peculiar mix of speculation and disdain as she pronounced that Jessie must make herself useful. After all, how could she possibly expect to remain at Lochrose unless she earned her keep? Of course, Jessie could do nothing but acquiesce.

Her father had agreed to the arrangement immediately. He was clearly pleased that Lady Strathburn had developed an apparent interest in his daughter. It also meant Jessie would be spending a considerable amount of time within the castle instead of hiding away in the factor's allocated residence, the Gate House.

And therein was the rub. Jessie strongly suspected her father still harbored the unrealistic hope that Simon Grant may take a romantic interest in her, and that perhaps in time she might make a well-placed marriage after all. But Jessie knew this would never happen—for two reasons.

Firstly, she had nothing to recommend her. A penniless, untitled lass was not marriage material for the Earl of Strathburn's heir.

And secondly, but most importantly, she couldn't stand the man.

Jessie hadn't yet told her father that the Master of Strathburn's interest in her was not the least bit seemly or well-intentioned. He'd had enough stress over the past year, and worrying about her wellbeing was the last thing he needed.

But today's encounter with Simon Grant had been the most invasive by far. Beneath her irritation, Jessie realized she was even a wee bit frightened. Right at this moment, fear prickled along her skin and her heart was hammering uncomfortably against her ribs. Her instincts told her to keep well back from the desk, out of Simon's immediate reach. She really couldn't wait to quit the otherwise deserted library.

"Mmm, the *Iliad*, the finest example of the epic poem I do believe," drawled the earl's son. Just like his mother, Lady Strathburn, Simon Grant affected the accent of the English upper classes. It made Jessie want to roll her eyes. "However," he continued, "I see this copy by Foulis is in ancient Greek. Tell me, Miss Munroe"—Simon's eyes swept over her again, a questioning smile curving his thin lips as he closed the book—"are you planning on *translating* it for my father?"

Of course I am. We kept scores of indecipherable texts in ancient languages in Dunraven's library. Jessie bit her tongue to stop the sarcastic retort escaping. *Keep ye counsel, lass. Ye dinna want to provoke him.* "I'm afraid my linguistic talents dinna extend to that language," she admitted through tight lips. "I wasna aware it was written in Greek, ancient or otherwise."

Simon's cool, calculating gaze dropped to her mouth. "My tongue, on the other hand, is adept, Miss Munroe. I would be delighted to improve your talents in that area, if you are so inclined."

When it's a cold day in hell. Jessie willed herself to ignore Simon's double entendre, but to her chagrin, her cheeks flushed hotly with both indignation and embarrassment. "I'm sure that will no' be necessary, sir," she replied, amazed how her voice kept steady. "But perhaps ye ken of another copy. An English translation?" If she could encourage him to look in the shelves, perhaps he would be diverted enough for her to beat a hasty retreat back to the drawing room and Lord Strathburn.

Simon rounded the desk then leaned his hip against it, all studied nonchalance. "I *may* have a copy myself. In my private collection," he said, tapping a finger against his lower lip. "Perhaps you could accompany me upstairs to my rooms to help me look for it?"

Jessie's stomach lurched with revulsion. Steeling herself to remain impassive in the face of such an inappropriate suggestion was proving no mean feat. Nevertheless, she lifted her chin and said, "Alas, I fear that I've been far too long already, and I'm keeping Lord Strathburn waiting." Her gaze darted to the desk as she weighed up the risk of taking the Greek version of the *Iliad* versus leaving it.

Simon's mouth curved into a knowing smile as he placed a proprietorial hand on the dusty cover of the book. He knew she wouldn't go back to his father empty-handed.

Damn him and this cat and mouse game he was playing. He was daring her to come closer to take it.

Well, dare away, sir. Jessie changed tack. "Perhaps I shall just take the other book Lord Strathburn requested. If ye will excuse me, sir." She bobbed a quick curtsy then crossed to the nearest bookshelf and pulled out a random volume. Shakespeare's *Macbeth*. It would have to do.

She was about to turn from the bookcase and head for the door when she felt Simon behind her, closing off her route. *Stupid, stupid.* How thoughtless of her not to have kept her eye on him. A cold frisson of unease slid through her, chilling her to the very bone.

Simon leaned over her shoulder. "*Macbeth*. Another tale of great passion and violence." He was so close, Jessie could feel the brush of his breath against the exposed nape of her neck. The sour odor of the claret he'd partaken with his lunch still lingered, and nausea roiled. She hated feeling so helpless—frozen, like a trapped deer, too afraid to move or breathe.

Where was her anger, now that she needed it?

A lock of her hair had escaped a pin and had fallen forward onto her cheek. At these close quarters, Simon had obviously noticed.

Reaching out, he tucked it back behind her ear, his long fingers trailing slowly down her neck before grasping her shoulder. "In the words of Macbeth, *'Let not light see my black and dark desires,'*" he whispered into her ear.

Jessie shivered even as her chest tightened in panic. Trapped against the bookcase, she did not dare to turn around.

"Are you cold, Miss Munroe?"

Simon's murmured question prompted a sudden idea to effect an escape. "I'm a wee chill perhaps, sir. I do hope I'm no' catching a cold," she replied then sniffed, loudly.

To Jessie's relief, her ploy worked. Simon immediately took several steps away from her, leaving her room to safely turn around without brushing against him. Lady Strathburn had alluded on more than one occasion that her precious son had a delicate constitution. Jessie had correctly surmised that Simon would be particular about not contracting sickness. *Macbeth* in hand, she hurried to the library door.

As she grasped the doorknob, Jessie turned her head to make sure

Simon wasn't following. Thankfully, he'd retreated to one of the window embrasures, his attention seemingly claimed by the view of Loch Kilburn.

Do no' linger, Jessie. Go. She quietly pulled the door open. But then it creaked.

Damn.

When Simon glanced over his shoulder at her, his gray eyes held a distinct, predatory gleam. *A wolf's stare.* Jessie's whole body instinctively recoiled and she stumbled over the threshold.

"Good day, Jessie," he murmured as she began to close the door.

She didn't bother to reply. An unwanted book in her hand, her heart in her mouth, she all but fled back to the drawing room.

As soon as Simon heard the door close behind Jessie Munroe, he pulled out a silk kerchief from his coat pocket then sat in the window seat behind his desk. His erection, straining painfully against his breeches, demanded immediate attention.

The maids wouldn't be in to tend the fire and light the candles for at least an hour or two, so he would not be disturbed. And if they did happen to poke their heads in—Simon smirked as he squeezed his rigid length through his clothes—perhaps they could lend him a helping hand.

He'd thought that slaking his lust with the red-headed lass he'd come across on a lonely country lane just outside of the village of Grantown yesterday evening would dull his appetite for Miss Munroe. If anything, it had just made the ache in his loins all the worse, especially when he recalled how the girl had initially struggled and begged him to leave her be.

He liked it when they fought back. He had no doubt that the high-and-mighty Miss Munroe would try to resist him too.

The throbbing in Simon's groin was now urgent. He swiftly unbuttoned the front of his black velvet breeches and closed his eyes, tugging frantically. As his release spread into his waiting silk kerchief, he shuddered and smiled with a mixture of satisfaction and anticipation. As luck would have it, Jessie's father was leaving tomorrow to collect rents and inspect the entirety of the Strathburn estate before winter descended. The excursion also included a trip to Inverness to attend to certain business matters. The journey would not be a short one.

At last, his pretty Jezebel would be alone. He would be able to do whatever he wished.

CHAPTER 3

On Jessie's return to the drawing room, it was to find Lord Strathburn fast asleep in his favorite chair before the fire. Beside him on the hearthrug lay his devoted deerhound, Caesar. Neither stirred at her entry. She'd obviously been too long in the library. Hopefully, the earl wouldn't be too annoyed with her when he awoke.

A half-drunk cup of tea sat on a small cherrywood table at Lord Strathburn's elbow. Sneaking a cup from the fine-bone china teapot to calm her jangled nerves was indeed tempting—Jessie's stomach still churned and her hands wouldn't stop trembling—but the risk of being caught taking such a liberty by the countess made her think better of it. She really didn't want to jeopardize her father's position.

With a shaky sigh, Jessie sank onto the window seat, discarding *Macbeth* onto the brocade cushion beside her. Outside, the mirror-like surface of Loch Kilburn reflected the fiery wooded braes and azure-blue sky. It was the type of autumn day just perfect for riding.

But not for her. Not anymore. Gone were the days when she could saddle Blaeberry whenever she liked to ride out and explore the country-side. The longing to be as free as the eagle presently swooping over the loch was suddenly so acute, tears misted Jessie's vision. Perhaps early tomorrow, before Lady Strathburn made a claim on her time, she could sneak away for a ride. It was also the day that her father would be leaving.

The thought passed like a dark cloud across Jessie's mind.

The idea of spending even a full day alone at Lochrose without her father's protection, let alone a fortnight, made her inwardly shudder, especially after Simon's lecherous conduct in the library just now. But to make matters worse—and despite her protestations—her father had arranged for her to stay not in the Gate House, but up at the castle during his absence. It would be almost impossible to avoid Simon.

Cold dread snaked down Jessie's spine at the thought of the coming days. And nights. She didn't know if she would be able to tolerate the man's unwanted attentions for much longer. The urge to knee him in the nether regions, or even plunge something sharp like a toasting fork into his person, was well-nigh overwhelming.

But for the sake of her father, she must bury her irritation and trepidation and carry on as though nothing at all was amiss. She didn't have the heart to tell her dear da about Simon's advances, just when his spirits seemed so much improved.

Why, only just this morning during breakfast he'd reported with a wide smile that the earl was a most canny and fair employer. Jessie knew that if she did tell her father what was really going on, he would be infuriated with the earl's son and would want to depart straightaway, effectively ending their employment. And then what would they do?

Positions such as these were few and far between, and destitution was hardly an inviting prospect.

With a heavy sigh, Jessie dashed away her useless tears and firmed her resolve. Regardless of how unpleasant life was at Lochrose, she would just have to swallow her frustrations and somehow soldier on.

Glancing over at Lord Strathburn, Jessie could see he was still snoring quietly. His head rested against the side of his leather wingback chair and a woolen blanket was draped over his knees. His silver-topped walking stick rested against the chair's arm. Despite her own cares, she smiled softly. He was a charming man—nothing at all like his son—and perhaps only a decade older than her father. Yet, in many ways, he seemed at least twenty years older.

The castle's cook, Mrs. MacMillan, had recounted the sad story of the earl's decline over tea and scones in the kitchen on Jessie's first morning at Lochrose.

"The good man never recovered after his eldest son, Robert, rode out with the Young Pretender at Culloden. It broke his heart when Lord Lochrose chose to join the Rebellion."

Oh... "Wouldna Lord Lochrose have put his family in jeopardy?" asked Jessie. "If the English forces suspected that Lord Strathburn was a supporter of the Jacobite cause as well?"

"Without a doubt," said Mrs. MacMillan sagely. "Only Lord Strathburn is canny and publicly disowned Robert. He didna really have any other choice, or else the entire estate could verra well have been forfeited to the Crown. Given that Robert has disappeared, Master Simon will undoubtedly inherit everything when the earl passes. Which I'm sure pleases her ladyship no end." The cook had winked at Jessie in a conspiratorial fashion. "Though ye didna hear that from me, lassie."

Curious about the fate of the earl's oldest son, Jessie had ventured, "I apologize if this question seems indelicate, Mrs. MacMillan, but... does the family know what became of Lord Lochrose at Culloden? I've heard it was a terrible battle."

Mrs. MacMillan patted her arm with a floury hand. "Och, it's all right to ask, lassie. It's no' often talked about here, ye ken, given what passed between Lord Lochrose and his father was such a tragedy—the way they fell out with each other. Rumor has it that the canny wee devil managed to escape the battlefield and left Scotland. But it's been ten years, so nobody really kens where he ended up or how he's fared after all this time." The cook's expression grew thoughtful. "If Robert *has* survived, I'm certain his lordship would be verra happy to have him home once more. But unless the Sassenachs take the price off his head" —Mrs. MacMillan shrugged—"he willna be able to set foot on Scottish soil again. Better to live in exile than end up meeting the same fate as poor Fraser of Lovat."

Jessie had to agree. Although she'd only been fourteen years old at the time, she still recalled how shocked her father had been when Fraser of Lovat, the chief of one of their neighboring clans, had been beheaded at the Tower of London in 1747 for his role in the Rebellion. The English did not easily forgive or forget Scottish traitors. In recent times she'd heard of pardons being granted in rare instances—young MacDonald of Clanranald had been one such case. But by and large, acts of clemency were few and far between.

"But thank heaven for small mercies." Mrs. MacMillan had given Jessie a warm smile. "I thank the Lord yer father has come. It's about time Lord Strathburn passed the runnin' of things over to a manager before Lady Strathburn and the young master go through the family's entire fortune and spend all our wages." The cook blew out a heavy sigh. "It never used to be this way, ye ken."

Mrs. MacMillan, obviously a keen orator, refilled their teacups at this point before continuing to reminisce. "It seems like only yesterday that Robert was here. A fine man in the making he was. He took after his lordship, in looks and temperament. Charming and full o' good humor. Fair minded with the staff and tenants and a natural born leader. Everyone thought verra well o' him." The cook's brown eyes twinkled. "A bonnie man to look at too, he was. Och, all the lassies were turning their heads for Lord Lochrose. Why, he even made an old piece o' mutton like me flush and jibber when he looked my way. Quite the rake he would have been. If he'd stayed, he'd be wed by now to be sure, with a few wee bairns underfoot."

She grasped Jessie's hand and looked her in the eye, suddenly serious. "Now Master Simon, he's quite a different kettle o' fish. Ye must needs be careful around him for if he likes the look of a bonnie lassie such as yerself... Weel, let's just say, the other female staff have dubbed him 'Master of the Wanderin' Hands' if ye ken what I mean. Though, ye have yer father here, so he may no' think it wise to try any such nonsense with you."

If only it were so.

The sound of a birch log falling in the grate pulled Jessie from her reverie. An early portrait of the earl hung over the fireplace in the drawing room. Tired of sitting idly, she crossed the room to study it.

It was hard to reconcile the weak and broken man slumbering behind her with the braw and confident looking clan chief in the painting. The younger version of Lord Strathburn had been very handsome, she decided. Even though the earl's countenance was now deeply lined with age, one thing about him hadn't changed—the deep blue eyes looking down at her from the portrait had a familiar lively spark in their depths. There was little resemblance between the earl and Simon, who favored his mother in looks.

She suddenly wondered what Robert Grant, Lord Lochrose, looked like, and if he had indeed been as attractive as Mrs. MacMillan claimed. Not that she would ever meet the man.

Turning to face the room once more, Jessie noticed that the earl had shifted slightly in his sleep and the blanket had slipped off his knees. As she bent to retrieve it, she spied something lying on the floor next to the earl's discarded walking stick. It was a small, round silver case, like a pocket watch, suspended from a chain. His lordship must have dropped it in his slumber.

Picking it up with the intention of returning it to the side table, the clasp unlatched in Jessie's fingers revealing not a timepiece, but a small portrait. It was of a young man in his late adolescence or early twenties. Perhaps this was the earl's long-lost eldest son...

If it was, Mrs. MacMillan had been right. Robert Grant, Viscount Lochrose, had been extraordinarily handsome. One might even say he'd been beautiful. Rather than wearing a powdered peruke like most aristocrats, Lord Lochrose had worn his dark brown hair clubbed at the nape of his neck. Just like the earl, he possessed arresting midnight-blue eyes that contained a devilish twinkle. In fact, as Jessie examined the miniature painting more closely, she could definitely see a marked resemblance between the young man's features and Lord Strathburn's. There was something similar in the lines of the straight nose and strong square jaw and the curve of his wide mouth—a mouth that was tilted into a lopsided smile as if he were secretly amused.

Without thinking, Jessie gently touched the portrait with the tip of her finger. She was sure Lord Lochrose would have made her blush and stammer, too.

The sound of Lady Strathburn's voice in the hall outside startled Jessie from her musing. She hurriedly clicked the portrait's silver case shut before depositing it into one of the earl's hands. Even though he was asleep, his fingers closed around the case reflexively, possessively.

Jessie stepped away just as Lady Strathburn swept into the room. In the countess's wake followed her harried looking seamstress.

"Now, Miss Munroe, what have you been up to all this while?" Lady Strathburn's cold gray eyes flickered over Jessie, then her husband who was now stirring. She didn't wait for Jessie to reply. "Not much I see. We must keep you busy. You can assist Mrs. Beattie with her sewing for the rest of the afternoon."

"Aye, milady." Jessie forced herself to bob a quick curtsy. It was difficult to maintain a respectful manner around the countess when she behaved so arrogantly...which was most of the time.

She began to take her leave, but the countess raised her hand. "Wait a moment." Lady Strathburn's eyes narrowed as she made a blatantly scathing appraisal of Jessie's serviceable gown of brown wool.

The countess herself was always expensively and tastefully dressed. A tall woman of middle age, she'd kept her handsome figure well. This afternoon she wore a panniered silk gown striped with lavender, cream, and leaf green. Cream Bruges lace cascaded from her sleeves and a fichu of lavender chiffon was pinned over her ample bosom with an elaborate pearl brooch. Like her son, she adhered to the fashion of wearing a powdered wig. Today her artfully arranged ringlets were dusted with a lavender hued powder to complement her dress.

Her perusal complete, the countess added in a clipped tone that brooked no argument, "Might I suggest you do something about the state of your own wardrobe, Miss Munroe? I have been meaning to mention it to you since you arrived. If you wish to continue attending on our family, you must attire yourself in something more suitable than drab gowns that have seen better days. Why, our scullery maid is more presentable. Have Mrs. Beattie measure you up for at least five dresses and matching accoutrements."

Jessie's cheeks flamed with barely concealed shame. "With the greatest respect, milady, I-I have limited means and canna afford more than a gown or two—"

"That is not my concern," Lady Strathburn said with a derisive sniff. "I'm sure the price of your new wardrobe can simply be deducted from your father's salary if you cannot pay."

"Caroline, you will do no such thing."

The countess whirled around to see that her husband had risen from his seat. Even though the earl was leaning heavily on his walking stick and his eyes were slightly puffy with sleep, his expression was nothing but determined.

Turning to Jessie, he addressed her in his soft Scots burr. "Choose anything you want, my dear lass, anything at all. Mrs. Beattie may just add it to Lady Strathburn's account."

Jessie shook her head. "That is far too generous, milord. I dinna think—"

"Now, now. Think nothing of it, Miss Munroe," the earl said with a smile, his eyes regarding her with genuine warmth. "Just indulge the whim of an old man who would've liked to have had a daughter of his own."

"Well…thank ye, milord." Jessie returned his smile. His unexpected kindness brought tears to her eyes and she curtsied with a bowed head so he wouldn't see her unseemly rush of emotion.

As Jessie turned to follow Mrs. Beattie from the room, her gaze locked momentarily with Lady Strathburn's. The look in the older woman's eyes was so venomous, Jessie's nape prickled with cold dread. The Countess of Strathburn did not take well to being crossed.

Life at Lochrose was proving to be more perilous with each passing day.

CHAPTER 4

With a groan, Simon finished throwing up into a chamber pot, then thrust the porcelain vessel at his valet, Baird. His head ached like hell. *Damned cheap Portuguese red wine.* Why couldn't his father afford to stock their cellars with something half decent from France?

The sudden racket coming from outside didn't help his already foul mood. Simon donned the silk banyan proffered by Baird then staggered to the bedroom window. Pushing back the heavy velvet curtains, he grimaced at the early morning brightness. Below, Alasdair Munroe was riding out of the gates of Lochrose with the earl's man of business and a small group of men-at-arms who would provide them with protection during their rent-collecting tour of the Clan Grant lands.

Despite the sickening pounding in his head, Simon smirked with satisfaction. Now he had plenty of time to do as he liked with Jessie. And there would be ample opportunities.

He'd been more than pleased to hear that Munroe had requested for his daughter to actually stay within the castle instead of remaining at the Gate House during his absence. *For her safety.* Simon's smile widened at the unintended irony.

Oh, his mother had been less than impressed by the arrangement, but at his insistence, she'd grudgingly acquiesced to install the girl in one of the east wing guest rooms instead of with the other staff in the servants' quarters. She knew it was useless to thwart his needs.

"For heaven's sake Simon, just don't get this one with child," had been her final words to him at dinner last night as his father had shuffled from the room on the arm of his valet.

Not that it would have mattered if his father had been there when dearest mama made her pronouncement. The doddering old fool usually didn't know what day it was, let alone what his son got up to.

A sudden flash of red at the corner of Simon's vision claimed his attention. Turning, he caught sight of Jessie riding out from the direction of the stables. Ah, the comely Miss Munroe was intending to take a morning ride.

Alone.

Simon watched as she ambled her mount across the wide stretch of lawn toward the trees and mist-veiled loch beyond. The lying hussy obviously didn't have the cold she'd purported to have yesterday, if she was up and about at this chilly hour.

Struck with sudden inspiration, Simon called over his shoulder to Baird to ready his riding clothes. Although it was early in the day, it was high time he made it abundantly clear to the chit what his expectations would be over the coming weeks. And that she should think twice about evading him.

Cupping his groin, Simon felt his already half-hard prick jerk in anticipation.

Not long now, my sweet Jezebel. Very soon, you'll be all mine...

⁓

The autumn morning was crisp and clear as Jessie set out for a long overdue, and much longed for, ride on Blaeberry. Lady Strathburn would not expect her presence until at least mid-morning, which meant she had at least an hour or two to herself.

Jessie had tried very hard to smile and chatter away as if she didn't have a care in the world as she'd bid her beloved father farewell in the stable yard. Now he was gone, her troubling thoughts returned full force to plague her. She prayed her ride would provide a welcome distraction. She really didn't want to think about Simon Grant at all this morning. There would be more than enough time to worry about Lochrose's resident reprobate later.

Blaeberry puffed white clouds into the frigid air and her hooves crunched the frost-rimed ground as Jessie gave the mare her head. In no time at all they reached the small stretch of woodland lining the shore of the loch. Entering the copse, Jessie slowed Blaeberry's pace to a sedate walk and let the mare pick her way through the ancient beech, chestnut, and oak trees. Wraithlike shreds of mist rising from the loch drifted around them as they drew closer to the water's edge. Aside from the quiet crunch of Blaeberry's hooves on the carpet of leaf litter and the occasional plaintive call of a bird, there was utter silence.

Once they reached the shore, Jessie slid from Blaeberry's back and found a smooth gray boulder to sit upon at the water's edge. She was determined to find some peace for at least a little while. Closing her eyes, she tried to empty her mind of everything except for what she could sense: the cool edge to the breeze lifting fine tendrils of her unbound hair off her face; birdsong and the sighing of the leaves in the woods behind her; and the intermittent jangle of Blaeberry's harness. She was so exhausted, her very bones ached. She'd tossed and turned, barely sleeping at all last night.

When Jessie again opened her eyes, the mist had fully risen and the loch's waters sparkled with dazzling light. The air was still frosty but huddled in her chestnut velvet riding habit and thick cloak of red wool, she felt warm enough. And contented. Blaeberry had wandered off a few yards to crop the lush grass on the bank. Somewhere in the woods behind them, a rook called.

When Blaeberry abruptly lifted her head and turned toward the trees, ears pricked, Jessie frowned and looked toward the shadowy copse as well. And then her heart seized. She heard it too.

The approach of another horse.

∽

Robert reined his hired mount to a stop within a dense coppice of Scots pines on a low ridge overlooking Loch Kilburn...and the home he thought he'd never see again—Lochrose Castle.

From this vantage point, he had a good view of where the castle's grounds ran into the waters of the loch, mist-shrouded at this early hour. Behind the adjoining woods, the two turreted towers of the castle were silhouetted against the peaks of the Cairngorms and the dawn-hued sky.

A range of emotions washed over him, but one surfaced above them all: a poignant yearning as sharp and strong as the slice of a dirk blade pierced his chest.

He had a powerful sense of homecoming, of belonging to this place, yet the scene before him also seemed slightly alien, different to how he'd envisaged it in his memories. And dreams. An odd sense of unreality clung to him and he had the urge to pinch himself, to make sure he was really here.

Ten long years he'd been gone...

Perhaps everything seemed different because he was now changed. He was no longer a hot-headed, adventure-seeking youth of one-and-twenty who thought he knew everything and took his responsibilities for granted, but a man of one-and-thirty. He'd certainly learned the hard way that honor and duty to clan and family were far more important than chasing phantasms of glory on the battlefield for James Stuart, the pretender to a long-lost throne.

He needed to right past wrongs. Indeed, he fervently prayed with his entire soul that he would be given the chance to do so.

Swallowing past a hard lump in his throat, Robert focused on how he could gain access to Lochrose undetected. The reason for this early morning foray was essentially for reconnaissance. He needed to minimize the risk of being caught when he attempted to reconcile with his father. Arrest was a very real danger, even after a ten-year absence. Although raw impatience clawed at his insides, he knew that walking straight in through Lochrose's front door in broad daylight would be beyond foolish. Simon and his stepmother, Caroline, would not let him escape this time.

Not when a fortune and title were at stake.

Robert surmised that the best time to reach his father without rousing anyone's notice would be at the crack of dawn or during the dead of night, when others such as his damnable brother and stepmother would likely be abed. Which meant he'd probably missed his chance of acting today. The sun had risen too high already and the mist was almost completely burnt off. But he could still scout closer to the castle.

With a shiver, Robert urged his horse down the slope. Here in the heavy bone-chilling shade of the trees, his dark brown wool coat and buckskin breeks failed to ward off the bite in the air. Although the morning was fine, he'd forgotten how damn cold it was in the Highlands. Thank God he and his squire, Tobias, had been able to hole up in his father's obviously long-abandoned hunting lodge last night. Robert's mouth tilted into a wry grin. Living in the Caribbean for so long had made him soft indeed.

About half-way down the brae, a flash of red across the loch caught his eye.

Dragoons? Surely not...

Pulse leaping, Robert halted and narrowed his eyes against the bright diamonds of sunlight dancing on the water. No, there weren't any cursed English soldiers skulking about the loch. There, on the bank, sat a woman in a scarlet cloak. Her horse, saddled and harnessed for riding, grazed nearby.

Who was she? From this distance it was difficult to make out anything in particular about the woman beyond the fact that she had glorious, red-gold hair. The only other thing Robert could deduce was that as she was obviously out for a ride, she definitely couldn't be one of the castle's servants.

Was she a visitor, then? Perhaps a guest of his father or stepmother?

His interest piqued to razor sharpness, Robert slipped from his horse and tethered the reins to a low pine bough. Thanking the Lord for his hard-earned soldier's stealth, he slowly descended the last part of the slope before silently threading his way through the trees by the bank, toward the solitary woman. When he was but twenty yards away, he took cover behind the thick trunk of an ancient chestnut tree, the golden and brown foliage of the low hanging boughs providing him with sufficient cover.

The woman was now slightly angled toward him. Her head rested on her knees, as if she were dozing, her unbound hair cascading like a waterfall of living flame around her. He silently begged her to look up so he might see her face.

And then she did, and his breath caught in his throat.

She was one of the most stunning women he'd ever seen.

Even from this distance Robert could see that her face was classically beautiful with a small straight nose, determined chin, and lush mouth. Her high cheekbones were blushed pink from the cold of early morning. He was too far away to discern the shade of her eyes, but he imagined they were brown, a rich warm brown. But it was her tumble of magnificent hair that transfixed him the most. He was suddenly filled with an inexplicable urge to run his fingers through its rich abundance. To bury his face in the curls at her neck and inhale her sweet scent. To taste her satiny skin and those delectable lips...

The woman was smiling serenely, gazing out across the water. Her beauty was so arresting, Robert suddenly fancied her to be a mystical creature like a naiad of the loch, or a lady of the lake. Something within him stirred, a feeling stronger than mere arousal. It was a longing so acute he wondered if he were bewitched.

He burned to know who she was.

The unmistakable sound of another horse approaching shattered the silence. *Damn.*

The young woman and her horse had heard it too. Cursing silently again, Robert retreated a little farther behind the tree. The girl stood in one swift, graceful movement, and despite the fact that she wore a cloak, he could see that she was as slender as a willow bough. She turned away from him toward the trees.

Horse and rider emerged.

Simon.

For a moment, time seemed to stop. Robert's blood pulsed hard and hot and every muscle in his body tightened, battle-ready. Simon slid from his horse and prowled toward the woman who remained silent. Motionless. Had she been waiting for him?

The answer came quickly enough when Simon greeted her. "Well met, Jessie my dear."

Jessie. The goddess had a name.

Robert's jaw clenched to the point of pain. Jessie and his brother knew each other, and obviously well, given they were on a first name basis. It suddenly occurred to him that he was witnessing an early morning lovers' assignation. Bitter disappointment churned in his gut. What the hell was such a goddess of a woman doing with his despicable brother?

Yes, despicable. Nothing that Robert had learned about Simon of late—via Lady Ogilvy, or Tobias, his squire—had indicated that his brother had matured in the intervening years. That he was now a man of principle and character rather than a self-serving scoundrel. He was clearly still a libidinous blackguard who loved nothing more than to tup the poor maids at Lochrose and waste a small fortune at bawdy houses.

By all accounts, Simon was *not* the sort of man who'd court a lovely young woman and do the honorable thing and take her to wife.

It took every ounce of Robert's mercenary training to keep his careening emotions in check while he continued to watch.

Stay Robert. Don't be a fool. You might learn something useful.

An expression which could only be described as lustful distorted Simon's features as he grasped the lass, Jessie, about the arms and pulled her hard against him. He spoke and Jessie replied, but at this distance, Robert couldn't hear the exchange. Nor could he see Jessie's expression, as she continued to stand with her back toward him. Resentment roiled afresh when Simon caressed the woman's cheek then pressed his face against her hair and whispered something in her ear. There could be no doubting their relationship now.

Then, just as he'd imagined doing only moments ago, his half-brother speared one hand into the fiery mass of Jessie's hair and crushed her lithe body even closer to his. Their kiss was long and intense. Passionate.

A lover's kiss.

Disappointment settled like a cold, hard stone in Robert's belly. He'd seen enough. Jessie was not for him.

With a snort of disgust, he turned away and quietly retreated back up the hill.

~

"Well met, Jessie my dear."

Jessie stood frozen, terror gripping her insides as Simon, the Master of Strathburn, stalked toward her.

She couldn't believe this was happening, that he'd sought her out like this. Her father had only been gone an hour and already the brute was upon her. Dreadful awareness of how isolated and vulnerable she was out here by the loch crackled through her mind. How stupid of her to have put herself in this position.

Well, she could be gormless no more. She would have to brazen out this encounter if she had any hope of remaining unscathed. Jessie instinctively knew that attempting to run from Simon would only inflame the situation, so she fisted her hands and lifted her chin—though she couldn't quite swallow the hard lump of fear clogging her throat as Simon stopped before her.

His silver-gray eyes gleamed with fierce hunger as they raked over her. A predator about to attack the lamb. Despite her mental bravado, Jessie's heart crashed crazily against her ribs. Her mouth was so dry it felt as if it were filled with sand. Try as she might, she couldn't formulate words. *God help her.* For the moment she was struck dumb with horror.

Then Simon reached for her, grasping her forearms roughly. His fingers were like claws, bruising her even through her clothes. He bent toward her, his face so close she could smell his hot, fetid breath. "I think it's about time you do something more to earn your keep here at Lochrose, don't you?" His tone both cajoled and threatened.

Jessie was sure that if he hadn't been holding her so tightly, her knees would have buckled beneath her. "Whatever do you mean?" *Damn it!* Her breathless voice betrayed her fear. Although her question indicated otherwise, she knew exactly what he meant.

Simon's smile was knowing as he stroked her cheek with the back of his gloved fingers in a mock caress. "Ah, still playing coy, are we?" His expression suddenly changed, grew harder, wolfish. "Make sure you

35

wear your prettiest night rail for me tonight, my sweet Jezebel. And if you please me, I might let your father retain his position." His gray eyes darkened and dropped to her lips. "Mmm, you are too delicious for your own good, Jessie Munroe." His mouth pressed against her ear as he whispered, "I could eat you all up right now."

One of his arms suddenly lashed around her waist, encircling her like a steel band, crushing her body against his. His other hand gripped her head and forced her to remain still as he violated her mouth, smothering her rising scream. He kissed her with such force, Jessie could only gasp with pain. His tongue plundered and his teeth ground so hard against her lips that she tasted her own blood.

When the brute finally raised his head, his cold eyes were filled with cruel triumph. "You will leave your door unlocked tonight or suffer the consequences. Do I make myself clear?"

Jessie nodded, still mute with terror. She instinctively knew that defying Simon Grant could be the catalyst for something much, much worse than the kiss she'd just been forced to endure.

However, Simon seemed satisfied with her response. He smiled his wolf's smile again. "Good. I'm pleased we now have this matter sorted out, my sweet Jezebel. I don't want to have to punish you for being disobedient." He trailed a gloved finger along her swollen bottom lip.

As if he cared. Jessie knew that a desire to inflict cruelty and fulfill his own indecent urges were the only motives behind Simon's actions.

As soon as he disappeared into the trees, Jessie ran to the water's edge and cast up the meager contents of her stomach. Her whole body shaking, she somehow dragged herself up and walked unsteadily toward Blaeberry. Her horse, clearly sensing something was amiss, nuzzled her gently.

"I...I would sooner die than let him come anywhere near me again," she whispered against the mare's neck as hot tears burned her eyelids. "Aye, I'll leave my door unlocked...but I willna be there."

When Jessie set foot in the kitchen an hour later, Mrs. MacMillan appeared to recognize that something was wrong with her straightaway.

The good woman dropped her rolling pin and enveloped Jessie in a warm floury hug. "Och, goodness gracious, lassie, sit down afore ye fall down. I'll fix ye some tea."

The motherly cook ushered Jessie to a wooden chair set at the large, well-scrubbed oak table in the center of the room, and quickly poured her a cup from Lady Strathburn's very own fine bone china teapot. Jessie began to stammer a protest but was duly ignored as Mrs. MacMillan added two lumps of sugar and cream to her tea. To her dismay, her hands trembled as she lifted the cup to take a sip.

Mrs. MacMillan frowned and shook her head, wild strands of her gray hair escaping the edges of her mobcap as she did so. She was clearly aghast at Jessie's state. "Ye're shakin' like the birks when there's a northwest wind a-blowin'. When ye're done with yer tea, ye must tell me what's happened. But I dinna think it will surprise me if it has somethin' to do with Master Simon."

Jessie nodded then dutifully drank the sweet, milky tea. Mrs. MacMillan set a freshly baked bap smothered in butter and blackberry jam in front of her, but Jessie couldn't bring herself to touch it. Her throat was tight and her belly still churned.

When she'd drained her cup, Mrs. MacMillan shooed away the two scullery maids who'd been stealing curious glances her way. "Now lass, ye must tell me exactly what that bastard has done," she said gravely, her shrewd gaze studying Jessie's face.

Jessie closed her eyes and swallowed back the tears which threatened to spill. She felt completely unlike herself—shaky, humiliated, and at the same time, angry as a wildcat caught in a rainstorm. *Damn Simon Grant to hell for making me feel this way.*

But she knew she must confide in someone. She wouldn't survive this situation unscathed unless she had help.

Taking a deep breath, she looked Mrs. MacMillan in the eye and proceeded to reveal the details of her recent encounter with Simon, as well as all her fears about tonight and the coming days. Try as she might, she couldn't keep the quiver from her voice.

Mrs. MacMillan's eyes flashed and her cheeks grew bright red with indignation as she listened. "Och, that sorry excuse for a man needs castratin' with my meat cleaver," she blustered when Jessie had finished. "I'd do it myself but for the fact that I'd end up swingin' for it."

Despite her distress, Jessie smiled a little at the thought of unmanning Simon. Though she was still astounded he had the audacity to believe he could behave in such an abominable way and get away with it. Mrs. MacMillan had warned her on her first day to be wary of him. But to go so far as to rape her under his parents' roof? How could he even consider such a thing?

"Do...do you think Lord and Lady Strathburn know of their son's... wicked tendencies?" she ventured.

Mrs. MacMillan's brows knitted together. "I would say that there would be little that escapes her ladyship's notice. She kens about her son's vices and does naught to stop him. As for the earl, I wouldna ken. He doesna have much to do with Simon, other than tryin' to limit his drinkin' and throwin' away the family's wealth. And he's ill, poor man."

Jessie was certain the earl would be appalled by his son's depraved behavior if he knew what was happening. It was a gamble, but she needed to consider entreating Lord Strathburn for aid as a course of action, if only to ensure Simon didn't have a hand in having her father dismissed. "What...what if I spoke to Lord Strathburn? Do ye think he might help?"

Mrs. MacMillan shrugged. "I dinna ken how he would react, to be honest. His lordship has always been a man of honor. But if ye kicked up a fuss and it was just yer word against Master Simon's...? Weel, I wonder if Lord Strathburn would think that havin' yer father and yerself here would be more trouble than it's worth, when all is said and done."

And that was exactly what Jessie feared. When it boiled down to it, she and her father had been at Lochrose for less than a month. Lord Strathburn may simply see her as a troublemaker. In the end, it was a chance she was unwilling to take if it meant her father would lose his position.

There was only one thing to do, as she'd known all along after Simon had threatened her at the loch.

I have to leave.

Mrs. MacMillan obviously knew that too. "Right m'lass, enough of this speculatin'," she said, her expression grim. "There's only one sure way to protect yerself. Ye must go, at once."

Jessie knew Mrs. MacMillan spoke sense, yet she was still torn between her sense of self-preservation and duty to her father. "I know I must, but how do I go about it without jeopardizing my father's post? That is still the question, isn't it? The master has threatened to have him dismissed if I do no'..." Her tongue stumbled, unable to complete the hideous thought.

"Dinna worry about yer father for the moment, lassie," the well-meaning cook said sternly. "Ye must only think of yer own safety now. Do ye no' have any other family or friends ye can turn to? Anyplace ye can go?"

Jessie considered her question. "When we lost Dunraven Hall, my da initially thought about sending me to Edinburgh to stay with my cousin, Maggie Henderson. She's married to a tea merchant and has three young children with another on the way. I am sure she wouldna mind if I came to stay, even for a wee while."

Mrs. MacMillan's face creased into a wry smile. "With that many bairns, I'm sure she wouldna mind if ye stayed a *long* while." Her expression changed, became serious again, and she reached out to squeeze Jessie's hand. "Now, here's what ye should do, lass. Ye must write yer father a note telling him that word has come from yer cousin, begging ye to come and stay at once to help with the wee ones and the bairn a-coming. I shall keep the note and give it to yer father when he gets back, so he willna fash himself about yer whereabouts."

"What shall I tell Lord and Lady Strathburn?" The earl's good opinion truly mattered to Jessie. She did not wish to come across as a flibbertigibbet and desert her position as his wife's companion without a credible reason.

"I will tell them the same story," replied Mrs. MacMillan, patting her arm. "The post arrived in Grantown earlier today, so they should believe ye about yer cousin sending word. Yer father canna be blamed for yer sudden departure if ye need to attend to a family crisis. The earl wouldna countenance that. And after all, yer father is a canny manager. Aye"—the cook nodded, her tone certain—"if ye go quietly and there isna a great to-do, I predict that all will turn out well. For both you and yer da."

Tears of relief and gratitude filled Jessie's eyes. "I...I canna thank ye enough."

Mrs. MacMillan pulled a handkerchief from her apron and offered it to Jessie. "'Tis nothing, m'lass. Nothing at all. Now, the only obstacle we have to overcome is how to get ye to Edinburgh."

Jessie frowned. "I dinna think it would be wise for me to ride all that way by myself. It's well over one hundred miles."

Mrs. MacMillan nodded. "The public coach from Inverness passes by the Strathspey Arms in Grantown, two days from now. At noon. It only goes by twice a month and it is verra slow, but respectable folk use it. Why, even Mrs. MacIntosh, the kirkman's wife, has traveled on it to visit her sister in Edinburgh. I would be happy to help ye with the money for the fare—a gift, or a loan if ye insist on payin' me back."

"No, that willna be necessary, dear Mrs. MacMillan." Jessie smiled. "Ye're too kind. I have a wee bit o' money set aside. Enough to cover a public coach fare at least. But the question is"—she sighed heavily—"what shall I do between now and when the coach leaves? I still need to avoid the master. If I stay here, or even at the inn at Grantown, I'm certain he will find me."

"Aye. He wouldna think twice about forcing himself on ye, even at an inn. Ye need to disappear." Mrs. MacMillan's brow dipped into a deep furrow as she thought a little longer. Then a mischievous smile creased her ruddy face. "I ken just the place, m'lass. Some place he willna look at all."

CHAPTER 5

Jessie paused beneath a ragged pine tree on a sharp ridge and wiped a trickle of perspiration from her brow. She'd been walking and climbing for over an hour, and aside from needing to catch her breath, she wanted to get her bearings before continuing on. The loch and the castle lay in the wide glen far below her. If she hadn't known any better, she would have thought it was a scene from a fairy tale, rather than the setting for the nightmare Simon had planned.

But she wouldn't stay at Lochrose to become Simon's unwilling plaything. She'd much rather scale mountains and traverse lonely upland moors any day.

Glancing upward along the ridgeline, Jessie could just make out the path leading to the isolated glen that was her ultimate destination. She prayed Mrs. MacMillan was correct in surmising that Simon wouldn't think to search for her at Lord Strathburn's old hunting lodge. Two nights—tonight and tomorrow—were all that Jessie had to brave alone before she made her way to Grantown on the other side of the range.

A solitary cloud passed across the midday sun and a chill breeze pulled at the loose curls which had already escaped Jessie's braid. It was time to press on. The weather was still holding relatively fair, but up here, the elements could change in the space of a moment. Jessie knew the sooner she reached the shelter of the hunting lodge, the better. With only her wren-brown woolen gown and scarlet traveling cloak to wear between here and Edinburgh, she really didn't want them to get ruined if she could help it.

Gathering her resolve, Jessie hitched her leather satchel higher on her shoulder before carefully negotiating the ridgeline and scaling the next slope, which was steeper still. Tumbled boulders and outcroppings of rock appeared and the wind-bent pines thinned out. The ground became less even and she had to take care where she stepped.

When Jessie at last reached the narrow pass curling between towering pillars of gray rock, her breath was coming in short, ragged pants, and her thighs ached with the exertion of climbing. She stopped for a brief rest, regretting that she'd packed her satchel so hurriedly; she'd forgotten to bring a water flask. But if she'd followed Mrs. MacMillan's directions accurately and was on the right track—and she fervently hoped she was—she would soon reach a burn.

The pass turned out to be more of a challenge than Jessie had initially anticipated. The path's uneven surface made it treacherous going, and on one occasion, she needed to scramble on her hands and knees between fallen, jagged-edged rocks. She was relieved that she hadn't ridden Blaeberry along this obviously long neglected route. Mrs. MacMillan had been right; she'd warned Jessie that it would be a difficult ride, even for horses used to the rugged terrain. Walking meant it would take Jessie much longer to reach the lodge and Grantown, but if it meant Blaeberry remained safe, it was worth it.

When Jessie at last emerged from the pass and skidded down a small gravel scree to the mountain burn below, she was both relieved and exhausted. The combination of poor sleep from the night before, little sustenance, and extreme physical exertion had left her weak and shaking. The terror which had filled her early that morning and the nagging fear that Simon *might* follow her—despite Mrs. MacMillan's assurances he wouldn't—probably weren't helping either. She dropped to her knees by the rocky stream and with trembling, scraped hands, splashed icy water onto her face before drinking her fill.

Her thirst quenched, she sat back on her heels and looked down the twisting, wind-blasted glen. The idea of walking for perhaps another hour across rough moorland to reach the hunting lodge at the far end seemed beyond her at this point. She needed to eat and rest for a while before she continued on. A little farther down the slope beside the burn was a small cluster of rowan and larch trees. The copse's foliage was a bright, welcoming blaze compared to the bleak gray rocks and expanses of bruise-colored heather and coppery deer grass. It would be the perfect place to take shelter.

Jessie rose unsteadily and on still shaky legs, picked her way along the edge of the burn toward the trees. She was only a few yards away when misfortune struck—she stumbled over a rock hidden in the grass and her right ankle twisted beneath her. She cried out as a tearing, agonizing pain assailed her.

Damnation. This was the last thing she needed.

Somehow, even though her vision was blurred by tears, Jessie managed to limp the rest of the way to the copse, ankle protesting with every ungainly step. When she reached the trees, she collapsed on the edge of the burn then gingerly removed her leather boot and woolen stocking to assess the damage. To her dismay, she could see her ankle was already beginning to swell. *Hell.* It was well and truly sprained. Gritting her teeth, she thrust her foot into the frigid water and prayed the cold would ease the swelling.

With clumsy fingers, Jessie opened her leather satchel and removed a little of the food she'd packed for the next few days—a nugget of sharp crumbly cheese and a hunk of dark rye bread. Although she didn't feel like it, she forced herself to eat. She was so tired and disheartened. What else could possibly go wrong?

Simon might find me.

No, she wouldn't think about what would happen if he did. With any luck, the blackguard probably wouldn't even notice she was missing until later on this afternoon, or even perhaps this evening. She must trust Mrs. MacMillan's assertion that Simon loathed hunting and hadn't set foot up here in these isolated upland moors for years.

For now she was safe. She had to be.

When Jessie could no longer stand the bone-chilling iciness of the burn, she removed her ankle and inspected the swelling. *Damn, damn, damn.* The cold water hadn't helped at all.

Trying but failing to stifle whimpers of pain, she pulled on her stocking, every little tug sheer agony. There was no way on earth that she'd be able to get her boot on, so she shoved it into her satchel. Getting to the hunting lodge suddenly seemed like an impossible feat. She bit her lip and willed herself not to cry. *'Tis a sprain, Jessie. Nothing is broken. You will live.*

She hobbled into the copse and carefully lowered herself onto a cushion of leaves, before leaning back against the black trunk of an ancient rowan. The wind had picked up and torn scraps of cloud scudded over the snow-capped peaks to the north-west. At least it didn't look like it was going to rain. Jessie gathered her scarlet cloak around her and closed her eyes. She would rest for just a wee while...

Jessie awoke with a start, face down in a pile of autumn leaves, her heart beating a wild tattoo. For one panic-filled moment, she had no idea where she was...then it all came back to her with heart-sinking clarity. Her flight from Lochrose and the long journey ahead that she must now manage with a badly sprained ankle. Indeed, it throbbed at the slightest movement. Sucking in a deep breath, she braced herself for the inevitable stab of pain and slowly sat up, her body stiff with cold.

She judged it to be late afternoon by the degree to which the autumn light had faded. She must have been asleep for hours. Looking beyond the copse, she noticed ponderous gray clouds had gathered over the mountains and a clinging, damp mist was beginning to gather in the glen. She should get up and keep moving before rain fell, but the thought of it was almost too much. The leaves above her and the moorland grasses shivered in a sudden gust of icy wind.

Jessie stiffened. Something had moved in the corner of her vision. She turned her head slightly to the left. On the other side of the rowan tree, partly shielded by a clump of bogmyrtle was a small, female roe deer. The doe was staring directly at her, its huge brown eyes wide with fear. A shred of mist drifted between them.

And then there was a deafening crack. Splinters of bark exploded around Jessie and a searing pain shot through her upper arm. As her own scream filled her ears, her world turned black.

~

Robert's heart froze, his blood turning to ice as he heard the scream—the terrified scream of a woman.

A woman?

The roe deer he'd been stalking for his evening meal bolted away at the same moment that the raw sound had split the silence. Through the drifting ribbons of mist, he could see no other signs of activity in or around the small cluster of trees. No horses or other voices.

What the hell had happened?

Beside him, in the shelter of the long grass lay his squire, Tobias, equally as stunned. The young man's face had blanched to the same shade of white as the snow-dusted Cairngorms behind them and his mouth had frozen to a round 'O'. "Who was that, milord?" he whispered.

"Christ knows." Robert slung the still smoking musket over his shoulder and in the next instant he was on his feet, half running, half leaping through the spent heather toward the copse where the deer had been. He splashed across the shallow burn into the trees and stopped dead.

There at his feet lay the gorgeous young woman he'd seen with his brother this morning, her scarlet cloak covering her body like a blood-red shroud.

Jessie.

Her eyes were closed and her face was deathly pale but for a trickle of blood at her left temple. *Oh God in heaven, what have I done?* Fear gripped Robert's gut anew. He prayed his flame-haired goddess wasn't dead.

He dropped to his knees in the leaves and felt her neck. Relief surged as he detected her pulse, still beating strongly beneath his fingers.

With swift efficiency he then untangled the cloak to check the lass's body for injury. He quickly ascertained that the gunshot wound she'd sustained was a graze along her left upper arm. The sleeve of her brown gown was torn and stained with blood. With unexpectedly trembling fingers, Robert gently probed the wound but there was no bullet. *Thank God.*

Looking up, he could see it had lodged in the rowan tree behind her. The blood at her temple came from a splinter of rowan bark that had superficially pierced the delicate flesh close to her hairline. Strangely, her right boot was also missing. *Curious.*

"She'll be all right, lad. It's just a graze." He addressed Tobias over his shoulder. His squire had entered the copse whilst Robert had been conducting his examination. "We'll need some water from the burn."

Tobias's voice shook. "I... She... Who...? What the hell is she doing here?"

Robert scraped a hand through his hair. "I have no idea."

His squire moved closer and dropped to his knees beside Robert. "Isna...isna that the lass ye told me about, the one that was with yer brother? What are we going to do with her?"

"Aye, I believe it's the same woman," replied Robert, shooting his servant a glance. "And to answer your second question, again I have no idea."

Just at that moment, Jessie began to stir. She moaned, eyelids fluttering.

Robert leaned closer and took one of her hands between his. *She was so cold.* "Open your eyes now, lass. There's been an accident but everything's going to be all right." He hoped his voice held the right amount of reassurance. The last thing he wanted to do was scare the poor girl to death.

Jessie's eyes flew open. He immediately noticed that they were honey brown, like the deep amber of whisky—more beautiful than he'd even imagined this morning. She gasped and struggled to sit up, to push away from him. She was clearly terrified but hampered in her efforts by her injury. She cried out in pain and clutched at her upper arm.

When she pulled her hand away, it was covered in blood.

CHAPTER 6

B*lood.*

There was blood on her hand and an excruciating pain—a breath-robbing, searing burn—in her left arm. Jessie stared at the bright red smear across her palm and fingers with incomprehension as rising panic constricted her throat. *What on earth?*

Her gaze darted to the dark-haired stranger bending over her. *Not Simon, thank God.* Deep blue eyes stared straight into hers, but try as she might, she couldn't make out what the man was saying. She felt muddled, light-headed, like her head was full of stuffing.

Another man with a mess of red hair suddenly appeared in her line of vision. He passed a flask to the blue-eyed man. "Here ye are, milord."

Jessie swallowed, tried to drag in enough air to speak. "What happened?" Her voice, when it emerged, sounded hoarse, foreign to her own ears.

The blue-eyed man spoke again and this time she understood. "You've been the unfortunate victim of a hunting accident," he said gently with only the barest trace of a Scottish burr. "Your left arm is injured, but not too badly."

At his words, memory flooded back. *There'd been a deer. And a loud crack. A gunshot.*

Jessie attempted to sit up again and gasped as a hot bolt of pain sliced through her arm making the simple action almost impossible. The movement also reminded her that her ankle was sprained, although at this particular moment, the throb of that injury was far less.

The man noticed her struggle also. He grasped her gently behind the shoulders and helped to ease her into a sitting position. When she was upright, he dropped his hands but didn't move away.

"Ye... Ye shot me." Jessie's voice emerged as a ragged whisper. As her gaze skittered over the stranger again, she noticed he wore a plain brown coat and tight-fitting buckskin breeches. A musket hung from his shoulder. Perhaps he *was* a hunter. Or a poacher...

The man drew in a deep breath and wiped a hand down his face, his expression more than a little contrite. "Aye," he admitted, meeting her gaze. "I'm so incredibly sorry. My companion and I, we were deer stalking. The deer I was after was in the copse with you, and in this mist... Well, you were neatly camouflaged, I'm afraid." His wide mouth suddenly tilted into a rueful half smile. "I'm obviously not as good a marksman as I used to be if I'm missing deer and shooting lasses instead."

Even though he'd shot her, and she had no real reason to trust this man nor his redheaded companion, Jessie could at least take him at his word about what had occurred. For one thing, his explanation made sense. She remembered the deer. And she'd deliberately worn colors that would blend into the autumn-hued landscape. A hunter probably wouldn't have noticed her in amongst the deer grass and the crimson leaves of the rowan tree.

But what if her fragile trust was misplaced? This man may have shot her by accident, but ownership of firearms was illegal for most Highlanders. So what on earth was this stranger doing up here, stalking deer on Lord Strathburn's lands in the first place? Who *was* he?

Despite his assurance that she would be all right, unease fluttered wildly in Jessie's belly. She was all alone and injured. Injured so badly she could not run. Vulnerable in the extreme. She tried to reassure herself that not everyone was like Simon—a cold, lascivious predator. Nevertheless, common sense dictated she should at the very least be wary of this man and his hunting companion.

Two of them, and only one of her...

Jessie glanced at the hunter's face again. He was kneeling very close, his deep blue eyes steadily watching her, obviously gauging her reaction to what he'd just told her. A strange frisson slid over her skin like a shiver of wind passing through the deer grass as it suddenly occurred to her that he was handsome, despite his rough appearance. His dark brown, almost black hair was tied back off his face revealing a strong angular jawline shadowed with the beginnings of a dark beard. Winged eyebrows, chiseled lips... She couldn't have said why, but she suddenly had the odd sensation that he seemed vaguely familiar.

The stranger spoke again, his pleasantly deep voice interrupting her blatant perusal. "Can you tell me your name, lass?"

Jessie considered his question and decided there was no reason not to share the information. She swallowed. Her throat was still so parched and tight she could barely speak. "Jessie...Jessie Munroe."

The man clearly noticed her need for a drink as well. He immediately produced the flask the redheaded man had given to him. "Just water," he said as if to reassure her yet again that he meant her no harm.

Jessie took it with shaking hands and sipped at the contents gratefully. Cold water slipped down her throat, easing the dryness. "Thank you," she said, handing the flask back.

The blue-eyed man took a swig for himself then poured a little water over his blood-streaked fingers.

Oh, dear Lord, it was *her* blood. Jessie swallowed down an unwelcome surge of queasiness.

The man recapped the flask and Jessie noticed that now the blood was gone, he had large, strong looking hands. Despite the fact his knuckles were scarred, his fingers were almost elegant with well-shaped nails. They were clearly not the hands of a crofter or brigand cattle reiver. More the hands of a gentleman, although the man's plain clothes and heavily stubbled jaw belied that particular station. He was an enigma to say the least.

It occurred to Jessie that she should ask the stranger for his name, but as she cleared her throat to ask her question, the man spoke again.

"Well, Jessie—you don't mind if I call you by your first name do you?—we're going to have to move to somewhere more sheltered. Night will be here soon, and it smells like rain." At that very moment, an ominous grumble of thunder sounded in the distance and a gust of wind sent a flurry of gold and scarlet leaves down upon them.

The blue-eyed man called out to his redheaded companion, who'd been standing at the edge of the copse all this time, watching. "Tobias, fetch the horses, will you?"

"Aye, milord," replied Tobias in a distinct Scottish burr before disappearing into the gathering mist and cloud.

The huntsman turned his attention back to Jessie. "There's an old, abandoned hunting lodge not far from here that we can use."

Well! Not only was this man stalking on Lord Strathburn's hunting grounds, but he also seemed to think nothing of using the earl's hunting lodge. It was a trespassing offence to say the least. But how on earth did the stranger know of its existence?

Her surprise at the comment about the lodge must have shown on her face as the stranger asked, "Do you know of it?"

She nodded, unable to prevent herself from saying, "It's owned by the Earl o' Strathburn. These are his lands."

The huntsman didn't seem at all rattled by her revelation. "Well, there's no possibility of us taking you anywhere else at present, given the weather setting in." His smile was wry as he glanced toward the lowering clouds. "I'm sure that like me, you'd prefer not to spend the night battling the elements." His eyes met hers directly again. "But before we move, Jessie, I'd like to take a closer look at your injured arm. You've lost a wee bit of blood and the wound may need bandaging." His gaze now held a light of earnest concern as he added, "I assure you, I have nothing but honorable intentions."

"Aye, verra well," Jessie said, steeling herself for what was about to occur. She supposed that if this man's intentions *were* dishonorable—if he meant to have her—she'd already know about it. Besides, if he really intended her physical harm, why bother attending to her arm?

The man laid aside his musket and, still on his haunches, leaned toward her. He was so very close. Jessie watched his face, unable to look down at her injury. His marked dark brows descended into a slight frown as he gently separated the torn edges of her sleeve to check the wound underneath. At these close quarters, she couldn't help but notice other particular details about the stranger. The skin at his throat and beneath his beard was tanned, like he'd spent a considerable amount of time in the sun. He possessed a long, straight nose and high cheekbones. *Definitely handsome,* she decided. *An elegant ruffian.*

Yes, he was a dark, handsome stranger and even though he'd shot her, he was now her rescuer. If she hadn't been in such a dire situation, she might have smiled at the irony.

"Jessie lass," the man said gently when he'd finished his inspection, "I'm going to use my linen neckcloth as a bandage to stem the bleeding. But in order to bind your wound properly, I'll have to cut away your sleeve. Would that be all right?"

Jessie nodded faintly even though her only gown for her journey to Edinburgh would be completely ruined. But she really had no other choice.

The huntsman pulled a dirk from his belt then began to slice through the already torn fabric that was obscuring her wound. Although he was gentle, she couldn't help but gasp. There was quite a lot of blood, more than she'd thought there would be. She closed her eyes and gritted her teeth, fighting a wave of nausea as the man proceeded to wrap a firm bandage around her arm. The slightest touch or movement triggered sharp flashes of white-hot pain. By the time the makeshift bandage was securely fastened, Jessie was shivering and a sheen of cold perspiration had broken out all over her skin.

The huntsman returned his dirk back to his belt. "You're a brave lass, Jessie Munroe," he said softly, as he studied her face. She thought there might even be a hint of admiration in the deep blue depths of his gaze.

To her annoyance, Jessie felt her cheeks grow hot, but before she could gather her muddled thoughts and form any sort of coherent response, the huntsman continued. "Now, I don't know if you've noticed," he murmured, the warm baritone of his voice as soft as a caress, "but you also have a rather large splinter at your temple that should probably be removed."

As his gaze moved to her forehead, he reached slowly forward and brushed her hair away from the left side of her face. For the first time, Jessie realized her brow was stinging. How had she not noticed that? She raised her right hand and gently probed the splinter, wincing slightly. Her temple was sticky with blood.

The huntsman gently tucked her loosened hair behind her ear. "The wound is quite superficial so it shouldn't leave any noticeable scar to mar your lovely face."

He thinks I'm lovely to look at? Surely he's jesting.

Even though she was still shivering, Jessie's face began to burn at his remark. "Considering ye mistook me for a deer, I suspect ye must be a wee bit blind," she said shakily, attempting a smile. "But nevertheless, I'm ready. Go ahead and do yer worst." As she closed her eyes to submit to the stranger's ministrations, he emitted a low chuckle.

Once the splinter was removed, the man stood up. He was tall, *very* tall. Broad shouldered and lean with long, muscular legs. Even if she'd been able, Jessie doubted she could outrun him.

"Jessie lass, I'm just going to leave you here for a moment to help Tobias with the horses," said the huntsman. Then, to Jessie's surprise, he shrugged out of his coat and draped it around her. She instantly noticed the smell of damp wool combined with the astringency of pine needles—and another note—the slightly musky scent of the man himself. It wasn't unpleasant. In fact, she rather liked it.

"I won't be long," he added, bending to retrieve his musket. And then he was gone.

The mist was growing thicker in the copse. The chill dampness seeped into Jessie's very bones. Shivering, she drew the huntsman's coat more closely around herself, trying to absorb the residual warmth. She closed her eyes, suddenly overwhelmed with fatigue. It was like the gathering fog had penetrated her mind.

As Jessie hovered on the edge of consciousness, she was suddenly plagued by doubts once more. She hated that she was now reliant on this handsome stranger. It was unsettling to be at such a disadvantage. She really knew nothing about this man, not even his name. Although the redhaired lad, Tobias, had called him *my lord,* an obvious mark of respect. Whether the huntsman was a nameless lord or a nameless poacher it really didn't matter, given her present predicament. Refusing his offer to take her to the hunting lodge would be foolhardy indeed. Besides, it was where she had been making for in the first place.

She prayed her initial instincts to trust him were right.

CHAPTER 7

"Jessie. Jessie, you need to wake up, lass." The huntsman was back again, speaking softly by her ear. One of his hands gently squeezed her right shoulder. "The horses are here."

With an effort Jessie prized her lids open.

"Do you think you can stand?"

Although dazed, Jessie found her voice. "I'm no' sure. I'll try."

"Good lass."

The man slid his arm around her waist to help her up, but as she started to rise, her temporarily forgotten sprained ankle protested. The sharp, shooting pain was so great she cried out in agony and clutched at the man's arm and shoulder. Her head swam with dizziness and dark spots appeared before her eyes.

"My ankle," Jessie gasped. "I-I sprained it earlier."

The huntsman's mouth quirked into a lopsided smile. "Ah, that explains the missing boot."

"Aye, I couldn't bear to put it back on." With her chin, Jessie gestured at the pile of leaves by the trunk of the rowan. "It's in my satchel, just there."

As she leaned against the tree for support, the man snagged the leather bag by the strap and slung it over his shoulder. Then before Jessie knew what he was about, he gently swept her up into his arms and carried her out of the copse and across the rocky burn to where his servant Tobias waited with two horses.

My goodness, he's strong. As the feelings of dizziness receded, Jessie became aware of the hard planes of the huntsman's chest as he cradled her in his arms. He lifted her onto one of the horses as if she weighed nothing at all.

"You're not going to faint on me again now, are you?" he asked, his hands lingering at her waist. Concern creased his brow.

"I-I think I'll be fine." Jessie grasped the pommel of the saddle, avoiding the huntsman's gaze. She was highly aware of the feel of his large, capable hands spanning her torso. Truth be told, she was more than a wee bit relieved when he released her to secure her satchel to one of his mount's saddlebags.

Thunder rumbled again, louder this time. Jessie shivered as an icy gust of wind tore down the glen. Despite the drop in temperature, she clumsily shrugged off the huntsman's coat and offered it to him. "I'm sure you would like yer coat back, Lord..." She looked down at the handsome stranger and arched a brow. After everything that had happened, she really wanted to know this man's name.

The huntsman smiled and the undeniably roguish tilt of his mouth made heat rise in Jessie's cheeks. "I'm flattered that you think me so distinguished. But I'm simply Mr. Robert Burnley. And you must call me Rob." His fingers brushed hers as he took his coat. "Thank you, Jessie."

The brief contact made Jessie's skin tingle in the oddest way, and to her consternation, her blush deepened. What on earth was the matter with her? For heaven's sake, she'd been kissed before—albeit quite chastely beneath the mistletoe last Christmastide by Duncan Ross. Simon Grant's supposed "kiss" this morning certainly didn't signify. At any rate, she might be a virgin, but she certainly wasn't a shy, *completely* innocent maid.

Mr. Burnley—or Rob as he insisted on being called—slipped his coat back on, then unsettled her yet again when he pulled a woolen plaid from the saddlebag. It was the hunting tartan of Clan Grant—a pattern of blue, green, and black checks. Jessie had seen a similar plaid blanket in

Lord Strathburn's study. The tartan worn by the local Black Watch regiment also had the same sett, the threads woven in much the same way.

Rob had noticed her frown. "I used to serve in the Watch hereabouts," he said by way of explanation as he wrapped the plaid around himself with sure efficiency.

A soldier, then. Her earlier observation had been correct. *If* Rob could be taken at his word, of course. But even if he'd served in the Watch, that was no guarantee she was in safe hands. Jessie had heard many a terrible story about the conduct of both dragoons and Watchmen during and after the Rebellion—tales of rape and pillage and murder which made her sick to the stomach. She prayed Rob was the man of honor he appeared to be and wouldn't turn out to be a violent brute of a soldier...or a man like Simon.

All further coherent thought scattered when Rob swung up behind her with easy grace. As one of his strong arms slid around her to hold her steady, Jessie appreciated how he was careful to avoid contact with her wounded arm. His other hand lazily flicked the reins and their horse moved forward toward the sea of impenetrable fog that cloaked the floor of the glen. Tobias trailed along somewhere behind them.

It wasn't long before a light, icy drizzle began to drift over them. Jessie shivered and at these close quarters, Rob immediately noticed her discomfort as well. He wrapped his plaid around her, binding her closer. Part of her knew she should be shocked at the flagrant intimacy of being pulled against him, but in truth, she was glad to be the recipient of the heat emanating from Rob's lean body.

To divert her attention away from the disconcerting yet strangely welcome sensation, Jessie focused again on the puzzle that was Mr. Robert Burnley.

"I take it ye're acquainted with the Earl of Strathburn and his family, Mr. Burnley?" she ventured, refusing to use his Christian name as he'd requested. She needed to put some sort of distance between them—to insert some semblance of formality into the situation, given there was nothing remotely appropriate about the way they were seated. With each swaying step of the horse, her back and rump pressed and rubbed up against the man.

There was a tense pause. Rob's fingers clenched around the reins, but he soon answered smoothly enough. "Aye, I am. Although it's been some time since I last encountered Lord Strathburn, I'm sure he won't mind that I'm using his hunting lodge. While we've drifted apart in recent years, our ties are...long-standing."

They both lapsed into silence. Jessie's mind wandered between thoughts and questions as insubstantial and half-formed as the roiling fog. She should ask Rob about the exact nature of his association with the earl and his family. For instance, was he an old friend of Simon's? Or perhaps he was a distant relation? Or...or could he actually be Lord Strathburn's long-lost son, Robert Grant?

Jessie knit her brows as she turned over the idea in her mind. Rob Burnley had blue eyes that were a similar hue to Lord Strathburn's... But then, many folk had blue eyes. Furthermore, the bearded, granite-jawed Scot who was currently sharing his horse and plaid with her bore little resemblance to the fresh-faced young man she'd seen in the earl's miniature portrait. She'd assumed the youth *was* Lord Lochrose, but perhaps it wasn't. Maybe it had been a picture of the earl himself in his younger days. Or his own father. She had no way of knowing.

In any event, Jessie was suddenly finding it difficult to think about anything except her own immediate discomfort. The unsettling physicality of the man behind her, the persistent pain of her injuries, and the bone-chilling rain were all beginning to wear on her.

Several quiet minutes passed before Rob startled her out of her fog of fatigue with a question of his own. "What were you doing up here all alone, Jessie?"

Jessie's pulse began to hammer and her mouth grew dry. What should she tell him? How much of her situation should she disclose? "I-I was... I was on my way to Grantown...and I—" She broke off and swallowed. "I enjoy long challenging walks and I wanted to see the countryside. But then, as ye know, I sprained my ankle." Her explanation sounded weak, implausible even to her own ears.

"Mmm, I see..." Rob paused and the taut moment stretched. "So I take it you reside nearby? You too seem familiar with Lord Strathburn and his family."

Rob's tone had been neutral, but even so, Jessie fought to control another surge of panic. She needed to think clearly. Although she was alone and essentially defenseless, if she implied a *close* sort of relationship with the earl—rather than revealing that she was only the factor's daughter and a mere companion to Lady Strathburn—Rob would believe she had connections in high places. While he hadn't behaved in an untoward manner—at least so far—she might be safer if the man believed she was under Lord and Lady Strathburn's protection.

"I-I've been... I've been staying at Lochrose Castle for several weeks," she stammered, silently cursing her incoherence. It made her sound like the nervous liar she was.

Rob's deep voice was at her ear. "And will not the earl and his family be expecting you home, then? I wonder why they've let you roam so far by yourself."

~

Though he waited, Robert did not receive an answer to his question. Tension seemed to be vibrating through Jessie's whole body. Not only was she shivering, but her spine and shoulders were as rigid as the stony peaks surrounding them. He'd obviously terrified the lass into silence by making such a point of her isolation.

Part of Robert regretted that this relentless line of questioning was destroying any hope of forging some sort of *rapport* between them—but he needed to know if Simon or anyone else would miss the young woman and come looking for her...and in doing so, find him.

He was just about to ask her something else, when Jessie spoke. "Aye, I expect Lord and Lady Strathburn will be verra worried by now," she said. "They may send out the Watch to look for me."

What a brave, clever lass she is. "Yes, I'm sure they will, Jessie," Robert remarked, if only to reassure the young woman that he meant her no harm. Other than what he'd already inflicted on her, albeit accidentally.

And all because I had a stupid bloody craving for venison.

Robert couldn't help but admire the lass's strategy of hinting that she had powerful allies who would be concerned about her welfare. Her choice of words was interesting too. She'd said that Lord and Lady

Strathburn would be worried. *Not* Simon... But he'd witnessed Simon and Jessie's tryst...

Robert seriously doubted that Jessie Munroe and his brother had any sort of formal understanding. For one thing, Lady Ogilvy hadn't mentioned that Simon was betrothed. Of course, their dinner party conversation in Jamaica *had* taken place a few months ago, so the situation *might* have changed. But Robert knew down to his very bones that Simon wasn't the marrying kind. And surely the lass would disclose such a significant relationship if she *were* actually engaged to the Earl of Strathburn's son.

Of course, Jessie might be his father's ward. In that case, the Watch and other clansmen would definitely be sent out to search for her.

Damn it. Robert gnashed his teeth together in frustration. He really didn't need this. But then, would the Watch or perhaps even Simon be out scouring these upland glens and corries on a diabolical evening like this? Despite the dangerous conditions they just might, but with any luck they'd wait until morning. In any case, to be on the safe side, he and Tobias would need to take turns keeping watch throughout the night.

The ride continued at a painstakingly slow pace. The freezing rain grew steadily heavier and the scudding clouds of thick fog made it impossible to see more than a few feet ahead. Every now and again, thunder growled and lightning briefly illuminated the clouds around them. The air was charged with strange currents.

Robert wrapped his plaid tighter around Jessie, hugging her close in an effort to share his body heat, but it was all for naught. It wasn't long before both of them were soaked and Jessie was quaking with cold. No doubt she was also experiencing a considerable degree of pain and even emotional shock.

Despite the abysmal conditions, Robert was astounded to find himself being overtaken by a powerful physical reaction to having Jessie so close to his own body. Try as he might, he couldn't ignore the soft swell of her breast rubbing against the inside of his arm as he held her securely on his horse, or the press of her lower back and the firm round-ness of her buttocks rocking rhythmically against his groin.

Christ, what am I thinking? Now was *not* the time to be experiencing any kind of lustful stirrings in his breeks. Besides, if he were to hazard a guess, the lass was only in her early twenties; she was not the sort of woman he usually dallied with.

Robert's thoughts continued to race as his horse trod steadfastly forward through the driving sheets of rain. What *was* Miss Jessie Munroe really doing up here all alone? She'd been essentially wandering in the middle of nowhere, with only a satchel containing a few pieces of food, some guineas, and underclothes. Robert had discreetly looked inside her bag as he'd secured it to the saddle. It was difficult to believe that she'd decided to negotiate such a challenging and largely inhospitable route through the mountains to Grantown on a mere whim, especially since there was a perfectly good road between Lochrose and the village. Surely his father or Simon would have offered the lass a carriage, or at the very least, a horse.

There *had* to be another reason as to why she'd ventured up here. A *significant* reason.

Robert's thoughts returned to Jessie and Simon's encounter by the loch. The pair *must* be embroiled in an illicit love affair. That was the only scenario that made sense. Perhaps they'd arranged a clandestine rendezvous at the hunting lodge. That would explain Jessie's foray up here and even the contents of her satchel. Indeed, Robert had used the lodge for such assignations on a handful of occasions in his youth. It was secluded—the perfect place for lovers to meet without fear of being disturbed.

However, Robert dismissed the notion that Simon would be anywhere about at the present moment. When he and Tobias had left the lodge mid-afternoon to go hunting, neither of them had seen a soul in the glen until they'd encountered Jessie. Unless Simon had changed dramatically in the last ten years, it was not likely that his lily-livered half-brother would be up here, particularly in this foul weather. He had neither the guts nor the stamina. He probably would've turned his tail homeward at the first spot of rain for fear of catching a cold.

The memory of Simon kissing Jessie so passionately—so possessively—invaded Robert's mind. Anger surged and he resisted the urge to pull this lovely young woman harder against him.

Don't be an idiotic fool, Robert. You don't know her. She's not yours. She can share her affections with whomever she pleases.

Precisely why he was so envious of Simon's claim on Jessie—formal or otherwise—Robert did not know. Right now, it was useless to examine his completely irrational feelings. He needed to focus his energies on working out how this unexpected turn of events—injuring and now taking care of Jessie—would affect his plans to reunite with his father, and ultimately his chance at securing a pardon. One thing was certain, given the appalling weather and Jessie's condition: there was no way in Hades he could return to Lochrose Castle tonight.

At long last Robert noticed the shadowy forms of trees through the driving rain and blanketing fog. They weren't far from shelter now. Jessie's head had lolled back against his shoulder some time ago, though he suspected she'd passed out rather than fallen asleep. Regardless of the risk to himself, and now regrettably Tobias through association, there was no doubt in his mind that he'd taken the right course of action in assisting the girl. He couldn't have left her at the burn, all alone and wounded. Especially not on a wet and freezing night like this. She could easily perish from exposure to the cold.

So now he faced a monumental dilemma: what was he going to do with Jessie after tonight? Rescuing damsels in distress had not figured into his plans whatsoever, especially damsels that may be in league with his half-brother. She was undoubtedly a canny lass. Even though she'd been gripped by pain and befuddled with shock and fear, she'd unerringly noticed Tobias's slip when the lad had referred to him as *my lord*. They both needed to be extremely careful about what they said around her. Robert would need to remind Tobias later to only ever refer to him as Rob. Her loyalties were unknown, and revealing his true identity to the lass could very well be a death sentence.

But that begged the question, did Jessie even know of the Jacobite, Robert Grant, the long-lost Master of Strathburn and Viscount Lochrose? That after all this time, he was still a wanted man with a price on his head? Now Robert had returned—and if she had clear designs on his half-brother—would she also see him as a direct threat to Simon's future claim to the Earldom of Strathburn?

Robert released a long, low breath. He was not sure how far he could trust Jessie Munroe, if at all.

CHAPTER 8

Even before Jessie opened her eyes, she was conscious of the fact that her clothes were soaking wet and she was colder than she'd ever been in her entire life. Not only were her teeth chattering, but her body was wracked with uncontrollable shivers. To make matters worse, her injured arm and ankle both throbbed in time with her heartbeat. Someone had placed a woolen blanket over her—it scratched beneath her chin—and her cheek lay against something relatively soft. A cushion or pillow, perhaps?

Forcing open her eyelids, Jessie confirmed that she was inside some sort of dimly lit dwelling. Lord Strathburn's hunting lodge, she presumed. And she wasn't alone...

Wariness prickled along Jessie's spine as her gaze found Robert Burnley. *Rob.*

He was but a handful of feet away, kneeling before a small fireplace. Poker in hand, he prodded the firewood to encourage the flames to take purchase. In the flickering light, it was clear he was also dripping wet.

Biting her lip to stop herself from whimpering, Jessie used her good arm to push herself up to a sitting position on the small settee where she'd been lying. A wave of dizziness assailed her and everything tipped crazily for a moment before righting itself. The stone-walled chamber—

a bedroom—was low-ceilinged and sparsely furnished. Apart from the settee, there was a simply carved four-poster bed opposite the now blazing fireplace. A large wooden chest stood at its foot.

Jessie's gaze skittered away from the bed and settled warily on Rob. *What is he going to do with me?* She really wished she had that poker in her grasp. *Just in case...*

"How are you feeling, Jessie?"

She started, her attention darting to Rob's face. His blue eyes were even darker in the uncertain light of the fire, his gaze intent—*speculative*—as he studied her in turn.

Jessie swallowed and found her voice. "A wee b-bit c-cold and sore," she said as she gathered the blanket about her. Despite her half-frozen state, her cheeks grew hot as Rob continued his quiet scrutiny.

"And I think that is a wee bit of an understatement, my lass," he said with a wry smile. "You must be chilled to the bone and in a *considerable* amount of pain. But I'll take good care of you. There's nothing to fear."

Strangely, Jessie was inclined to believe Rob's last pronouncement. She detected no menace, only compassion in the man's gaze as it briefly lingered on her face before raking over the rest of her in an assessing sweep. What a sight she must present, shaking, and dripping, and blood-ied. As weak and defenseless as a lamb.

Rob, on the other hand, seemed anything *but* defenseless. Even though he was as completely sodden as herself, he looked so blatantly masculine and powerful—indeed, so physically attractive—Jessie's heart hammered against her ribs. He'd removed his plaid and coat and was now simply clad in buckskin breeches and a shirt. The wet, almost trans-parent linen clung to the broad expanse of his well-muscled chest, impossibly wide shoulders, and sizable biceps. She recalled the feel of their steely strength when he'd carried her, how it had felt to be pressed against his hard, warm body with his arm around her on the ride here. She blushed again at the memory.

Stop staring like yer daft, Jessie Munroe. Say something. "Aye, I b-b-believe you, sir," she forced out between her chattering teeth.

"You mean, Rob," he said, his wide mouth tilting into an appealing grin, his even teeth a flash of white against the stubble darkening his tanned jaw.

"R-Rob," she conceded, attempting to smile back. The man's charm was infectious. And dangerous. She attempted to pull the blanket more firmly around herself to still her shaking, but winced as a hot knife of pain sliced through her arm.

Rob noticed her discomfort immediately. He frowned with what appeared to be genuine concern. His next words however, sparked alarm. "Jessie, you're going to have to get out of your wet things and let me take a closer look at your injuries."

Jessie shook her head emphatically. *Like hell.* "N-N-No. If I sit b-by the fire I'll b-be all right."

"No, you won't," he said firmly. "You've been through quite an ordeal—not to mention you've been exposed to the elements—and I have no idea how much blood you've lost from the wound in your arm. I think my bullet only grazed you, but I need to be sure. You need to get dry and warm and bandaged up properly."

He said this with such quiet determination that Jessie knew he spoke sense. But she was *not* going to undress in front of him, a complete stranger. *A dangerously attractive man.*

Rob seemed to guess the reason for her reluctance. "Well. I'll leave you here to change. Unless you'd like some help...?"

Certainly no'. We're in a bedchamber for heaven's sake! Jessie shook her head and sat up a little straighter. "N-N-No, thank you. I think I'll be able to manage."

Rob's eyes narrowed slightly in apparent disbelief, but he inclined his head. "As you wish," he said, standing up and heading for the door. "Your satchel is on the small table beside you, and there's a linen towel, dry shirt, and plaid at the foot of the bed. I'll just be in the next room, so call if you need anything else."

No' bloody likely. As soon as the door clicked shut, relief washed over Jessie. She knew she should do as Rob had suggested. And seeing all the items he'd laid out for her, she couldn't help but be touched by how thoughtful he was. She decided then and there that she would accept that he was just trying to help. Not every man was like Simon.

She slowly pushed herself to her feet. Although she still felt slightly unsteady and could barely put any weight on her ankle, Jessie didn't think she would topple over or fall into a faint. Dropping the already damp blanket along with her sodden cloak onto the wooden floor, she limped to the bed to begin the painful process of undressing without assistance.

One thing at a time, Jessie. She sat on the wooden chest and dried her face, neck, and hair as best she could with the coarse linen towel. Somewhere along the way she'd lost her ribbon, and her curls were a snarled, dripping mess. Bending down, she tried to remove her remaining boot, but even that simple act left her dizzy and gasping in pain. Her frustration ratcheted even higher when she discovered the ribbon garters securing the tops of her stockings just above her knees were hopelessly knotted. Her half-frozen, trembling fingers could not prize them undone, no matter how hard she tried.

The task of removing the rest of her soaking wet clothes suddenly seemed beyond her. Untying her gown's laces would be impossible to manage one-handed. Jessie raised a shaking hand to the back of her bodice, but as she suspected, her efforts were ineffectual. Tears of frustration pricked behind her eyelids.

A light knock made her jump like a startled rabbit. "Just checking if you're all right," Rob called through the door.

"Ye...ye m-may come in." Jessie hastily dashed away her tears as he entered.

He frowned when his gaze settled on her, though whether it was because of her inaction or the fact she'd been crying, she couldn't have said. He'd evidently had no trouble changing out of his wet things into a loose, white linen shirt, fresh buckskin breeches, and black leather top boots. His dark hair, still noticeably damp, hung loose to his shoulders.

"I c-canna seem to manage, after all." She gestured at her bandaged arm by way of explanation for not having undressed.

Without a word, Rob crossed the room and knelt before her. His eyes held hers for one long moment, and Jessie couldn't help but wonder what he was thinking. Even though his expression was unreadable, his tone was gentle when he spoke. "Let's take a look at your ankle first, lass. I don't think it's broken, but let's see what damage has been done."

Jessie nodded. She closed her eyes, and her whole face burned with embarrassment as Rob carefully lifted her skirts and began to unfasten the ribbon ties of her stockings. Gripping the edge of the wooden chest, she swallowed past a tight throat. She couldn't believe she was letting this complete stranger touch her in such an intimate fashion.

But the most incredible thing of all was that her body was reacting in a completely different way to how it usually did when Simon Grant took liberties. While she felt oddly unsettled, she was not repulsed by Rob's hands on her bare skin. Her flesh tingled wherever his long, capable fingers grazed her. And warmth—something like desire—began to bloom low in her belly.

Of all the strange and unexpected events that had occurred today, the fact that she *wasn't* filled with the overwhelming impulse to shrink away from Mr. Rob Burnley was perhaps the most bizarre of all.

God's teeth, how am I supposed to help Jessie undress with any semblance of composure?

Robert's blood began to pound hard and fast through his veins as he bent to the task of lifting Jessie's skirts and exposing her legs. When he'd first entered the room and been struck with the full realization of what he must do, he'd been determined to steel himself against his body's primal urges. He'd sternly reminded himself that this woman was quite possibly Simon's paramour and he could not trust her. He must not fall beneath her spell.

Yet despite his resolution, he was swiftly becoming hopelessly aroused...and unaccountably nervous. His hands were shaking. Even the pace of his breathing had accelerated.

For Christ's sake, control yourself, Robert Grant. He was reacting like a green, unskilled youth, not a man of one-and-thirty years who'd undressed and bedded his fair share of women.

Inhaling a bracing breath, he tried to concentrate on simply undoing Jessie's garters and rolling down her wet woolen stockings one by one. He would *not* dwell on the fact that her legs were impossibly long, pale, and slender. Or that wherever his fingers brushed, a trail of light goosebumps was left in their wake.

Carefully lifting her naked right foot, Robert placed it on his buckskin clad thigh then probed the swollen tissues of her ankle with gentle fingers. The brave lass answered his questions as he moved the joint this way, then that, tolerating his examination with nary a complaint. Not even a whimper.

While the base male in Robert would like nothing more than to kiss Jessie's delicate arch and run his tongue along the silken skin behind her knee, he crushed the errant thoughts and instead placed her foot gently on the floor.

"Good news," he said gruffly without looking at her whisky-hued eyes. "No broken bones, as far as I can tell. It's just a sprain. I'll strap your ankle after I attend to your arm."

He swallowed hard and stood up. Thank heavens his long linen shirt hung loose, hiding his unruly cock straining against the front of his breeches. He did not want Jessie to be alarmed. "Do ye think you can stand so I can help with your gown?"

"Aye. The fastenings are at the back of my bodice." She rose slowly then turned, presenting her slender back to him.

Robert suddenly wondered if Simon had ever undressed her in this very room. His eyes darted to the four-poster bed in front of Jessie. Had they lain together right here, too?

The same frustrated anger he'd experienced that morning at the loch lanced through him, hot and sharp. What could this gorgeous lass possibly see in his half-brother?

Somehow tamping down his illogical ire, Robert unclenched his fists, blew out a breath, then willed himself to get on with the job at hand. The sooner she was undressed, the sooner she could be clothed in warm, dry clothes, and he'd never have to touch her in such an intimate way again.

So he could gain better access to the ties at the back of Jessie's gown, Robert carefully brushed the heavy curtain of her damp curls over one of her shoulders, releasing a tantalizing scent of fresh rainwater and something else that was floral and wholly feminine.

Bloody hell. His cock grew even harder. At this rate, he'd spend in his breeches before he'd even removed her gown.

Gritting his teeth, Robert steadfastly ignored the pale-as-cream skin at the nape of Jessie's neck and the elegant line of her spine which was gradually exposed as he loosened the laces. As gently as he could, he eased the ripped bodice over her injured arm. Even so, she flinched and sucked in a sharp breath as the sodden wool slid over the bloody bandage. The remaining sleeve slipped off easily and then her gown fell to the floor. Her petticoats quickly followed.

Jessie now stood before him in only her wet shift and stays. God help him—he'd never been so physically affected by a woman in all his life. Too scared to make another move in case it was the wrong one, he ran a hand through his damp hair, waiting for some further direction from the lass.

Even though her back was still toward him, Robert could tell she was fumbling with another set of ties.

When Jessie spoke, her words would surely bring about his undoing. "I'm afraid the laces o' my stays are at the front, and they're knotted too tightly. My...my fingers do no' seem to be working verra well." Her whole body was trembling, and her voice was little more than a husky whisper.

And then Robert's breath snagged inside his chest as Jessie turned to face him.

Christ, she's beautiful.

He was stunned. *Enthralled.*

Her luscious figure and wild red hair were bathed in golden firelight. And her lovely face... Her eyes were cast downward, her cheeks flushed, and her full lips slightly parted. Above the damp, almost transparent linen of her shift, the plump mounds of her breasts rose and fell with her rapid breathing. Rogue that he was, he burned to know the color of her nipples.

Thanking the Lord she couldn't hear his rampantly lustful thoughts, Robert raised his hands and proceeded to untie the stay's stubborn laces. When his knuckles accidentally brushed the soft, full underside of Jessie's breasts, he almost groaned. As soon as the task was accomplished, he turned abruptly away from her and strode over to the fireplace on the other side of the room.

The logs weren't the only things in this bedchamber that were aflame. Robert gripped the rough stone mantelpiece as though he were about to rip it apart. He was going to need a dram of whisky, or to go out into the freezing rain—or perhaps both—before he would be able to attend to Jessie's arm.

Behind him, he heard the soft plop of wet garments on the floor then the rustle of dry fabric as Jessie pulled on the clothes he'd provided—a linen shirt like his own and a Clan Grant hunting plaid. He was relieved his family's plaids hadn't been confiscated by the dragoons hereabouts. Since the Rebellion, the wearing of tartan cloth had been banned except for members of the Black Watch. Still safely folded in the chest at the end of the bed between disintegrating bunches of dried lavender, it looked like the clothing hadn't been disturbed for years.

Perhaps ten years.

When Robert turned around, he was surprised at how much it pleased him to see Jessie in his clan's colors. They suited her well. But then, she'd look gorgeous in a sackcloth and ashes.

He forced himself to meet her wary gaze. She was obviously waiting for his next move. Smiling in an attempt to affect a calm he in no way felt, he said gruffly, "Right, Jessie. Let's get this arm seen to."

Jessie nodded, too overwhelmed to speak. She didn't think she'd ever endured anything so disquieting before. The stranger who'd accidentally shot her had just undressed her. Instead of being horrified, she'd all but welcomed his touch.

Good Lord. What did that say about her? When had she become such a wanton?

Indeed, she couldn't meet Rob's eyes when he swung her up into his arms and carried her through into the next room.

Could one die from mortification?

The hunting lodge seemed to consist of two main areas: the bedchamber they'd just quit, and the room they were presently in—a relatively spacious kitchen-cum-dining-room. It was furnished with a large oak dining setting, a matching dresser, and several armchairs and a low table were arranged before the fireplace. Through an open doorway on the far side of the room, Jessie also spied a smaller chamber which appeared to contain little more than a single pallet bed. Saddlebags were piled near another door that she presumed led outside. Tobias, now also dry, stood by the fire, lighting candles upon the mantelpiece with a taper.

The young man sent her an uncertain smile as Rob conveyed her over to the sitting area and placed her gently in the armchair closest to the hearth. It was only then that Jessie noticed the curious array of items covering the low wooden table: several large bowls, one filled with water; a towel beside several torn strips of linen; a small leather pouch and a silver clan brooch; and finally, a pair of glass tumblers and a bottle of whisky.

Jessie bit her lip as trepidation nipped. She suddenly felt nervous. *Very* nervous.

Rob, his expression now grave, sat on a padded footstool to her left. He clubbed his hair back with a leather tie, all business. "All right, lass. Let's roll up that sleeve."

Before she could even say aye or nay, he pushed the loose fabric up to her shoulder and pinned it out of the way with the silver brooch. It was disturbing to see how much blood had seeped through the makeshift bandage. Jessie bit her lip harder and tried not to whimper as Rob unwound the linen. Every movement increased the throbbing.

When the bandage was off, she stole a glance at Rob's face. His brow had knitted into a deep frown. "How bad is it?" she whispered. She swore that she could feel fresh warm blood oozing down her arm.

"Deeper than I thought, but I've seen worse." Rob looked straight into her eyes. "Jessie, you're going to have to be brave for a wee bit longer."

Her stomach flipped like a landed salmon. "Wh-What do you mean?"

Rob squeezed her hand, the heat of his touch nothing now compared to the panic rising within her. "This may sound odd, but I've learned from experience that wounds should be thoroughly cleaned to avoid any purulence developing. For some reason that I cannot explain, the *uisge beatha*"—he nodded at the bottle of whisky—"seems to do the trick. Once that's done, I'll...I'll have to put in a few stitches. Five or six at most."

Jessie closed her eyes and nodded. She did not like the sound of this at all.

"I want you to drink this first." Rob was offering her a tumbler with a sizable dram of the whisky in it. She took a tentative sip. It tasted of peat and honey as it burned a warm trail down her tight throat.

"All of it, lass. It will help."

Jessie obediently tossed it back. The whisky was potent stuff and made her cough a little. On an empty stomach, it was already going straight to her head. Not only that, but an odd warmth seemed to be penetrating her limbs, making her feel as limp and relaxed as a rag doll... until Rob glanced at Tobias who'd been hovering nearby and said, "Can you hold her lower arms, lad?" Rob's eyes returned to hers. "I won't lie to you, Jessie. This bit is going to hurt."

Jessie's heart crashed against her ribs and her throat constricted as Tobias reached from behind and firmly held her forearms against the arms of the chair. With horrified fascination, she watched as Rob poured out another measure of whisky into a clean tumbler. He dipped a pad of folded linen into it. Then, with a steady hand, he pressed the whisky-soaked pad against her open wound.

Jessie couldn't contain her scream. Excruciating fire ripped through her and she bucked against Tobias's hold. Her breath came in short, ragged gasps and nausea swelled within her. "I'm goin' to be sick."

Rob was ready for her. He calmly and swiftly placed an empty bowl in her lap and held back her hair as she brought up the meager contents of her stomach. When she was done, he wiped her face gently with the clean towel and offered her a tumbler of water to rinse out her mouth.

"All right, the worst part's almost over, lass," he said, compassion lighting his eyes. "Tobias will hold you still again while I put in the stitches."

Jessie nodded, too weak to speak. She was trembling from head to toe. Would this nightmare ever be over?

Rob opened the small leather pouch and threaded a needle with fine cotton. These he also doused in whisky before he proceeded to stitch the laceration. It hurt like the very devil and brought stinging tears to Jessie's eyes, but Rob had been correct when he'd said that the worst part was almost over. He was efficient and in no time at all, the stitches were in. To finish, he applied another bandage of fresh linen, then let down her sleeve.

When he was done, Robert sat back and wiped a hand down his face. For all his outward calm, his fingers were now slightly shaking too.

He offered her a weak smile. "We're nearly finished."

Jessie swallowed hard. "What do ye mean, *nearly?*"

Rob moved even closer to her and gently pushed her drying hair away from her left temple. "I wanted to check the graze from the splinter." With a fresh damp cloth, he carefully wiped away traces of dried blood which the rain obviously hadn't washed away.

His face was very close. *Too* close. Jessie's gaze dropped from his dark blue eyes to his wide sensual mouth, just inches from her own. *What would it be like to be kissed by those lips?*

Although heat flooded her cheeks at the errant thought, she couldn't seem to tear her gaze away. *What in heaven's name was wrong with her?* Shock and the whisky had clearly addled her brain.

Tobias cleared his throat. "Och...weel, I'll just clean up a few things, shall I, milord? I mean, Rob. And then I'll ready supper."

Rob shook his head a little as if he were waking up and a wee bit dazed. He drew back slightly then nodded curtly at Tobias who was already beating a hasty retreat outside with the discarded bowl and used tumblers. A gust of freezing wind blew in from the night, and the candle flames and fire guttered before the door slammed shut. The strange mood was broken.

Rob turned back to Jessie, all business again. "Well, let's bind this troublesome ankle before supper, shall we? I don't know about you, but I'm famished."

Jessie couldn't have said why, but the mischievous imp inside her that was forever getting her into trouble, decided to show itself. She affected a sigh then curved her mouth into a rueful smile. "Such a shame we're no' having venison."

Rob, clearly startled, raised his eyebrows then threw his head back and laughed. "I couldn't agree with you more, Jessie Munroe," he said, amusement and perhaps even admiration dancing in his eyes. "I couldn't agree more."

CHAPTER 9

Despite her hunger, Jessie had only been able to stomach a little of the rye bread from her satchel. She willingly shared the rest of it, her wedge of cheese, and the apples with Rob and Tobias. For their part, they were happy to share their stash of salted beef and oatcakes. It wasn't a grand supper by any means, but it would do.

In the end, Jessie was too exhausted to ponder the enigma that was Mr. Rob Burnley for too long. Perhaps he *was* just a poacher who was pretending that he knew the earl. While he did seem familiar with the lodge—and appeared quite comfortable inhabiting it, almost like he belonged here—that wasn't so odd if he'd used the place as a secret hunting base before. These upland moors were quite deserted after all.

The second dram of whisky she'd had with her meal sat much better than the first. Indeed, a heavy, pleasant warmth spread through Jessie as she sat before the fire, tucked up in the plaid and a thick woolen blanket. Even though her arm and ankle still pulsed with steady pain, it wasn't long before her eyes grew heavy and her head began to nod.

She could hear Rob and Tobias in quiet conversation as they sat nearby at the scrubbed oak dining table, their voices nothing more than a murmur above the steady tattoo of heavy rain on the roof. Perhaps she even drifted into a light doze—for how long she wasn't sure—but something roused her to full consciousness again. She was aware of the two men still talking. Then Tobias said her name and her breath hitched in her throat.

They were discussing her. Her eyes were closed so they clearly thought she was sound asleep.

"What do ye think she was really doing up here, milord?"

"After what I saw this morning by the loch, I can only assume that she and Simon must have been planning another assignation. But the inclement weather has clearly put him off."

"So do ye think they're definitely...lovers?"

There was a taut pause before Rob answered. "What I witnessed was more than just a friendly embrace, Tobias. The questions I keep asking myself are: how did Jessie come to be at Lochrose, and how significant is her connection to Simon? Most importantly, can I trust her?"

God in heaven. Rob had been at Loch Kilburn this morning and had seen her with Simon! More than that, he'd witnessed Simon *kissing* her. But Rob had misinterpreted everything.

Why had he been at the loch in the first place?

Aside from that, both Rob and Tobias *knew* Simon.

Before Jessie could even think on what she'd learned, Tobias asked another question that set her heart galloping. "What are ye going to do with her, milord?"

Jessie's breath froze in her lungs as she waited for Rob's reply. *Why didn't he respond? Was it really that difficult a question?*

"I don't know yet," came his low answer eventually. "It's a complicated situation to say the least. If Jessie goes back to Lochrose, there's a good chance she'll tell Simon about us. Of course, he'll easily put two and two together and set the Watch or dragoons on me. I can't risk being arrested."

"Do ye really think Simon would do that?"

"It's more than a definite possibility. I'd wager my soul it's exactly what he'd do."

Breathe, Jessie, breathe. Don't let them know ye're eavesdropping. There was another short pause in which she heard the clinking of glass followed by the glug of liquid from a bottle.

Rob spoke again. "She's a problem I wasn't expecting," he said softly. "And it could be my downfall."

"Do ye think Simon will be out looking for her tonight or on the morrow then, milord?"

There was a low chuckle. "Well, I suppose it depends on the weather." A serious note returned to Rob's voice. "But it's likely that the Black Watch will be out and about at any rate if she *was* expected back at the castle tonight."

"She's a comely lass, milord. Perchance she's nowt but a tumble in the hay for Simon?"

"Mmm. That is one possibility. But I think she's maybe a little more than that. She's refined. She speaks and dresses well and there were guineas in her satchel. The horse she rode to the loch this morning was the mount of a genteel woman. She's not just a lass from the village or a servant at the castle. I *did* wonder if she might be my father's ward."

"Perhaps I could ask my cousin Annie, or the other staff at the castle about her."

"On the surface that sounds like a reasonable course of action to take, Tobias. Perhaps tomorrow, but only after we've discussed a line of questioning that won't arouse suspicion. We need to exercise caution whatever we decide to do about Jessie. If we let her go, she'll undoubtedly tell Simon about us..." There was a slight pause then Rob added in a low voice, "We might appear to be poachers, but there's a very good chance that he might work out what is really going on when she provides him with a description of me."

In the heavy silence that followed Rob's pronouncement, the crackle of burning logs in the fireplace and the drum of steady rain were the only discernible sounds. All the while, Jessie's thoughts tumbled over each other as her mind worked furiously to make sense of what she'd just heard. Even with her eyes closed, she sensed Rob's attention was on her. It was like she could feel his stare—as if he were actually touching her. She strove to stay perfectly motionless, to control her breathing, to keep her expression neutral. She must have succeeded in convincing him she was still asleep as he soon resumed the speculative discussion...about her.

"On the other hand, if we keep Jessie with us, we also run the risk of

Simon, or others who care for her, sending out a search party. Either way, we'll have the Black Watch or the dragoons on our tails."

"I dinna think she will take kindly to being held against her will."

"Aye, I believe you may be right on that score, Tobias."

"She kens too much, milord."

"Aye, she does. She's definitely a complication we could do without."

"Maybe it would be easier if we just—" Tobias suddenly broke off.

A chair scraped on the wooden floor and footsteps approached.

Jessie's pulse bolted clean away. What if they could tell she'd been listening all this time? Her heart was thudding so violently in her chest, she was certain they must be able to hear it. What had Tobias meant when he'd said it would be easier to...what? Do away with her?

They see me as a threat of some kind.

A complication.

Had fear registered on her face? Had she given herself away?

A shadow moved across her and she swallowed a scream.

"Jessie?" It was Rob.

Despite her best efforts to control her breathing, it was rapid and shallow. He would know—he would know she'd heard everything! What were they going to do—

Rob's hand was on her knee. "Jessie lass, wake up."

Jessie's eyes flew open and she gasped. Rob was bending over her, his far-too-handsome face was very close to her own.

"It's all right, lass," he said softly. "You must have been having a nightmare."

Jessie nodded. *Aye, she was trapped in a nightmare.* A waking nightmare. But the cold fear gripping her heart was all too real.

"I'll carry you to bed," Rob continued in a soothing velvet voice. "You'll sleep better there."

As he effortlessly lifted her up, Jessie started to protest, but he simply cast her a lopsided grin. "It's no trouble at all, lass." His warm breath caressed her ear. "You don't want to be putting weight on that ankle yet. You've been hurt enough for one day."

His tone and expression were completely at odds with what he'd just been saying to Tobias, and that unnerved Jessie even further.

How could Rob dispassionately discuss holding her captive—perhaps even *disposing* of her—in one moment, then utter honeyed words delivered with a charming smile in the next?

With equal measures of trepidation and disappointment welling within her, Jessie realized that Mr. Robert Burnley *was* dangerous after all. A true wolf in sheep's clothing.

Rob carried her through to the main bedchamber and placed her gently on the large bed so that she reclined against the pillows. Then, without invitation, he sat down beside her. "I'm afraid the bedding is a bit dusty and in need of a good airing. But at least it's warm and dry," he said.

Jessie nodded, not trusting herself to speak. She was so disconcerted, only heaven knew if she'd be able to produce more than a rush of panicked gibberish. She didn't *think* Rob was deliberately trying to intimidate her by sitting so close. There was no threat evident in his voice or expression, and since she'd been injured, he'd shown her nothing but kindness. But was it all a ruse? Was he trying to lull her into a false sense of security whilst he worked out how to dispose of the problem she was assumed to be? She was so confused and heartsick. And more than a wee bit frightened.

Jessie dropped her gaze to the bedclothes. She couldn't look at him.

Rob continued to sit on the edge of the bed, watching her. Was he waiting for her to say something? Jessie wanted to reassure him that she wasn't a threat, that she had no allegiance to Simon Grant whatsoever. She didn't want him to believe she was Simon's paramour, despite what Rob thought he'd seen by Loch Kilburn.

More than anything she wanted him to know the truth—that the thought of being Simon's lover made her feel ill.

But how could she speak of such awkward, degrading things when she hardly knew Rob? Would he even believe her? He had no reason to trust her. Perhaps he would think she was denying a tie to Simon simply to save her own skin. Jessie worried her bottom lip whilst she tried to work through all the twists and turns of her thinking.

Perhaps if...if she just expressed how grateful she was for his care. Surely if he understood she hadn't taken all he'd done for her thus far for granted—that she felt indebted to him—he might consider the possibility that she was actually an ally, at least on some level.

With some effort, Jessie pushed herself upright against the pillows and tried to ignore the press of Rob's long muscular leg against her own through the folds of the plaid. *She needed her wits about her.* She drew a shaky breath and forced herself to meet Rob's eyes. "I-I want to thank you...for helping me. I appreciate all that ye've done to take care of me since the accident. Ye've been nothing but kind and a...a gentleman, in every way."

Rob smiled at that, and she blushed as she remembered how he'd helped her to undress.

Pushing such unhelpful thoughts steadfastly away, Jessie garnered the remnants of her courage and continued. "I-I'm sorry to have caused ye so much trouble. If there is anything at all I can do to repay ye...ye only need to ask."

Jessie's breath caught as Rob's gaze immediately dropped to her lips. His eyes narrowed slightly and heat flared in their midnight blue depths. For a moment she had the impression that he was going to kiss her. Surely he didn't expect her to show gratitude in *that* way.

But what if he did? Jessie's pulse began running wildly and that warm flutter of desire she'd felt earlier stirred between her thighs. She was clearly daft. At the very least, she should be shocked, perhaps even outraged that Rob *might* actually be a ruthless rogue. The sort of man who'd take advantage of a woman in a vulnerable position. *A man like Simon Grant...*

But heaven help her, she wasn't shocked or outraged at all.

"Mmm," Rob murmured. He reached out and gently lifted her chin with a crooked finger so she was forced to look straight into his eyes. "You must not think that way, *mo ghaoil.* In fact, I'm the one who should be begging for your forgiveness for having hurt you so. If anyone needs recompense, it is *you,* Jessie Munroe."

With that, Rob got to his feet then carefully spread a thick quilt over her legs. "What's *most* important right now," he added, his manner full of soft reassurance, "is that you get some sleep, so I will bid you good-night." In the next instant he was gone, the door snicking shut behind him.

With a great shuddering sigh, Jessie sank back down onto the bed, thoughts too numerous to count spinning about in her head. Even though she was spent, sleep seemed impossible. She resolutely pushed away all thoughts about kissing Rob. Dwelling on that was *not* going to help her escape this predicament.

Regardless of everything that had befallen her today, her focus still needed to be on getting herself to Grantown to catch the public coach to Edinburgh as she'd planned. But that would be impossible if Rob decided to keep her captive or subdue her in some other way...

Yet he'd called her *mo ghaoil*. My dear.

She ruthlessly crushed the notion that Rob cared even a little about her. He'd used the Gaelic endearment simply to dupe her into trusting him.

With a frustrated groan, Jessie wrenched her mind back to the problem at hand. She reviewed all that she'd learned from the exchange she'd overheard between Rob and Tobias. She now strongly suspected that these men were not mere poachers, but fugitives of some kind. Why else would they be taking such great pains to evade the Black Watch and the dragoons? Rob Burnley especially.

But why? What had he done that was against the law?

Somehow, Rob knew Simon well. He was even aware of Simon's particular dislike of unpleasant weather. Indeed, the man seemed to think—for some reason that was completely unfathomable to her— that *Simon* was his biggest threat. And because of Rob's mistaken belief that she was in some kind of relationship with the vile rogue, he was now going to assess how much of a potential threat she was to his safety also.

But she was no threat at all.

Jessie again contemplated confessing that she and Simon were not lovers. That in actual fact, she was running away from Lochrose Castle *because* of Lord Strathburn's horrid son. At least then Rob might believe she had no loyalty to the odious Master of Strathburn.

But if she were honest and revealed she was just the factor's daughter, with no one really searching for her, Rob may see her as even more dispensable. It would be easier to remove a complication if that said complication wouldn't be missed at all. If she pretended to be someone of some importance to the earl and his son, it may stay Rob's hand in acting to silence her.

Jessie closed her eyes and tried to slow her breathing. Tried desperately to quell the maelstrom of panicked thoughts whirling through her mind.

Perhaps she should just run now? Perhaps when Rob and Tobias were asleep, she could sneak out and take one of the horses and ride to... Where? Lochrose and back to Simon Grant? She'd sooner die than return to him. And if she stayed at the Strathspey Arms, there was still the distinct possibility that Simon would find her there too.

Oh, blast it all to hell. Flight would be a near impossible feat, given her injuries. And then there was the problem of her lack of suitable clothes. Her gown was ruined, and she doubted she'd be able to put it back on. Wearing a hunting plaid which was proscribed was not conducive to remaining inconspicuous. She'd be noticed and apprehended on sight by any dragoons or Black Watch in the area.

Jessie pulled the quilt up to her chin. The rain lashed the hunting lodge's windows and the occasional flash of lightning lit the room. It was certainly not a night to be outside, especially considering her current state. Any attempt to leave here would be doomed to failure.

There was no feasible way of escape and no safe place to go. Her father, who could be anywhere right now, had no idea of the danger she was in and wouldn't worry about her for at least a fortnight...

Jessie had never felt so alone in all her life. Tears spilled out from under her eyelids. For a long time she watched the fire dying in the grate, until at last she succumbed to exhaustion.

When Robert entered the bedchamber again sometime later, it was to discover that Jessie was fast asleep. And she'd been crying. By the light of the candle he held aloft, he could detect the faint glimmer of half-dried tears on her cheeks.

Although he couldn't say for certain, his gut told him that the lass had been listening when he'd been talking to Tobias earlier. What a fool he'd been to let his guard down. When he'd approached Jessie, he hadn't failed to notice the tension in every line of her face, her erratic breathing, the alarm in her eyes. She'd been terrified. Now she probably knew he'd seen her with Simon. Knew he was contemplating what to do next. That he was a wanted man. But did she yet know he was Robert Grant, the Jacobite, heir to these lands? If he didn't lose his head on the executioner's block of course...

The fire had died to a low reddish glow. Robert placed the candle on the mantel, and after throwing another pine log into the grate, he absently watched the sparks fly up the chimney. Behind him, Jessie stirred slightly. He turned to look at her again. The sight of her in sleep made him ache in a way he didn't like. She was dangerous this woman, dangerous beyond imagining.

When he'd put her to bed earlier and she'd betrayed her nervousness by biting her fulsome bottom lip, it had taken every ounce of restraint he possessed to stop himself from seizing her then and there and kissing her senseless. The lustful male in him wanted to wake her now and join her in the bed, to make her want him as much as his body seemed to want her. Yet part of him also longed to lie beside her and fall asleep with his face buried in her luxurious hair. To take comfort from the simple pleasure of cradling this beautiful Highland lass in his arms.

Even now, the scent of warm, sleepy female beckoned to him like a siren's song. But he knew he would not share a bed tonight, or indeed any night, with Jessie.

She belonged to someone else.

His brother.

It suddenly occurred to Robert that his urge to possess Jessie sprang from an entirely selfish need—that perhaps she could somehow fill the gaping black void within him. That by getting lost in mindless pleasure, she'd help him forget his fears and assuage his ever-present guilt about his past failures.

But then again, perhaps he simply wanted her because he couldn't stand the idea of her being with Simon. The previously indefinable emotion that sliced through Robert whenever he pictured Jessie with his half-brother was jealousy, pure and simple.

Jealousy that twisted in his gut like a Highlander's dirk.

Frustrated by his conflicting thoughts and his mad, aching desire for a woman he couldn't have, Robert sighed heavily then threw himself onto the settee before the fire. He would stay by Jessie's bedside tonight. Given her injuries and the wild weather, it was unlikely she would run... But still, he couldn't take that chance.

Regardless of what she did or didn't know about him, or what she might guess, he was now certain he couldn't let her go.

~

Simon stood before the drawing room window of Lochrose, watching the storm lash the castle grounds and the woodland beyond. Every now and again, lightning illuminated the loch and the brooding mounds of the surrounding braes. The night perfectly matched his own foul mood. His Jezebel had gone and was nowhere to be found.

He'd given up the search for her about Lochrose when the bad weather had set in, late in the afternoon. He'd also sent Baird, his valet, to Grantown to look for the girl, but the man had returned alone.

Simon was certain Mrs. MacMillan was somehow involved in the girl's sudden disappearance. The old cow had been questioned by his mother but to no avail. The woman was sticking to her story that Jessie had been urgently summoned to Edinburgh to assist some cousin.

Simon didn't believe the tale for a minute.

Impotent anger as black and volatile as the storm clouds outside churned inside him. He tossed back another glass of cognac, but like always, the alcohol did little to douse his fury. His Jezebel was out there somewhere, somewhere close, he could feel it. The public coach for Edinburgh didn't pass through Grantown until the day after tomorrow, and the chit hadn't taken her horse or any other mount from Lochrose's stables.

She was hiding from him, but he would find her.

And when he did, he would make her so completely his, she would never dare to defy him again.

CHAPTER 10

When Jessie awoke the next morning, it was to discover that Rob had slept in the settee by the fire, only a handful of feet from the end of her bed.

Her breath caught at the unexpected and wholly overwhelming sight of him. Even though he was still asleep, he presented a formidable figure stretched out along the settee—all long, muscular legs encased in tight, buckskin breeches and black leather boots. His loose, linen shirt spread open at the neck and she glimpsed a deep inverted triangle of surprisingly tanned, taut skin that extended across his collarbones and down to the apex at the center of his breastbone. A pale ray of sunlight filtered through a gap in the window shutters behind him and caressed the dark stubble across the line of his strong jaw.

Despite her uncertain, perhaps even precarious situation, Jessie's thoughts slid into even more perilous territory as she couldn't help but wonder how Rob would look clean-shaven. It would be far easier to sustain her justifiable wariness if the man wasn't so devastatingly handsome. She simply couldn't think straight when she was around him. Why, he had the ability to turn her into a henwit, even when he was asleep. And when he smiled... Jessie shivered. Did he know what power he had over her? Did he wield his charm with calculated purpose? To disarm her so she would let down her guard?

Remember he's a fugitive, Jessie. He's dangerous. You cannot trust him.

You need to leave...

But how? She didn't even know if she could walk.

She carefully pushed herself up to a sitting position. Her arm still throbbed and the stitches tugged sharply, but thankfully her ankle seemed stiff rather than acutely painful. She was about to pull the covers back so she could slide out of bed when Rob stirred.

Damnation.

It took a moment for her darkly handsome captor to rouse completely. He rubbed the back of his neck as he sat up straight, then yawned, pushing his brown-black hair away from his face. The action made him seem strangely vulnerable.

Until his deep blue eyes focused intently on her. "Good morning, Jessie. I trust you slept well?"

Jessie swallowed, the sound audible in the silence. Rob's question threw her. A polite inquiry as to how she'd rested seemed completely out of place, given that the man had effectively stood guard over her all night. But she wouldn't show him that she was rattled.

Somehow she summoned a wry smile. "Better than you, I suspect."

Rob flashed a smile in return at her retort, his eyes traveling over her disheveled form. She blushed and snatched the quilt up to her chest as she realized her linen shirt—like his—had become loosened at the neck and she'd been displaying far too much cleavage.

Annoyingly, his smile widened. "Hmm, I think you may be right. But tell me—even though you *look* very well to me—how are your injuries?"

As Jessie described how her arm felt, Rob rose and moved over to the bed. "Let me take a look at your stitches. We can't have your wound getting gangrenous now, can we?"

She reluctantly proffered her arm and winced as Rob gently pushed up her sleeve and loosened the linen strip to check his handiwork. Apparently satisfied that everything was fine, he rewrapped it. "You'll have a slight scar I'm afraid."

Jessie shrugged. "It doesna matter." She pushed down her sleeve, confused as to why he showed such an ongoing concern for her welfare, even though last night he and Tobias had unmistakably marked her as a threat. Could Rob have had a change of heart? Perhaps he would let her go after all. She bit her lip as worry gnawed at her belly. She trusted she would be able to deal with any contingency.

She had to.

Rob's gaze ran down the length of the quilt to her feet. "Shall I check your ankle, lass?"

Jessie shook her head firmly. "No, that willna be necessary. It's much improved. I should be able to get about without a problem today."

"Well, I shall leave you to freshen up. I hope you don't mind, but I laid your gown and...and other wet things out by the fire last night. I imagine it may be a while before they're in a state that's comfortable to wear. Just call if you need me to assist."

After the door closed behind him, Jessie shook her head in bewilderment. She couldn't believe Rob had tried to dry her clothes for her and was concerned they may still be damp. Yet again his actions confounded her. If he meant her ill, why worry about the state of her attire?

But puzzling over unanswerable questions wasn't going to get her out of this mess. Getting dressed would be a good place to start.

Dragging in a fortifying breath, Jessie struggled out from under the bedclothes and warily tested her ankle. It was very stiff and painful when she bore weight on it, but she could manage.

There was a chamber pot beneath the bed and a pitcher with ice cold water in it by the hearth. After attending to her ablutions as best she could, Jessie changed into her fresh shift and spare woolen stockings (which she'd packed in her satchel) before confirming her gown was in no fit state to wear, wet or not. Aside from missing the entire left sleeve, the brown worsted wool was bloodied and stained with mud. Her red woolen cloak, also grubby, would be serviceable, but as it was still too damp, she left it by the hearth.

Which meant she would be wearing an unusual combination of garments, to say the least. *Better to be fully clothed than no'*, she told herself as she surveyed what was on offer.

In the end, Jessie settled for donning her stays, the linen shirt she'd worn during the night, and her almost dry cambric petticoats. She then wrapped the plaid around her waist and over her shoulder in the style of an arisaid before securing it with the silver brooch Rob had used to pin up her sleeve last night. She noticed for the first time that it bore the Clan Grant crest—a burning hill with the motto *Stand Fast* above it. How ironic, given her circumstances. However Rob Burnley had come by it, she did not think Lord Strathburn would mind if she borrowed it.

A sudden gust of wind rattled the window, drawing Jessie over to take a look at the day. Throwing open the inner shutters, she found the panes were rimed with frost, but she could see enough of the view outside to ascertain that it was a fine, blustery morning. The strong wind had cleared the sky of all traces of cloud and fog. The nearby trees bent against the onslaught, their branches raining fiery flurries of gold, burnt orange, and scarlet leaves to the ground. Even though it was clear, it would be cold.

Catching sight of her faint reflection in the windowpane, Jessie barely stifled a shriek. Her hair was a mass of wild snarls and tangles. Indeed, her appearance was something akin to a fiery Medusa. Although she tended to eschew personal vanity, she blushed to think that Rob had seen her in such a state of disarray. The heat in her cheeks crept across her whole face when she recalled how Rob had already seen her in a worse state of undress when she'd stood before him, all wet and bedraggled and half-naked last night.

To take her mind off the mortifying memory, Jessie hastily dug out her comb from her satchel and attacked her hair with vigor. A few leaves fell to the floor—*good Lord*—but she made steady progress and felt remarkably more human as her curls were wrestled into submission. As she had no idea where her ribbon had gone, she settled for leaving her hair unbound. Errantly curling hair would just have to do.

As Jessie began to turn away from the window, she suddenly sensed a movement in her peripheral vision. It was Tobias, riding away from the lodge. His horse cleanly cleared a small burn before disappearing into the trees. Frowning, she realized the lad was probably heading to Lochrose to question his cousin, just as he'd mentioned last night.

Of course, that meant Tobias would soon discover she was only the factor's daughter and not the earl's ward. He probably wouldn't glean much else about her, though. She trusted Mrs. MacMillan would never divulge any of the sordid details about Simon's pursuit of her. And the other staff would not be privy to what had really precipitated her flight from Lochrose. Aside from Mrs. MacMillan, everyone else at the castle would have heard how she'd been summoned to Edinburgh to assist her cousin.

It also meant that no one would confirm or deny that the factor's daughter was Simon's lover. Rob might still assume she was his mistress.

Unless I confess all to him.

Right at this moment, she and Rob were all alone. Now would be as good a time as any to tell him the truth.

Squaring her shoulders, Jessie crossed to the bedroom door, pushed it open...then bit back an involuntary gasp. There before the fireplace knelt Rob, naked from the waist up, sharpening his dirk on a whetstone. His linen shirt was tossed carelessly over the back of one of the oak chairs at the table. He glanced up, but he didn't seem perturbed at all that she'd come upon him in a shirtless state.

The shameless rogue nodded at the armchair nearby. "Why don't you take a seat and warm yourself by the fire? It's damnably cool this morning."

Cool? Jessie felt anything but cool. Her pulse skittering and her cheeks flaming, she reluctantly limped to the chair Rob had indicated and sat down with a small indignant huff. How was she to profess her true situation to him and seek to enlist his support when...when he flaunted himself thus? Yet again he'd thrown her off balance and rendered her all but speechless.

Rob was facing her, his head bent forward. He'd tied his hair back with a leather strip, but a stray lock kept falling forward over his forehead. His naked torso was so close, if she leaned forward and reached out she would be able to touch him, trace the hard lines of sinew, muscle and bone. Jessie fisted her hands into the wool of her borrowed plaid, determined to ignore the wanton impulse. Instead, she tried to marshal her thoughts into some semblance of order.

But it was a hopeless enterprise. Never before had she seen a man in such a state of undress. She felt stunned and awed and awkward all at the same time. She determinedly tried not to look at Rob's wide, powerful shoulders and the hard planes of his chest. She desperately tried to ignore the ripples down his lean stomach and the defined, well-developed muscles in his upper arms. Instead, she studied the flames jumping in the grate and contemplated how she was to broach the subject of Simon and her desperate need to get to Edinburgh. Her cheeks still blazed, but not from the heat of the fire.

Rob appeared to stay focused on his task of sharpening the dirk on the moist surface of the stone. Every now and again he tested the blade on his thumb before returning to the process of honing it to razor sharpness.

Jessie cleared her throat to speak but halted, suddenly apprehensive about why he was taking such care in sharpening the knife—the same one that he'd used yesterday to cut her sleeve away. Dear God, surely he wouldn't use it to threaten her, or worse...

She dragged in a breath and found her voice. "Wh-What are yer plans for the day, Mr. Burnley? After you've finished sharpening yer dirk?"

~

Robert smothered a smile as he tested the blade of his dirk. Jessie was visibly uneasy, no doubt because of his semi-clothed state. Well, let the lass look her fill. He'd certainly had his turn to see her half-naked. It was only fair he returned the favor.

But then, what if she were instead unsettled by the task he was engaged in? Robert frowned as he scraped the blade along the whetstone. Surely she didn't think that he would physically harm her.

Well, more than he'd done already.

Since the hunting accident, he'd done all he could to make amends for the damage he'd inflicted.

Of course, the last thing he wanted to do was frighten the lass. Robert lifted his gaze and whatever he'd been about to say stuck in his throat. Even dressed in a haphazard array of garments, Jessie's beauty stole his breath. Struck him to the very bone. Her cheeks were flushed, and her beautiful red-gold hair curled around her face like a bright halo. A memory of how she'd looked last night in nothing but her wet shift burst into his mind and his cock twitched. God, how he wanted her.

But he couldn't have her. Disappointment settled heavily in his chest.

Jessie was frowning, her whisky-brown eyes wary as she waited for him to answer.

Guilt—for his less than chivalrous conduct and wholly lustful thoughts—suddenly writhed in Robert's gut. He really should put the lass at ease.

"Any plans I have are not untoward, I assure you," he replied, failing to hide the huskiness in his voice. But he cast her what he hoped was a reassuring smile. "As for my dirk, I'm just making sure the blade is razor-sharp so I don't cut myself when I dispose of this." He ran a thumb across the thick stubble on his jaw. "Just because we're out in the wilderness, it doesn't mean that I should go around looking like a savage Highlander."

"I see," Jessie responded and he noted a sudden spark lighting her eyes as she delivered her next comment. "Might I suggest an addition of a shirt might assist in yer transformation as well?"

He chuckled at that and noticed how the tension in her posture began to ease. A moment later, her stomach grumbled loudly. "There's an apple left over if you'd like to break your fast." Robert nodded toward the oak table where it sat between the candles. "Tobias has ridden out to forage for more food. He shouldn't be too long."

Jessie doubted that food was all Tobias was gathering. Nevertheless, she took a seat at the dining table. Truth to tell, she was relieved to be farther away from Rob. He made her feel more ruffled than a Highland loch in a storm, and she badly needed to think.

As she bit into the apple, she mulled over in her mind how to tackle the topic of her...situation. First and foremost, she needed to convince Rob to trust her. If she could succeed in this, perhaps she could negotiate with him to stay here at the hunting lodge until she could catch the next day's public coach to Edinburgh as she'd originally planned. She was in no hurry to get to Grantown quite yet.

But she would not begin the conversation she needed to have until the man was decently dressed. She needed her wits about her.

Despite her resolve *not* to look at Rob, her gaze kept straying toward the fireplace where he was now shaving. He'd propped a small looking-glass on the stone mantelpiece and had lathered his jaw with soap—the small cake sat beside a basin of sudsy water on the hearthstone. She watched in fascination as Rob held the skin of his face taut and ran the wickedly sharp dirk blade over it, revealing smooth tanned skin underneath. With his hair pulled back, she could clearly see the ripple of his defined arm and back muscles whenever he moved.

He'd told her he used to be in the Black Watch. Indeed, he had a warrior's body. Aside from his powerful musculature, there were obvious marks of old, healed battle wounds on his skin. Her gaze traced along the ridge of a particularly nasty looking scar—a long slash that ran across his left shoulder blade down to his rib cage—and she wondered how he'd sustained it. It must have been excruciatingly painful. Her bullet graze was nothing compared to that.

Look away, Jessie Munroe. Now. But her eyes wouldn't obey. Her gaze strayed lower to Rob's lean hips, and she couldn't help but notice how his buckskin breeches hugged the firm curves of his buttocks and muscular thighs.

She bit down hard into the apple to stifle a purely wanton and unladylike groan. Heavens above, Rob was too...too beautiful, too powerful, too captivating. Yet again desire flickered and pulsed deep inside her and she felt disconcertingly slick between her thighs.

Ugh. Flustered, and feeling more than a trifle guilty for ogling the poor man, Jessie was about to look away when she noticed the reflection of his eyes in the mirror, staring back at her with an expression of wry amusement.

Robert Burnley was laughing at her! *The rogue!*

Anger and embarrassment sparked within Jessie. With a muttered curse, she deliberately shifted her position in the chair and gave the odious man her back. How dare he parade himself in front of her like a...a damn peacock and not expect her to gawp at him? It was audacious to say the least. She would *not* look at him again until he was fully clothed.

Unfortunately, Jessie had forgotten that Rob had tossed his shirt over the back of a chair on the other side of the table. When he finished shaving, the irritating man walked over to stand directly opposite her. Even though Jessie focused all her attention on nibbling the last remnants of flesh from her apple, out of the corner of her eye she spied the handle of Rob's dirk jutting up near the outline of his lean hipbone. He'd sheathed the knife in a scabbard secured to the waistband of his breeches.

Oh God, dinna stare at the front of his breeches, Jessie Munroe.

"How's the apple?" Rob asked, his tone laced with amusement.

Jessie narrowed her eyes and tossed him a withering look...but then her eyebrows shot up. "Oh, my Lord," she gasped, dropping the apple core. It rolled off the table and onto the floor entirely unheeded.

Rob stared, his brow furrowed in apparent confusion. "Are you all right, lass?"

No, no' at all... Jessie stood up so abruptly, her chair tipped over with a crash. "Ye're Robert Grant," she whispered as the truth slammed into her, stealing her breath. "Viscount Lochrose. The Master of Strathburn."

How had she been so blind? It *was* the same man she'd seen in the miniature portrait belonging to Lord Strathburn. The man before her was obviously older than the handsome youth rendered in the painting. The lines of Rob's face were now leaner, more defined, harder some-how. But she could plainly see that they both shared the same striking features, now the beginnings of Rob's beard were gone. She recognized the same clean square jaw, the wide mouth, the strong blade of a nose, and of course, the man's startling blue eyes.

Other pieces of information came back to her that fitted her construct. This man obviously used to be a soldier, he seemed thoroughly familiar with this countryside and the lodge. He knew Simon's character through and through. How had she not realized it before?

"Ye...ye've come back," she added uselessly as she took a step away from the table, almost tripping over the upended chair.

Rob—or Robert, Lord Lochrose—inclined his head, a sardonic twist to the corner of his mouth. "So it would seem."

"But... It all makes sense now, about ye and Simon. Oh God,

Simon... He... When ye and Tobias were speaking last night... When ye were at the loch... Simon and I... Ye mustna believe... It's no' what ye think..." Jessie knew she was babbling, but she couldn't rein in her riotous thoughts or control her runaway tongue as she backed away.

Oh God. There was a hard set to Robert Grant's mouth as he followed her around the table. Fear gripping her heart, she bumped into the wall behind her. What would he do now that she'd recognized him? Now she definitely knew too much?

Robert towered over her, his gaze suddenly hard and assessing. A muscle worked in his cheek. "So tell me, Jessie Munroe, how are things really between you and my half-brother? How am I supposed to trust you?" He leaned forward and rested a muscled forearm against the wall beside her head, his eyes boring into hers. "He's your lover, is he not?"

Jessie swallowed, barely able to breathe. Robert's bare chest was a mere inch or two from her, her lips were just above his collarbone where his pulse beat. Now was the time to tell this man the truth...but she was too ashamed. And she feared he wouldn't believe her.

Hot tears flooded her eyes and threatened to spill. Robert was so close, she could feel the handle of the dirk pushing into her abdomen. Feel the heat radiating from his long hard body. She recalled his words last night. They echoed in her head.

She was a threat. A problem. A complication.

I'm in danger.

"Well, Jessie?" Robert gripped her jaw, forcing her chin up. His gaze searched hers for a moment, then dropped to her mouth. Panic flared. Stole her breath. His mouth hovered over hers.

Oh God, he was going to kiss her. And the kiss would not be kind.

No. Not like this.

Anger rose swiftly, overtaking Jessie's fear, overwhelming her original intentions to be truthful. "Simon and I are handfasted. So I'd suggest ye leave me be, Robert Grant," she all but hissed against his lips.

Robert froze. His eyes darkened to the blue-black of storm clouds and he abruptly released his uncompromising hold on her jaw. Then without a word, he turned on his heel, grabbed his shirt off the chair and marched outside. Through the wide-open door, she saw him stride over to the burn and drop to his knees before sluicing water over his face.

Jessie sank to the floor, her whole body shaking. There was no way to tell if her mad bluff would make things safer for her. She simply prayed that if she was seen as important to Simon, someone of consequence, surely...surely Robert would not harm her. He would assume that Simon would be searching for her sometime today. He would have to move on, or risk capture. But would he let her go?

Dear Lord, what had she done? Why had she jumped straight from the frying pan into the fire? She felt tarnished, tainted, as if she'd sold her soul to the very devil himself.

And Robert probably thought that about her too. Oh, she was a foolish henwit indeed.

CHAPTER 11

The icy cold water of the burn shocked Robert into a semblance of calmness. *Damn it all to hell.* Things were worse than they seemed.

Jessie's admission about her betrothal to Simon hurt as acutely as any bayonet slice, but there was no time to dwell on his feelings right now. There was no doubt in Robert's mind—his half-brother would be looking for this woman. The question was, how much time did he have before Simon ventured out on his search with or without the Black Watch or even the dragoons?

Either way, Jessie would be coming with him, wherever he moved onto next. Robert couldn't afford to leave her behind. She would surely divulge his presence in the area, now she had recognized him. For now, his only advantage was that no one except Jessie knew of his return to Scotland.

Robert stood and threw on his shirt. He judged that they may still have a wee bit of time between now and when any search for Jessie was conducted up here. It was early and it would take some time for any sizable search party to negotiate the steep terrain and narrow mountain pass that was the only way into this isolated glen. In fact, Tobias was scouting the area right now for any signs of activity.

The time to question Jessie Munroe further had undoubtedly arrived. Robert needed to know exactly who she was and why she'd been up here alone in the first place. If she *was* betrothed to Simon, why hadn't she mentioned it yesterday when she'd claimed an acquaintance with his father and stepmother? Something about the lass's story didn't make sense.

Yes, it was definitely time for Miss Munroe to stop playing games and reveal the truth.

~

The sound of approaching hooves roused Jessie from where she sat on the floor. Even though her knees still shook and her ankle was stiff, she managed to stand. Through the open door she could see Tobias astride his horse, talking with Robert. Tobias glanced toward her as the two men spoke, then just as quickly, averted his gaze. The servant nodded at something Robert said before dismounting and leading his horse away.

Jessie thought she would be sick waiting to see what would happen next.

Robert also disappeared from her direct line of sight. As Jessie hobbled toward the door, Tobias appeared on the threshold. Gone was his affable expression of the evening before. He gave her a token nod by way of greeting before walking to the dining table where he carefully placed a small parcel of foraged food—several duck eggs and a small quantity of late season blaeberries. He obviously hadn't been to Lochrose Castle yet.

Jessie had no idea what to do, so she sat at the table and watched Tobias crack the eggs into a skillet over the fire. As the eggs began to crackle and spit, Robert returned, shrugging into his brown coat. He'd also tied a simple linen cravat around his throat. As she surreptitiously studied his face and his aristocratic bearing, there was no doubt in her mind he was Robert Grant, the attainted Viscount Lochrose and Master of Strathburn.

A Jacobite with a price on his head.

Robert turned his gaze on her. "I suggest you finish getting dressed and collect your things," he said curtly. "We'll be leaving soon."

We? Was that all three of them? Was she now Robert's prisoner? And *where* were they going? Jessie simply nodded in response. She wanted to ask the questions hovering on the tip of her tongue, but something in Robert's expression stopped her. His eyes were as cold and dark as the sky at midnight. It was a stranger's gaze, and it surprised Jessie how much the change in the man's demeanor stung. But what else had she expected after uttering such a lie about her relationship with Simon?

Silly, silly girl.

Without a word, Jessie returned to the bedchamber. Regardless of whether she went with Robert Grant or tried to escape, she would need her belongings.

She stuffed her still damp shift and stockings from yesterday into her satchel, then fed her ruined gown to the fire. There wasn't much point in taking it with her, and she didn't want to leave evidence of her stay behind.

She would not cry. She refused to. The tears that blurred her vision, Jessie assured herself, were simply triggered by the sharp pain in her arm as she carelessly threw her scarlet cloak around her shoulders. Then there was the agony of thrusting her sprained ankle into her boot. Her tears were absolutely *not* provoked by anguish or fear about what was going to happen next.

Of course, what she *needed* to happen next was to get to Edinburgh.

On returning to the main room, Jessie discovered that both Robert and Tobias had gone outside. Indistinct snatches of their murmured conversation drifted through the open doorway. A plate of food had been left for her—a fried egg, an oatcake, and a handful of berries. Although her appetite had all but gone, she forced herself to eat. Who knew when her next meal would be?

As she picked at the last few berries on her plate, she observed that the fire had been put out. Damp ash and a few wisps of smoke were all that remained. She shivered, but it wasn't only the chill of early morning that was responsible for the feeling of cold and miserable dismay seeping into her bones.

A grim-faced Robert suddenly appeared in the doorway with a bucket and without even a glance at her, strode past before disappearing into the main bedchamber. Water splashed and then there was a faint sizzle as the last of the coals and embers were extinguished. They must be leaving immediately. While Jessie didn't seem to be in any immediate danger, God only knew what Robert was planning.

Perhaps she should sneak out the door and try to take one of the horses while the men were distracted. She could—

At that moment, Robert returned.

Damn and double damn.

He leaned against the table next to her, arms folded across his chest. His expression was inscrutable, and Jessie's heart sank as heavily as a stone. She was a fool indeed to think she had any chance of stealing away.

"Now, Miss Munroe, the time has come for plain speaking," he said, his voice edged with steel. "I need to know exactly what I'm dealing with here. I suspect my brother will be out looking for you this morning. Wouldn't you agree?"

Jessie licked her lips, her throat dry. *Miss Munroe*, was it? Robert was clearly angry and distancing himself from her. If she couldn't escape, she needed to retract her lie, no matter the cost. Convince him that she wouldn't betray him. That she was no threat to him. "Perhaps he will... I do no' ken for certain," she said, unable to hide the tremor in her voice. "Ye see, I need to explain...about yesterday and what ye saw at the loch—"

"I know what I saw."

"But it's no'—"

Robert cut her off with an impatient huff. "How long have you and Simon been betrothed?"

He won't believe me, not now. The painful realization sliced into Jessie as sharply as the blade of Robert's dirk. She swallowed past the tight ache in her throat and resumed her charade. She hated lying, but refuting her claim that she was engaged seemed all but useless. It was too late. "No' long," she whispered.

"You are not from the area. Where are your kin?"

Jessie drew a breath. At least she didn't have to lie about her family. "My father is Alasdair Munroe, younger brother of the former Laird of

Dunraven in Cromartyshire, Dugald Munroe. He's all the immediate family I have."

"And where is your father?" demanded Robert, his gaze hard. "I assume he will be out looking for you too."

Jessie shook her head. "N-No, he won't be. He doesna even know that I left Lochrose. He's touring all the villages on the Strathburn estate, collecting rents, and then he intends to visit Inverness. He'll be gone for a week, at the verra least. Most likely two."

Robert raised an eyebrow in query.

Jessie continued, her eyes locked with his. "He's recently taken up the position as factor for yer father. My Uncle Dugald...he incurred considerable debts and his estate became forfeit to the bank. Despite the family's loss, our solicitor, who's also Lord Strathburn's, recommended my father for the position at Lochrose. Ye see, the loss of the Munroe fortune wasna attributable to my father, but to my uncle because he refused to give up his profligate ways. My da is a canny manager and as yer father needed assistance with managing his estate's affairs"—she shrugged a shoulder—"it seemed like a match that was meant to be."

It was a relief to share something with Robert that was true.

Jessie just prayed he would believe her.

Robert studied Jessie's face. His gut instincts told him that she was telling the truth about where she hailed from and how she came to be at Lochrose. Her voice was stronger, the glint in her eyes sharper, when she spoke of her family. It certainly fitted with his theory that she was gently reared, not a servant. He was sure there was more to her family's story, but now was not the time to pursue that particular topic further.

What did surprise him though—in light of what he'd just learned—was that Jessie and his brother *were* actually betrothed. While it would not be out of character for Simon to dally with someone like Jessie, it was not the sort of match he would have expected Simon to make, nor one his stepmother would condone for that matter. As for their father, Robert frankly didn't know what he would make of such a union.

Indeed, given the avaricious nature of both Simon and his mother, surely an aristocratic young woman, or at the very least a wealthy merchant's daughter, would be the only sort of bride they would consider "suitable" for the son of an earl. It certainly wouldn't be the niece of an impoverished laird, no matter how well bred or comely the lass.

Unless...unless of course the lass *had* to get married for some reason. Robert wouldn't put it past Simon to have compromised Miss Jessie Munroe. *Or* was it the other way round?

Robert frowned. It wasn't unheard of for a woman to snare herself a wealthy, titled husband by such means. In any event, he knew his father would insist Simon do what was right and honorable and marry the lass.

The cynical part of Robert couldn't help but wonder how important it was to Jessie that her husband-to-be was the Earl of Strathburn's heir. Was she eagerly anticipating becoming the next countess? No doubt Jessie's father was well pleased at the match, given the man and his brother had recently lost everything. Perhaps the girl had thrown herself at Simon, with her father's blessing. Perhaps that was why they had come to Lochrose in the first place.

However, there was still one part of Jessie's story that Robert didn't quite understand. "Miss Munroe, why were you really up here yesterday?"

Jessie's head had been bowed all this time while he'd considered her story thus far. She surprised him when she took a deep breath and looked him directly in the eye. "I-I received word from my cousin in Edinburgh. She's married to a tea merchant and has three young children, with a bairn on the way. She's been unwell of late and asked me to stay with her to help with the babes but...but Simon...he was unhappy that I was leaving. In fact, he didna want me to go at all, but I have to. It's my duty. So I decided to travel to Grantown to catch the public coach to Edinburgh. It leaves at noon tomorrow. Unfortunately, I sprained my ankle and rested for a while, and then... Well, ye know the rest."

Robert frowned. Most of Jessie's explanation made sense. He could well imagine Simon being the possessive, jealous type. He would resent the fact that she was needed by someone else. But Robert still didn't understand why she'd chosen to travel to Grantown by such a circuitous route. "Wouldn't it have been easier to take the road from Lochrose to get to Grantown?"

"Simon was so verra angry when he...when he heard my plans," said Jessie quietly. Her brow pleated into a frown as she added, "I thought he might try to stop me, so Mrs. MacMillan—ye would remember her of course—suggested I travel this circuitous way and spend a few nights at the hunting lodge instead of at the Strathspey Arms where Simon would be sure to look for me. She didna think Simon would search up here straightaway, if at all."

Robert smiled inwardly. *Mrs. MacMillan, always the mother hen.* He was glad she was still there to look out for others, as she'd looked out for him. He would make sure Tobias had a careful word with her when he paid the castle a visit later today, to see if she could corroborate Jessie's version of events. Even though he'd been reluctant to seek assistance from others, Mrs. MacMillan might even help him reunite with his father.

Robert was rapidly realizing that as much as he wanted to gain entry to Lochrose all by himself—he most definitely did not want to place anyone at risk on his behalf—it was becoming an increasingly difficult prospect.

But right now, they must get moving. Despite what Mrs. MacMillan thought about the unlikelihood of Simon searching for Jessie up here, he knew his brother and how single-minded he could be. If Simon wanted the lass—and that was undoubtedly the case if the kiss Robert had witnessed was anything to go by—his brother would leave no stone unturned until he found her.

Robert caught Jessie's eye. "I don't agree with Mrs. McMillan. Simon may very well look for you up here, particularly now the weather has cleared up. We must leave immediately."

He straightened, preparing to check on the horses, but Jessie reached out and grasped his hand, staying him. Her slender, elegant fingers were pale against his tanned skin and yet again, the unwelcome sensation that this woman was not his burst through his chest, leaving a bittersweet ache in its wake.

"Will you help me make the Edinburgh coach?" asked Jessie, a pleading note in her voice. "I assure you, it isna my intention to expose you."

Robert studied the lass's expression as he considered her request. Her face was pale and her brow furrowed, but her eyes were as clear as the water in the burn outside.

It puzzled him that she was still intent on leaving Lochrose. That sharing her newly found knowledge of his existence with Simon was *not* uppermost in her mind. Perhaps she wasn't a grasping, social-climbing female who would see him as an obstacle to her ambition to become a countess. Perhaps—and the thought sat like a leaden weight in his stomach—she truly cared for his half-brother...

"I can't make any promises," Robert replied, foolishly relishing the feel of her fingers as they clasped his. "Surely you can understand that. I'm a wanted Jacobite. An enemy of the Crown. At the moment, it's vitally important I'm not apprehended. I don't wish to end up with my head on the chopping block or in the hangman's noose just yet. Reconciling with my father is the only way I'll ever have the chance of gaining a pardon. So you'll need to forgive me for not acceding to your wishes, given your allegiance is with Simon. I'm sure you well know that there is no love lost between my brother and me."

Jessie nodded, her expression grave. She released his hand. "I understand, Lord Lochrose."

It hurt that she'd decided to use his old title. But then, he'd also felt compelled to call her Miss Munroe, had he not? The budding camaraderie and teasing humor which had hovered between them at times was gone. An awkward silence extended and was not broken until the chink of bridles and the crunch of leaves heralded the arrival of Tobias with the horses.

Jessie's gaze darted to the door. "Where are we going?"

"Somewhere safe," said Robert heavily. "That's all you need to know."

He helped Jessie to her feet and escorted her outside, before boosting her up to ride pillion with him again. Joining her in the saddle, he pulled her close—selfish brute that he was. That's when he noticed that she was as tense as a bowstring and was, quite literally, quivering.

"Dinna fash yerself now, lassie," Robert murmured against her hair, feeling like the worst kind of heel. For some unfathomable reason, despite all that Jessie had revealed and the danger she posed, it was still important to him that she didn't fear him.

His comment seemed to work. She grasped his forearm and her body relaxed into him a little. Grinning like the idiot he undoubtedly was, Robert flicked the reins and then they were off—across the burn and through the trees, cantering toward the upland heath and craggy mountain glens where Simon wouldn't have a hope in Hades of finding them.

~

It was early afternoon when Simon and four men from the local regiment of the Black Watch cantered across the rough moorland toward his father's old hunting lodge. All morning he'd been searching with them. *All fucking morning.*

He'd scoured the village of Grantown and questioned the staff at the Strathspey Arms himself, but to no avail. He'd even ordered some of the local crofters' huts to be searched. Despite his threats of violence, despite the military presence he'd brought with him, everyone denied having seen Miss Jessie Munroe. Simon had been about to have the innkeeper from the hovel that passed for a coaching inn at Grantown flogged when MacTaggart, the Captain of the Watch, quietly suggested looking in and around the hunting lodge instead.

It had not occurred to Simon to search up here, and although he was kicking himself for stupidly overlooking this location, his anticipation sharpened as they drew closer to the small copse where the lodge was hidden.

God, how he hated this place. He'd only visited the hunting lodge a handful of times when he was a youth. His father and Robert had once taken him deer stalking and he'd loathed every moment of it, crawling around in the boggy undergrowth, swatting at midges, getting scraped and covered in mud. To make matters worse, he'd come down with a terrible ague which had left him bedridden for several weeks afterward.

When the small stone building came into view, it appeared completely deserted—the shutters were closed, no smoke spiraled from the chimney. But the girl was canny—too canny for Simon's liking. She could just be taking extra care.

As Captain MacTaggart ordered his men to search about the lodge and the woods, Simon dismounted and threw open the door. There was a faint, acrid smell in the air and MacTaggart, who'd followed him in, pointed out damp ashes and coals in both of the fireplaces. Someone had indeed been here recently.

But there was no sign of Jessie. *Damn her to hell.*

"Master," called one of the young Watchmen from the main bedchamber. Simon entered the room to find the man brandishing a long, brown velvet ribbon. "I found this under the bed and there are a few strands of red hair on the pillow."

Simon snatched at the ribbon and balled it up in his fist. The bitch had been here, there was no doubt about it. She'd traveled by foot, so even if she'd set out at first light, there was only so far she could go, especially in this upland terrain of moors, bogs, and mountains.

He smiled. It would not be long before he found her.

Simon's deliciously dark musings were interrupted by the excited call of another Black Watchman who'd been searching outside. He and MacTaggart rushed out to find a young corporal pointing at a space on the ground from which he'd cleared a pile of leaf litter. "Horse dung, Captain, and fresh too."

Fuck. Simon ground his teeth so hard his jaw cracked. Where the hell had the chit obtained a horse? From the Strathspey Arms, or one of the estate's tenants? God knows where she could be if that were the case.

Damn her.

"What now, sir?" asked MacTaggart.

Simon exploded. "How the bloody hell should I know? She could be anywhere by now!"

MacTaggart did not flinch at all. "Perhaps we could return to Grantown and question the stable hands at the inn a wee bit more. I can also send word to the regiments at Fort George and Braemar to keep an eye out on the roads to Inverness and to Edinburgh. If she has a horse, she may be headed for her cousin's house as her note suggested."

Simon flung out another violent string of curses. The urge to smash his fist into something was almost overwhelming.

How he hated feeling thwarted. Made a fool of. What the captain had suggested made perfect sense, but as black rage pumped through his veins, he needed a physical release. Simon briefly contemplated taking a swing at the captain's face, but the man looked as solid as the stone wall of the lodge behind him. Clenching his fists, Simon instead envisioned what he'd do to Jessie Munroe when he found her.

A slow smile crept across his face. This frustrating chase would all be worth it, when he claimed what was his due.

CHAPTER 12

Christ, this water's cold.

Despite the fact that Robert was thigh deep in a lochan and quite literally freezing his arse off, he remained stock-still. The surface of the ice-cold water rippled in the moment before he felt the smooth slide of the trout against the back of his bare knee, then his waiting palm. *Yes.* It had been a decade, but he still had the knack of catching a fish with his bare hands. Grinning, he held the slippery, writhing trout aloft for Jessie to see. They might be going to sleep in a cave, but at least they would eat well tonight.

Jessie's mouth twitched in an answering smile. "Ah, so ye *can* hunt after all. And without injurin' any young ladies, I notice."

"Wicked wench." Robert splashed her and she squealed as the icy droplets rained down on her face and hair. He laughed and waded out of the water onto the mossy bank, tossing the trout onto a nearby rock for gutting and scaling with his dirk. "You should be thankful I can, otherwise it would be salted beef again, Miss Munroe."

She pressed her lips together as if attempting to look contrite, although she couldn't quite hide the gleam of mischief in her eyes. "I am grateful, truly, milord. I'm so hungry, I would've been happy if ye'd caught a hedgehog for dinner."

"They're a wee bit tough and have nowhere near enough meat on them. And stop calling me 'my lord.' Rob or Robert will do just fine."

Jessie looked up at him from her perch upon a boulder and arched a fine brow. "Well, ye only have yerself to blame. Ye keep calling me Miss Munroe."

"Aye, I do." Robert wiped his wet palm on his plaid, then proffered his hand. "Shall we call a truce for this evening then, Jessie?" After her incendiary revelation about her betrothal earlier in the day, he was relieved that the icy distance between them had at last begun to thaw a little.

She narrowed her eyes but there was no heat in her quelling look as she grasped his hand. "Agreed. But only if ye stop prancin' about half-dressed. There is only so much informality a lass can take, Robert Grant."

~

Jessie tried to keep her gaze averted as Robert dried off his very tanned bare legs and feet with his plaid before pulling on his buckskin breeches. Of course, he probably wouldn't mind if she openly ogled him, in view of his behavior this morning. Why, the man was utterly shameless, the way he'd stood in the water clothed only in his shirt and plaid, the kilted fabric rucked up around his bare muscular thighs, like a Highland warrior of old. At one point she'd even caught a glimpse of one taut buttock cheek.

But aren't ye shameless too, Jessie Munroe? If she were truly honest with herself, she couldn't deny her mouth was watering, and not because of the promise of a trout meal. Even Robert's long bare feet were attractive. Who'd have thought one could be aroused by such things?

Despite the fact they'd called a truce, she wasn't looking forward to spending another night alone with Robert in close quarters. Not because she was afraid of the man. No, it was because her stomach fluttered madly with butterflies whenever she so much as looked at him. Her father would be horrified if he knew. At least Tobias would be returning soon—Jessie assumed he'd gone to finally speak with his cousin at the castle—and would act as a chaperone of sorts. She shuddered. A male chaperone didn't really count though, did it? Oh, she could never tell her father about any of this, *ever*.

With any luck she'd be on the public coach for Edinburgh tomorrow and the last few days would just be a bad memory, nothing more.

A bitterly cold wind suddenly tore through the shadowy glen, pulling at Jessie's hair and cloak. Heavy gray clouds were rapidly piling up along the granite peaks surrounding them. She glanced at Robert, who was seated on the hard ground, tugging on his boots. "Ye must be freezing."

Robert stood and pulled on his coat. "Aye. And you soon will be too. I can smell snow. As soon as I've cleaned this trout, we'll need to get back to the cave."

Jessie frowned. "And ye're certain we canna spend the night at the lodge?"

Robert shook his head, the line of his mouth grim. "I didn't tell you this before, but Tobias spied a search party of Watchmen—and your *fiancé*—in the glen earlier this afternoon. I just can't take that chance, Jessie. Who knows where or when Simon will turn up again looking for you. Hopefully Tobias will be back from Lochrose soon with more news."

Oh God, Mrs. MacMillan had been wrong. Simon *had* been looking for her up here.

An icy tendril of fear, colder than the gale whipping about them, snaked down Jessie's spine, raising gooseflesh. What if Simon found her?

No, she couldn't think about it. She was safe here with Robert.

Her captor. Who thought she was engaged to the man she was truly fleeing.

What a tangled mess she was in.

A strange urge to laugh suddenly gripped Jessie. She must be slightly mad. She dragged in a shuddering breath and deliberately tried to calm her breathing, to slow her racing heart.

She mulled over the other piece of information Robert had shared. So, Tobias had definitely been to Lochrose. By now he would have discovered that no one at the castle had any knowledge of her "betrothal." It suddenly seemed ridiculous to persist with the lie. Robert wouldn't hurt her, she was certain of it.

She drew in another steadying breath. "Robert..."

He looked up from his quiet task of scaling the trout and cocked an eyebrow in query.

She swallowed. *Speak, woman!* "Robert, I wanted to—"

Just then, a frigid squall of stinging rain and sleet hit, taking Jessie's breath away. Robert swore and sprinted over to the pine tree where his horse was tethered.

Huddling into her cloak as she limped after him, Jessie gritted her teeth against the biting cold and her frustration. It seemed her confession would have to wait.

What are ye waiting for, Jessie?

Less than an hour later and seated on her balled up, ruined cloak—a poor cushion substitute but it was better than nothing to ward off the hard chill of the cave floor—Jessie held her numb fingers out to the small fire Robert had built, deliberating whether now would be the right time to set things straight with him. Perhaps more importantly, negotiate her freedom to leave tomorrow.

Their truce had held throughout the last half hour as they'd trekked through the rain to the cave, then finished setting up their makeshift camp. But now, as Jessie eyed the far too-handsome Lord Lochrose over the fire's leaping flames, she found the momentary spurt of courage she'd felt by the lochan had completely deserted her. Indeed, it had been missing ever since they'd returned to the cave and she'd been forced to contemplate the long cold hours ahead...and what was to become of her. It seemed anxiety had frozen her tongue and was eating at her as steadily as the hunger gnawing at her belly.

Robert also seemed pensive, his brow furrowed deep in thought as he turned the trout on the spit he'd deftly crafted from birch branches. Jessie wondered what he was thinking but wasn't game enough to ask. Instead, she watched the flames twist and dance and the smoke spiral upward, toward a narrow fissure in the cave's ceiling that served as a natural chimney. Every now and again, a gust of wind sent flurries of snowflakes through the cave's entrance, but tucked away toward the back of the deep yawning space, she and Robert were relatively well protected from the sharp-as-a-knife draft.

Evidently Robert was highly familiar with this eyrie-like hiding place in the side of the mountain. The rocky, narrow path his horse had followed to reach here was well secreted—almost impossible to locate unless you knew what you were looking for.

She would be safe from Simon. But would she survive the night with Robert?

Jessie's gaze darted to the very back of the cave where a bed of bracken and spent heather lay piled. Robert and Tobias had gathered sheaves of the fronds earlier in the afternoon, before Tobias had headed off to the castle. Not for the first time, Jessie silently questioned precisely what the sleeping arrangements would be for tonight. There did not seem to be a large enough pile of bedding to accommodate... well, more than one person. She certainly wasn't going to share. She didn't know if she would feel more or less awkward if Tobias returned. Perhaps both men would be chivalrous and let her use the bed. Perhaps they could take turnabout.

If Tobias returned. Dusk had long since descended into the inky blackness of night and Jessie prickled with unease, wondering if Tobias was all right and how he would find them again. Negotiating the mountain trail would be treacherous at the best of times. In the dark, whilst it was snowing, it would be a certain death trap.

Robert suddenly turned to her, startling her out of her worried musings. "Jessie, perhaps you could turn the trout once every so often, so it doesn't burn?" He then rose in one swift movement and strode toward the mouth of the cave.

"Ye're leaving?" Jessie couldn't keep the slight note of panic from her voice. Was Robert returning to Lochrose tonight after all? She knew he was anxious to reconcile with his father, but surely he wouldn't leave now.

Contrary creature that she was, she was worried about spending the night alone with him, but absurdly, she didn't want him to go either. It was far too dangerous out there.

Foolish, Jessie. Ye dinna ken what you want.

Even in the gloom, she could make out the flash of Robert's white teeth. "I'm just going to retrieve my saddlebags and attend to my horse. The snow seems to be getting heavier and I want to make sure he's well sheltered. I won't be long."

Jessie sighed with relief when, true to his word, Robert returned but a few minutes later, saddlebags slung over one shoulder and a half-full bottle of whisky in his other hand. He tossed the bags down beside the fire before shaking the snow off his coat and dark hair.

He waved the whisky at her. "We'll be needing a few drams of this tonight to keep us warm. Tobias definitely won't be back now, so there'll be more for us." He sat down beside her and, with a wolfish grin, offered her the bottle.

So they *would* be all alone. *All night.*

Jessie's relief dissipated as quickly as the snowflakes melting on Robert's broad shoulders. She licked suddenly dry lips. She really didn't think she should be drinking whisky, not with Robert smiling at her like that. She shook her head. "No' for me, thank you. But perhaps ye wouldna mind sharing yer water instead."

Robert shrugged and rummaged around in his saddlebag before passing his water flask to her. As Jessie took it, their fingers brushed— the light contact making her skin tingle and a shaft of heat shoot all the way down to her lower belly. Resisting the urge to squirm to ease the disconcerting feeling, Jessie instead busied herself with drinking from the flask and turning the fish so it would continue to roast evenly.

Out of the corner of her eye, she saw Robert loosen the linen cravat at his throat before taking a swig of whisky straight from the bottle. After a short pause, she felt his gaze settle on her.

"How is your arm holding up?" he asked quietly.

She grimaced, keeping her eyes on the trout. "To be honest it's quite sore, but I dinna think it's worth worrying about."

Robert frowned. "Hmm. Nevertheless, I'll take a quick look and change the bandage, just to be sure. In hindsight, you've probably been more active today than was wise."

He hid it well, but he must be frustrated in the extreme having to play nursemaid as well as guard. It was delaying his reunion with the earl.

Before Jessie could reiterate that checking her wound *really* wasn't necessary, Robert had moved closer and had gently rolled up her sleeve. His hands were surprisingly warm on her bare skin as he unraveled the linen.

"All's well," he concluded after a close inspection. His eyes held a spark of amusement. "You can look, you know. It's not as bad as you think. I'm quite a good seamstress if I do say so myself."

Jessie sucked in a deep breath and looked down at her arm. He was right. The wound was sutured with six neat stitches into a straight red line, about an inch or so long. There was no sign of swelling or angry purulence. It would heal cleanly.

She touched it tentatively. "I take it ye've had some experience with this sort of thing before."

"A little." Robert pulled the loosened linen cravat free from his throat and proceeded to carefully rewrap her arm. The intimacy of the gesture made Jessie's pulse quicken and heat flooded her cheeks, but thankfully, Robert didn't seem to notice. "During the Rebellion," he continued, "and then, when I served with the French army."

Surprise sparked within Jessie at this disclosure. "You served with the French?"

Robert shrugged a shoulder dismissively. "For three years. After Culloden I went to France. I had to make a living somehow."

So Robert Grant had been a soldier for three years. That would explain a few things about him—his strong build, his ability to move about as silently as a lion on the hunt, his calmness under pressure. And his battle scars.

Jessie stole a glance at his profile as he continued to bandage her wound. There were many complexities to this man. She wanted to ask him what else he'd seen and done in the intervening years. His tanned skin suggested he'd been living in much warmer climes. Why had he left it so long to return to Lochrose? Why had he let the estrangement with his father continue when it was something he regretted? He'd been effectively disowned by Lord Strathburn in favor of Simon, obviously to prevent the Strathburn estate being forfeited all those years ago. It was a situation he now clearly wanted to reverse.

From what she recalled of Mrs. MacMillan's account, Robert had played a relatively minor role in the Rebellion. It was not unheard of for pardons to be granted by the King if the supplicant was sufficiently penitent and had the advocacy of a highly ranked sponsor. It suddenly occurred to Jessie that if Robert were pardoned and returned to the family fold, then Simon would become second in line to inherit the earldom once Lord Strathburn passed. And then only if Robert himself didn't produce a male heir.

Was that the cause of such obvious enmity and distrust between himself and Simon? Did Robert really think Simon would have him, his long-lost brother, apprehended just to hold onto the title Master of Strathburn and remain the only heir to the earldom?

He undoubtedly did.

Jessie contemplated discussing the issue with Robert, but for now, the topic seemed too difficult to broach, along with all the other issues she needed to discuss. She was suddenly reluctant to ruin the return to easiness between them. It was too fresh, too fragile.

She was undoubtedly a coward. She didn't want to see the hardness in Robert's eyes she'd seen this morning, or watch him sink into the brooding mood that had overtaken him only moments before.

Perhaps after dinner she'd feel brave enough to have a frank discussion with the man. She probably needed a dram or two of whisky after all.

Robert completed his task and eased her sleeve back into place. Outside the cave, a gust of wind howled past, and another flurry of snowflakes drifted in. The fire guttered and the roasted trout crackled and spat.

Her far-too-mercurial captor tested the fish with the blade of his dirk. "I think our dinner may be ready, Jessie," he said with a smile. "Ready enough for me, anyway."

He portioned up the fish onto a pair of small tin plates he'd pulled from the saddlebags. She gratefully accepted one, and ignoring the pain of burnt fingers, began to pick at the succulent coral flesh.

Robert attacked his serving of trout with relish, all the while conscious of Jessie sitting beside him. The *sangfroid* he'd fought to armor himself with since this morning rapidly evaporated as he noticed her delicately nibbling at her portion with even white teeth.

But it didn't seem to matter how many times he told himself, *she's not for you, she's dangerous, she belongs to your brother.* It mattered not at all when her pink tongue darted out to capture the juices from her full bottom lip and the corner of her mouth, or when she set about licking and sucking her moist fingertips. It took everything in him to stop himself groaning aloud like a wild beast.

God in heaven, everything this woman did seemed to make him burn. He was as hard as the honed steel blade of his dirk with wanting her.

When he'd finished eating, Robert wiped his fingers on a clean corner of the discarded linen bandage and slugged back several mouthfuls of whisky to calm his raging urges. He offered Jessie the bottle again. This time, to his surprise, she took it and threw back a decent swig. Her cheeks were flushed with high color and in the fire's glow, her eyes were the same deep, amber-brown as the whisky.

Robert could see why Simon should want the woman so badly. God help him, he wanted her too.

He took back the bottle and drank some more. When his body began to relax—including his errant cock—he got up and re-stoked the fire, then dug out a blanket for Jessie and another Black Watch plaid for himself. He draped the blanket around her shoulders, and she smiled at him in thanks. He decided then and there that he would have to sleep on the hard, stone floor of the cave by the fire, rather than beside her on the bed of bracken and heather.

As he wrapped himself in the rough wool plaid and returned to his place before the fire, Robert fell to contemplating the conundrum of Jessie's betrothal to his half-brother. Something didn't ring true about the situation.

Perversely, the question which seemed to plague him the most at this particular moment was, did Jessie love Simon? She'd never once mentioned that she cared for him. Robert examined her actions since he and Tobias had first discovered her in the copse yesterday. Not once had she actively fought to escape or demand that she be returned to Lochrose. Neither had she threatened to bring down the full weight of the law upon them if he and Tobias were caught. Her actions did not seem to be consistent with those of someone who was deeply in love. Wouldn't she want to return to the side of her beloved *fiancé* if that were the case?

But maybe this was all just wishful thinking on his part...

What he *did* know to be true was that Simon was actively searching for Jessie. It was clear his brother wanted the lass back. Robert now dismissed the theory that Simon had been manipulated into a betrothal by Jessie or her father, for surely his brother would be glad to wash his hands of her rather than pursue her.

Jessie had also asserted that she genuinely needed to leave Lochrose to travel to Edinburgh as she felt duty bound to assist her cousin and her brood of bairns. Of all the things she'd told him so far, Robert did believe this one thing to be true.

But regardless of what had precipitated Jessie's flight from Lochrose yesterday, or how much or how little she cared for Simon, would she still betray him, Robert, if the opportunity arose? She may, if she really did aspire to be the next Countess of Strathburn. Surely she would want to warn Simon of his return. Whether she was a grasping jade, or devoted wife-to-be, or something else entirely, it really didn't matter.

Any way Robert looked at it, letting Jessie go was still a huge risk. He couldn't afford to take any chances.

He ran his gaze over the lass again as he took another slug of whisky. The sight of her as well as the *uisge beatha* heated his blood. His inner voice whispered to him again.

She's not for you. She's dangerous. She belongs to your brother.

~

A heavy silence stretched out between Jessie and Robert, broken only by the occasional spit and pop of the fire or the howl of the wind.

Jessie squirmed. The strange tension in the atmosphere was

becoming more palpable with every passing minute. She occasionally cast a glance Robert's way, but he was staring fixedly at the flames, lost in thought—dark thoughts, judging by his scowl. She wondered what had triggered such a change in him. He did not seem himself at all.

Putting aside her now empty plate, Jessie determined that she couldn't put off speaking with Robert any longer...especially now the whisky bottle was only a quarter full. If Robert were too far gone in his cups, her task would only be harder.

Tamping down her unease, and scraping her courage together, Jessie took a deep breath and looked at him squarely. "I-I wondered if we might speak of what will happen tomorrow. The coach to Edinburgh leaves at midday..."

Robert barely spared her a look. "I know." He drank more whisky.

Jessie frowned and bit her lip, struggling for the strength to stop herself from saying something she would regret. Or worse still, hurling the contents of the water flask over Robert to knock him out of this morose mood. To chase away the uncommunicative oaf he'd become. Common sense dictated she should own up to her falsehood, but it was hard to talk about Simon's degrading demands when Robert seemed so remote, even hostile. But then, she was partly to blame for that, wasn't she? She was going to have a hard time gaining Robert's trust.

But she had to try.

Perhaps it would help if she struck some kind of bargain with him. Offer him a gesture of support, a show of goodwill. Sucking in another steadying breath, Jessie resisted the urge to twist her hands. "Robert, I know that ye have no reason at all to trust me. But perhaps if I promise to help you, ye would feel more inclined to help me..."

Robert leveled his gaze on her. His dark blue eyes were almost black, their expression unreadable.

She swallowed to ease the tightness in her throat. "I've been thinking about why ye've come back after all this time. Mrs. MacMillan has told me a wee bit about what happened ten years ago—when ye left to rally to the Stuart cause."

Robert's face was like stone. "Has she now?"

Jessie rushed on, feeling awkward and nervous under his cold stare. "Aye, she has. Mrs. MacMillan speaks very fondly of you, by the way.

Anyway, what I was trying to say was, I ken how verra difficult it must be to return here. No doubt ye're concerned about being recognized... and then arrested for taking part in the Rebellion. But having lived at Lochrose, I ken the routines of the household and everyone's schedule. I...I could perhaps help ye to enter the castle undetected so ye could see yer father..."

Robert's eyes narrowed. There was a sudden intensity in his scrutiny of her.

At last, he was interested.

Encouraged, Jessie leaned forward and continued to plead her case. "I know I have no right to speak of such things, but I'm sure yer father misses ye too. Although I have no' heard him speak of you, I know he has a miniature portrait of you that he carries about with him. I've seen it. That's how I recognized ye this morning. Mrs. MacMillan says yer father was heartbroken after Culloden, that he's never been the same since yer estrangement. After all these years, I'm sure that he would give anythin' to see you again..." She faltered, at a loss what to say next as Robert's reaction to her words mystified her.

He bowed his head and pinched the bridge of his nose as if a great surge of emotion overwhelmed him. A muscle worked in his jaw.

When he raised his head, Robert looked straight at her. His eyes were hard and cold with withering anger.

Heavens, what have I done?

"How can I believe a single word you say, Jessie?" he bit out. "You're betrothed to Simon, the pair of you are set to become the next Earl and Countess of Strathburn. Why would I trust you to help me, when doing so ruins both your chances of inheriting that glittering prize?"

Did Robert really think so badly of her? Ignoring the lurch in the pit of her stomach in the face of such ire, Jessie somehow summoned her voice. "Ye believe Simon would betray you, but do ye really credit it? Surely after all this time he would welcome—"

Robert laughed, but there was no mirth in the sound. He raked her with a look that could only be described as scathing. "Of course he would betray me. I'm surprised he hasn't recounted the whole sorry story to you. How his bloodthirsty and glory-seeking older brother, ignoring the entreaties of their wise father, rushed into battle in support of the evil Pretender and squandered the lives of six-and-thirty good clansmen."

Jessie shook her head, tears pricking her eyelids. "I-I had no idea ..."

"What? You don't know that after the villainous Jacobite managed to escape capture by the English on the field at Culloden, he retreated to Lochrose, craven cur that he was? And that the steadfast, obedient younger son had him locked up in the wine cellar, ready for the dragoons to take away, because of course, that was the noble and right thing to do, wasn't it?"

Jessie was stunned. If what Robert had just told her was really true, Simon had set out to maliciously betray his brother. *What sort of a ruthless monster was he?* It took her breath away. "What a heinous betrayal... I didna know... Mrs. MacMillan never told me that..." Jessie trailed off, utterly lost for words.

Robert was still looking at her as if she were some low creature that had just crawled out from beneath a rock. Of course, in his mind, she and Simon were both fashioned from the same mold, and she couldn't blame him for that. She drew in a shaky breath, wanting to know more. She wanted to understand. "But ye managed to escape."

Robert snorted. "No thanks to Simon. Even though I'd defied my father, I suppose he took pity on me. Either that or he couldn't bear to see our family name dragged through the mud any more than it had been. Better to have a son in exile than one who had been executed for treason. At any rate, my father arranged for one of the local Black Watchmen whom he trusted to stitch me back together—"

"Ye were wounded?"

Robert shrugged. "You've seen my shoulder. A bayonet sliced me open. I don't even remember when it happened during the battle. Anyway, the Watchman, MacTaggart, put me back together and released me from Lochrose's cellar. Along with Tobias, he helped me to get to the coast and onto a fishing boat without being intercepted by the King's men. It was more than I deserved." Robert gulped down more whisky before he continued. "Tobias, the poor bastard... He lost his older brother Hamish, you know. All because of my cock-headed idiocy. Why the lad never held it against me, why he bothered to come with me, I'll never know." He shook his head and stared into the fire, the flames casting strange patterns of light and shadow over the strong planes of his handsome face.

Jessie watched his expression grow distant, his thoughts obviously turning inward.

"I should have died. I deserved to." Robert's voice was laced with bitter self-recrimination. "I was so bloody stupid."

It was shocking to catch a glimpse of this man's inner pain. Jessie recognized immediately that the scars Robert carried from that long-ago battle were more than skin deep and they had not healed. He was still deeply wounded to the depths of his very soul.

At the risk of being subjected to his disdain again, she rallied her courage to speak, to break the taut, painful silence, to draw Robert back from whatever horrors he was currently reliving in his mind. She knew she could never offer him comfort, but at least she could convey her sympathy.

Jessie watched him quietly and waited until he met her gaze again. "I know I couldna even begin to understand what Culloden has cost ye, Robert," she ventured gravely, her heart clenching for him. "But I want ye to know that I...I'm truly abhorred by the knowledge of what Simon did to you."

Her bid for reconciliation failed dismally. Robert stood abruptly, looking down at her with nothing but contempt in his eyes. Jessie shrank back, pulling her blanket about her tightly, as if it could provide her with protection.

Robert raised the whisky bottle in a mock toast. "Here's to you, Jessie Munroe, and your betrothal to the *honorable* Simon Grant, Master of Strathburn and heir to the Earldom of Strathburn. I wish you well." He drank from the bottle then strode to the entrance of the cave. Leaning against the rock wall, he gave his back to her and stared out into the bitterly cold night.

Jessie watched his rigid form. His derision stung more than she cared to admit, but it was undeniably her own fault that Robert viewed her with such enmity. She persisted in perpetuating the lie about her relationship with Simon.

She suddenly couldn't bear the idea of being associated with such a low, despicable creature any longer. Once and for all she needed to set things straight. Tell Robert the truth, no matter how ashamed she felt.

Although stiff and cold, Jessie dropped the blanket and pushed herself to her feet. Robert half turned his head as she drew close. His face was in darkness. She sensed rather than saw his animosity. It fairly vibrated off him.

She dragged in a shaky breath. "Robert..." To her dismay her voice shook slightly. He turned around and stared at her, his eyes like deep black hollows. She tried again. "Robert, there's something ye should know. It's difficult for me to talk about..."

Except for the frigid wind, lifting the lock of hair over his brow, Robert remained motionless. *Enough, Jessie.* She would not be intimidated by his dark mood. *This must be done.*

"I'm ashamed to admit that I havena been completely honest with you. I must explain—"

Robert laughed, a short, sharp derisive bark. "Well, I must say that doesn't surprise me, given the company you keep." He dropped the now empty whisky bottle, pushed away from the cave wall then took a step toward her.

Despite the quaking in her bones, Jessie held her ground. Snowflakes swirled in the air between them.

"What continues to surprise me though," Robert all but growled, "is that you find my brother even remotely worthy of your attention. I mean, what the hell do you see in him? Can you just explain that to me, Jessie, because I'd really like to know."

Jessie swallowed hard, forcing herself to hold Robert's searing gaze. "I... It's no' what ye think... When ye saw Simon with me, yesterday morning—"

"You're lovers. Don't deny it." Robert moved closer and Jessie stepped back until her shoulders met the rough stone of the cave wall.

She had nowhere to go. She closed her eyes as a deep chill ran through her. *This wasn't going well at all.*

Robert was relentless. "So what is it about Simon that attracts you so, Jessie? Is it his fine form, charming personality, and sparkling wit?"

Jessie shook her head. "Ye dinna understand..."

Coherent thought had fled. Robert was so close now, he was almost pressed flat against her. The scent of him—pine needles, wood smoke, whisky, and something else that was essentially male—surrounded her. Drugged her mind. He leaned forward and placed his forearms against the cave wall behind her. Framing her.

Trapping her. She couldn't breathe, couldn't think.

Robert bent low, his voice a heated rasp against her ear. "Or is it his wealth and promise of a title?"

"No," Jessie whispered, her own voice little more than a whimpered breath. She was torn between wanting Robert and wanting to push him away so she could explain. "No, it's no' like that at all."

Robert traced a finger down the side of her cheek and along her jaw, down to her collarbone. His touch was like fire upon her skin. Jessie's whole body trembled from head to toe and her heart slammed frantically against the wall of her chest. Whether it was from fear or anticipation, she hadn't a clue.

Robert's mouth was so close to her parted lips, his frosted breath mingled with hers. "Or is it the way he kisses you, Jessie, that has you so enthralled?"

Before she could utter a sound, Robert clasped her jaw and claimed her mouth in a bruising kiss. His lips were hard, demanding, as they crushed against hers. Hot anger flared within Jessie, dousing any fear.

How dare he kiss her like this? He was as despicable as Simon!

But even as Jessie tried to wrench her mouth away, hot liquid warmth coursed through her, as potent as the whisky they'd shared. She futilely pushed her hands against Robert's chest, but his lean, rock hard body crushed her hard up against the cold stone. She felt hot and cold all at once as if she were overcome with some strange fever.

Robert buried both hands in her tangled hair and deepened the kiss, his mouth moving urgently over hers. Never before had Jessie experienced a kiss like this, and never before had her body responded in such an inexplicable way.

A firestorm raged inside her. Fury at Robert for taking such liberties, yet deep, pulsing arousal beyond anything she'd ever known swept through her. When Robert's tongue traced the seam of her lips then pushed inside, she gasped at the invasion—but she soon yielded to the intimate stroking of his tongue against hers, even tasting him in return.

It was as though her body had surrendered even though her mind resisted. Gradually, by degrees, her ire started to dissolve into the molten heat throbbing through her veins. Ignoring the pain in her wounded arm, she grasped the back of Robert's neck with both hands and pulled him closer. A moan, desperate and needy, spilled from her throat.

And then Robert pushed her away. He roughly pulled her hands from his neck and clasped them up against her chest. He was panting raggedly, his breath a harsh sawing sound. "So tell me, Jessie...does he kiss you that way?" Robert's dark, smoldering gaze searched hers. "Is that what you love about him?"

She shook her head, aching and angry and wanting, and oh, so confused. "Please... I—"

"Or does he kiss you like this?"

Again Robert took her mouth, but this time the kiss was slow, sinuous, teasing. A hot, satiny glide. He released her hands and cupped her face gently. His thumbs softly stroked the sensitive flesh beneath her jaw and down the sides of her neck. He broke the contact briefly to draw breath, before lowering his head once more. The tip of his tongue ran over the swell of her bottom lip before pushing into the recess of her mouth again, tasting her as if she were the most exquisite delicacy.

Jessie was melting. If Robert's body hadn't been pressing against hers, holding her up, she would have slipped to the ground. Her hands curled into the wool of his plaid, pulling his body closer. One of his muscular legs pushed between hers and she half stood, half straddled him. Even through the layers of her cambric petticoats, the heat of his body penetrated through to her own.

When Robert pushed closer into her, his pelvis gently thrusting against her hip, she moaned again, breasts aching, mound throbbing. Heaven help her, she was completely overwhelmed. A warning bell clamored somewhere at the back of her mind. *This had to stop... Had to stop before—*

With a shudder, Robert ripped his mouth away, panting hard. He pushed away from her, and Jessie felt like she'd been doused with a bucket of cold loch water. "I won't dare ask if there's anything else you love about my brother." His tone was harsh, bitter. He turned abruptly and stalked off into the darkness outside.

A soft sound almost like a sob escaped Jessie's swollen lips. She touched them with shaking fingers. *She wouldna cry. She. Would. Not.*

But she couldn't hide from the fact that yet again she'd failed to tell Robert the whole truth. Any of it. Damn her weakness. And damn Robert Grant for making her feel this way—frustrated and yearning and desperate and as furious as a wildcat. She hoped he froze to death out there.

Too exhausted to examine the tangle of her thoughts and emotions, Jessie decided to opt for the welcome oblivion of sleep. She returned to the fire, now slowly dying, and retrieved her blanket and cloak before struggling to the bed at the back of the cave. It was icy back there away from the fire, but she was beyond caring. Wrapping herself tightly in her makeshift bed covers, she sank onto the bracken and heather, and willed herself to sleep. She would have to try and reason with Robert in the morning, when he was sober and she wasn't...wasn't whatever she was in this moment.

Failing that, she'd just take the wretched man's horse.

Robert stood outside in the swirling snow, kicking himself for his brutish treatment of Jessie. He shouldn't have drunk so much whisky. He'd let his guard down and succumbed to his own base desires. The need to make Jessie his own, to steal her from his brother if only for a moment or two, had overtaken all rational thought.

The lass must now think he was the worst kind of lustful beast.

What he hadn't been expecting was Jessie's seemingly inexperienced response to his kisses. Of course, he'd anticipated angry resistance for his presumption when he'd initially forced himself on her. And she had resisted...at first. But when she'd yielded to him, her kisses were not those of a well-practiced lover, but those of a tentative novice.

Robert raked a hand through his snow-covered hair. Yet again he was confounded by the woman. Had he...was it possible that he'd misinterpreted the seemingly passionate kiss he'd witnessed between Jessie and Simon? He closed his eyes and although it hurt, he revisited what he'd seen. There was no way to tell. In hindsight, he'd been an idiot not to stay longer to watch more of their exchange. But handfasted or not, he'd wager a good deal that Jessie had little to no experience when it came to lovemaking.

But then, why should he care at all about her innocence?

Because Simon has a cruel streak and he will debauch her, you know it.

Frustration that bordered on anguish twisted inside Robert, the emotion stronger now he'd tasted Jessie's sweetness himself. He wished Simon to hell. He wished Jessie was his. Most of all, he wished he hadn't begun to care for her.

But he had.

He did.

The snowfall continued unabated. The frigid cold had rapidly sobered Robert up and he realized he needed to return to the cave. To Jessie. Heaving a deep sigh, he wrapped his plaid tighter about himself and trudged back up the path.

Jessie had disappeared from view. Her confession that she hadn't known of Simon's duplicitous role in his arrest after Culloden confused him also. Her shock then compassion had seemed genuine. He wanted to trust her, but dare he?

She'd offered to help him gain admittance to Lochrose, even though she would be risking her own chance to make her way to Edinburgh tomorrow. But was her offer just a ruse to lure him into the path of Simon? Was she complicit in his half-brother's games, or innocent?

Perhaps when Tobias returned, Robert would have the answers he needed to solve the mystery that was Miss Jessie Munroe.

As he shook the snow off his hair and clothes at the cave's entrance, he immediately noticed that Jessie had already retired to the makeshift bed. Was the lass already asleep or was she just foxing, so she wouldn't need to speak to him? His mouth kicked into a grim smile. He wouldn't blame her in the least if she was quite literally giving him the cold shoulder.

The temperature in the cave had dropped significantly so he threw a few more hunks of wood and branches onto the fire. Despite his earlier resolution to sleep on the floor of the cave away from Jessie, he decided it would be sheer folly to do so. It was freezing and they would both end up suffering from exposure if they didn't take precautions—which meant they needed to share their body heat beneath their meager collection of blankets and wrappings.

Hell's bells.

Squaring his shoulders, Robert steeled himself to approach Jessie. He knelt down beside her then gently touched her arm beneath the covers. "Jessie lass. You must wake up."

Her eyes flew open immediately and she pushed herself up in a panicked gasp, wrapping her cloak and the blanket defensively around her shoulders. She looked exhausted and wary, her mouth a tight line, her eyes red-rimmed from crying. Tears he'd undoubtedly caused.

Guilt tugged at his heart. She stared at him, waiting.

Robert swallowed, struggling to find the words to apologize and somehow repair the fragile rapport he'd well and truly crushed. She'd never agree to his proposal otherwise. "Jessie, I...I'm so sorry for my behavior before. It was completely reprehensible, not to mention entirely inappropriate for me to...to take advantage of you in such a way. I have no excuse, but I hope you will consider accepting my sincere apology."

Jessie looked down and brushed her wildly curling hair behind her ear as she shivered. He held his breath, waiting for her to speak.

"I accept," she said quietly. She then raised her face, and he could see her beautiful brown eyes glowed with a quiet, determined strength. "But there's something I want *you* to understand. After tomorrow, ye must let me go. My only wish is to go to Edinburgh, to stay with my cousin. I swear to ye that I willna say a word to Simon or Lady Strathburn for that matter, about yer return. And my earlier offer, to help ye see yer father again, was sincere and still stands. I realize that ye have no real reason to trust me, but I ask that you do. Perhaps we can even make a deal... I will assist ye to enter Lochrose undetected in exchange for my freedom to leave. What do ye say?"

Robert extended his hand. "Agreed, Jessie Munroe."

Jessie clasped his hand and shook. Her skin was so cold, Robert had the sudden urge to place her hand under his shirt against his chest to warm it. Instead, he enveloped it with his other hand and began to gently chafe and massage her icy fingers.

She closed her eyes and sighed. "Why are ye so warm, Robert? It doesna seem fair."

Robert smiled, encouraged that Jessie hadn't ordered him to bed down with his horse. But he needed to do more than hold her hand to keep her warm. How would she react to his next suggestion?

He drew a fortifying breath, preparing himself for a stinging rebuke. "Jessie lass...it's as cold as Hades tonight, and I fear that we will both suffer if we do not take extra measures to keep ourselves warm."

She opened her eyes and regarded him warily. But she did not pull her hand away. "Well, ye drank all the whisky. What are ye suggesting?"

Robert held her gaze. "What you are wearing is nowhere near adequate for this kind of weather. I can feel how cold you are already and it's only going to get colder in here."

A small frown of suspicion creased her brow. "Aye..."

He took another deep breath. *In for a penny, in for a pound, Robert.* "We should lie together and share our body heat beneath the blanket and our plaids."

As he spoke, Jessie's eyes grew wide. She shook her head vehemently and wrenched her hand away. "You and I... I dinna think that would be appropriate. *At all.*"

"Jessie, I swear this is not some ploy to seduce you. If we don't do this, we may very well freeze to death. You must believe me."

She bit her lip and stared hard into his eyes, searching. She must have been satisfied with what she saw as she moved over to give him room beside her on the heather and bracken bed. "All right, Robert Grant. But if I catch yer hands wanderin' where they should no', I'll use yer own dirk on you. Do ye understand?"

Robert held up his hands in a gesture of surrender. "Understood. I shall be nothing but the perfect gentleman from now on." He eased himself down next to her and tucked his plaid and the blanket around them. Jessie lay stiffly beside him, barely touching him. She was still trembling and her teeth had started to chatter.

This wouldn't do. Slowly, carefully, Robert gathered her into his arms, the front of her body pressing against his side. He heard her sudden intake of breath, but she didn't try to pull away.

"It's better this way," he whispered softly against her ear. Her hair smelled faintly of heather and wood-smoke. "You'll tell me if I'm hurting your arm, won't you?"

Jessie nodded, her hair tickling his cheek. "I'm all r-right," she whispered. Her breath was warm against the hollow of his neck.

Robert fought the familiar urge to kiss her, but vowed to himself that he would not do anything to break her trust. He prayed she wouldn't notice that his rebellious cock had already started to grow stiff...and not with cold. *Blasted, brainless, obstinate thing.*

"Goodnight, Jessie," he murmured and slowly, he felt the tension ebb from her body. She relaxed into his embrace and her shivering eased as she quietly drifted into slumber. The palm of her left hand drifted upward to rest against his heart, and with a faint smile on his lips, Robert closed his eyes and let sleep claim him.

CHAPTER 13

W hen Jessie awoke the next morning, it was with the startling realization that her limbs were entwined with Robert's—and that she was warm, even comfortable.

In fact, she was *too* comfortable.

Curled into Robert's furnace-like heat, her head rested against his shoulder whilst one of his thighs lay over her hip. Even more shockingly, one of Robert's hands gently cupped her breast. She should be affronted and swat his hand away, untangle herself from his legs and use his dirk on him like she'd threatened to last night. But she didn't want to. The thought disturbed her, more than just a little. Robert had been joking yesterday, but perhaps she *was* a wicked wench.

She moved slightly and Robert stirred. His hand moved away from her breast to brush her hair away from her cheek.

"This seems to have become a bit of a habit, us spending the night together. How did you sleep?" His voice was low and husky, a caress against her ear.

Jessie found her voice, also husky with sleep and another emotion she didn't care to name. "Better than expected... And you?"

"I slept well," he murmured, sliding his hand from her head to her shoulder, then down to the curve of her waist. "Better than well."

127

Oh my. Jessie pushed away from him, attempting to create space between them, to break the intimacy. But then she saw Robert's face and she stilled. Her breath caught. His blue eyes were soft and dark in the dim light of dawn, his smile languid. No one had a right to look so handsome first thing in the morning. She swallowed, dragging her gaze away from his mouth. *His wide beautiful, inviting mouth.* She was definitely wicked. And this was dangerous—very dangerous. She needed to get up. Start the day. Get away.

Get to Edinburgh.

Robert's thoughts must have drifted in a similar direction. He sighed then dropped a quick kiss on her forehead. "As much as I would enjoy lying here all day like this, I think we really should get up. Besides, Tobias may be back at any time and—"

"Good mornin', milord. Miss Munroe."

Tobias!

Jessie shrieked and scrambled awkwardly from the bed, ignoring the pull of her stitches and the soreness of her sprained ankle. Her face blazed as she adjusted her plaid and wrapped her cloak tightly about her. Tobias hovered awkwardly at the entrance of the cave.

"Ah, good morning to you, Tobias." Robert followed Jessie out from underneath the bedclothes and stretched lazily, seemingly unperturbed by being caught abed with a woman. "I trust your fact-finding trip was worthwhile."

"Aye, milord." Tobias, his face beetroot red, looked only at his master. "I do indeed have news that I believe will interest ye."

Robert glanced back at Jessie. His expression had turned serious. "If you'll excuse me, Miss Munroe." He inclined his head toward the entrance of the cave. "Lad, how about you and I go and check on my horse?"

Heart sinking, Jessie watched the men disappear into the early morning fog drifting in the frigid mountain air. Despite the deal she'd struck with Robert last night, he still didn't trust her. After all, some of Tobias's intelligence must be about her. At least there would be independent corroboration of her claim she *was* the factor's daughter and that she'd been summoned to Edinburgh by her cousin—even though that, in and of itself was a lie.

What a muddle.

But she prayed the information Tobias had gleaned would improve Robert's opinion of her, even just a wee bit. Which meant he might still uphold his end of the bargain.

God willing, in a few hours, she would be on the public coach to Edinburgh.

She had to be.

~

The fog remained impenetrable as Jessie, Robert, and Tobias descended with painstaking slowness from the snow-shrouded upland glen to the lower wooded braes and Loch Kilburn. Jessie rode with Robert, his arm encircling her. She wasn't sure if it was for support or restraint.

After the men had returned to the cave, Robert had been subdued and distant. Every now and again, Jessie had caught him looking at her speculatively, making her worry anew about what he'd learned about her, and whether or not he would abide by their bargain and let her go.

In the rush to leave the cave, there hadn't been an opportunity to talk with him about her ideas for gaining safe entrance into the castle, or what her role would be. As they drew closer to Lochrose, Jessie found herself more than a little frustrated with Robert for not sharing his thoughts about the morning ahead. But railing at him wasn't an option, not when stealth and subterfuge were paramount.

Thankfully, they encountered no one along the way. The world around them was still, silent, and gray. Trees loomed out of the fog like ominous specters. Robert had insisted she leave her scarlet cloak behind as it would be too noticeable against the snow-dusted landscape. Even though he shared his plaid with her now, Jessie shivered with cold...and bone deep dread.

She was acutely aware that every step of Robert's horse brought her closer to Simon. Anxiety tied knots in her belly and frayed her nerves to the point that she felt nauseous. It probably didn't help that all she'd had for breakfast was a small portion of salted beef. But even if a feast awaited her at Lochrose, she doubted she could have eaten a thing.

At last she began to identify familiar landmarks as they materialized out of the fog. They were skirting the loch, heading for the direction of Lochrose's main gate and the Gate House. She clutched the pommel in front of her and began to gnaw at her bottom lip. The going had been so frustratingly slow, she was now terrified that time was slipping away from her. She estimated she only had a few hours at most to get to Grantown to catch the coach. She really couldn't stand not knowing the plan any longer.

Jessie turned back toward Robert. "Where are we headed?" she asked quietly over her shoulder, hating that she couldn't hide the breathy edge to her voice. "I canna imagine that ye're going to ride straight up the drive."

Robert waited a heartbeat before responding softly against her ear. "Your house, Jessie."

"Oh." Her brow plunged into a deep frown. He'd truly surprised her. "But why? Are ye going to share yer ideas so I can help? Dinna you remember our bargain?"

"Of course I do. But all will be revealed in good time."

Jessie hoped so. She *really* hoped so. There wasn't much time left.

When they got to within fifty yards of the Gate House, Robert and Tobias reined in and tethered the horses within a dense copse of larch and fir trees at the dwelling's rear. Robert helped Jessie to dismount, and she found herself pressed up against the hard planes of his body, his hands lingering at her waist. Despite her trepidation, Jessie immediately responded to his nearness. Her breath hitched and though she was chilled to the bone, warmth suffused her cheeks. Her physical attraction to Robert must be mortifyingly obvious. And despite the wide gulf of misunderstanding and mistrust that stretched between them, she also sensed that Robert desired her too.

The passionate way he'd kissed her last night certainly suggested he wanted her... And the way he'd gazed at her this morning when they were abed—the expression in his eyes so meltingly soft, she felt like sun-warmed butter...

She chanced a glance at his face and the corner of Robert's mouth inched upward into a smile. "It's been a long time since I've been this close to home, Jessie," he murmured as his eyes locked with hers. "I'm trusting you not to give me away."

Jessie's heart leapt in the oddest way. She offered a small smile in return, hoping Robert could see she was truly sincere. His good opinion of her mattered, more than she had hitherto realized. "I willna let ye down. And in case ye've forgotten, we can enter the Gate House from the back. I left the rear door unlocked when...when I left for Edinburgh."

Robert glanced at Tobias who stood nearby, seemingly busy with his mount's harness. A silent communication passed between them. The servant nodded and Robert turned back to Jessie. He took her hand. "Lead the way then, *mo ghaoil.*"

The cozy two-floor house was deserted but it was obvious someone had been there at some stage since Jessie had left. Someone who'd been very, very angry.

The hair at Jessie's nape stood on end as she took in the sight of a kitchen chair which had been upended, and her father's whisky bottle smashed on the stone floor. Even more disturbing was the state of her bedchamber upstairs. There looked to have been a rough search through her belongings. Her chest of drawers had been opened and items of her clothing had been tossed about the room.

Robert, standing beside her in the doorway, raised an eyebrow. "Simon?"

Jessie nodded, clutching the doorjamb, willing herself to swallow the surge of bile rising to her throat.

"He must be frustrated indeed that you left him, Jessie." Robert paused for a moment, frowning as he considered her face. Concern shadowed his eyes. "I imagine you would like to change, now you've access to your clothes. Will you be all right if I leave you for a few minutes?"

She found her voice although she couldn't hide its tremble. "Aye, aye, of course. I'll be fine. I willna be long, I promise."

Robert gave her a reassuring smile. Reaching for her shoulder, he gave it a gentle squeeze. "Good lass. Call me if you need anything."

Jessie nodded then he disappeared down the stairs.

Although her nerves were completely tattered, and she had precious little time to waste—the clock on her mantel indicated it was almost nine o'clock—Jessie didn't wish to squander this opportunity to wash and change into fresh clothes. It mattered not that the water she'd left in the pitcher several days ago was icy-cold as she splashed it over her face. With as much haste as she could manage, she shed her hodgepodge of filthy garments before grabbing fresh undergarments from the clothing strewn about on the floor. She shuddered to think of Simon touching her most private things, but she had no choice other than to use what was at hand.

From her wardrobe, Jessie selected a thick black wool cloak and her spare riding habit of emerald-green worsted wool trimmed with black velvet; it would serve just as well as a traveling gown. The tailored jacket and matching waistcoat—which she wore over a lace-trimmed linen shirt—buttoned up the front, so it was a relatively easy ensemble to don.

Although her ankle was still stiff and sore, she managed to pull on soft, black leather ankle boots without too much difficulty. She also fished out a pair of black kid gloves which she shoved in her habit's pocket along with a small purse containing her guineas for the coach fare. She wouldn't bother with a hat. It would just be something else to worry about.

Then she glanced at the clock. *Five minutes past nine.*

Her hair... Well, her hair was a disaster. Jessie sat before her dressing table mirror and dragged a brush through the tangled mess before pulling the curls into a low arrangement of sorts with a leather tie and black velvet ribbon. There were dark shadows under her eyes, but at least she no longer looked like some wild harridan. She was presentable enough to catch a public coach, at the very least.

If she made it in time. As long as she left by eleven o'clock and rode like the wind, she should be able to get to Grantown by midday. All going well.

And if Robert keeps his promise.

And if I do no' meet Simon.

Tears pricked and Jessie scowled at her reflection. *Stop it, Jessie. Ye dinna have time to cry.*

～

When Jessie went downstairs, Robert was standing by one of the mullioned windows in the small front parlor, scanning the drive.

In the weak light that filtered through the window, she immediately noticed that Robert had also taken the opportunity to improve his appearance for his upcoming reunion with his father. Although he hadn't shaved away the dark shadow of his morning stubble, he'd clubbed his hair back with a black velvet ribbon. He'd discarded his rumpled, travel-stained plaid and now wore buckskin breeches tucked into his black and tan top boots, a fresh white linen shirt with an elegantly tied cravat, and his brown hunting coat. Even though Robert's attire was simple, one couldn't fail to notice his innate air of authority.

Robert Grant, the gentleman Jacobite. A worthy bearer of the titles Master of Strathburn and Viscount Lochrose. Jessie prayed the earl would see that too.

She drew closer to the window. "'Tis fortunate the fog is lingering. Is there any sign of movement outside?"

Robert frowned, his mouth a hard line. "Four Black Watchmen rode by, headed for the castle but two minutes ago." His gaze met Jessie's. "Simon is persistent, I'll give him that."

Jessie clutched her black traveling cloak closer, her skin prickling with unease. She'd considered stealing outside and taking one of the horses under the cover of the fog, but she was beginning to question whether it was all that wise to go anywhere unaccompanied, given that Simon was still actively searching for her. In fact, she was starting to wonder whether she might be better off staying with Robert and not traveling to Edinburgh at all. Despite the mistrust between them, despite her initial doubts about him, she couldn't deny that he, above all others, made her feel safe.

Robert suddenly reached out and lifted her chin with gentle fingers, forcing her to look at him. "What is it, lass?" His voice was soft and low, but his gaze was searching. "Why are you so—"

The creak of the kitchen door opening made Jessie jump and Robert curse beneath his breath. He immediately tugged Jessie over to the parlor door and shielded her with his body. Her breath seizing, her heart crashing against her ribs, she watched Robert silently draw his dirk. His lightning reactions and apparent calmness in the face of possible danger were nothing short of impressive. Yet as his hand gripped hers, Jessie was also conscious of tightly reined in energy. He was the epitome of a battle-hardened soldier about to strike.

"'Tis only me, milord."

Only Tobias. Thank God. Jessie sagged against the wall, her knees almost buckling beneath her.

Robert visibly exhaled also and gave her a tight smile before sheathing his dagger. He stepped into the kitchen. "How goes it out there, Tobias?"

"No' verra weel, milord. Yer brother is still abed—he was up drinking until the wee small hours according to his valet, Baird. But there are four verra impatient Watchmen waitin' in the forecourt for him to rise. But Baird doesna ken when that will be. No one is game enough to wake him. My cousin Annie says that ever since Miss Munroe left"—Tobias flicked Jessie a glance—"the young Master has been in the foulest temper she's ever seen."

Robert ran a hand down his face and sighed heavily. "You know, Simon will probably have the coaching inn watched, Jessie," he said tightly, a dark frown creasing his brow. "He is relentless. He's making it almost impossible for you to catch that public coach."

"I know," Jessie replied in a small voice, fear and despair clogging her throat. She hated being the fly in the ointment, ruining Robert's plans. Even worse was the knowledge that her own plan to escape was destined to fail. She'd had no idea that Simon would be so...so dogged.

She closed her eyes and dug her fingernails into her palms, willing herself to swallow her tears, not to give in. She needed to think. And she didn't want to break down in front of Robert.

Robert gently touched her shoulder. "Perhaps my father can intercede. For both of us."

She nodded weakly. *Perhaps... What other choice do I have?*

"Are ye ready then, milord?" Tobias asked.

Ready for what? Although her vision was blurred with tears, Jessie narrowed her gaze on Robert. "I think it's about time ye shared yer plan, milord."

~

Robert rubbed his jaw, guilt gnawing at his belly. Jessie regarded him warily, eyes glistening with unshed tears and sharp suspicion. She knew something was afoot, and now was the time to tell her what was in store. The problem was, he knew she wasn't going to be happy.

He drew a deep breath and looked at her squarely. "Jessie, I'm going to leave you here with Tobias while I sneak into Lochrose. You'll be perfectly safe."

Her face blanched. "Ye dinna trust me, do you? Please...I beg you, let me go with you. I give ye my word, I willna betray yer presence."

Robert hesitated. Jessie was all but quaking with terror. It had initially occurred to him that perhaps she was play-acting, that her previous show of fear was just an elaborate hoax to get him inside the castle so she could alert Simon—or his stepmother—about his return. But now, studying her ashen face, he discarded the idea.

Why was Jessie so afraid to be left here with Tobias? If Simon was such a threat to her departure, surely it was safer if she stayed here, where she was hidden?

"It's better for everyone if I do this alone," he said carefully. "If something goes wrong, it's better if you and Tobias are not implicated in aiding a wanted man. You're both innocent. Tobias will look out for you."

Jessie swallowed and licked dry lips, her fear palpable. "I just want to help you. That was our deal. I must get to Edinburgh and I do no' care how. But if Simon comes here looking for me again...I dinna think he will let me go."

"Jessie, it is more likely that you will encounter Simon *inside* the castle than if you remain here. Tobias will protect you."

But the lass shook her head and grasped his hand, desperation clouding her golden-brown eyes. "Please, I would rather stay with you."

Robert searched her troubled face. Something clearly wasn't right. Not at all. He glanced around the room at the smashed bottle and tipped over chair. "Why are you so frightened, lass?" he asked gently. "Has Simon done anything to harm you? There's something you're not telling me, I know it."

Her eyes grew wide for an instant, her pupils dilating in panic. Then her eyelids fluttered downward. She wouldn't look at him. "It doesna matter." Her voice was barely above a whisper. Her cheeks had turned a burning red.

She was ashamed to tell him.

Anger flared inside Robert, hot and bright. Simon had hurt Jessie in some way, he was sure of it, but whatever it was, she was obviously reluctant to confide in him. More than ever, he was determined to find out what was really going on.

But now was not the time to question Jessie further. With every passing minute, it was more likely that Simon—and for that matter, his stepmother—would be rousing for the day. With that would come increased activity in and around the castle.

Robert made a snap decision. "All right, Jessie, you can come with me."

She grasped his arm, almost collapsing with relief before him. "Thank you, Robert," she murmured on a shaky exhale. "Ye willna have any cause to regret yer decision, I swear it."

Robert glanced over to Tobias who'd been trying to remain as inconspicuous as possible during the tense exchange. "You may as well head off. The rest of the plan remains the same."

The young man looked uncertain but nodded. "If ye're sure, milord."

"I am, Tobias." Robert crossed the room and placed a hand on his shoulder. He knew the best and safest place for the lad to be was far away from him, should anything go wrong. His family had already lost so much. "You've done more than enough to help. There's no sense in waiting around for my father's verdict on whether he'll assist me or not. It's best you go back to the *Phoenix*. Besides, if all does go well for me, I'll be seeing you and Drummond in Edinburgh before you both set sail again."

Tobias bowed his head. "As ye wish, milord. Godspeed to you."

Robert smiled and gave him one last clap on the shoulder. "Good lad. Give my regards to Drummond, won't you? Godspeed to you too, Tobias."

Once the back door clicked shut, Robert barred it against any other unexpected visitors, then turned to Jessie. "Is there a lantern or an oil lamp about, lass?"

She narrowed her eyes and looked quizzically at him for a moment, but quickly retrieved a lantern, as well as tinder from a dresser near the fireplace. "We are going somewhere dark, I take it?"

"Very." Robert smiled back at her before swiftly striking the tinder and lighting the lantern's wick. "You're not afraid of dark tunnels, are you? Or secret passages?"

Jessie eyed him suspiciously. "Nay... Ye really didna need me to help ye at all, did you?"

Robert ignored her question and flashed her a grin instead. He was pleased to see she was no longer shaking, and she even blushed a little at his smile. Picking up the lantern in one hand, he grasped Jessie's hand firmly with the other, and led her toward the Gate House's cellar door. "Come with me."

CHAPTER 14

Robert's grasp was warm and reassuring as they descended into the cellar.

Although Jessie had been more than a little frustrated with the man for taking so long to reveal his secret strategy—a strategy which had involved leaving her behind—Jessie cared not a fig where he was going to lead her now. She trusted him.

After all she'd been through over the last two days, she now knew without a doubt that she could count on this man to keep her safe. Her initial reason for claiming she was handfasted to Simon—to protect herself from Robert—now seemed utterly absurd. After Robert was reunited with his father, she swore she would tell him the truth.

She watched with interest as Robert went to one of the far dark corners of the cellar. After placing the lantern on a disused crate, he ran his hands along the roughly hewn bricks until he located one that seemed to be loose, and without too much effort, levered it out. He put his hand inside the dark recess and pressed down on something that made a decided click. A part of the back wall immediately grated open a fraction.

Robert replaced the brick and beckoned to her. "Do you think your ankle is up to this, Jessie?"

"I think so." She would not be left behind. "I will do my best no' to slow us down."

"I believe you, lass." He gave her a quick smile and then took her hand again to guide her into the underground tunnel beyond.

A blast of stale, frigid air immediately hit Jessie. When the door closed behind them, they were plunged into inky blackness save for the pale flickering flame of the oil lantern. Jessie couldn't quite suppress a shiver.

As if sensing her unease, Robert drew her close and squeezed her hand. "Courage, Jessie. Tobias was down here yesterday and he assured me the way is clear."

"Where does the passage lead?" she asked, following Robert through the heavy darkness. The stone floor of the tunnel was uneven and sloped slightly downward. The ache in her ankle made her concentrate on each step.

"To Lochrose's wine cellar. When my great-grandfather had the castle constructed, he insisted on escape tunnels in the event of an attack. There's another tunnel that forks off this one to the loch, but Tobias says part of its wall has collapsed and would need digging out. Rising damp from the ground near the loch has probably weakened the mortar." Robert glanced back at her, and she caught the flash of his smile even in the weak light. "But never fear. That's not the case with this tunnel."

They continued walking for an indeterminate amount of time, Robert carefully leading Jessie around the occasional protruding rock or warning her to duck when the ceiling became low. The cold was damp and penetrating. By the time they reached another bricked doorway, Jessie was shivering in earnest.

Robert located a latch and the door reluctantly scraped open. Stepping through, Jessie could see that they were indeed within a wine cellar. Rows and rows of casks and bottles lay neatly stacked in racks that stretched away into the darkness. She heard the dull thud of the door closing behind them, and then Robert was leading her toward a set of stone stairs at the other end of the chamber.

"Careful where you step." Robert indicated a pile of rusted chains and manacles in their path.

Jessie looked down and stopped as the import of their presence here struck her. "This—this is where Simon had ye chained up? Like an animal?" She gripped Robert's hand as tears welled in her eyes. "Oh my God, Robert. How could he? And ye were wounded…" Even in the dim light, she could see the mortar between the flagstones was stained, undoubtedly with Robert's blood.

Bright, white-hot anger sparked in Jessie's heart. The tangible evidence of Simon's cruelty took her breath away.

Robert shrugged, reaching out and brushing a thumb across her cheek, wiping away a spilled tear. "It was long ago, lass. Dry your tears. I'm not worth it."

Without thinking, Jessie pressed his palm against her face. "Aye, you are, Robert Grant. What Simon did was wrong. Verra wrong."

Holding her gaze, Robert drew her hand to his lips and glanced a kiss across her knuckles. His mouth was warm, his lips oh, so soft. This time when Jessie shivered, it wasn't with cold. Heat scalded her cheeks, and she couldn't rip her gaze from Robert's.

If only things were different, for both of us. If I were a fine lady, if Robert Grant wasna a wanted Jacobite, he might just be the man to win my heart and hand…

The lantern's flame momentarily dimmed, and Robert sucked in a breath, shaking his head as if waking from a dream. "Come, let's go, *mo ghaoil*. It's time I stopped putting off this meeting with my father."

Instead of taking the stone stairs, Robert led Jessie to the alcove beneath them where several barrels were stacked. After she took the lantern, he pushed the barrels aside then pressed on a wooden panel— another door swung open, revealing a narrow staircase concealed behind the wall. "This will take us to the hall where my father's rooms are," he said, reaching for her hand again.

Although he appeared outwardly calm, Jessie could sense a growing tension in Robert. A muscle worked in his jaw and his grip on her hand was so tight, it was almost uncomfortable.

With a jolt, she suddenly realized the source of his disquiet. "How do ye feel, seeing yer father after all this time?" she asked softly.

To her surprise, Robert's mouth pulled into a lopsided grin. "Nervous as hell," he admitted. "But there's no going back now." He took the lantern then ushered her into the stairwell, encouraging her to lead the way. "You set the pace, Jessie. I wouldn't want you to trip if I hurry you along too much."

Jessie nodded. Lifting her skirts, she began to scale the steep and narrow stairs.

The lantern gave off just enough light that she could see where she was going without too much trouble. However, her ankle soon started to give her grief. Ignoring the sharp twinges as best she could, she continued to climb. At one point she stumbled, gasping with both pain and alarm. Robert caught her, holding her steady against the solid wall of his chest.

"I've got you. How's your ankle?" His breath was warm against her ear.

"A wee bit sore but I'll be all right," Jessie whispered back, thankful he'd suggested she go first. He must have anticipated something like this. "Thank ye for catching me."

She felt his lips curve in a smile against her ear. "It's my pleasure, Jessie. It's not every day a bonnie lass falls into my arms."

"Hmph. That's what *ye* say, Robert Grant, but I'm no' inclined to believe you," Jessie rejoined, trying to ignore the fluttering of her pulse in response to his words. The feel of his strongly muscled arm about her waist was equally disconcerting. "Yer rakish smile is far too well-practiced. I'm sure bonnie lasses fall for ye all the time." When she pulled away, she strongly suspected that Robert had muttered that she truly was a wicked wench. She couldn't help but grin.

By the time Jessie reached the top of the stairs, she was breathless but relieved the painful climb was over. If for some reason she had to run, though... She closed her eyes, praying it wouldn't come to that. She had to trust that Simon was such a slugabed that he wouldn't have risen yet—and now was definitely not the time to lose her nerve. She drew the hood of her black wool cloak over her telltale hair, preparing for the next, most hazardous part of their mission.

Robert gently pushed past her to carefully hang the lantern on a small hook above her head. The wicked wench within her suddenly had the urge to throw her arms around his broad chest and draw in his masculine scent, to take pleasure in his strength one last time.

But she didn't. She didn't want to distract Robert or seem any more of a burden. Even in the dim, flickering light she could see that the tension within him had not lessened. His expression was drawn, his mouth a tight line.

He placed his ear to the panel-like wooden door in front of them. "Fingers-crossed it's all clear, Jessie," he whispered. Then he released the catch and pushed.

~

The door swung open onto a wide hallway which was heartbreakingly familiar. Robert paused on the threshold, his heart clenching in the oddest way.

He was home.

He glanced up and down the corridor, thanking God it was completely deserted. As he stepped out, Jessie followed closely behind. She'd done well to make it this far with him. Her resilience and determination astounded him. Robert looked her way, and she gave him a tremulous smile. Beneath her veneer of courage, she was obviously as nervous as he was.

It was utterly silent up here where Lochrose's main bedchambers lay. The thick Turkish carpet muffled their footsteps as Robert and Jessie quickly traversed the long hall, heading toward his father's suite.

Nothing much had changed. The stone walls between each bedchamber door were still hung with fine tapestries and paintings of Highland landscapes. The other side of the corridor was interspersed at regular intervals with arched mullioned windows, through which he could see that the fog hadn't yet dissipated. With a sharp pang of regret, Robert realized he couldn't see the rose garden his own mother had installed so long ago when he was but a wee babe.

They passed Simon's suite of rooms. Not a sound emanated from within. Robert prayed the cur was still abed, not just for his own sake but for Jessie's as well.

At last. Robert drew Jessie into the shelter of the window embrasure directly opposite the last set of paneled oak doors at the end of the hall. The Earl of Strathburn's suite. He threw Jessie the devil-may-care smile she'd teased him about, as much to reassure himself as well as her. "Well, here we are."

Jessie smiled back. "Aye."

A pale ray of sunshine which had managed to penetrate the dense fog highlighted flecks of gold in her whisky-hued eyes. Robert decided he could happily drown in those eyes. His gaze dropped to Jessie's bewitching mouth. Scoundrel that he was, he suddenly couldn't resist the sight of her full, oh-so tempting lips. And this might be his last chance to ever kiss them, if the following meeting didn't go well.

"Kiss me for luck?" Robert whispered and before Jessie could reply, he dipped his head and kissed her once, gently.

He needn't have worried that she would not be acquiescent. She responded immediately, her lips parting slightly in complete acceptance of the stolen kiss.

Surprise sparked and Robert was tempted to press her for more, to deepen the kiss and taste her fully. But as much as he wanted to, this was not the time or place to linger in an embrace. Reluctantly, he mastered his desire and started to pull away...only to find that Jessie had fisted her hand into his lapel and was pulling him back down. She crushed her lips against his in a brief but fiery kiss of her own. When she broke the contact, her eyes were glowing. "Good luck, Robert. Ye deserve to be happy."

"Thank you, *mo ghaoil*." Inhaling a steadying breath to marshal his courage, and with Jessie's hand still in his, he stepped toward the door and tried the brass handle.

It had been ten years since Robert had last been here and fought so bitterly with his father. Ten long years since he'd foolishly stormed out this very door and slammed it behind him. For ten years he'd waited for this moment—a moment that in dark periods of despair he'd feared would never come.

The door swung open silently. Heart in his mouth, Robert crossed the threshold, gently pulling Jessie with him.

They were in his father's sitting room. A cheerful fire crackled in the grate and the dusky blue velvet curtains at the window were pulled back to allow the weak morning light to filter in. It took a moment for Robert's eyes to adjust to the dimness as he scanned the room. On first glance, it appeared empty of occupants. The furniture and fittings were exactly as he remembered them—fine walnut tables and several leather wingback chairs graced a deep burgundy and blue patterned Turkish rug before the fire. Bookshelves and a walnut desk flanked the wall opposite the fireplace. Between them was a closed door leading to his father's dressing room. Beyond that was his father's bedchamber. It was like stepping back in time.

Then Robert noticed a movement by one of the wingchairs and a strange whine.

He froze. His heart slammed against his ribs.

"Caesar. Yer father's deerhound," whispered Jessie. "I'm sorry, I didna think..."

The huge hound loped to its feet and stood staring at Robert, its gaze intense. It sniffed the air.

Robert swallowed. "Caesar," he whispered.

The animal whined again and began wagging its tail. Then all at once, the great shaggy hound launched itself at Robert, its great front paws coming to rest upon his shoulders as it madly licked his face.

Robert laughed, rubbing the hound's back. "I don't believe it. You remember me, Caesar."

Jessie shook her head, clearly astounded. "He knows you."

Robert nodded, attempting to push the exuberant dog down. The hound's tail whipped back and forth wildly. "Father gave him to me when I was but nineteen. He was my dog for two years, before I left. It's incredible that he still recognizes me."

"Caesar!" A voice crackled with age sounded behind Robert and his pulse leapt.

Father. Robert couldn't quite believe it. After all this time, there he was, but a few feet away.

The Earl of Strathburn stood in the doorway of his dressing room, leaning heavily on a walking stick, a dark scowl marring his brow. He looked between Robert and Jessie. "Miss Munroe, what on earth are you doing here in my quarters with this strange man?" he demanded. "I thought you'd gone to Edinburgh. Please explain yourself. At once."

Ignoring the twisting in his gut, Robert stepped forward and sought his father's gaze. The lines of his father's face were familiar, and yet so changed. He'd changed too. "Father...it's me... Robert."

Lord Strathburn's look of annoyance was replaced with one of anger. "What do you mean? How dare you come in here, claiming to be my son. Robert is dead." He took several faltering steps toward Jessie. "Miss Munroe, what is the meaning of this?"

Jessie lowered the hood of her cloak and then crossed the room, taking his father's shaking hand—an old man's hand. His father seemed to have aged at least twenty years rather than ten. A great wave of sorrow welled up inside Robert, for all that they'd both suffered and lost. His vision blurred.

Jessie was murmuring in a low, gentle voice. "Lord Strathburn, 'tis true. This is yer son, Robert Grant. He's returned home to Lochrose."

His father stared at him a moment longer, studying his face, then took another step closer. His rheumy blue eyes drifted to Caesar, who was still licking Robert's hand. Tail wagging, Caesar whined and looked at the earl.

Robert swallowed past the tight ache in his throat. It was a struggle to keep his voice calm and even as he said, "Caesar remembers me, Father. After all this time...it's amazing, isn't it?"

"Robert?" his father whispered. His face blanched like he'd seen a ghost. "Robert...it *is* you. Oh, my God. My son." He dropped his cane and stepped forward at the same time that Robert crossed the floor to embrace his father.

As they grasped each other tightly, as Robert felt his father shuddering against his shoulder, he could scarcely believe it. His father hadn't turned him away.

He called me son.

"Robert, my lad. My boy." His father's voice was choked with raw emotion. He pushed Robert away to hold him at arm's length, staring fervently into his eyes, tears streaming down his face. "Let me see you. Speak. Tell me this is not just an old man's dream. Tell me again it's really you."

Robert blinked away his own tears. His voice, when he managed to speak, was little more than a thick rasp. "Aye it's me, Father. Robert.

Not a ghost or hallucination. It's me, in the flesh—ten years older and battle-scarred—but me, all the same."

His father crushed him in a fierce hug again. "I can scarcely fathom it. You've been gone so long, I thought you must be dead. Why did you stay away so long, my son?"

Robert closed his eyes. The guilt and shame of what he'd done still dwelt within him, a painful, cankerous wound. He gently pulled away from his father's tight embrace and met his gaze. "I'm so sorry to have defied you. I was such a bloody, idealistic fool—the worst kind of fool. I should have listened to your counsel but I was too arrogant. I thought I knew what was best for the clan. But I was wrong. And our men died because of what I did—" His voice broke. He couldn't go on.

His father, grabbed his shoulder, shook it gently. "Robert, you were young and hot-headed, yes, but you are not to blame for the mistakes of that fool Prince you followed into battle, or the brutality of the English on Drumossie Moor that day. Tell me...tell me you didn't stay away all this time because of some foolish words I spoke in anger to you."

Robert wiped his eyes roughly with his sleeve. *Damnation, he'd promised himself he wasn't going to cry.* "It wasn't just your ultimatum, Father, that kept me away. I couldn't come home because I couldn't face you—or the clan—not then at any rate." He raised his gaze to his father's. "But I've been a coward for far too long. I have a debt of honor that needs to be repaid to all of the families that lost a son, a husband, or a father. I don't expect forgiveness, from you or from them, but I need to try to make amends...if you will let me."

His father placed his hands on Robert's shoulders and looked at him squarely. "Son, I forgive you. You must believe me. I thank God that you have been returned to me. Now, come sit with me and tell me more. We both have a decade's worth of tales to tell."

CHAPTER 15

Jessie hovered at the edge of the room, unsure of what to do as she watched Lord Strathburn and Robert take seats before the fire. The earl settled into a leather wingback chair while Robert sat close by on a silk-upholstered settee. Quite touchingly, Caesar lay at Robert's feet, his muzzle on his boots.

She surreptitiously wiped away the involuntary tears that had slipped down her cheeks as she'd witnessed the bittersweet reunion between father and son. She felt like an intruder watching such a private moment. While she wanted to let Robert and his father have some time alone, she could hardly leave. The risk of discovery by Simon or Lady Strathburn, or even one of the other servants, was too great. It would be inappropriate for her to retire to the earl's dressing room or bedchamber. So she stayed near the double oak doors attempting to remain as inconspicuous as possible.

And it did indeed seem that Robert and the earl were oblivious to her presence for the moment.

At his father's urging, Robert briefly recounted the sequence of events which had followed his escape from Lochrose ten years ago. He spoke quietly, his low voice weighted with leaden remorse. "I took you at your word, Father, when you told me I was never to return—for a very long while at least. MacTaggart got me to the coast where I managed to persuade the captain of a fishing boat off Nairn to take me as far as Skye. From there I made my way to Ireland and thence to France. You'll be pleased to know my new identity as Robert Burnley held up even under the scrutiny of a commander of an English frigate that intercepted the boat to Ireland. Your magistrate did a sterling job, Father. The commander believed my papers to be legitimate. If it weren't for you and MacTaggart—"

"I still cannot believe Simon had you chained up in the wine cellar to hand you over to the English." The earl's face had turned dark red with anger. "No matter that you defied me, I couldn't let Simon betray you like that. It was abominable." His fist struck the arm of the wing chair and Caesar lifted his head and whined.

Robert reached out and grasped his father's hand. "Steady, Father. You must not stress yourself too much. I couldn't bear it if anything were to happen to you, now we've found each other again."

Lord Strathburn patted Robert's arm. "I'll be all right, son. Mrs. MacMillan has been taking good care of me with her special tea of comfrey and willow bark. I swear that woman has a touch of the wise woman in her." His high color began to fade as he added, "But pray, continue with your tale."

Robert's expression grew grim. "I'm...I'm not proud of how I spent the next few years. Suffice it to say, I didn't much care where I was or what I put my hand to."

"Whatever you've done in the past, Robert, it doesn't matter to me. It's all over now," said the earl, compassion lighting his eyes. "I will listen to anything you wish to share."

Robert studied his father's earnest expression for a moment then sighed. "I effectively became a soldier for hire, a mercenary with the French Army. Fighting was the only thing I was fit for."

Lord Strathburn reached out and squeezed Robert's shoulder. There were tears in the old man's eyes. "You wanted to die, didn't you, my son?"

Robert dropped his gaze to his tightly fisted hands in his lap. "Aye. For a long time, life didn't seem to be worth living anymore."

Shock stole Jessie's breath and her vision swam with tears. Robert had opened up his very soul to reveal his deepest pain and her heart wept for him.

The earl spoke again, his voice gentle. "So what made you give up the fighting?"

"I wish I had a better, more noble reason but frankly, I just grew tired of it, Father," Robert said thickly. "The pointless messy, bloody insanity of it all. And I don't know why, but I seemed to have the devil's own luck on the battlefield. Aside from the occasional superficial injury, nothing ever seemed to touch me."

Lord Strathburn nodded. "Either that or you were a damn good soldier. MacTaggart always maintained you were a fine marksman and an even better swordsman. What did you do next?"

Robert grinned shyly, surprising Jessie. He looked almost boyishly proud. "I settled in the Caribbean. Jamaica to be exact. While I've been parading around as the very English Mr. Robert Burnley, respectable merchant ship-owner for the last four years, I've also been undermining the English Crown in other ways." He shrugged a wide shoulder. "I'm afraid the Scots rebel in me cannot help it."

"Really?" asked Lord Strathburn, curiosity tinging his voice. "Given that devilish twinkle in your eye, I'm almost afraid to ask."

"Aye, perhaps you should be," said Robert. "Only a trusted few know this, but I've been secretly working as a spy and rogue 'privateer' so to speak." His expression hardened, the light from the window high-lighting the smoldering anger in his eyes. "After Culloden, I couldn't let the English get away with blue murder. I also couldn't let them exploit my fellow Scotsmen who'd been indentured into hard labor in the Colonies after the Rebellion—or anyone else who's been sold into slavery, for that matter. It's beyond despicable that the English make coin off the blood, sweat, and tears of captured souls who are treated like chattel. So I decided to employ my merchant ship, the *Phoenix*, and my corsair's vessel, the *Griffon*, to eke out some natural justice. I trade shipping information with England's enemies and when I'm at sea, I free the enslaved. It was the *Phoenix* who actually brought me home. She's currently anchored in Edinburgh."

Jessie couldn't contain a small gasp. Robert was not only a Jacobite rebel, but a spy and a pirate? Goodness gracious, he'd led a dangerous existence. But he was also a champion of those who needed help. She was nothing but impressed.

Lord Strathburn seemed impressed too. He returned his son's smile. "You're an adventurer down to your very bones, my boy, and far too noble for your own good. But I'm grateful you're home now and rest assured, I will never break your trust. Your secrets are safe with me. I've missed you. More than you could ever know."

Robert smiled then, and his eyes seemed to glow with genuine happiness. "I've missed you too, Father," he murmured. But then a shadow crossed his countenance. "One of the reasons I ventured home was that a few months ago, I heard a rumor or two suggesting the estate has not been faring well of late. Is it true?"

Lord Strathburn's chest rose and fell with a weary sigh. "Indeed. As much as I hate to admit it, that is in fact the case. Your stepmother and brother..." A rueful smile twisted the earl's mouth. "Well, let's just say I've got a firm hold on the purse strings at the moment, and they are none too happy about it. Things started to go awry about a year ago when I began to hand over the management of the estate to Simon. I thought I was doing the right thing, trying to keep him busy and out of trouble. It was a grave mistake. But now I have a new factor—Munroe is his name—keeping an eye on things, the situation is starting to improve."

Robert nodded and glanced over toward Jessie. Their eyes met briefly and heat flashed through her, but as was so often the case, she could not read his expression.

The moment passed and Robert turned his attention back to his father. When he spoke, his voice was imbued with quiet determination. "As I said, that was part of the reason for my return. I couldn't bear the thought of leaving the Strathburn estate and the fate of our clan in Simon's hands. I know you may need time to think about it, but if there's any chance at all that you could find it in your heart to forgive me, I would like to try to repair all the damage I've done." He drew a deep breath. "Father, will you let me come home and take my place at your table once more?"

Lord Strathburn gripped Robert's hands. "Of course. Nothing would make me happier than to see you back here at Lochrose. I wouldn't have it any other way." He pushed himself up from his seat. "Let me call my valet, MacGowan, so he can make your old room ready for you."

"Father." Robert rose and clasped the earl's shoulder, staying him. "That would not be wise. Not quite yet at any rate."

Lord Strathburn frowned. "What do you mean?"

"There might still be a price on my head. If Simon and my step-mother learn of my return, they might seek to have me arrested again."

The earl scowled. "They wouldn't dare. I'd have them cast out from here faster than they could blink. The cheek—"

"Nevertheless, Father, I feel we need to exercise the utmost caution. I'm a known Jacobite—a traitor to King George. I need to seek a pardon. Until then, I will not be safe."

Lord Strathburn sighed heavily. "You're right. I have been caught up in the moment and the joy of your return. I'm not thinking clearly." He stood and clasped Robert's arm. "I will write a petition straightaway that you can present to Lord Arniston, the Lord Advocate, requesting clemency. Even if you are not absolved immediately, at the very least you may be released into my custody."

As Lord Strathburn began to walk hesitantly toward his desk, Jessie came forward, limping slightly herself. She retrieved the earl's walking stick and offered it to him. His eyebrows lifted in surprise. "Miss Munroe, I've been so distracted that I'd forgotten you were here." He took the cane from her and patted her hand.

"That is perfectly understandable, milord, given the circumstances," said Jessie with a smile. She was awash with both relief and happiness for Robert. To see his father welcome him with open arms was heart-warming indeed.

Concern clouded the earl's eyes as his gaze traveled over her. "I notice you are limping, lass. Are you hurt?"

"Only a wee bit." Jessie was understating the degree of pain she was now in. In fact, her ankle was fairly throbbing. "Perhaps if I could sit..."

Robert stepped forward. "Of course, Jessie. You should've said something sooner." He crossed the room, then with his arm about her waist, effortlessly guided her to the settee.

As Jessie sank onto the cushioned seat, she chanced a glance at Lord Strathburn, and oh dear... His brow had plunged into a fierce frown.

"Miss Munroe, how is it that you have come to be here with Robert?" he asked with a sternness that made Jessie's heart sink with dismay. "Lady Strathburn informed me that you left for Edinburgh two days ago, as there had been a family emergency of some kind."

"That is so, milord." Jessie hoped she sounded convincing. After all, she was not being *entirely* untruthful. There had been an emergency of sorts...but it had been her own. "I was plannin' to leave for Edinburgh to help my cousin who's taken ill. Unfortunately, the public coach doesna leave until noon today."

"But where have you been in the meantime?" Lord Strathburn demanded. "And how did you meet Robert?"

Robert placed his hand on her shoulder, as though he wanted to protect her from his father's display of irritation. "It's complicated, Father," he said carefully.

"Well perhaps one of you can enlighten me," said Lord Strathburn looking from one to the other, his gaze growing flinty. He was clearly unimpressed.

Quick thinking was undoubtedly required. Jessie swallowed, praying she wouldn't sound nervous. She had nothing to be ashamed of, after all. *Not really...* "Milord...I left here to travel to Grantown the day before yesterday," she explained. "As you can see, I was injured—"

The earl's manner softened a little. "How so?"

Jessie hesitated. *Hmm, what do I admit to and what do I leave out?* "I sprained my ankle along the way and...Lord Lochrose and his squire came to my aid," she said. She certainly didn't want to complicate matters further by confessing that she'd also been shot in the arm. By his son.

Lord Strathburn's frown returned. "So you've been staying in Grantown with Robert all this time? At the Strathspey Arms?"

Jessie blushed. "No, milord. No' in Grantown. Mrs. MacMillan suggested that I stay at yer hunting lodge rather than at the inn. I know I'm only a veritable nobody—just yer factor's daughter—but I ken it would be improper and perhaps even a wee bit risky for me to stay in such a public place on my own. I apologize if it was inappropriate of me to use yer lodge, without yer express permission."

Lord Strathburn's eyes narrowed with suspicion. "Miss Munroe, I'm beginning to suspect your sudden departure from Lochrose had less to do with an imminent family crisis and more to do with my younger son, Simon. You've been hiding from him, haven't you?"

Jessie's heart began to pound as heat scalded her cheeks. She was loath to answer. If the earl continued along the same vein, Robert would soon know she had continually lied to him about her fictitious betrothal to his half-brother. Now the moment was upon her, she couldn't bear it.

Worse still, she could feel Robert's gaze on her face and a wave of humiliation swept over her. If only the floor would swallow her up whole.

Lord Strathburn continued when she didn't respond. His voice was now surprisingly gentle. "I may be old, Miss Munroe, but I have ears and eyes. This is not the first time something like this has happened. I know what...what Simon is like. Unfortunately, you're not the first to have been the recipient of his...unwanted attentions." He moved closer and sat in his nearby wingchair. "Believe me, my dear, I understand the situation better than you think."

Scraping together what was left of her courage, Jessie raised her eyes to the earl's. "I think it would be best for everyone if I went to stay with my cousin, milord."

Lord Strathburn nodded. "If that is what you wish, Miss Munroe, I shall do my utmost to make it so. I only wish you had come to me for help sooner."

Jessie sighed shakily. Robert's continued silence felt like a physical weight on her chest. "I didna want to create a fuss, milord, or make things difficult for my father," she said at length, her tone more than a wee bit defeated. "It just seemed easier to leave..."

At last, she glanced up at Robert. *What was he thinking?* His posture was rigid, virtually motionless save for the twitch of a muscle in his jaw. He was angry with her, and she couldn't blame him. What a daft fool she'd been.

As her gaze skipped away, Robert squatted down before her. "Is all of this true, lass?" he asked gently, reclaiming her attention. "Has Simon been forcing unwanted attentions on you?"

His deep blue eyes bore into hers and Jessie knew there would be no escaping the truth this time. Sucking in a breath, she hiked up her chin and resisted the urge to look away. "Aye, 'tis true."

Confusion flickered in Robert's eyes. "So you lied to me about being handfasted to Simon. Why did you do that? I don't understand."

"What? Simon and Miss Munroe are handfasted?" Lord Strathburn exclaimed.

Robert glanced at his father. "I was led to believe they were betrothed." To Jessie he said, his tone grave yet gentle, "Tell me honestly. Is the betrothal all a lie?"

Jessie lifted her chin a fraction higher, steeling herself to admit her perfidy. "Aye, I lied. But I prefer to think of it as...self-preservation." Now her deception had been revealed, it was as though she were daring Robert to censure her for her actions.

"So I misinterpreted everything I saw at the loch," Robert said gruffly.

"Aye," she admitted, stomach twisting into a tighter knot with every word. "I...I tried to explain what had really happened that morning so many times, but I was alone and injured, and to be honest, more than a wee bit frightened. I didna know if ye intended me harm. Then when I discovered that ye perceived me as a threat to yer safety, I didna think ye'd believe me if I denied what ye had assumed to be true—that I was Simon's paramour. I know it sounds foolish and illogical, but I believed that if ye thought I was someone important, Simon's betrothed, perhaps you would see me as less...dispensable."

"Och, Jessie lass. I must've come across as the worst kind of barbarian if you thought I would harm you, just to protect myself from discovery." Robert's voice was laden with remorse. "You should've told me I was wrong about what I'd seen the other day." He suddenly gathered her into his arms and gently kissed her hair.

"I couldna do it," Jessie whispered into his shirt, hot tears stinging her eyelids. "I was too...too ashamed..." Now Robert understood how precarious her situation had been, the reason for her duplicity, an overwhelming relief washed through her. Feeling stronger, she raised her head from Robert's shoulder and sought his gaze again. "That morning by the loch, Simon told me that if I didna do as he wanted, he would see that my father lost his position here. But I couldna bring myself to give in to his demands...so I left. And you know the rest."

Robert stroked her hair away from her face, then gently wiped a tear from her cheek with the back of his fingers. "You will never have to suffer his presence again, Jessie. I will make sure of that."

She gave him a watery smile. "I believe you."

Lord Strathburn cleared his throat pointedly. "Robert, please tell me you haven't been staying *alone* with Miss Munroe for the last two nights."

Och, no. Jessie's stomach dropped. Was Lord Strathburn about to make an enormous mountain out of a molehill?

Robert rose slowly and met his father's gaze directly. "Circumstances beyond our control forced us together," he said, his tone measured. "But let me reassure you, nothing untoward has occurred."

"But you have spent two nights together," persisted Lord Strathburn, his brow knitting into a deep frown. "Isn't that so, Miss Munroe?"

"I'm afraid so, milord." Jessie's whole face burned with embarrassment. "The first night we stayed at the hunting lodge. There was nowhere else to go. And I was injured... Although we were no' entirely alone. Tobias, Robert's squire, stayed at the lodge too. Then last night, when Robert and I stayed in the cave—"

Lord Strathburn's eyebrows shot upward. "I beg your pardon?"

Robert's brow furrowed slightly. "I was concerned that Simon would be out looking for Jessie with the help of dragoons or the Black Watch," he explained calmly. "We moved to somewhere more isolated last night to avoid detection. An encounter with the King's men was the last thing I needed. We remained safe and no harm has been done. You need not be so concerned."

Lord Strathburn's expression was grim. "Robert, regardless of the reason, you cannot overlook the seriousness of this situation. What will Jessie's father think when he hears of this?"

Jessie took a deep breath, praying for patience. "Lord Strathburn, as

Robert said, no' a thing occurred between us that would be of any concern—"

"Miss Munroe, the mere fact you've been virtually alone in the company of my son for two nights is enough to completely ruin you," Lord Strathburn said stiffly. "And while I may not be as sprightly as I used to be, I am neither blind nor deaf. I can see by the way Robert looks at you—and touches you—that you have shared some degree of affection. You cannot deny it. It's obvious, even to an old fool like me. Your father will be livid you've been compromised, even by reputation only. I know he has high hopes of you marrying well one day. If you were my daughter, I would too."

"Perhaps it would be better if her father did not know then," Robert said carefully.

Jessie glanced up at Robert. The very idea that the earl would think that they had already been intimate... That Robert had seduced her... Her face flamed. But nothing had happened! Nothing of import in any event.

Lord Strathburn shook his head. "Lying by omission will not change the reality of the situation, Robert. I ken you are an honorable man at heart. You cannot want the lass's reputation to be harmed."

Robert exhaled sharply; he was clearly irritated by this turn in the discussion. "You're right. But why upset Jessie's father needlessly if *nothing*—and I say that without a word of a lie—has happened? Miss Munroe's virtue has *not* been tarnished."

"Are you sure about that?" returned Lord Strathburn hotly. "Despite your assurances to the contrary, it looks to me as if something quite significant has transpired between the two of you."

"What are you suggesting then?" returned Robert, a note of impatience hardening his voice.

"There is only one way to set things to rights," said the earl gravely. His steely blue gaze was uncompromising as he glanced between Robert and Jessie. "You two will have to be handfasted."

Jessie gasped. *Oh Lord, surely the earl was jesting.*

Robert obviously thought so too. "You cannot be serious," he burst out.

"Oh, but indeed I am, my son," said Lord Strathburn, mouth set in a determined line. "There is no other course of action open to you and Miss Munroe, considering the circumstances. I will not stand by and let this poor lass be ruined. You will be handfasted in this room, this very day, before you leave here."

"But, Father," began Robert urgently, retreating to the edge of the hearth...away from Jessie. "Surely that is not fair on Miss Munroe, given that my future is far from bright at the present moment. I'm a wanted man. A traitor. I'm sure Mr. Munroe would be far from happy to have his daughter betrothed to someone like me—"

"You will be pardoned, Robert," the earl declared as confidently as if he were simply stating a universal truth. "Lord Arniston is an old friend of mine. There won't be a problem. And after that, you two can return here to be wed at Kilburn Kirk. And besides"—the earl smiled down at Jessie—"it is a fine match for Miss Munroe. She will be a viscountess after all. Her father will be delighted."

Jessie's mind was reeling, her heart thudding wildly against her ribs. This attempt at matchmaking by Lord Strathburn was completely unexpected. True, it was heartening that he seemed so concerned for her reputation and welfare, but to suggest she should wed his son—it seemed unwarranted in the extreme.

And besides, one of the party seemed resolutely against it...

She risked a glance at Robert. *What must he be thinking?* He'd dragged a hand through his brown hair, loosening a thick lock which fell haphazardly across his brow. Judging by his deep scowl, he was exasperated at the very least. Perhaps even furious.

When he spoke, it seemed to Jessie that he was struggling to keep his tone even and measured, which could not be a good sign. "Father, despite your faith in the Lord Advocate, there is still a significant chance that things could go awry. As I said before, I'm sure Jessie and her father would both prefer that her *fiancé* wasn't a Jacobite-on-the-run wanted for treason. I understand your concern for Jessie's reputation, but perhaps it would be safer and wiser for a betrothal to take place after I've been pardoned."

Robert leveled a heavy look upon her. "And of course, if Jessie and her father consent." He arched a dark eyebrow. "What say you, Jessie?"

Jessie looked away from his questioning gaze, trying to think clearly.

She could scarcely believe this was happening. Handfasted to Robert Grant—a Jacobite and roguish pirate adventurer—it was madness!

But deep in her heart, she wasn't completely shocked by the earl's suggestion. A part of her thrummed with excitement at the thought of being joined in wedded union to such a man. Although she'd only known him for a few days, she couldn't deny her deep attraction to Robert Grant. She wanted to be near him. *With him.*

But how did Robert feel about her? He seemed to care a *little.* He would surely not be considering this if he did not desire her a *wee* bit. Even the earl had noticed that his son seemed to show a genuine concern for her.

Was that enough of a basis for a marriage? Especially to someone like her, a virtually penniless woman who was essentially a servant?

Jessie bit her lip, fervently wishing she had more time to contemplate the matter. Things were happening too quickly, events slipping through her fingers, spiraling out of control. Perhaps, when Robert was free and if *he* chose to propose, she could seriously consider such an offer. Even then, she hoped love might be part of the equation—a condition not always necessary for marriage, especially for members of the nobility, but in her mind, affection and a degree of devotion were highly desirable. Especially when the man in question clearly had a strong streak of "rakehell" running through him...

She couldn't give her whole-hearted consent, not now. She doubted Robert could either. Indeed, neither of them should be forced into a betrothal. And then there were the wishes of her father to consider. What would *he* want for her future?

Jessie was conscious of both men staring at her, waiting for her to respond to Robert's question. She lifted her gaze to the earl's and cleared her throat. "I agree with Robert, milord. I see no need to rush into anything. And I would prefer to have my father's blessing before I accept any offer of marriage."

Lord Strathburn's gaze softened as he regarded her. "I understand, lass, but as the Chief of Clan Grant of Strathburn, and guardian of all those within my household, I have a duty of care that I cannot ignore." He reached out and took her hand. "I would much prefer that you were within the safe care of Robert on your way to Edinburgh. I cannot allow you to make that long journey by yourself. Indeed, I could never forgive myself, and I very much think your father would hold me to account, if you were left unprotected. You've already suffered enough as it is, no thanks to Simon." Lord Strathburn stood and faced his son, an obstinate set to his jaw. "Robert, I insist that you and Miss Munroe are handfasted before me, right now. I will not write the request for clemency until you do."

Even Jessie could see that the Earl of Strathburn would not be swayed. The determined look in his eyes, the rigidity of his bearing, spoke of a formidable spirit. She suddenly had an inkling of how he must have appeared ten years ago when he'd forbidden Robert to lead out the clan to war. No wonder Robert had been certain he would not be welcomed home.

Robert sighed heavily and dragged a hand across his jaw as if suddenly resigned to his fate. Like a man about to walk the scaffold. "As you wish Father," he replied gravely. "We will be handfasted. But"—he turned to Jessie—"only if you consent."

Jessie stared at the breathtakingly handsome man on the opposite side of the hearthrug. A sliver of dismay penetrated her chest as she noted the fine lines of tension radiating from the corners of his eyes, bracketing his perfectly sculpted mouth. There was a muscle ticking in his jaw while he waited for her reply. Her answer would determine whether or not Lord Strathburn would help him gain his pardon. The earl was essentially holding Robert to ransom. It was hardly fair.

And yet what other choice did she have?

She raised her chin. "I had no' anticipated this turn of events, Robert, and I'm truly sorry to have placed ye in such a situation." She paused for a moment before she stepped over the precipice of no return. Her heart began to beat faster, an unsteady gallop within her chest. She sensed Robert was holding his breath. "But as I do no' wish to stand in the way of yer chances at obtaining clemency, I...I will agree to be hand-fasted to you as well."

Robert inclined his head, the corner of his mouth lifting in a slight smile. A smile which only reinforced how reluctant he was to make this commitment.

Jessie suddenly felt lightheaded as the enormity of what she had agreed to do hit her in the chest like an unleashed cannonball.

Apparently oblivious to the mood in the room, Lord Strathburn rubbed his hands together and grinned broadly. "Excellent, all will be set to rights." As awkward silence reigned, he crossed to his desk and retrieved a long, fine wool scarf of Clan Grant tartan from a drawer. "For the binding of hands," he remarked as he returned to the fireside.

Robert assisted Jessie to her feet. The touch of his hands on her arm and at the small of her back burned through to the flesh beneath her clothes. She recalled how Robert's hands had felt on her skin when he'd helped her to undress in the hunting lodge. When they were married, it would be his right as her husband to touch her in any way that he liked. A shiver—whether of anticipation or trepidation she couldn't have said —slid through Jessie at the thought.

When Robert and Jessie took up positions before Lord Strathburn on the hearthrug, she stole a glance at her husband-to-be's face. It was as though his features were cast in stone, the look in his eyes grim. This was not how she imagined her betrothal would be. She'd always wanted smiles and heart-fluttering joy, not awkwardness bordering on outright unwillingness...

Inhaling a fortifying breath, she forced herself to focus on what Lord Strathburn was now saying.

"Robert and Jessie, I want you to join hands," he said smiling at them both.

At least someone is happy, thought Jessie darkly as Robert threaded his fingers through hers. The earl then carefully wrapped the tartan scarf around their wrists and hands, binding them together.

"Now, Robert," the earl continued, "I want you to repeat the following words after me."

Robert dutifully and solemnly repeated the simple vow of betrothal. His dark blue eyes held Jessie's as he spoke. "I, Robert James Alexander Grant, the Viscount Lochrose and Master of Strathburn, promise to take you, Jessie Munroe, to be my wife." He squeezed her hands gently beneath the tartan and gave her a brief half-smile of encouragement. It was gone so quickly, she couldn't tell whether the smile had reached his eyes.

Now it was her turn. Jessie's mouth was as dry as the nearby hearth-stone, but somehow she managed to speak. "I-I, Jessie Elizabeth Munroe promise to take you, Robert James Alexander Grant, the Viscount Lochrose and Master of Strathburn, to be my husband." She tried to smile back at Robert but only managed a tremulous quiver of her lips.

Lord Strathburn addressed them again. "As the Chief of Clan Grant, I have born witness to your promises to each other, and I now declare you to be handfasted."

Robert took a step forward and raised their tied hands to his lips. Between the folds of tartan, he placed a gentle kiss on her fingertips.

"*Mo nighean ruadh mhaiseach,*" he murmured in Gaelic, his wide mouth lifting into a soft smile. *My beautiful red-haired one.* "I will protect you and care for you, from this day forward."

But would he love her?

Even more importantly, would Robert ever be free to love her?

With all her heart, and every fiber of her being, Jessie prayed that he would.

CHAPTER 16

Simon froze in the doorway of his room, blood rushing straight from his head to his groin in a red-hot torrent of furious lust.

He couldn't believe it. After the merry dance Jessie had led him for two whole days and nights, here she was, right under his very nose. His quarry, emerging from his father's sitting room as bold as you please, skirts swaying around her ripe, completely fuckable arse.

He couldn't wait to bend her over and swive her senseless.

"Jessie!"

She turned, her full mouth a wide "O" of surprise. He grinned. *Imagine what it will feel like when you force her to use her mouth on your—*

But wait... Who the hell was she with?

Before Simon had time to even think on it a second longer, her companion—a tall, wide-shouldered, dark-haired man—turned and fixed him with a cool, hard stare.

Shit. Simon's world slipped sideways. He clutched at the doorjamb as his heart crashed inside his chest. *Fucking no. No, no, no.*

Robert. He must be dreaming. It couldn't be Robert. Robert was supposed to be dead. *What the devil?*

Even more incredible, the whore—his very own Jezebel—was

holding hands with the bastard. Despite the denial roaring through Simon, a small part of his brain knew he wasn't seeing his half-brother's ghost.

Somehow, he scraped his voice together, the vitriol swirling inside him roughening his voice. "Robert!'

As Simon took a shaky step toward the pair, he saw without a shadow of a doubt that it *was* Robert—only this man was broader and harder in body than the youthful Robert of ten years ago.

Before he could draw another breath, the more mature version of Robert released Jessie's hand and closed the remaining distance between them as swiftly and silently as a predatory lion. Even the way the cocky bastard walked hadn't changed. It made Simon want to puke.

"Simon, I suggest you let us be on our way," drawled Robert with all the arrogant nonchalance that Simon remembered. "No need to make a fuss."

Robert's smooth, confident tone immediately fueled Simon's ire to blazing proportions. He snorted and clipped his hated brother's shoulder with the heel of his palm. *As if I would ever let you go. Never again.*

"Fuck you, Robert," Simon growled. "You've come crawling back to lick Father's boots, have you? Well, I won't let you. You're nothing but a foul traitor. A disgrace. You're not wanted here." He shot a look over Robert's shoulder, straight at Jessie. "And where the hell have you been all this time, you bitch—"

Robert's punch was so swift, Simon didn't even see it coming.

He staggered back into the window embrasure and slid down the wall. Eyes shut, struggling to suck in air, his body was paralyzed by an all-consuming combination of shear incredulity, blazing anger, and thought-robbing pain. He clutched at the heavy velvet curtains so hard he almost rent the thick fabric from the curtain-rod. With his other shaking hand, he gingerly probed the left side of his jaw where Robert had landed his bone-shaking blow.

Before Simon even opened his eyes, he knew Robert and Jessie were gone.

Shit, shit, shit. Head still swimming, he pushed himself up and collapsed onto the window seat and spat out a mouthful of blood along with a piece of cracked tooth. He shook his buzzing head, attempting to clear his vision, then scanned the now vacant hallway. Try as he might to convince himself he'd only seen his brother's ghost, the reality of his throbbing face belied that idea.

Robert had definitely returned.

His half-brother most certainly wasn't dead as his mother had foolishly convinced him over the years. Simon had always suspected his father had engineered Robert's inexplicable escape from the wine cellar ten years ago, but he'd never been able to prove anything.

Not that it mattered now. No, the only thing that mattered was that Robert was indeed back, and Father had never followed through with his threat to have his eldest son officially disinherited through an Act of Parliament because he was a traitor. Or have him legally declared dead. Right at this present moment, Simon would've been more than happy to make sure his brother was dead in truth.

To protect his own interests, Simon would have to take action. *Now.*

Holding onto the sagging curtains, he pulled himself to his feet and swallowed back a scudding wave of nausea.

Another confounding thought suddenly occurred to him: where exactly had Jessie been hiding for the last two days, and how in the devil's name had she become acquainted with Robert?

The image of them holding hands sprang into his mind's eye again.

With a roar that shook the very glass of the window, Simon ripped the curtain away. Shaking with rage, he turned towards his father's rooms. Robert might have risen from the dead, but he'd make damn sure he stopped his brother from staking his claim on the title, Master of Strathburn, and ultimately his inheritance of the earldom... And Jessie Munroe.

"Father!" Storming into the earl's chambers, Simon could tell immediately that he was expected. His father stood before the fire and even though he leaned on his walking stick, there was a steely look in the old man's eyes. His gaze was cool, disdainful. His father had always despised him. Simon had never been enough and never would be.

Not like fucking Robert.

Simon sucked in a ragged breath, a sliver of agony searing his abused jaw. Somehow he managed to resist the urge to punch his father in the face and jabbed a finger toward him instead. "You can't let him come back. I won't let you."

Caesar gave a low growl. If Simon were holding a pistol, he'd have shot the bloody dog—*Robert's* dog—on the spot.

His father didn't even flinch. "Leave it be, Simon. He's back. He will be pardoned. The new Lord Advocate is a personal friend of mine."

Simon clenched his fists. "You know the law is on my side," he gritted out, jaw throbbing with every sound uttered. "Robert's a God damned trait—"

His father snorted and drew back his shoulders. "You don't care about the law. All you care about is making sure you inherit the fortune that funds your mother's and your own dissolute way of life."

True. But the money—everything—*should* be his. Simon had to make his father see that. "But Robert disobeyed you." Oh God, he sounded like he was whining. "He doesn't deserve a second chance."

"Once! He disobeyed me only once!" their father roared, his face turning a dark shade of puce. As he poked his walking stick at Simon's chest, Caesar leapt up and lunged toward Simon, teeth bared and snarling. "What do you think you've been doing every single day for the last ten years, if not more? You don't care about me. You don't care about the estate or the clan. Like a spoiled child, you only care about yourself."

Fuck this. Simon stormed over to the door. Ironic that a display of temper seemed to be the only thing he had in common with this foolish old man. As he turned the handle, painful, long-buried memories of Robert burned through Simon's mind like acid: images of his older brother outriding him, thrashing him at fencing, outsmarting him during lessons with their tutor. He swallowed past the hard, bitter lump in his throat and glanced back at his father.

A strange red, blurry haze of hatred and anguish blurred his vision. "Mother's right. I'm never good enough, am I? I never will be. It's not fair. I've always been second best to you."

"You take and take, Simon. You never give. It's *you* who doesn't deserve a thing. Time after time I've given you the opportunity to prove yourself. But you choose to squander everything. If I let you have free rein, you'd ruin us."

"Yet it was Robert who charged off, led countless others to their deaths, and risked bringing ruin upon us all." Simon wrenched open the door. "I won't let him get away this time and there's not a God damned thing you can do about it."

He charged out of the room as if Caesar or the hounds of hell themselves were at his very heels. Robert and Jessie had a fifteen-minute head start on him at most. He'd take MacTaggart and his Black Watchmen. Gather a group of Redcoats from somewhere.

He'd see Robert dead if it was the last thing he did.

The fog was starting to clear when Robert and Jessie finally emerged from the Gate House. It was mid-morning and a meek sun appeared intermittently between swathes of scudding gray clouds. After their encounter with Simon, they had all but run down the secret stairs to the wine cellar and back through the passage to the factor's residence.

Robert's eyes scanned the leaf-littered ground between the house and the copse of trees where he'd left his horse. There was no sign of the Watch, thank God. He had no idea how much time they had, now Simon had seen them both.

Simon. Robert's jaw clenched as he recalled the lewd sneer on his brother's face when the brute had laid eyes on Jessie. Though reluctant to use force, as soon as the cur had insulted her, Robert hadn't been able to hold back. He judged there had been enough force behind the punch to incapacitate his brother for at least a little while. With any luck, they would have gained enough time to get clean away before Simon set out after them. Better still, Robert hoped their father would stay Simon from pursuing them at all...but he couldn't count on it.

He glanced at Jessie—his betrothed—as she stood beside him in the doorway, clutching at the door frame, catching her breath. He could hardly fathom that she was promised to him. A tempest of conflicting thoughts battered at his brain, but there was no time to sort them out now. Their priority was to get away safely.

He grasped Jessie's hand and caught her worried gaze. "Are you ready to make a run for the trees?"

She offered him a grim smile. "Would a fast hobble suffice?"

Robert squeezed her hand and nodded. "That will do."

As planned, MacGowan, his father's valet, was waiting for them behind the copse with Jessie's mare, saddled and ready to go.

"Blaeberry," Jessie breathed, her face lighting up with joy. The horse snickered in return and rubbed its nose against her.

"You'll be right to ride on your own?" Robert asked. "We have a long, hard ride ahead if we've any hope of evading Simon and making it to Edinburgh in good time." Since their handfasting, it had been decided that it would be foolhardy for Jessie to catch the public coach. Lord Strathburn had agreed there was a good chance Simon would have already sent out local Watchmen to monitor the coaching inn and the comings and goings along the road to Grantown. Riding was the best option. And the fastest.

Jessie's eyes shone. "I will be fine," she reassured Robert. She patted her horse's flank. "And I willna slow ye down at all. Blaeberry will keep up, so dinna worry about that."

Robert thanked MacGowan for his assistance.

"Anytime, milord," replied the gray-haired valet bowing. "And if ye dinna mind me saying so, it's verra good to see ye back, hale and hearty. If there's anythin' else I can do..."

Robert grinned. "Perhaps you could see to it that my brother's horse needs re-shoeing right about now. And if the other horses just happen to be out to pasture, perhaps in one of the far paddocks, that would also be most helpful."

MacGowan nodded and returned Robert's grin. "Of course, milord. I wish ye and Miss Munroe swift and safe travel to Edinburgh."

They rode hard the rest of the morning, only stopping to rest and water the horses briefly when Robert judged they were safely away from Clan Grant land and were not likely to encounter any men from the local Black Watch or dragoon regiments.

On resumption of their fast and furious flight, Robert began to reflect on the unanticipated turn of events that had thrown them together. They were handfasted—promised to each other—but the timing could not have been worse. Guilt gripped his heart. How could he, if he had any sort of conscience, promise to marry a woman when he could very well be arrested and thrown into prison, or worse, executed?

One thing was clear in his mind: he would do what was right and honorable. Even though he and Jessie were handfasted, he would not take her to bed, no matter how much he desired her—not until he had been pardoned and they were lawfully wed before a minister. If things should go awry, he wanted Jessie to be able to walk away unscathed. He would not compromise her any further than he already had.

I just have to avoid temptation tonight.

And that was going to be difficult. He wanted Jessie badly, more than any woman he'd ever encountered. Even now as he watched her slim hips rise up and down in the saddle as they cantered across a lonely stretch of moorland, he could feel the tension building in his loins. Never before had he been overwhelmed by such a fever of longing. Indeed, he'd felt this way since the very first moment he'd laid eyes on her.

There had to be a rational explanation for his need, and the most likely reason was that he'd simply been without a lover for too long. It had been at least six months since he'd last sought pleasure with a mistress. Physical release long denied could do strange things to a man. Besides, he and Jessie had shared nothing but intense experiences over the past few days, full of pain and danger and for the want of a better word, adventure. Perhaps that was why he'd developed such strong feelings for the lass.

He really couldn't be falling in love with her. Not after a handful of days... Surely his heart was too battle-scarred, his spirit too broken for any sort of sentimental emotion like that. Or was that just a convenient lie he'd latched onto to avoid forming any sort of romantic attachment to anyone for the past decade?

If Robert were *truly* honest with himself, he'd own that he was attracted to Jessie beyond her breathtaking beauty. In their short time together, he'd learned that not only was she quick thinking and intelligent, but bold of spirit and steadfastly loyal to those she cared for.

Most important of all, despite their shaky start, she was someone he could trust.

As Jessie glanced his way and flashed him a shy smile, Robert couldn't help but wonder if the potent mixture of emotions swirling in his chest—passion, admiration, a compelling need to protect Jessie—were indeed the first stirrings of love. He'd never actually been "in love" before, so had nothing to compare his present feelings to. Never in all his years of exile had he ever let his guard down around a woman. In fact, all his relationships had been short-lived, emotionless affairs because in his mind, the taking of a wife had always been inextricably linked with the impossibility of his return to Lochrose.

All going well with the Lord Advocate, he may have at long last gained both: Jessie Munroe, a woman he could wed and grow to love; and the freedom to reclaim all he'd lost...his birthright and home.

~

It wasn't until mid-afternoon, when they stopped to rest again, that Jessie noticed how sore and swollen her ankle had become. As Robert helped her to dismount from Blaeberry, she cried out sharply and gripped his wide shoulders, barely able to put any weight on her foot.

Robert swore beneath his breath. "Jessie lass, you should've told me that your ankle pained you so," he admonished.

Before she could protest, he swung her into his arms and carried her over to the shallow, peaty burn that gurgled and splashed its way past a knot of twisted birks and pines. He gently lowered her onto a tussock of frost-burned grass, then dropped to his knees on the ground beside her.

"Right, let me see, lass," he said gently, one of his strong hands heading toward the hem of her gown.

Pulse pounding, Jessie held her skirts firmly around her ankles. "I will be all right," she said, not sure if she would be able to withstand Robert's hands on her naked skin in broad daylight when they were all alone. Not without making a complete fool of herself.

Her heart was already racing, her stomach fluttering—and she was only just thinking about it. Heaven knew how she would react when he actually *did* touch her. Although they were now engaged, the knowledge that Robert would soon have the right to explore her body intimately when he became her husband in truth made her feel strangely hot and achy and needy all over.

"You're not going all shy on me, are you?" Robert asked with a half-smile. "Remember, it's nothing I haven't seen before. And, after all, we are handfasted now. Your injury needs examining."

Damn his canny ability to read me like an open book. But Jessie knew Robert spoke sense. With a sigh of resignation, she reached under her skirts, eased off her boot and then carefully rolled down her stocking. Biting down hard on her bottom lip, she tried to ignore the pain as much as the tingling sensation Robert's touch aroused as he gently probed the bruised and swollen flesh.

"This is my fault, Jessie," he said ruefully, after he'd completed his inspection. "I should never have taken you to Lochrose this morning. You've been on your feet far too much."

Jessie frowned, surprised at his self-recriminating tone. "But I made ye take me," she countered. "Besides, 'twas part of the deal we struck."

Robert regarded her with such compassion, it warmed her all the way to her very toes. "As soon as I saw your reaction to the mess Simon had made in the Gate House, I knew something was wrong. It was clear you were terrified. I couldn't refuse your plea to accompany me to the castle. But I'm also truly sorry, for the trouble that *I've* caused you. I never meant to drag you into the mess of my life." His mouth tipped into a wry smile. "I'd wager that being engaged to a traitorous fugitive was probably never in your plans for the future, was it?"

"No, no' really," she admitted, face heating. Robert's display of tenderness was playing havoc with her pulse, making her blush. "But then, I'm sure you were no' planning on being handfasted to someone like me either." On an impulse, she reached out and caught Robert's hand, curling her fingers around his. "Ye shouldna blame yerself for things that ye are no' responsible for, Robert Grant. And my life was verra much a complicated mess as well, even before I met you. The way I see it"—her eyes met Robert's directly—"if it weren't for you, I wouldna be safely away from Lochrose right now."

Robert slid his large hand over hers then brought her fingers to his lips. "You are too generous, *mo ghaoil*." His tone was as gentle as his caress.

Jessie shivered and for a moment she fancied that he was going to kiss her, but he rocked back on his heels and began to focus on the task of binding her ankle.

Disappointment tugged at her heart. Truth to tell, she yearned to be kissed by Robert again—and to kiss him back. But she didn't know how to tell him. Or show him. Although she possessed some basic knowledge about what occurred between a man and a woman in the marriage bed —cousin Maggie had explained such things to her once in practical terms—Jessie had no idea how to initiate even the most innocent of seductions.

She guessed that perhaps Robert's newly gained knowledge about Simon's forced attentions tempered his actions. Part of her—the wanton part that thrilled to Robert's touch and his kisses—wished he wouldn't be so solicitous of her feelings.

But would he be so solicitous tonight?

After they'd set off again along the rough military road heading south across the moors, Jessie's thoughts kept returning to the unforeseen complication their handfasting represented—and what the future, for both of them, might look like. She still couldn't quite believe this was really happening. Everything had transpired far too quickly. Her mind was awhirl, a veritable maelstrom of complicated thoughts and extraordinary feelings...the foremost being shock at the thought of being engaged to a man whom she barely knew.

She fell to the task of carefully trying to catalogue what she did know about Robert, this beautiful man who made her tremble inside and blush so easily. She considered his behavior since they'd crossed paths. Right from the very beginning, he'd shown her nothing but consideration. Well, except for shooting her, but that, after all, had been an accident. Even when he'd believed she was handfasted to his brother, he'd tended to her injuries and done his utmost to keep her from harm. Though she strongly suspected he desired her, he did not seem intent on seducing her. At least, not for the moment.

But would he want to make love to her now they were handfasted?

Although handfasting was viewed by many Highlanders as a

marriage of sorts—and was legally binding if the couple physically consummated the union—in her mind, it wasn't the same as being wed before a minister of the kirk. A kiss was one thing, but anything else... Tonight she must be strong and not betray her beliefs, no matter how much her treacherous body ached for Robert. Or how impressive the rakish wiles he might employ to seduce her might be.

Jessie slid a glance Robert's way. He was riding beside her, his long, lean, muscular body moving in perfect unison with his cantering horse, the wind whipping his dark hair off his too-handsome face. Although he lacked a plaid, he was a Highland warrior in every other sense.

My warrior.

Perhaps...

If Robert wasn't granted clemency, this might be one of his last days of freedom. Her blood suddenly ran colder than an icy Highland burn at the thought. She couldn't bear to think of him captured and locked away in Edinburgh's Tolbooth, or the notoriously harsh prison at Fort George, near Inverness. Or even the Tower of London where noble traitors were sometimes sent. Worse still was the thought that he could be executed. It was not outside the realms of possibility for the crime of treason.

Jessie shuddered at the thought. It would be such a waste of a good man's life. A man she could easily fall in love with.

When Robert turned his head toward her and flashed her a grin, her heart danced wildly within her chest.

Perhaps she'd started to fall in love with him a wee bit already...

CHAPTER 17

On dusk, as they rode by the Braemar Castle Garrison on the outskirts of the tiny hamlet of Invercauld, Robert noticed how Jessie fought to stay upright in her saddle.

He dropped back to ride alongside her. "It looks like there is a small but respectable inn up ahead, Jessie. I'm counting on the fact that Simon will think we've taken the shorter route to Edinburgh through the Pass of Drumochter. With any luck, he won't search for us here, and I'm loath to press our horses any farther in the dark. A warm meal and a soft bed are what we both need right now."

Jessie frowned. "But are ye no' worried about the garrison? Surely there will be dragoons about."

Robert shrugged. "They will not be on the lookout for me just yet. They do not know me here. Besides, I have papers stating I am the very English Mr. Robert Burnley."

Jessie arched an eyebrow. "Ye dinna sound verra much like a Sassenach."

Robert grinned. "Oh, but of course I do, my dear," he said in his best clipped upper crust accent. "It's how I survived for near on a decade."

When Jessie gawped at him like a caught salmon, Robert couldn't help but laugh.

Within a short time, he'd secured a private room at the relatively secluded Invercauld Arms on the banks of the Clunie Water. Thankfully Jessie had seemed too exhausted and distracted to question the arrangement of sharing a room. She did blush a fiery shade of red however, when Robert presented her to the innkeeper and his two daughters as his new wife, Mrs. Burnley.

The innkeeper smiled knowingly at them. "I will send Mary up to attend to yer bedchamber directly, Mr. and Mrs. Burnley," he said. "We have a bonnie private dining room, but perhaps ye'd prefer supper trays in yer room...?"

"Yes, that would be excellent," responded Robert with a smile, continuing his charade of the dashing English gentleman. It was a mantle that still fit very well. "My bride and I are a trifle tired from traveling, and given the circumstances, we would very much like a little privacy." He handed over an additional handful of guineas. "For your... discretion, shall we say," he added with a wink.

"Och, of course, Mr. Burnley." The innkeeper beamed. "And if there's anythin' else, just let my daughters ken. Mary will take ye up now."

During this exchange, Jessie had started to lean heavily against Robert, and he'd slid his arm around her slender waist to support her. Her ankle and arm were probably aching like mad, and the instinct to care for her appeared embedded deep within him. As the girl Mary started up the stairs toward the guest rooms, he carefully scooped Jessie up into his arms.

"What on earth do ye think ye're doing?" Jessie hissed into his ear.

"Sorry, my sweet Scots wife," Robert whispered back as he followed the innkeeper's daughter. "Just putting on a bit of a show. The innkeeper may be less likely to divulge details to anyone who did happen to make enquiries if he thinks we truly are the newly wedded Burnleys."

Jessie scowled but nevertheless relaxed in his arms...until they entered the room, which was obviously a bridal suite. "Ye could put me down now, ye ken," she whispered, her body stiffening again as soon as Robert had crossed the threshold.

"But I like holding you," he said, carrying her to the wide four-poster bed that dominated the room. "And remember, such is the custom of the newly wedded."

Jessie blushed again. She was such an innocent, his *fiancée*. She was obviously acutely aware, as was he, that they were soon going to be alone with the whole night ahead of them.

Robert prayed he had the strength to resist her allure. No matter how much of a temptation she presented, he would try to take the honorable course and behave like a perfect gentleman.

Once the candles and the fire were lit, Robert was surprised, and more than a bit pleased, to see the chamber was well-appointed for such a small inn. The four-poster bed where Jessie reclined, was covered in a deep blue damask counterpane with an abundance of plump white pillows piled against the carved walnut bedhead. Opposite the foot of the bed was a decent sized fireplace with a pair of matching armchairs and a small oak table arranged before it. To one side of the fire, by the shuttered windows, was a washstand with a large porcelain basin. The apartment was fit for King George himself.

Mary hovered by the door. "Would ye like Elspeth and I to bring ye hot water, and towels after yer dinner?" she asked quietly. "We often do for the couples stayin' here."

Robert glanced at Jessie—who was still bright red—before returning his gaze to the young maidservant. "I think that's a splendid idea. Thank you indeed, Mary."

Mary bobbed a curtsy and once the door snicked shut, Robert turned back to Jessie. *They needed to talk.*

"I-I wasna expecting anythin' like this," Jessie said, gesturing about the room, looking everywhere but at him as he approached. Why, she was as skittish as a wildcat. "A nice dry pile o' straw in a barn would have been sufficient."

Robert sat beside her on the bed and took one of her hands in his. Jessie bit her lip, further betraying how nervous she actually was... *of him.*

"Jessie lass, we need to discuss our...situation," he began, then stopped, not sure how to continue such a delicate conversation. Several moments passed in which the heavy silence was broken only by the crackle of the growing fire and the rattle of the window as a gust of wind battered against the panes.

It might have been a false start on his part, but it was enough of a prompt for Jessie. She drew in a shaky breath then at last, lifted her eyes to his. "I would like that," she said quietly, attempting a smile. "Neither of us was expecting anythin' like this to happen...and now we are both wondering—"

"What will happen next," Robert finished. He was heartened to see Jessie's smile widen.

"Aye," she agreed. "That's it exactly." Her forehead pleated. "So... what *will* happen, Robert?"

Frowning as well, he shrugged. "I don't know what tomorrow will bring. But as for tonight ..." Robert held Jessie's gaze, hoping she would see the sincerity in his eyes. "I'm not sure what you were expecting, but I want you to know, you mustn't feel beholden to me even though we've been handfasted. I assure you, I will not try to take advantage of you." He offered her a half-smile. "Well, at least not until we're properly wed."

A deep sigh of relief escaped Jessie's lips and her stiff posture visibly relaxed. He realized he'd been right in speaking so plainly about something which had clearly been worrying her. Easing her concerns by making a veiled reference to Simon's demands and emphasizing that he, Robert, did not expect anything like that from her, had undoubtedly helped.

"Robert, I understand what ye're saying," she said, squeezing his hand. "And thank you. I feel safe with you. I ken ye are an honorable man."

Robert let his gaze wander over Jessie as she sat propped against the pillows, her tousled red-gold curls framing her face, her whisky-brown eyes glowing with warmth. If she only knew how inviting she looked, sitting there on the bed, how much he wanted to seduce her...she would not feel so secure.

He inhaled a calming breath, his conscience warring with his baser instincts. "Hmm, safe. I've never been described quite that way before." He cocked an eyebrow. "So much for my reputation as a rebellious rogue."

Jessie smiled back, her eyes dancing with mischief. "Och, ye have roguish charm aplenty, Robert Grant. But I'm trustin' ye to keep yer promise, that ye will not try to use it on me until after we're married." Her smile then faded and another frown creased her brow. "Whilst we're being frank, I also wanted to clear the air...about Simon. It's difficult to talk about yer brother and what he did..." She trailed off, absently plucking at the blue counterpane, as if searching for the right words.

"You don't have to talk about it, Jessie. It's all right," said Robert gently. He could see this was awkward for her, but he also understood that perhaps sharing her experience with him would ease her mind. It would hopefully stop him from imagining the worst. Hypocritical though it was, given his own past actions, he was having a difficult time dealing rationally with the knowledge that Simon had even kissed Jessie against her will. If anything else had happened... He would need to be physically restrained from tearing Simon apart when next their paths crossed.

Jessie lifted her chin, looking him straight in the eye. "No, I need to, Robert. I want ye to know that Simon only ever kissed me that one time at the loch. Nothing more. I left before he could force me to...submit to any of his other demands. At any rate, I just thought ye should know."

"I understand," Robert replied softly, anger still churning in his gut for what Simon had put her through. But he was also relieved that the swine hadn't harmed her in any other way.

"But that's no' all," Jessie added, a pink blush blooming in her cheeks. "I also want ye to know that when ye kissed me last night, and this morning, that it was different. To be perfectly honest with ye, I liked the way it felt... Perhaps too much..." She trailed off, biting her lip momentarily before she took a steadying breath. "I wanted ye to know that too, seeing that we're now handfasted."

"I see," Robert said, his heart racing.

This was dangerous, very dangerous indeed. He was having a hard enough time dampening his desire for Jessie without this admission; an admission that sent a sudden rush of heat coursing through his veins, straight to his groin. He shifted uneasily on the bed, hoping like hell Jessie wouldn't notice the telltale sign of his burgeoning arousal.

But he needn't have worried. Jessie's gaze was cast downward at the quilt she'd returned to plucking. "I'm sorry," she said quietly. "I've shocked ye with my forwardness, haven't I?"

Guilt pricked Robert's conscience. The lass had obviously mistaken his silence for disapproval. He reached out and gently tilted her chin upward to capture her gaze again. "No, I'm not shocked, Jessie. I appreciate your honesty. You must know that I want you too, but I do not think it would be wise to compromise your virtue more than I already have. Not when my future is so uncertain."

He wouldn't go back on his word, no matter how hard he got, or how much his balls ached.

It was going to be a very long night.

~

Compromise your virtue...

Heart pounding with longing beneath his focused regard, flesh tingling beneath his touch, Jessie decided that maybe she would like to be further compromised by her handsome-as-sin *fiancé*. Her common sense had clearly flown out the window. She might be safe from *him*, but was she safe from her own weak and wanton self?

"Tonight will be difficult for both of us it seems," she said without thinking—then blushed to the very roots of her hair when Robert's gaze sharpened on her face.

Stop behaving like a vixen on heat, Jessie Munroe. Robert was right. Neither of them could afford to give in to their desires. Not when Robert's situation was so precarious.

A knock at the door saved her from making any further revealing admissions. After checking who was there, Robert unlocked the bedroom door to admit Mary and Elspeth with their dinner. Jessie's stomach growled noisily as the maids set out everything on the small table beside the fire. It had been three days since she'd had a decent hot meal. At least there was *one* type of hunger she could sate tonight.

Once the innkeeper's daughters had departed, Robert helped Jessie to the table then played servant, pouring red wine as well as ladling out steaming portions of jugged hare into bowls for each of them.

"*Slainte.* To our health, Jessie." Robert smiled as he touched his glass of claret to hers. His eyes were as warm as the deep blue of the sea on a midsummer's day.

Oh, my goodness. Jessie really wished Robert wouldn't look at her like that. She cleared her throat. "*Slainte,*" she responded, not surprised at all when her voice emerged with a husky edge. "And might I also add, here's to yer bid for clemency and safe return home."

Robert inclined his head, the corner of his mouth tipping into a breath-stealing smile. "Thank you, *mo ghaoil.* That is one of my deepest desires."

Only one of them? Jessie really shouldn't dwell on what any of Robert's *other* desires might be as his attention focused on her mouth. Instead, she dropped her own gaze to the bowl in front of her and began to attack her fragrant stew with relish.

During the meal, and afterwards as they dallied over a platter of autumn pears and cheese, Jessie found herself both entertained and enthralled by Robert as he regaled her with amusing anecdotes about his experiences in France and his life in the Jamaican colony. She thought he must find her terribly provincial given that she'd spent most of her life in the far north of Scotland. Indeed, the largest city she'd ever visited was Edinburgh, and that was only to see cousin Maggie's first bairn. But Robert never showed any indication—by way of comment or expression —that he found her as dull as ditchwater. In fact, she felt as if he were watching her closely and paying attention to her every word.

"Tell me more about your family, Jessie," Robert said, refilling her wine glass, his eyes barely leaving hers.

"There's no' much to tell really. It's always just been my father and me, for as long as I can recall." Jessie paused as a wave of sadness washed over her. "My mother, Elizabeth was her name, passed away when I was but three years old."

"You have my sympathies." Robert's gaze was compassionate as it rested upon her face. "It seems we have that sad circumstance in common. My mother died within a few months of my birth. I think that's the reason my father remarried so hastily. But your father—Alasdair, is that right?—he never remarried?"

"No..." Jessie fiddled with the stem of her glass. Robert's eyes were drawn to the play of her fingers and she suddenly felt far too warm, like she was sitting too close to the fire. She took a hurried sip of her claret and Robert's gaze returned to her face. "I'm no' sure that he ever really stopped grieving for my mother, and he was always so busy with estate business. For my uncle, the laird."

"Your father sounds like a resourceful man," Robert observed. "It's obvious my father thinks very highly of him.'

Jessie smiled, unaccountably pleased that Robert had taken note of her father's reputation. "He is a wonderful da and the most giving man."

"And a canny manager by the sounds of it."

"Aye," Jessie agreed. "If it wasna for his skill, Dunraven, my uncle's estate would have collapsed long before it actually did. This is difficult to speak of but...my uncle, Dugald Munroe, was an inveterate gambler —a proclivity he concealed for a verra long time. By the time my father found out the extent of the problem it was too late. In the end, it was only because of my father's generosity that my uncle didna end up in debtor's prison. My father used his own savings to cover a sufficient amount o' the debt to prevent that." Her mouth tightened with disapproval. "The sad thing is, I dinna think my uncle, my aunt, or their three daughters will ever really appreciate the sacrifice he made for them all. Or be in a position to repay him."

Robert nodded. "Where are your uncle and his family now?" he asked.

"Quietly living in the depths o' the Yorkshire countryside I believe, with my aunt's family," replied Jessie. "No doubt they're all pining for a taste o' London society by now. I ken my aunt—her grandfather was a baronet—had high hopes that my cousins would make well-placed marriages. She will be bitterly disappointed at their downturn in circumstances. 'Tis a shame for all concerned."

Robert took a sip of his claret, studying Jessie over the rim of his glass. "It might be indelicate of me to say so, but I imagine your family's loss also affected your plans for the future. Someone as lovely as you must have had a suitor or two at the very least..."

"One or two." She smiled, taking a sip of her own wine. "And yes, it is indelicate of ye to discuss such things, Robert Grant. I dinna intend to ask ye about yer past dalliances. I'm certain ye would have had quite a few more than one or two."

Robert's mouth curved into a rakish grin, and he raised his glass to her. "*Touché.*" He suddenly reached across the table and clasped her hand. "I want you to know, I care not a whit about your family's fall in fortune. Or that your tocher probably went toward clearing your uncle's debts—I notice how you don't mention it. *You* are all that matters, Jessie. Only you. I want you to remember that."

Jessie shivered, yet her face was hot. She didn't know what to say. Robert's perceptiveness and kindness had surprised her yet again. She took a large sip of her wine, trying to hide her discomposure.

They were just sharing the last of the claret when there came another knock at the door.

Robert rose from the table. "I suspect it is the serving girls with our bathing water."

Sure enough, Mary and Elspeth entered to deposit a large pitcher of steaming water, a bundle of towels, and soap on the washstand, before discreetly quitting the room.

As soon as the door shut, panic began to dance a wild reel inside Jessie's belly. There was no screen to speak of in the room, and there was no way on earth she was going to bathe in front of Robert.

Robert turned to regard her, a reassuring smile tugging at the corner of his mouth. "Don't look so alarmed, *mo ghaoil*. I will go down to the taproom for half an hour so you may have some privacy... Unless you feel you need my help of course..." Wicked amusement gleamed in his eyes. "I'm very good at loosening stays as you well know...and washing backs."

Such impudence could not go unpunished. "So much for yer vow to keep yer hands to yerself, Robert Grant," Jessie chided with a mock scowl as she lobbed the remnants of her pear core at him.

He dodged away easily, laughing. "Well, I suppose I have my answer then. Enjoy your bath, *mo nighean ruadh*." With a wink and another annoyingly rakish smile, he departed, locking the door behind him—no doubt to ensure she wouldn't be disturbed while she washed.

Jessie heaved an exasperated sigh and tossed back the last of her claret. Robert Grant was a Jacobite rogue and seafaring pirate and gentleman all rolled into one. He was, quite frankly, irresistible.

Damn him.

And damn her errant lust.

It was surely going to get her into trouble. Someone was definitely going to have to sleep on the floor.

~

When Robert eventually returned to their room, more than a half hour later, it was to find Jessie sound asleep, her wildly curling red-gold hair tangled across the white pillows, the quilt tucked up around her chin. Her cheeks were flushed with sleep and her breath sighed gently between her slightly parted lips.

So beautiful. Robert puffed out his own heavy sigh, resisting the urge to stroke a lock of hair away from her cheek. She was clearly exhausted, poor lass.

A quick glance around the room revealed that she'd placed several blankets and a pillow by the fire. His mouth kicked into a grin. She was also a canny lass.

His amusement quickly died when he also spied Jessie's green riding habit, petticoats, stays, and stockings draped neatly over one of the chairs. That meant, beneath the covers, Jessie only wore her linen shift. And Robert knew *exactly* how she looked in only a shift.

His cock twitched at the vivid memory. *Damn.* He was going to have to suffer more than a hard floor. He prayed exhaustion would win out, otherwise he'd probably get no sleep at all.

With another heavy sigh of resignation, he shrugged off his coat then took a seat by the fire and tugged off a boot. Clumsy with fatigue, he dropped it. *Bloody hell.* The sound of leather hitting the wooden floor was loud in the silence. His eyes flew to Jessie. Had he woken her?

Murmuring and turning over in her sleep, his betrothed did not wake but the quilt slipped. Robert swore again as he caught a breathtaking glimpse of bare shoulder and the gentle swell of a breast.

His blasted cock stood to full attention.

There was only one thing for it. He was going to have to scrub away his ardor. There was probably warm water left in the pitcher. Enough to bathe and do what he needed to do to get some relief.

But he didn't want to disturb Jessie. Or worse, shock her, should she wake to discover him slaking his lust by his own hand.

Treading carefully, Robert silently approached the four-poster bed and drew the heavy damask curtains across the end...

Drifting on the edge of a dream, Jessie stirred from sleep. Water splashed in the distance, and she fancied herself by the shore of the Cromarty Firth, at home, at Dunraven. Sighing, wanting to recapture the dream, she rolled over...and a sudden stab of pain in her arm brought her crashing back to reality.

She wasn't home. She wasn't even at Lochrose.

She was...was staying at an inn. The name drifted back to her... Invercauld. With Robert.

But where was he? Had he come back to their chamber yet?

Jessie gingerly pushed herself up and swept a wave of tangled hair out of her eyes. The room was still suffused with the warm glow of fire and candlelight but strangely, the curtains had been drawn across the end of the four-poster bed. She frowned, nerves prickling with anxious curiosity. Tired though she had been when she'd collapsed onto the mattress, she was certain she hadn't done that.

All senses on alert, she sat up straighter. In a narrow gap between the swathes of dark blue bed hangings, Jessie sensed a movement—then bit back a gasp when she caught an unexpected glimpse of Robert, his upper torso naked, his breeches slung low around his lean hips. He was by the washstand, his back to her. He must be bathing.

She should close her eyes, at the very least avert her gaze, but she could not.

She was transfixed.

Surely he wouldn't mind if she admired his physique, not after his shirtless parade before her yesterday?

Through the opening Jessie could just see a section of Robert's back and lean waist. The firelight limned smooth flesh and sleek muscle with a golden glow. She unconsciously licked her lips, mouth suddenly dry, heart pounding. He was magnificent. A dark-haired Apollo. Her fingers itched to touch him, explore his sublime body.

Then he turned slightly, and she saw him. *All of him.* And her breath caught in her chest.

He wasn't washing himself...

Robert's eyes were closed while his hand was curled around his manhood, stroking the shaft. His rock hard, impossibly *long* shaft. As he squeezed his staff's ruddy head, he groaned soft and low, biting his lip as though in pain...

What in heaven's name was he doing?

The answer hit Jessie like a bolt of lightning.

He's pleasuring himself, you ninnyhammer. Remember Maggie told you. It's what men do.

This time, she couldn't stifle her gasp.

Robert immediately turned his head directly toward the end of the bed. "Jessie?" he called over his shoulder

Jessie was speechless, gawping. He would know that she'd been watching him. Her cheeks flaming, she squeezed her eyes shut as Robert drew the curtains back. She couldn't look at him.

"Jessie, I'm... Damn, I'm sorry if I startled you, lass." There was the sound of something rustling. "You can look now."

She cautiously opened one eye and then the other to find Robert standing at the end of the bed, his buckskin breeches re-buttoned and in place. *Thank the Lord.* Although acute embarrassment still twisted uncomfortably inside Jessie, she couldn't stop herself from running her gaze over Robert's beautiful body: his heavy pectorals with their light dusting of black hair, the hard ridges of his stomach, and then even lower to the suspicious bulge beneath the placket of his breeches.

She caught her lower lip between her teeth. She now knew what was in there. Apprehension and desire in equal measure, curled her toes.

Wicked, wicked, Jessie.

"Are you all right?" Robert asked.

She doubted that it was only concern that gave the man's voice a husky edge. Jessie swallowed then somehow managed to drag her gaze back to his face. "I-I woke and I could see yer...ah, yer back through the curtains... And ye were... Ye seemed to be—" She bit her lip again. She couldn't say what she'd *really* seen.

Robert cocked an eyebrow, a glint of amusement lurking in his eyes. "Washing?" he suggested.

"Aye," she huffed, prickly with indignation now. "We'll say ye were just doing that." The man was hateful when amused at her expense. "But ye're also half... Ye ken..." She gestured at his bare chest.

Robert's smile grew broader. "Half-naked? Like you?"

Jessie glanced down at herself and squealed. Her linen shift had slipped to an alarmingly low level, revealing far too much of her breasts. Why, her nipples were practically spilling out. Blushing furiously, she belatedly hauled the bedcovers up to her chin. "Ye should've said something sooner," she accused.

Robert winced, his expression approaching contrite. "Yes, I should have. I shouldn't tease you. And I apologize for waking you. If I somehow startled or offended you for any other reason, I offer you an apology for that as well. We men are very basic creatures sometimes... Well, I assure you, it won't happen again."

So Robert did suspect she'd caught him in the act of self-pleasuring. Jessie willed herself not to blush again, but his apology dispelled some of the tension crackling between them. She let out a shaky sigh, and at last had the courage to fully meet his gaze. "Thank ye, Robert. Yer apology is accepted."

"Well"—Robert rubbed the back of his neck—"I suppose it's time for bed."

Jessie grimaced. "About that..."

Robert gave her a reassuring smile. "Don't worry. If you can spare another pillow, I'm quite happy to sleep on the floor. It was always my intention."

Guilt twisted in Jessie's belly. She suddenly felt quite mean, and she didn't like it. "Here ye are then," she said needlessly, pulling one of the pillows from behind her and thrusting it toward him when he approached her side of the bed. "Are ye sure this is all ye need?"

"Quite sure." As Robert's fingers innocently brushed against hers, Jessie's breathing faltered. Even that brief contact set her skin aflame, made her pulse race. This yearning ache inside her was almost too much to bear.

A pillow might be all Robert needed, but she definitely needed something more. Something she'd promised herself she wouldn't have.

The question was, would Robert give it to her?

Robert hovered by Jessie's side of the bed, pillow in hand, in a definite quandary. Should he kiss his innocent *fiancée* goodnight or beat a hasty retreat to the fireside?

He truly regretted how Jessie had caught him *in flagrante*. He wasn't sure how much she'd actually seen, but judging by her reaction, it was sufficiently shocking. She might have accepted his apology, but there was still a strange awkwardness between them. Indeed, the very air around them seemed to vibrate with it.

Perhaps a brief goodnight kiss would help to alleviate the tension.

After all, they *were* handfasted.

He glanced down at Jessie. She'd begun to worry her bottom lip with her teeth again. The urge to soothe her poor abused mouth with his own was strong, but he wouldn't. He would keep the kiss light and amicable—and away from her delectable lips.

"Well, *mo chridhe*," Robert murmured. "I'll bid you goodnight then."

Leaning down, he aimed chastely for Jessie's cheek but somehow it all went wrong. In the moment before he kissed her, Jessie turned her head and his lips found her soft, lush-as-a-ripe-peach mouth instead. Her lips moved imperceptibly against his and desire sparked.

Had she done that deliberately? Stunned, Robert broke the contact and sought her gaze.

There was neither censure nor trepidation in the golden-brown depths. Indeed, Jessie's eyes looked almost drowsy with longing. Her lids were heavy, her pupils dilated. She'd told him earlier that she enjoyed his kisses. Would she welcome another?

God forgive him, *he* definitely wanted another.

He cleared his throat. "Jessie, what happened just now—"

"It's all my doing, Robert," she said in a breathless rush. "I wanted ye to kiss me... I just didna know how to tell ye."

Christ. She really meant it. Despite catching him in the midst of a crude act, despite all of his provocative quips, she still wanted him. It was more than he deserved.

Robert dropped the pillow and sat down on the edge of the bed. Jessie did not draw away. If anything, she leaned closer, her attention completely focused on his mouth.

One more kiss, that's all he needed. One more kiss and he would be sated.

What harm could it do when they were practically wed?

His throat suddenly tight with longing, he murmured, "Jessie, may I kiss you again?"

The tip of her pink tongue darted out, moistening her lips. "Aye," she whispered, her eyes dark as molten honey. "I thought ye'd never ask."

~

At long last, the moment she'd been waiting for all afternoon, and the best part of the evening, had arrived.

Jessie held her breath as Robert slid one of his hands into the tangle of curls at her nape, then oh, so slowly bent his head to claim her. His mouth slanted over hers, hungry, yet gentle. His lips were satiny smooth yet firm. This kiss...it was delicious. Intoxicating.

Exhilarating.

Jessie pushed herself against Robert's naked chest and the potent scent of him—warm, clean, aroused male—wrapped around her, flooded her senses. Her head spun as she breathed him in. She slid her hands over his hot skin, and his powerful muscles flexed and rippled beneath her touch.

She couldn't touch him enough. Couldn't taste him enough.

Robert was holding back, taking too much care with her, she could sense it. And she didn't want him to. She wanted passion and blinding heat, all the sensations he'd aroused when he'd kissed her the night before in the cave.

Boldly, instinctively, Jessie slid her tongue between the seam of his lips. With a deep throaty growl that sent a deep thrill right down to her toes, Robert returned the thrust, his tongue stroking and tasting her in return.

It was divine, heavenly, but all too soon it ended. With an agonized groan, Robert suddenly dragged his mouth away and grasped her questing hands between his. He was breathing heavily, his blue eyes as dark as a turbulent storm-tossed loch. "Have mercy, lass. If we keep on like this much longer, we'll both burst into flames."

Jessie looked down at their entwined fingers resting against his thigh and immediately noticed how the kiss—how *she*—had affected Robert. His impressive erection strained against the fall of his buckskin breeches.

He noticed where her gaze had traveled and smiled, almost sheepishly. "There's no hiding your effect on me, Jessie. I apologize if my state frightens you."

"No, it doesna frighten me," she said shakily, answering his smile with one of her own. In fact, the sight of Robert's great need only served to increase hers. Her body was aroused in its own disconcerting way. Her nipples were hard and aching, and the secret place between the apex of her thighs felt heavy, pulsing with strong desire. They couldn't stop here. She didn't just want the taste of Robert's mouth, she wanted to taste and explore all of his sleek hardness.

And she wanted him to touch her in return.

When had she become so brazen and wanton?

Although Jessie understood why Robert had brought a halt to their passionate exchange, it also occurred to her that should their plans go dreadfully awry, this might be one of the last opportunities he would ever have to be with a woman. The only opportunity to be with *her*.

Truth be told, this was an experience she did not want to miss either, despite the consequences, despite her promises to herself.

And so Jessie took a deep breath. "Robert," she began. She disengaged one of her hands from his and stroked his stubble-shadowed jaw. He stared at her with such heated intensity, she thought she might catch alight. "Robert...I ken we should wait to consummate our handfasting. But after tomorrow, or even the next day...it may be too late. If this is one of yer last chances to spend a night with someone... With me..."

Robert pressed a finger to her lips. His smile was tender, his eyes filled with regret as he spoke. "Christ alive, woman. As much as I want you, it would not be right for me to take your maidenhead. Not when my future is so uncertain. If I am locked away or even worse, executed..." He inhaled a deep shuddering breath then stroked her cheek with the back of his fingers. "It's a risk I won't let you take."

She shook her head. "I understand yer concern for me, but ye're too noble for yer own good." On an impulse, she leaned forward and kissed the side of his neck and was thrilled to feel him shiver, hear his sharp intake of breath.

Robert's groan thrummed through her. "Jessie, if you had any idea how much I want you, how hard it is for me to resist making you mine this instant, you would not be so bold."

In mute response, Jessie raised her head and kissed his jaw and the side of his mouth. The strength of her own desire was making her reckless and she did not care.

"I want ye, Robert Grant," she whispered against his mouth. "More than anything I've ever wanted before."

~

Robert's mouth crushed Jessie's in a hard, almost bruising kiss. A possessive kiss. *She wants me as much as I want her.* His blood sang at the heady realization.

If he were a better man, he would not be doing this: kissing Jessie like this, pushing her shift off her shoulders, raining hot, open-mouthed kisses along her neck and collarbone, down to the deep shadow of her cleavage. But heaven help him, he wasn't strong enough to resist her blatant invitation.

And Jessie was right. He may never have this chance again.

But he would not take her virginity. He would satisfy her need, and his own...but he would not risk getting her with child, not tonight.

Robert broke their kiss briefly to carefully ease Jessie down onto the pillows. The sight of her full breasts straining against the thin white fabric of her shift made his cock grow harder to the point of pain. But as much as he wanted to tear the garment from her body, and despite her declaration that she wanted him to make love to her, he didn't want to frighten her. For all her enthusiasm, she was still an inexperienced novice. He would take his time and follow her lead.

He wanted her to enjoy this as much as he was going to.

~

Jessie's heart burst into a wild unbridled gallop as Robert eased himself onto the bed to lie beside her. Her heart-stoppingly handsome, considerate *fiancé* was going to make love to her. She could barely believe it.

She could hardly wait.

"Jessie, you must tell me when you want me to stop," Robert murmured, his voice rough with emotion. "I won't do anything you don't want me to do."

She nodded, too breathless to speak, but seriously doubted she'd want him to stop. Ever.

"You are so, so beautiful, *mo chridhe*." *My heart.* Robert's passion darkened gaze slid from her face to her breasts. "Everywhere."

He thinks I'm beautiful. Jessie's heart thrummed with unexpected delight. "So are you," she whispered and placed a hand against Robert's bare chest. She swore she could feel his heart pounding beneath the hard plane of muscle, an echo, a mirror of her own heartbeat.

Unable to resist exploring Robert a little more, she ran her fingers through the fine dusting of dark hair along his pectorals, smiling when his nipples contracted.

Robert shuddered and on a broken groan, buried his face in her hair. Pushing the tangle of curls away from her neck, he inhaled deeply before pressing a hot kiss in the hollow just below her ear. Encouraging his exploration, she arched her neck, marveling at the delicious, tickling sensations his clever mouth provoked as he nibbled and licked his way down her throat until he reached the edge of her shift.

Then he paused. Robert raised his head and his eyes locked with hers. "Let me see you," he whispered.

Jessie didn't hesitate. With trembling fingers, she clumsily loosened the ribbons at her neckline, all the while watching Robert's expression.

His eyes were dark, heavy-lidded with desire and when her shift gaped open to reveal her breasts, he swallowed.

"I was right. Beautiful," he murmured reverently, trailing a fingertip down one breast to her tightly furled, aching nipple. She closed her eyes and whimpered, arching toward his hand. The hot restless ache in her was too much. She needed more.

And, thank the Lord, Robert obliged. He lowered his head and when his lips closed around the exposed bud, she cried out in agonized pleasure. Hot, dark desire swirled through her as he mercilessly suckled and teased her breasts with his tongue, lips, and fingers. She writhed beneath him, tangling her fingers in his hair, unsure if she could take much more of this exquisite torture, not when the throb in her sex was growing with each passing minute.

At length, Robert raised his head and smiled at her, a wicked, entirely self-satisfied smile. Through her thin shift, he stroked gently across her ribs and down to her belly, making her quake.

"Please dinna stop," Jessie breathed. She was unsure what he would exactly do next, what she needed to ask for, but she hoped he would focus his attention on that part of her where her unsatisfied need throbbed the most.

"I won't." Robert dipped his head and kissed her on the mouth again, tenderly this time as he gently lifted the hem of her shift.

One of his hands stroked slowly up the inside of one thigh and then the other. She instinctively parted her legs, straining toward his teasing feather-light touch. When his fingers slid up and down, between her most secret folds, warm and slippery with moist need, she gasped with the unexpected pure pleasure of it.

She was indeed wanton. *Wild.* She didn't care, not when Robert could make her feel this way.

But it wasn't the end, far from it. With unerring accuracy, the pad of one of Robert's fingers found the focus of her pulsating desire. Jessie jolted and gasped but his teasing, circling caresses didn't falter in rhythm. As he expertly built the intensity of the exquisite sensations inside her to fever pitch, she panted and moaned in utter abandonment, unsure how much more she could take. She was spiraling higher and higher toward some hitherto unknown heavenly world where agony and pleasure coalesced.

And only when she thought she could take no more did her reality explode into ecstasy. Jessie cried out again and again with the shattering power of her very first release. By degrees, she floated back to earth and became aware of Robert kissing her neck, her jaw, her cheek, her eyelids. She was completely boneless and replete and awed all at the same time.

Body humming with contentment, her mind hazy, she opened her eyes and smiled drowsily at Robert. "Thank you," she murmured. "I had no idea... That was... What ye did was amazing... I canna describe it any other way." She reached out and placed a hand on Robert's chest, not wanting to lose contact with his hot skin. "Is it like that for ye too?"

"It can be," he murmured before kissing her hair and drawing her close into his arms.

Jessie felt his erect manhood pushing hard up against her belly. Robert had satisfied her, yet his need was still great. She couldn't let him suffer so.

"Mmm, I think it is yer turn to be satisfied now," she said, kissing his neck where his pulse beat a strong and steady tattoo. Yet despite what they'd just shared, and as much as she wanted to please Robert, uncertainty pinched. She had no idea what she should do next.

She ran one of her hands languidly down Robert's chest to the taut plane of his stomach, pausing at the waistband of his breeches. Biting her lip, she wondered how to proceed. She'd seen how Robert had stroked himself...

Tentatively, Jessie placed her palm against the large, swollen length of him covered by the leather of his breeches. Would he let her see him, touch him, pleasure him there? She flexed her fingers experimentally, and Robert sucked in a harsh breath, pushing against her.

Jessie smiled to herself. *Perhaps he would.*

"I havena ever done this before," she said softly, meeting Robert's intent, dark-as-midnight gaze. "Ye might need to show me the way."

Robert chuckled gently. "I think you've found the right place," he said, then kissed her lightly. "Are you sure you're ready for this though? I can wait...if you are unsure about continuing."

Jessie's cheeks burned but she didn't look away. *This was what she wanted.* He *was what she wanted.* "Aye, I'm sure. I want ye to feel the way ye made me feel."

Pushing herself up, she took a deep breath and began unbuttoning the front of his breeches, exposing the mysterious swelling. At such close quarters, the sight of Robert's fully erect member jutting up from the thatch of dark curls at his groin quite took her breath away. He was powerfully, rampantly beautiful.

And tonight, he was all hers.

~

Robert's breath caught at the sight of Jessie, breasts still exposed, staring with rapt fascination at his raging erection. She evidently hadn't been put off by his earlier display of randy behavior.

Her tongue suddenly darted out to moisten her already kiss-bruised lips and Robert nearly choked.

No, his sweet yet daring *fiancée* clearly wasn't perturbed at all.

God help him, Robert was so aroused, he wasn't entirely sure that he wouldn't explode like a green lad as soon as she touched him.

Jessie reached out and ran a tentative fingertip down his straining shaft, as if testing the feel and texture of him. When she encircled him with her whole hand near his base then ran her hand up his pulsating length to the dripping head, he groaned and fisted the sheets, willing himself not to spill yet. She repeated the action, sliding her hand up and down, over and over again. *How had she learned to do that?* Her rhythm and the way she squeezed him was damned near perfect. Maybe she'd seen more of his failed self-pleasuring attempt than he'd thought.

"Tell me when ye want me to stop," she whispered with a satisfied coquette's smile. She was evidently pleased at his reaction so far.

"Jessie," Robert growled. "Don't you dare stop."

Of their own volition, his hips began to move in time with her rhythmic stroking and squeezing. Closing his eyes, he gritted his teeth. Sparks flew behind his eyelids. He wasn't sure how much longer he would be able to hold back.

And then her hair caressed his thighs and her tongue flicked over him. She'd suckled him. Suckled his cock!

Christ. Robert bucked and his eyes flew open.

"I-I'm sorry," Jessie stammered. Her eyes were wide. "I didna mean to startle you. Or offend you."

"No need to apologize, *mo ghaoil.*" Robert's voice was little more than a breathless rasp. "And I'm not offended at all, far from it. It's just that I wasn't expecting you to...kiss me like that." His mouth hitched into a smile. "And if you continue, you'll soon see how much I really do like it, and I don't know if you're quite ready for that experience yet." He reached for her hand that still grasped him and guided her back to the sliding rhythm she'd started before, only a little faster.

A few more strokes and he'd be there.

"Jessie," he groaned and pulled her beneath him, wanting to take her mouth, plunder her with his tongue as he pushed his rigid throbbing length against her smooth belly. Her sweet taste, the musky floral scent of her recent climax engulfed him.

Within a handful of thrusts, glorious oblivion rose up to claim him. Shuddering, gasping Jessie's name into her sweet-smelling neck, he undulated his hips and jerked against her soft silken flesh until he was quiet and spent.

Jessie's passion, her sensual curiosity...she was a revelation. Robert's heart and body thrummed with the deepest contentment he'd ever known. If the worst happened, and there was no tomorrow for him, he would die a happy man.

But there would be time enough to worry about his future tomorrow. He still had the rest of the night to share with Jessie.

Robert kissed Jessie's delicate earlobe. "Thank you," he murmured, catching her warm as honey gaze. "You have no idea how much this has meant to me." Then, because he was greedy and because he couldn't resist, he stole another kiss. "Now, let's make use of that pitcher of water before it turns to ice."

He slipped from the bed and returned with a damp washcloth. Once he'd wiped Jessie's stomach and himself clean, he put her shift and his breeches to rights.

"Well, goodnight again." Robert bent down to kiss her forehead near the scratch left by the rowan splinter. He then retrieved the discarded pillow from the floor.

Jessie caught his hand. "Dinna go. Sleep here, with me," she invited. "Ye'll be more comfortable and we have another long day of riding ahead of us."

"As long as you promise to behave now," he teased with a mock frown.

"I promise," Jessie said with a solemn smile and moved over to make room. Robert climbed in beside her and pulled her firmly against his side, reveling in the way her body immediately molded to his. Her cheek rested against his bare chest and her fingers curled around his shoulder. This felt so right to have her here in his arms.

As Robert watched Jessie drift into sleep, he prayed this would not be the last time.

CHAPTER 18

"The Invercauld Arms is just up ahead, Master."

Simon slowed his exhausted horse to a trot and glanced back at the English dragoon who had addressed him. "Thank you, Captain Slater. I'm counting on our quarry being holed up here."

Simon would actually wager his soul that he was correct. In his quest to locate Jessie, he'd had the foresight to post lookouts on all the roads leading south from Lochrose and Grantown. Indeed, if he hadn't been so astute, he wouldn't have known that his cursed half-brother and Jessie had taken the longer route to the south-east along Caulfield's Road toward Pitlochry. With any luck, they may have stopped in Invercauld for the night. The dragoons from the Braemar Castle Garrison had been most interested to hear that they might have a wanted Jacobite right under their very noses.

Even if Robert and Jessie *weren't* at the inn and had decided to seek shelter in a barn or crofter's hut, the locals must have seen them pass through the village. With her blazing red hair, his Jezebel would have caught some man's eye.

"Perhaps we could change our horses here, sir," suggested MacTaggart as their sizable party—Baird, three other Black Watchmen, and four dragoons—all clattered into the inn yard. "It's probably the only place with decent mounts hereabouts."

Simon hated to admit it, but MacTaggart was right. The sun had set behind the Cairngorms several hours ago and all they had to light their way was a ponderous yellow moon. It would be foolish to travel any farther along the narrow, rutted Highland road on fatigued horses. Simon certainly wasn't going to break his neck on Robert's account.

The inn, although small, was still serving customers at this late hour. Leaving the business of stabling the horses and questioning the stable hands to most of the Watchmen, Simon headed for the taproom with Baird, MacTaggart, Captain Slater and his lobster backs. To Simon's annoyance he found the dimly lit room was nearly filled to overflowing with men who looked like off-duty soldiers, dusty travelers, local crofters, and drovers on their way to the Edinburgh markets. He'd be hard pressed to find a table without having to spend a coin or two.

He scanned the room and noted the only women present were two comely serving girls waiting on the tables.

There was no sign of Robert.

He informed the dragoon captain, who nodded and sent his men to question the taproom staff and the bar's patrons.

Simon turned to address MacTaggart over the noise of the rowdy throng. "I want you to go and question the innkeeper about who has sought accommodation for the night. Be quick about it."

MacTaggart's eyes narrowed, but nevertheless the insolent son of a bitch acquiesced. "Aye, sir."

Once the Watchman had departed, Simon pushed his way to the bar. At least he could partake of an ale or two whilst he waited for news. He spied a buxom, red-headed serving girl passing by with a tray of food. He smiled to himself. If his Jezebel wasn't here, he could always sample whatever the tavern wench had to offer.

Either way, he wouldn't leave here until he was satisfied.

Despite his exhaustion, it didn't take Robert long to realize that sleep would elude him as long as Jessie's soft curves pressed up against him and her warm breath sighed gently across his chest. His body was already taut with desire for her yet again.

With a frustrated sigh, he gently eased himself away from her, then quietly rose from the bed and dressed. A wee dram or two of whisky would probably relax him enough to sleep. Although there was still likely to be plenty of patrons in the taproom, he wasn't concerned. His strategy of hiding in plain sight had worked remarkably well over the years, and he had no reason to believe it would fail him now. A decade after Culloden, Invercauld was hardly a hot bed of illicit Jacobite activity. And as he'd told Jessie earlier, as Simon probably wouldn't think to search along this route, the local Redcoats wouldn't be on the lookout for the Jacobite rebel Robert Grant.

Aside from that, Robert doubted that Simon possessed the physical stamina to travel this far south in one day. He'd never been much of a horseman growing up at any rate.

Yes, Robert would bet his life that both he and Jessie were safe tonight.

As he eased on his coat, Robert noticed the slight crinkle of parchment in the inner breast pocket—his father's letter of appeal to the Lord Advocate. After checking it was securely in place, he glanced at Jessie, still soundly asleep. A soft smile curved his lips while he contemplated what it would feel like to be a free man: free to truly offer Jessie his hand in marriage. And how wonderful it would feel if she said yes.

The smile was still on Robert's face as he pushed his way toward the bar. The crowd had thinned a little and aside from a few off-duty soldiers, there was no sign of the Watch or anything or anyone else he'd consider untoward. Whisky in hand, he was about to turn around to find a dark corner in the taproom when someone grabbed his shoulder in a tight almost painful grip. A sharp click and something hard and metallic, possibly a pistol muzzle, jabbed into his lower back in the vicinity of his left kidney.

A low voice hissed in his ear. "Well, well, Robert. If it isn't the prodigal son himself."

Fuck. Simon. There was no mistaking his half-brother's venomous tone.

Robert froze, inwardly cursing himself for being too cock-sure and letting his guard down. Clearly he had seriously underestimated his opponent.

Carefully placing his whisky on the counter, he turned slowly, palms upraised in a gesture of surrender. Sure enough, a smirking Simon stood before him.

Robert noted with a small degree of satisfaction that his brother was only able to manage a somewhat crooked grin given that his left jaw was empurpled and swollen with a rather impressive bruise. "Simon," he said dryly. "Fancy meeting you here."

Simon sneered. "Judging by the look on your face, it appears as though you didn't expect me to turn up in Invercauld, did you, dearest brother?" he taunted as he pushed the pistol into Robert's stomach.

"No..." Robert quickly scanned the room and swore under his breath when he took in four dragoons standing at the ready near the doorway, and another three Black Watchmen hovering behind Simon. How had he not noticed them when he'd first entered the tap room? He'd been well and truly ambushed. There was no way he could take on that many men, even without a cocked pistol pressed into his abdomen.

Bloody, bloody hell. What a blind fool he'd been. The stakes were high and he'd made a grievous miscalculation about Simon's capacity for vengeance.

And Jessie is in danger. Fear, like nothing Robert had ever experienced before, ripped mercilessly at his gut. If Simon found Jessie upstairs, alone, asleep...

Simon's gloating face reclaimed his attention. "Don't even think about making a break for it. As you can see, there is no way that even a legendary Jacobite such as yourself can escape this time."

"I'm afraid this will all come to naught, Simon," Robert replied smoothly, repressing any hint of fear from his voice. "Father will be lodging an appeal for clemency with the Lord Advocate. Any hope you had of seeing me executed for treason is dead."

Simon's snort approximated a laugh. "Well, I have to admire your optimism, if nothing else." His expression suddenly turned sly. "Or perhaps there is something else of yours I admire. Something which is actually mine." He glanced meaningfully toward the ceiling.

Robert's stomach twisted with a potent combination of cold dread and blazing anger. "What do you mean?" he ground out, clenching his fists, envisioning the pleasing sight of pounding the lascivious smile from Simon's face.

Simon's gaze returned to Robert's, his eyes glittering with malicious intent. "I know which chamber she's in, and there's nothing you can do to stop me having her."

⁓

Jessie started awake, her heart pounding. Something had woken her.

For a moment she was disoriented. She sat up, awareness rushing back as she took in the four-poster bed, the washstand, the dying fire... and the fact she was alone again.

Why had Robert left and for how long had she been asleep? A rising wave of panic was exacerbated tenfold when there came a knocking at the door.

It couldna be Robert. He had a key.

The knocking halted and a gruff male voice called out. "Miss Munroe? Miss Munroe, ye must wake. My name is MacTaggart. I'm a captain with the Black Watch and I work for Lord Strathburn. I must speak with ye urgently."

Oh God, something has happened. Please let Robert be all right.

Heart crashing against her ribs, Jessie slipped from the bed and began to throw on her riding habit. As she frantically tried to button the undershirt with trembling fingers, the man's voice came again.

"Miss Munroe, I have with me one of the innkeeper's daughters, Mary, to show you I mean ye no harm. I ken ye are frightened but please, ye must believe that I have nothin' but honorable intentions. Please let us in."

A young woman then spoke. "'Tis true what he says miss. I'm Mary. I served ye earlier."

Ignoring her protesting ankle, Jessie crossed to the door as fast as she could. Even as a maelstrom of thoughts and questions whirled about her head, she was not ready to open the door yet.

She spoke through the heavy wood. "MacTaggart, ye say?" The man's name was vaguely familiar for some reason. Did this man really work for Lord Strathburn, or was he in the pay of Simon? Could she trust him? She dare not ask him directly about Robert lest she give away his presence. "What on earth is going on? Why exactly are ye here?"

MacTaggart's next words struck a cold hard blade of fear through Jessie's heart. "Miss Munroe, Mr. Simon Grant is downstairs and is at this verra moment apprehending Lord Lochrose. He has several dragoons and some of my men with him. I have grave fears for yer safety."

Jessie slumped against the door, a lump of ice-cold fear lodging in her throat. *Simon was here. He had Robert. Oh, this must be a nightmare.* Any moment she would wake up and find herself nestled with Robert in the bed beside her. But something MacTaggart said was telling... "*Mister* Grant?" she said. Of course, now Robert had returned to reclaim his place, Simon would no longer have any claim to any of Lord Strathburn's courtesy titles. Robert was the viscount *and* master again.

"Aye, Miss Munroe. I believe Lord Lochrose's brother will be paying ye a visit verra shortly. I assume ye've been abed...? If ye open the door, Mary will help ye get dressed."

Jessie swallowed. MacTaggart was right. If Simon came upon her in her current state of *dishabille*, the situation didn't bear thinking about.

With shaking hands, she unlocked the door to reveal a tall, heavily built man in a Black Watch plaid. A quivering Mary stood beside him.

The Watchman gave a small bow. "Thank ye, Miss Munroe. I will wait outside. I suggest Mary remain with ye for the rest of the night."

Jessie nodded. MacTaggart's face might be battle-scarred and ferocious looking, but he had kind brown eyes, eyes that shone with concern, not cruelty. She was inclined to take him at his word. "Thank ye for yer kindness, sir. I'm verra grateful. I will be sure to commend ye to the earl and to my father, Alisdair Munroe."

MacTaggart bowed his head. "*Tapadh Leibh.*" Thank you.

Before Jessie closed the door, she had one last question. Her throat was so tight, the words barely came out. "Wh-Where will they take Lord Lochrose?"

The Black Watchman met her eyes directly. "To the Braemar Castle Garrison, and tomorrow, they'll likely set out for Edinburgh where his lordship will be incarcerated in the Tolbooth Prison. I will do what I can to help him, but now there are dragoons involved, I'm verra afraid that it willna be enough to save him."

Which was what Jessie dreaded too.

～

After the dragoons carted Robert away, Simon impatiently scanned the taproom for MacTaggart. No doubt the man was still upstairs locating Jessie for him as he'd instructed. Robert, the fool, had denied Jessie was here at all. In fact, he'd insisted she'd taken the public coach from Grantown. But Simon knew it was a lie.

Jessie was here, he sensed it. It was only a matter of minutes before he would have the girl all to himself.

He downed Robert's discarded whisky in one gulp and headed for the inn's upstairs rooms. Gaining the head of the staircase, he spied MacTaggart standing before one of the doors. *Excellent.* The Watchman had found her. Simon's ballocks grew heavy and tight with anticipation. *Finally, after all this time.*

"That'll be all, MacTaggart. I'll take care of Miss Munroe from here." Simon held his hand out for the key to the room but instead all he received was a stony-faced glare from the burly Black Watchman. Impatience spiked. "MacTaggart. Give me the damn key."

The Watchman stared back, clearly unfazed. "I'm verra sorry, Mr. Grant. Miss Munroe has retired for the evenin'. Her attending maid informs me she willna be available to meet with ye until tomorrow mornin'."

"Damn you to hell, MacTaggart! What are you playing at?" roared Simon. "I don't care if my brother is back. You'll address me as Master! Now step aside and open the fucking door."

The door to the bedchamber suddenly cracked open a fraction and a timid mouse of a maid slipped out, clearly terrified. "Ah, M-M-Miss Munroe says she will receive ye, Mister...I mean, Master. As long as the door stays ajar and Captain MacTaggart stays close by."

"I'll have you stripped of your rank for this, MacTaggart," Simon uttered savagely under his breath as he pushed roughly passed the captain and the serving girl into the room beyond.

To his further annoyance, Jessie was fully dressed, seated in a fireside wingback chair behind a small table. She sat ramrod straight, chin upraised, eyeing him with defiance. Oh, how he would enjoy wiping that look from her face.

Simon raked her with a deliberately lewd gaze before casting a meaningful look at the rumpled four-poster bed. "Shame you're not still abed, Miss Munroe. But no matter. I'll soon have you back there."

She didn't respond, just raised her chin a little higher, her eyes glittering.

Anger flashed through Simon, hot and fierce. He threw himself into the armchair opposite Jessie, leaning back with his legs extended, his booted feet crossed at the ankle beneath the table. He rested his chin on his steepled fingertips and studied her through narrowed eyes. Her face was pale except for two flags of bright color across her high cheekbones. *Good.* Despite her outwardly holier-than-thou manner, he had rattled the little bitch.

But he wanted to cow her even more. When he spoke, he imbued his voice with soft silken menace. "I have a proposition for you, Miss Munroe. Spend the night with me and do my bidding...or I shall have you arrested by the dragoons and thrown into prison for aiding and abetting a wanted fugitive and traitor."

I'll spend the night with ye when pigs fly.

Jessie bit back the retort and glared at Simon, anger smothering her fear. She'd had enough of this man's bullying and whilst she had the advantage of MacTaggart's support, she intended to show some backbone. Having Robert's dirk in her hand beneath the cover of her skirts also emboldened her. Thank heavens he'd left it behind on the washstand.

Simon picked at non-existent lint on his cuff, obviously affecting a nonchalance he didn't feel. His mouth was compressed into a grim line and a muscle ticked in his jaw. "I'm waiting for your answer, Miss Munroe," he said, his tone dark and dripping with disdain. "Unlike you, I don't have all night. What's it to be?"

Jessie gripped Robert's dirk tighter, grateful for the feel of the cold steel hilt in her sweat-slickened palm. Her voice, when it emerged, shook only a mite. "Ye'd best send for the dragoons then. I would much rather sleep on a cold stone floor with lice and rats as companions than spend one more moment with you."

She'd pushed him too far.

With a growl, Simon launched himself from the chair, knocking over the table between them. Looming over her, his hands on the arms of her own chair, his face hovered mere inches above hers. Even though Jessie recoiled on a gasp, another part of her was infuriated. Perhaps even emboldened. At these close quarters, she could plainly see the aftermath of Robert's punch along his jaw. It reminded her that Simon wasn't all-powerful.

Courage, Jessie. She firmed her grip on the dirk. She would use it against this vile, sorry excuse for a man if she had to. No matter the consequences.

"Now listen to me you little b—" began Simon.

"No, ye listen to me," returned Jessie, so furious she could spit. "I suggest ye move away from me at once, or I will summon MacTaggart to arrest ye for threatening assault." Her instincts told her that she would be able to count on the good captain for aid.

Simon instantly pushed himself away and glared, his rage barely contained. His hands were bunched into fists and his gray eyes flashed with ice-sharp anger. He reminded her of a wolf about to attack its prey.

Despite her trembling legs, Jessie stood and faced him, the dirk still in her hand. She had something else she needed to say, and she would do so at eye level. She would not cower before him. Never again. "I think ye should also ken that this verra morning, yer father handfasted Robert and I. As soon as Robert is pardoned by the Lord Advocate—and he will be—yer brother and I shall be wed. I'm sure Lord Strathburn would be none too pleased with you, if he was to hear that yer behavior toward me, as my future brother-in-law and his future daughter, was nothing less than exemplary. Dinna ye agree?"

"Well, haven't we done well for ourselves, my dear Jezebel?" Simon's voice was brimming with mock politeness. A narrow smile, like a grimace, twisted his thin lips. "I was right about you all along. You are nothing but a greedy, grasping harlot."

He stalked toward the door but paused and looked back over his shoulder. His parting shot chilled Jessie to the bone. "But what will become of you, Miss Munroe, when my brother's head is on the chopping block? I'll still be here...waiting. Remember that, won't you, my dear, as you fall asleep tonight, all alone."

~

"I'd bid ye good night, *milord*, but I ken ye willna have one." The dragoon's gruff laughter echoed about the stone walls of the completely bare cell in the Braemar Castle Garrison—Robert's "room" for the night.

Well, that's hardly surprising. Sighing heavily, Robert tipped his head back against the rough bricks behind him as the soldier slammed the heavy, wooden, iron-studded door shut. He already knew he wouldn't be able to sleep during what was left of the night.

It wasn't the biting coldness of the air around him, or the hard stone floor beneath him that destroyed any hope of rest, but the nauseating fear and acrid self-recrimination that clawed his insides to shreds. His surroundings brought to mind his long-ago confinement in Lochrose's wine cellar...only this time, there was no chance of drowning himself in whisky in a feeble attempt to deaden the dark, disturbing train of his thoughts.

His worst nightmare had come to life. He'd been captured, and tomorrow he'd be transported to the Edinburgh Tolbooth, God help him. And may God help those he cared about.

What plagued Robert the least was thoughts of his own mortality. He'd stared the specter of Death in the face countless times before. Indeed, since Culloden, and during his time as a mercenary and more recently as a Caribbean "corsair," Death had been an ever-present companion. No, he'd made peace with the idea of dying long ago.

What he couldn't bear was the overwhelming sense of failure swamping him. It crashed down upon him so heavily, it felt as though he could no longer draw breath. Or that his heart had been crushed to a lifeless, flat stone within his chest.

If he were found guilty of treason and executed, it would spell certain disaster for his family. Simon was nothing but a drunken, self-serving lecher, and Lady Strathburn was as rotten and avaricious as the famed Lady Macbeth herself. There was no doubt in his mind that the pair would ruin the estate. They would destroy his aging father and lay waste to the clan as surely as a contingent of dragoons on a rampage. The clansfolk would be cleared from their villages and crofts, the land sold. And Jessie...

God, Jessie!

Since he'd been hauled from the taproom by the dragoons out into the night, Robert had not seen hide nor hair of Simon, which probably meant his despicable brother had gone after Jessie, just as he'd threatened. Bile burned the back of Robert's throat and his gut clenched.

If Simon harmed a single hair on Jessie's head...

He struck his fists against the unyielding stone-flagged floor, perversely taking joy in the sharp pain ricocheting up through his protesting knuckles.

Jessie was strong, capable, smart. But would she be able to fend off Simon if caught unawares? Sweet Jesus, when Robert had left her, she'd been sleeping soundly in their bed...

I'm still as thoughtless and hot-headed as the upstart I was a decade ago. I've learned nothing. I let my balls get in the way of rational, strategic thinking and let complacency get the upper hand. If anything happens to Jessie, it's all my fault...

It was a useless enterprise attempting to stem the hot slide of tears down his face. Tears of guilt, shame and desperate anger. Of all the things Robert had done wrong, this was the one thing he would never be able to forgive himself for—failing his sweet, sweet Jessie.

He dashed his shirt sleeve across his eyes. The Redcoats had taken his jacket when they'd searched him for weapons. His father's letter, his only hope of salvation, was gone. He could only pray it had been given to Captain Slater. He seemed like a reasonable man, despite the fact he was a Sassenach. He would take note of the seal of the Earl of Strathburn and the intended recipient of the missive, the Lord Advocate himself. Perhaps the captain had taken heed of his father's elevated rank already... This tower room might be as icy as Hades and devoid of furniture, but at least Robert hadn't been chained up in some dank, filthy dungeon. On the surface, it appeared to be a concession of some kind.

But if Father's letter falls into Simon's hands...

Robert closed his eyes and gritted his teeth against the familiar swirling of black despair in his chest. *Hope.* He must remember there was hope. God knew why, but his father still believed in him. And didn't he owe it to his father and the clan, and to Jessie, not to give up?

When pale, tremulous morning light began to filter in through the small, barred window above his head, and the rusty scrape of bolts being drawn back dragged him back to full alertness, Robert had already firmly engraved his resolutions into what was left of his heart.

I will not die. When I get out of this, I will be the son I should have been. The leader I want to be. I will honor my commitment to Jessie. And with God as my witness, I will make sure Simon never hurts her or anyone else again.

CHAPTER 19

After Simon Grant's departure, Jessie spent several fruitless hours trying to rest. Fear for Robert's safety constantly needled her brain, making sleep impossible. The innkeeper's daughter, Mary, seemed to have no such trouble. More than a few times, Jessie cast an envious glance over to the young maid sleeping soundly in a narrow pallet bed beside the four-poster.

Eventually Jessie had given up on sleep altogether and had spent the rest of the night in one of the armchairs before the dying fire. She'd tried to piece together some sort of plan to save Robert, but in the end, she knew there was nothing she could accomplish on her own in the dead of night. Liberating Robert from a locked cell in a castle garrison was definitely an impossible feat.

At the back of her mind, a prickle of a thought had also irritated. Why had Robert left her alone in the room? MacTaggart had told her he'd been arrested in the taproom, so perhaps he'd had trouble sleeping. After all, he had a lot weighing on his mind. But a small, vulnerable, wholly feminine part of Jessie hoped Robert didn't regret their physical encounter. Or worse, was having second thoughts about being hand-fasted to her at all. Surely he wouldn't abandon her here...

Jessie quickly dismissed the nonsensical notion when she looked around the room and noted several of Robert's possessions: a linen cravat, his plaid and saddlebags, and of course, his dirk. He wouldn't have left any of those things behind if he'd been intending to leave. There must be some other logical explanation for his departure. Perhaps he'd simply wanted a drink to settle his nerves. Whatever it was, worrying about it further wouldn't help the situation.

Eventually Jessie determined that even though traveling alone would be dangerous, there was no other real course of action open to her. Remaining here in Invercauld was *not* an option.

Yes, despite the risk, she *must* return to Lochrose to inform Lord Strathburn of Robert's plight. She fervently prayed the earl would be well enough to journey to Edinburgh to plead Robert's case to the Lord Advocate in person.

She also hoped to God that when she *did* set out, Simon would be heading in the opposite direction—to Edinburgh. If she encountered him alone on the road somewhere... She shuddered and pushed the gut-wrenching thought determinedly away.

As soon as dawn broke, Jessie gathered up her satchel and what remained of Robert's belongings—Mary and her sister helped with the saddlebags—then descended to the inn's vestibule. To her surprise, she found a young Black Watchman waiting for her.

"Miss Munroe," he said with a polite bow, his cheeks slightly pink. "My name is Corporal MacGillie. I hope ye dinna mind, but Captain MacTaggart asked me to escort ye safely to Edinburgh."

"Oh." Tears pricked Jessie's eyes at the knowledge MacTaggart was still looking out for her. She had not expected such support and suddenly felt quite overwhelmed. "Thank you, but I think it would be best if I returned to Lochrose Castle. I need to see Lord Strathburn."

The Watchman's brow crinkled in confusion. "Oh, I thought ye knew. The earl is heading to Edinburgh as well, via the Pass of Drumochter. Captain MacTaggart mentioned he was traveling that way before we set out from Lochrose. With any luck, we might cross paths with his lordship on the road south to Perth. I assume ye'll want to head that way too?"

Jessie blinked in surprise. If Captain MacTaggart had mentioned that last night, it might have spared her quite a bit of worry. But then, perhaps he'd been prevented from saying too much in front of Simon.

She thanked Corporal MacGillie for the information.

"'Tis no trouble, miss," the young man said with a bashful smile. "It seems Lord Lochrose settled yer account last night when ye arrived, and I've had yer horse brought round already. So if ye're ready to leave..."

Jessie nodded, swallowing back another wave of grateful tears. "Aye, of course, Corporal MacGillie. Let us be on our way."

They made good time. The road south of Invercauld was much better maintained than the previous stretch Jessie had traveled along the day before with Robert. She and Corporal MacGillie managed to reach the outskirts of Pitlochry just as dusk was descending.

They'd started to round a bend in the road in a wooded stretch by the luscious banks of the river Tummel, when Jessie heard the unmistakable crunch of carriage wheels approaching. Slowing Blaeberry's pace, she veered close to the grassy verge just as a fine carriage pulled by four fine bays appeared around the corner.

As the carriage drew alongside, Jessie immediately noticed the Strathburn coat of arms emblazoned on the oaken carriage door. Relief surged, especially when she sighted Lord Strathburn peering out, his eyes wide with surprise. Within a few moments, the carriage had drawn to a halt and the earl's man, MacGowan, had jumped down from his position beside the driver and had thrown open Lord Strathburn's door.

"Miss Munroe, my lord would see you," he called.

Jessie urged Blaeberry over to the carriage and MacGowan helped her to dismount.

"My dear, Miss Munroe, come inside at once and tell me what has happened," urged the earl, his face creased with anxiety. "Where is Robert? Dear Lord, has Simon intercepted you?"

"Yes milord, I'm afraid so." Jessie took a seat in the carriage opposite the gray-faced nobleman and a glowering Lady Strathburn. She noticed the earl had a white-knuckle grip about the silver head of his walking stick and there were dark shadows beneath his worried eyes. Lady Strathburn, on the other hand, appeared deeply affronted by Jessie's "intrusion." The woman remained steadfastly silent, her lips drawn tight in a thin line, her gaze as grim and unwelcoming as any Highland granite peak.

Whilst relieved to have come across Lord Strathburn so soon, Jessie was also saddened to be the bearer of bad news. Ignoring the countess, she turned to the earl to explain all that had transpired. "Captain MacTaggart thinks Robert will be taken to the Tolbooth," she concluded.

"I think he may be right, my dear," said Lord Strathburn on a deep sigh. "I only pray the dragoons do not mistreat him. Do you know what happened to my letter addressed to the Lord Advocate?"

"It was no' with Robert's things at the inn, milord," replied Jessie. "I believe that Robert kept it in his coat. He must have had it with him when he was arrested."

"Perhaps it will help him in some small measure until I can speak with Lord Arniston myself," said Lord Strathburn. "It was foolhardy of me to send you both away on your own, especially after your"—he glanced at Lady Strathburn before returning his attention to Jessie—"inopportune encounter with Simon before you left Lochrose. I heard everything from Simon himself. As soon as he declared that he would pursue you and Robert, I knew I must follow straightaway. I may be frail, but I simply cannot let Simon play judge, jury, and executioner all over again." The earl leaned forward and squeezed Jessie's hand. "You have been very brave to come this far all by yourself."

Jessie smiled. "No' quite on my own. Thanks to you and Captain MacTaggart, I've been well looked after. After Robert was taken, MacTaggart arranged for Corporal MacGillie"—she gestured toward the young Watchman outside—"to escort me the rest of the way to Edinburgh."

Lord Strathburn nodded. "MacTaggart is a good man. I've always been able to rely on him to do the right thing. Thank God I managed to get word to him about what was afoot before he and his men left Lochrose. Even so, I wonder that you did not have more trouble with Simon."

At this comment, Lady Strathburn threw a withering look her husband's way. "Really, William. As if Simon would trouble himself with *her*."

Lord Strathburn scowled. "Don't be ridiculous, Caroline. You know how entrenched your son's proclivities are. I suggest you pay more respect to Miss Munroe. Need I remind you that she will soon be your step-daughter-in-law?"

"Yes. So you keep telling me." Lady Strathburn glared at Jessie, her gray eyes glacial with hostility before she turned away to contemplate the scenery outside her carriage window.

Jessie sighed heavily. It was going to be a very long and uncomfortable journey.

The earl, ever perceptive, caught Jessie's eye and winked. "You must be exhausted, my dear child, and we have a long way to travel yet. But we will stop in Pitlochry to have dinner and change horses so we can continue throughout the night. The sooner we reach Edinburgh, the better."

Jessie smiled back at Lord Strathburn, grateful for his unfailing kindness. She couldn't have agreed more.

CHAPTER 20

Strathburn House, The Canongate, Edinburgh

Night had well descended when the Strathburn carriage reached the earl's townhouse in Edinburgh two days later. At the outskirts of the city, MacGowan had been sent on ahead to ensure the staff had made the house ready for their arrival. The brownstone, three-storied residence—rather grander than many of the other closely cramped buildings along the Royal Mile—was located at the end of Auldgate Close, a small cobble-stoned courtyard just off the Canongate and only a short distance from the Palace of Holyroodhouse. In fact, from what Jessie could recall from a previous trip to the capital to visit her cousin, the Tolbooth Prison was also within walking distance of Strathburn House—scarcely a half mile up the hill.

When Jessie stepped from the carriage, she was sorely tempted to turn away from the wide-open doorway no matter how inviting the candlelit vestibule looked beyond. The pull to make her way up the Royal Mile toward the prison was so much stronger. Aside from the fact that her ankle was definitely not up to the task, there was no guarantee Robert had even *reached* Edinburgh yet. She would just have to be patient and wait for tomorrow to find out exactly where he was.

Lord Strathburn had just begun to escort Jessie up the short flight of front stairs—Lady Strathburn had already swept on ahead and disappeared inside the townhouse—when a silhouette appeared in the doorway beside Strathburn House's butler.

"Good evening, dearest Father, Miss Munroe," drawled a familiar voice.

Jessie froze, icy dread spearing through her. Simon stood on the threshold, leaning negligently against the doorframe, a grin that was almost a sneer stretched across his face. Why hadn't it occurred to her that Simon would be staying here, in his family's home, as well? She pressed her lips together, trying to tamp down a burst of breath-stealing panic and frustration. Would she never be free of this man's unwanted attentions?

Yet again she had the impulse to turn and flee up the Mile. Perhaps she could ask for a horse to be brought round and she could make her way to her cousin Maggie's house in the Grassmarket? It surely wasn't far from here. Lord Strathburn would understand.

Simon seemed visibly amused by his disconcerting effect on them both. His grin grew wider as he raised a glass of liquor, possibly brandy, in a mock toast. "Welcome to Edinburgh." He pushed away from the door and affected a clumsy bow. He was clearly more than a wee bit drunk.

Lord Strathburn's arm stiffened beneath Jessie's hand. "What on earth do you think you are doing here under my roof, Simon?" demanded the earl, voice shaking with anger. "What makes you think I would permit you to stay here after what you have done to Robert and Miss Munroe? Your audacity astounds me."

"But, dear Father, I'm not the fugitive on the run, the traitor to the King, the disobedient son. Are you disowning me for simply upholding the *law*?"

Lord Strathburn straightened and pointed his walking stick at Simon. "Get out of my sight," he ground out. "Get out, and do not return until I permit you to do so."

Simon shrugged a shoulder. "No matter. I'm sure the White Horse Inn has a suite of rooms, and no doubt, the innkeeper will accept your name as a guarantee." He passed his glass to the hovering butler. "Fetch my coat, Gordon. I think I fancy a stroll down the Canongate. Oh, and send my man Baird on with my things, will you?"

Coat in hand, Simon deliberately brushed past Jessie as he descended the stairs, his breath hot and fetid in her ear. "I'll be sure to blow a kiss up the hill to where your beloved resides, sweet Jezebel. Sleep well, sister-to-be."

Jessie closed her eyes and shuddered—but as the sound of Simon's footsteps faded into the cold dark night, she smiled to herself. At least she now knew Robert was definitely here.

She would be able to see him tomorrow.

Despite her anxiety about Robert's fate over the past few days—who knew how the dragoons had treated him?—Jessie quickly descended into an exhausted sleep once she retired for the evening.

Lord Strathburn had seen to it that she was accommodated in one of the townhouse's well-appointed guest rooms. A young maid named Alison had even been assigned to act as her lady's maid. As an added precaution against any attempted nocturnal visits by Simon—who undoubtedly still had his own set of keys to the townhouse—the earl had ordered that the maid spend the night on a pallet bed in her room. It was a gesture much appreciated by Jessie, and she hoped the maid didn't mind.

Jessie was not certain if Alison or any of the other household staff had been told of her betrothal to Robert, or of his capture and imprisonment. On arrival, she had simply been introduced as Miss Munroe without further explanation. Although she suspected Simon would have crowed about his brother's dramatic fall from grace to all and sundry.

When Jessie rose early next morning, she was delighted to discover that a small traveling trunk containing some of her things—undergarments, several gowns, and another pair of shoes—had been delivered to her room. According to Alison's intelligence via MacGowan, Lord Strathburn had arranged for one of Lochrose's maids to pack the trunk at the Gate House prior to their departure. She would never be able to thank the earl enough for his thoughtfulness, but she would certainly try.

But first, she had other things to attend to. Her priority was to do anything she could to aid Robert, and that would require a walk up the Mile to the Tolbooth.

Fortunately, her ankle was much improved. The gash on her upper arm was also continuing to heal well beneath Robert's careful stitches. Alison's eyes had widened in surprise when she'd seen the wound but she did not remark on it, much to Jessie's relief. Instead, the maid quietly fetched a pitcher of warm water and after gently bathing the wound, applied some lavender oil and a fresh strip of linen.

Once Jessie's arm was re-bandaged, Alison had then assisted her to wash and don her Sunday-best gown—a becoming one of royal blue wool, trimmed with black velvet at the neckline, cuffs, and around the hem. It was only a little worn at the elbows, and hopefully the creases that had resulted from it being bundled up in a trunk would soon fall out.

Alison also seemed to have a remarkable talent for styling hair. The young girl quickly and effortlessly arranged Jessie's unruly curls into a becoming upswept style with a few curling tendrils artfully escaping about her neck. Aside from the slight blue smudges of fatigue under her worried eyes, Jessie thought the young woman staring back at her from the looking glass looked decidedly civilized—a far cry from the travel-stained, careworn character she'd become over the past few days. Not that her appearance mattered to her that much. But she did wish to appear at her best when she next encountered the earl.

And of course, when she went to visit Robert.

Robert... Jessie's heart clenched with both trepidation and joy every time she thought of the man. *Her* man. The need to see him, to hold him, to make sure he was all right was a constant ache.

But the anxiety she suffered would be nothing compared to what Robert must be enduring. Aside from having to deal with the horror of being incarcerated, he would no doubt be tormented with worry about her fate as well. She was certain Simon would have taunted him with lies about what had happened to her, the brute. But if she could see Robert today, she could at least put his mind to rest on that score.

As Alison fussed about her hair, adding extra pins to her curls here and there, Jessie couldn't help but smile at the memory of her last few hours alone with Robert. She did not regret a single moment. Never before had she felt so wanted and—she hardly dared to think the word —so loved. In her heart of hearts, she would secretly acknowledge that she wanted Robert to be pardoned more than anything. Though Lord Strathburn had bound her and Robert together due to some misguided sense of propriety, she would hold to her vows of handfasting, come what may.

She just prayed Robert felt the same way.

At any rate, she would soon find out...if her plan for the morning worked out.

"Ye look lovely, miss," offered Alison shyly as she finished nestling a black velvet ribbon in amongst Jessie's curls. "If ye dinna mind me saying, I think yer intended will think so too. Are ye going to see him up the Mile today?"

Jessie found herself blushing. "How did you ken about my engagement to Lord Lochrose?"

Deep color stained Alison's already rosy cheeks and she began fiddling with the tendrils around Jessie's neck. The girl was clearly embarrassed as well. "Ah...Mrs. Bowie, our cook, has been speaking with Lord Strathburn's man, MacGowan. I'm sorry, miss, if I've offended ye with my prattle. Lady Strathburn doesna like the staff to gossip."

"It's all right, Alison." Jessie was quick to reassure the maid. She did not want the girl—she couldn't have been older than seventeen or eighteen—to get in trouble with the countess on her account. "But perhaps I could ask ye to help me this morning...?"

Alison's reflection nodded.

"We will need to be discreet," Jessie cautioned.

"Of course, Miss Munroe. I willna breathe a word."

~

The hall clock on the landing of the stairs was striking eight when Alison led Jessie to the kitchens below.

"Are ye sure ye only want a cup o' tea and an oatcake?" queried the middle-aged cook, Mrs. Bowie.

She seemed more than a little bemused to find the earl's guest visiting her kitchen, but when Jessie explained her plan, the good woman was more than happy to fulfill her requests. Jessie was delighted to discover that the cook was in fact the younger sister of Mrs. MacMillan—it certainly explained the similarity in facial features and welcoming manner. Jessie could not help but hope that the woman was just as good a cook as Mrs. MacMillan.

A short time later, a small basket laden with food on her arm and her purse tucked into the pocket attached to her petticoats—no doubt guineas would be needed to gain entry into the Tolbooth—Jessie quietly left Strathburn House with Alison accompanying her.

The morning was chill and gray as they stepped onto the busy Royal Mile. At the bottom of the hill, Jessie could see the elegant spires of Holyrood Palace, the former headquarters of the foolish Bonnie Prince Charlie. To the south-east towered the sheer cliffs of Salisbury Crags and Arthur's Seat.

Blowing out a sigh, Jessie turned and faced uphill where the brooding bulk of Edinburgh Castle loomed at the very top of the Royal Mile. Robert was somewhere up there in the Tolbooth. He was so close, yet all of a sudden seemed so very far away.

As she set off with Alison, Jessie pulled her black traveling cloak tightly around herself to ward off the biting wind that whipped down the hill and caught at her skirts and hair. It had rained overnight and the cobblestones were slippery. While they'd been washed clean of some of the mud and filth that usually filled the gutters, she would need to take care that she didn't slip and twist her sprained ankle now it seemed to be improving. Their progress up the Mile would not be as swift as she would have liked.

"Miss, perhaps...perhaps we could secure a pair of sedan chairs to take us up the hill," suggested Alison. She'd obviously noticed her new mistress's limp. "Lady Strathburn has a verra good sedan, but I dinna think she would be inclined to let ye use it. But with yer sore ankle and all...weel, the hired chairs are not verra expensive. It willna take more than a wee moment to hail one or two."

"Sedan chairs. What an excellent idea." Jessie cast Alison a smile. She didn't know why she hadn't thought of it herself. Edinburgh's closes and wynds were often so narrow and winding, particularly in this part of the capital, it was almost impossible for a horse-drawn vehicle of any kind to negotiate them. But sedan chairs could go practically anywhere. She'd never taken one before, to be sure, but if it saved her from having to negotiate the hill with a sprained ankle, she was more than happy to hire one with a little of her coin.

As Alison predicted, it didn't take long for two burly chairmen to trot by with an empty sedan chair suspended between them on sturdy wooden poles. The men stopped at Alison's call, a fee to their destination was agreed upon, and Jessie climbed through the door at the front into the small space to take a seat. Once she'd seen that Alison was climbing into a second sedan chair, Jessie indicated that she was ready to set off, and they did. Indeed, her pair of chairmen took off at a cracking pace up the hill, weaving their way through the bustling crowd of pedestrians, other sedan chairs, open carts, and carriages also traveling up and down the steep thoroughfare.

The towering spire of St Giles Cathedral was sounding the nine o'clock bell when her sedan stopped at the gates of the grim Tolbooth Prison. Jessie climbed out, settled the fee with the chairmen, and stared up at the imposing gray brick edifice whilst she waited for Alison to arrive. Somewhere, locked inside these cold and miserable stone walls, was Robert.

She clutched her cloak around her and bit her lip, suddenly beset by a wave of despair and stomach-churning nervousness. What could she possibly say to the prison guards that would make them admit her to see Robert? She didn't even know if there were visiting hours, or if visitors were allowed at all. She should have waited for Lord Strathburn.

"Are ye all right, miss?" Alison was at her shoulder. Jessie hadn't even noticed the maid's arrival.

"I... I'm no' sure if the guards will permit me to visit Lord Lochrose." Heart sinking, Jessie turned away from the iron gates and looked back down the street toward the Canongate. "I fear I've acted too hastily. Perhaps we should go."

Alison stepped closer to Jessie and lowered her voice. "Now dinna fret, miss." The corners of her mouth lifted into a conspiratorial smile. "I should've mentioned before, my Uncle Angus is the head warden here. He'll make sure the turnkey lets us in, dinna ye worry. Just let me do the asking. Ye'll see."

The maid was as good as her word. She spoke with the sentry on duty and within a few minutes Angus McDonald, Alison's uncle, was ushering them through the gates and into the dark and fetid interior of the jail.

Jessie held her cloak to her nose to try and dissipate the rank stench around them as she followed Mr. MacDonald down shadow-filled corridors and up narrow, twisting stairwells. Truth be told, her stomach became increasingly knotted and unsettled the farther they progressed. It could have been the frigid, foul air that made her feel so, or the pitiful moans and desperate calls emanating from behind the bolted cell doors.

Her heart ached at the thought of Robert, and the many other poor souls, locked up in these inhumane, squalid conditions. She silently prayed her *fiancé* would soon be released from this hellish place.

Before too long, they emerged onto a fourth-floor landing that was relatively well lit compared to the lower stories. The air was remarkably fresher too. Surprisingly, there was only one guard on duty on this level. He stood by the iron-barred door where they'd entered, and after a quick cursory search of Jessie's food basket, he escorted them down the narrow corridor.

As Jessie passed a barred window, she could see down below to the bleak cobblestones of Parliament Square where the convicted were executed at the Mercat Cross. Her cousin had once told her that in the case of beheadings, the victim's heads were displayed on spikes along the north wall of the square. There were no such obscene displays today at least. Jessie shivered and hurried on.

"Here we are then, miss," Mr. MacDonald said almost jovially to Jessie when they stopped before one of the doors. But then he frowned as he observed her face. "Ye are verra pale, miss." He turned to his niece. "Ye ken, I'm surprised ye didna think to bring summat sweet smelling with ye, Alison. Ye should ken better than that. Yer mistress here looks as if she's about to faint dead away."

"I'm quite fine," said Jessie quickly, afraid Alison's uncle would suddenly curtail her visit if he thought she couldn't cope. "How long can I visit with Lord Lochrose?"

"A quarter of an hour 'tis all that's permitted I'm afraid, lass," he replied. "Mr. Cameron"—he gestured at the guard with his chin—"the door if ye please."

The guard did as he was bid. "Lochrose, rise n' shine. Ye have company," he announced unceremoniously into the gloom beyond. "I hope ye're decent. They're ladies."

Her knees trembling, Jessie stepped forward and peered into the dark interior. Although the cell was larger than she'd expected, its only source of light was a high, narrow-barred window that let in a thin strip of weak gray light. In the far-left corner, obscured by shadow, she discerned movement. *Robert.*

He was seated on a narrow bunk, rubbing his hands down his face as if he'd just woken. His voice was husky with sleep as he said her name. "Jessie?"

Jessie wanted to go to Robert, throw her arms around him, but she stayed hovering in the doorway, suddenly unsure of herself...and of him. In the dim light, it was difficult to discern his expression.

"Aye, Robert, 'tis I," she murmured, her voice cracking. She took another tentative step into the cell at the same moment Robert rose to his feet. She could see his features now, and her heart clenched. Her *fiancé* looked drawn. Brooding. His jaw was covered in thick stubble and his unbound hair tumbled across his forehead and onto his shoulders. Despite his dishevelment, or perhaps because of it, he was both darkly handsome and forbidding, all at once.

She was about to close the short distance between them, but Robert's next words halted her, taking her completely aback.

"Christ, Jessie. I can't believe you're here." He pushed his hair away from his face with a shaking hand, his gaze raking over her. He was frowning, clearly shocked. "You shouldn't have come."

Jessie's breath hitched. She opened her mouth to speak but the words jammed in her throat.

He didn't want her here. What had she been thinking? Perhaps he'd meant to leave her at the inn in Invercauld after all. She'd obviously been mistaken about his feelings for her.

Hot tears scalded her eyelids. She knew she should go, but she couldn't move. She was frozen to the spot by Robert's penetrating blue gaze.

She felt Alison at her elbow. "Lord Lochrose," the maid said, taking the basket from Jessie and depositing it just inside the cell door, "Miss Munroe thought ye might like some provisions to...to make yer stay more comfortable."

Robert acknowledged the maid with a quick nod before she beat a hasty retreat into the corridor. Then, within the space of a heartbeat, he took a handful of strides toward Jessie and gathered her into his arms, burying his face in her hair.

"Jessie, Jessie my love," he murmured against her ear. One of his hands stroked up the length of her back before his fingers curled about her nape. "I'm such an idiot. I didn't mean I didn't want to see you. I...I just can't believe you would set foot in this godforsaken prison. After all you've been through, this is the last place I would want you to be. You simply could have sent word to me that you were here in Edinburgh."

Jessie drew a ragged sigh, relief flooding through her as she sagged against Robert. He'd called her *my love*. He cared for her. He was worried about her. She pressed her damp cheek into his linen shirt, breathing in the musky scent of him, drinking in the warmth of his hard chest as he crushed her against his body.

"I wanted to see that ye were all right," she whispered. "I just had to know."

Robert gently pushed her away from him, his eyes searching hers. "You had to know if *I* was all right," he said, shaking his head. The corner of his wide beautiful mouth curved up into the lopsided half smile she adored so much. "Jessie, if you only knew how worried I've been about you. At the inn, when Simon had me arrested, he knew you were there also. I've been going mad, not knowing what happened to you." Robert's eyes sparked with blue fire and his grip on her grew harder. "Tell me, Jessie, did he touch you? Did he hurt you? I have to know. Because if he did…" The unspoken, deadly intent was clear in Robert's expression.

Jessie reached out to stroke his stubbled cheek, relieved she could put his tortured mind to rest. "He didna hurt me, Robert." She quickly explained what had happened at the inn—how MacTaggart had woken her to warn her about his arrest and Simon's imminent visit, and then how the chivalrous Watchman had protected her. "If it hadna been for Captain MacTaggart, I can barely stand to think what might have happened. I was hoping he'd somehow gotten word to ye to let ye know that I was safe. He must have been prevented from doing so."

Robert raised a sardonic eyebrow. "Simon's interference no doubt. I'll make sure my father gives the good captain a commendation. If I ever get to see my father again, that is…"

Jessie smiled, her heart lighter with every passing breath. "Yer father is here in Edinburgh, Robert. He left Lochrose with yer stepmother soon after Simon mounted his pursuit. He suspected trouble and wanted to be able to plead yer case in person with the Lord Advocate if it should come to that. Which indeed, it has."

"How do you know all this?" asked Robert smoothing one of her wayward curls behind her ear.

Jessie closed her eyes briefly, relishing Robert's gentle touch before she answered his question. "After ye were taken, I decided to travel back to Lochrose to ask yer father for help. But I learned that he was on his way to Edinburgh and as luck would have it, I met him along the road near Pitlochry. I journeyed the rest o' the way here in his carriage and stayed at yer family's townhouse in Auldgate Close last night."

Robert's eyes narrowed with concern. "And where precisely did Simon stay? He's here in Edinburgh attempting to orchestrate my demise no doubt."

"Yer father ordered him away as soon as we arrived," she replied, smoothing her hand against his cheek. "He was intending to secure lodgings at the White Horse Inn."

"Hmm, I knew my dear brother would be lurking somewhere close to gloat over my misfortune," said Robert with a cynical twist to his smile. Turning his back on the guard just outside the door, he suddenly pulled Jessie hard against him and pressed a kiss to her forehead. "You should go, my love," he murmured. "You've lingered long enough in this dreadful place."

"There's no place I'd rather be right now," Jessie whispered, turning her face upward, willing Robert to kiss her. She didn't care that Alison and the guard waited nearby.

It seemed Robert didn't either. She saw the smile in his eyes in the moment before he lowered his head to take her willing mouth in his.

Who'd have thought heaven could be found in a jail cell? Jessie sighed and melted into Robert, parting her lips as his tongue gently explored her mouth with slow, deep, tantalizing strokes. She cradled his roughly bristled jaw, winding her fingers into his dark hair, pulling him closer, wanting this bittersweet kiss full of promise and yearning to go on and on, to never end. All the while she prayed this would not be their last kiss.

But all too soon, Robert gently untangled her hands from his hair and broke the contact of their mouths. Like her, he was slightly breathless...and smiling.

The guard pointedly cleared his throat. "Time's up, I'm afraid, Lochrose," he called.

Jessie felt herself blushing. She reluctantly stepped away from Robert, but he did not release her hands.

"Goodbye, my beloved," he murmured as he kissed her fingertips.

"Do no' say goodbye, Robert." Jessie put a finger to his lips. "I couldna bear it if this was goodbye. Ye will be pardoned. I'm certain of it." With great effort, she withdrew from Robert's embrace and moved toward the door. When she turned to look at him one last time, he smiled. Then the guard swung the cell door shut.

The resounding clang seemed as final as any death knell.

Alison touched her arm. "Come on, miss."

Jessie followed the girl along the corridor to where her uncle waited to escort them out. Catching sight of the Mercat Cross again, Jessie paused. As an unbidden image of Robert kneeling before the execution-er's block appeared in her mind, pain lanced through her heart and tears stung her eyes. *Robert couldn't die.* She did not think she could bear it.

And then she realized with heart stopping certainty that she was in love with this man.

Completely and utterly.

No matter that they'd only spent a few days together. She knew she was in love with him as surely as night follows day.

Then and there, she decided to do whatever was within her power to save Robert from a traitor's death, even if that meant pleading with the Lord Advocate himself. And before she returned to Strathburn House, she would visit St Giles and pray for Robert with all her heart and soul. It was the least she could do.

CHAPTER 21

When Jessie returned to the townhouse in Auldgate Close, she found Lord Strathburn had already been busy making arrangements of his own—to meet with the Lord Advocate.

"Two o'clock this afternoon, Jessie my dear, that's when we'll get this all sorted out," he announced with a smile when she entered the drawing room.

To her surprise the earl looked remarkably well, despite the long and exhausting journey from Lochrose. Indeed, ever since Robert's return, it appeared that a great burden had been lifted from the old man's shoulders. There was now a twinkle in his eyes and a healthy color in his face. Although it was puzzling in the extreme that Lord Strathburn did not seem the least bit concerned his son was incarcerated, awaiting trial for treason. Jessie marveled at his absolute certainty that everything would work out.

"So, I hear you have been to visit Robert," the earl said, gesturing for her to take a seat opposite him before the fire. "You were very brave to go there, my child. How did you find him? I trust young Alison's uncle, Angus, is looking after him?"

Jessie nodded, impressed by Lord Strathburn's intelligence. "He seems well enough, my lord." Her brow furrowed with concern. "But I believe he's worried that he willna be so easily pardoned. As am I."

Lord Strathburn smiled reassuringly. "As I've mentioned before, Lord Arniston and I are very good friends. He will be sure to secure a pardon from the King. And while we wait for that, I'm sure he will release Robert into my custody. By this evening, he will be here with us in Strathburn House, just you wait and see."

"Oh yes, I can hardly wait." Lady Strathburn's voice dripped with sarcasm as she glided into the room.

Jessie immediately rose to her feet and bobbed a small curtsy as the countess installed herself in the wingback chair beside her husband. As Lady Strathburn smoothed the skirts of her jade green silk gown, Jessie was reminded of a deadly snake, poising itself to strike.

Sure enough, she did not have to wait long for one of the woman's venomous comments. Fixing her frost-laden gaze on Jessie, Lady Strathburn's thin lips twisted into what could only be described as a cruel smile. "I'm looking forward to Robert's return almost as much as your marriage to my stepson, Miss Munroe. A Jacobite traitor and a factor's daughter. Won't that be the social event of the season?"

Heat crept into Jessie's cheeks as she hovered by her chair, uncertain whether to stay or go after receiving such an insult. Humiliation and rising anger tangled up inside her. She was already highly aware that she was marrying above her station, but she didn't appreciate being addressed in such a contemptuous fashion. And she especially didn't want to hear Robert being slighted.

Lord Strathburn glared at his wife. "Now see here—"

"My dearest husband," Lady Strathburn cut in, seemingly unconcerned by the earl's irritation, "when will you allow our other son to return home, seeing as you unceremoniously cast him out into the streets last night?"

Lord Strathburn rose to his feet and looked down upon his wife, his eyes narrowed to thin slits. "When hell freezes over, as far as I'm concerned," he grated out, his voice shaking with scarcely concealed contempt and fury. "After all the lies and betrayal, not to mention his dissolute ways, Simon will be lucky to even get an allowance off me.

And I'll thank you to remember just who funds your extravagant ways also, *my lady*." The earl flicked the hem of his wife's lavishly flounced skirts with his walking stick.

Lady Strathburn's face grew visibly paler beneath her powder. For once, the malicious glitter in her eyes was replaced with a look of fear.

The scene was almost too much for Jessie to witness. She swallowed and looked away, awkwardness prickling along her skin. Even though the countess certainly deserved to be brought down a peg or two, Jessie felt conspicuous. Like an intruder.

Still seemingly oblivious to Jessie's presence, the earl continued, "Yes, you had better bite your viper's tongue, dear wife, or you'll soon find yourself mucking in with the horses in nothing but a burlap sack." Finished, with his scolding, he crossed over to Jessie and offered her his arm to escort her from the room.

When Jessie chanced a fleeting glance back at Lady Strathburn, the undisguised look of hatred the woman shot her filled her heart with foreboding. She feared that when the viper struck again, it would be far worse than a barbed comment.

It didn't take long for Lady Strathburn to retaliate. Not long after Jessie retired to her bedchamber to rest a little before the appointment at Parliament Hall with the Lord Advocate, the countess entered her room without knocking, taking Jessie completely by surprise.

She rose from her shepherdess chair hurriedly and curtsied. "Milady?" she enquired. Apprehension trickled like ice water down her spine.

Lady Strathburn raked her with a disdainful gaze, looking at Jessie as if she were something repulsive which had become stuck on the sole of her well-heeled shoe. "I have no idea what Lord Strathburn sees in you. Or how you have bewitched him," she began coldly.

Calm, Jessie. She bit her tongue, certain that if she said anything, it would contain more than a few choice expletives. Lady Strathburn was clearly determined to belittle her and put her back in what *she* considered to be her rightful place—that of the hired help. Even though she knew it would provoke the countess, Jessie couldn't resist the urge to raise her chin defiantly.

Lady Strathburn didn't miss the silent insult. She narrowed her eyes, her stare positively poisonous. "I can understand to a degree why my own son wishes to...dally with you," she continued. "You obviously possess certain attributes—quite tawdry and obvious in my opinion—that men find alluring. But the thought of *you* as my daughter-in-law, the wife of Viscount Lochrose, is quite laughable."

Even though heat scorched Jessie's cheeks, she was determined this woman would not intimidate her. She had nothing to be ashamed of. "Well, yer husband and my Lord Lochrose obviously disagree with you, milady," she replied tightly.

Lady Strathburn smirked. "Oh, you think you have made quite a catch, don't you? If my stepson escapes the executioner's axe, that is. But what do you really know about your betrothed, Miss Jessie Munroe?" She took a few swift steps closer and grasped Jessie's upper arm, her fingers cruelly digging into the soft flesh right where Jessie's bullet wound lay.

Jessie gasped and tried, without success, to pull away. Tears of pain welled.

Lady Strathburn's face was an ugly leering mask. "Did you know your beloved Robert was quite the rakehell, just like his brother Simon? Before the Rebellion, I couldn't count the number of young women my stepson bedded then discarded. What makes you think it will be any different for you? From what I hear, my husband forced Robert into this ludicrous betrothal in a vain attempt to curb his tomcat tendencies. Robert may think you a comely lass, but once he's had you—if he hasn't already—he'll soon grow tired of you. Just like my Simon will."

The countess abruptly released Jessie's arm then sashayed to the door, jade silk skirts practically hissing as they swept across the floor. She paused on the threshold and flicked one last barb Jessie's way. "It's my hope that you won't even be wed to begin with. Either Robert will be executed, or he'll come to his senses and end this farce of an engagement. In any event, I won't have to suffer your presence in my household any longer."

Only when the door slammed shut did Jessie give in to the quaking in her legs. Sinking back onto her chair, she pressed her trembling fingers to her lips. The strength of Lady Strathburn's animosity terrified her right down to her very bones. Indeed, what lengths would this woman go to, to remove her and perhaps even Robert, from her life?

One thing was certain: Jessie did *not* want to find out. But she feared that very soon, she just might.

By the time the mantel clock in her bedchamber struck half-past one, Jessie's nerves were stretched as tautly as a bowstring. As she waited beside the earl for the carriage to be brought round to the front of the townhouse, she was grateful Lord Strathburn was happy for her to accompany him to his meeting with the Lord Advocate. Action of any kind felt better than sitting around on tenterhooks, waiting to find out what Robert's fate would be. Action would keep her from dwelling on when Lady Strathburn's axe might fall. And whether Simon might return unexpectedly to Strathburn House too...

Although there was nothing substantial she could do or say to influence the Lord Advocate's decision to grant Robert clemency, the earl had been quick to assure her that her presence would make a difference.

"I happen to know that Lord Arniston would find it difficult to resist the request of one so fair," he said with a reassuring smile once they were both installed in the carriage. "And as long as Robert expresses a suitable amount of contrition and the intent to settle down, a pardon will be granted. I'm certain of it."

The trip to Parliament Hall, located directly across from St Giles Cathedral and the Tolbooth Prison, flew by. The carriage drew to a halt on the cobbled square before an equestrian statue of the mounted form of King Charles II.

It was with no small degree of apprehension that Jessie stared up at the Parliament's grim gray brick façade. The dour-faced, black-robed and white-wigged court officials bustling in and out of the main entrance did not instill a feeling of confidence within Jessie either. She consciously tried to slow her breathing and relax her fingers as she gripped the handle of the carriage door.

Lord Strathburn leaned forward and squeezed her other hand. "Courage, dear child. All will be well."

On alighting from the carriage, Lord Strathburn and Jessie were immediately greeted by a bewigged and elegantly robed gentleman who introduced himself as the secretary of the Lord Advocate. He was to escort them both to Lord Arniston's chambers.

If Jessie had been less nervous, she would have been able to admire the high vaulted ceiling of oak beams and magnificent stained-glass windows as they traversed the main hall of the Parliament building. As it was, it took some effort—given the earl's tendency to become short of breath and Jessie's still considerably sore ankle—for them to keep apace with the secretary as he led them through a series of corridors and up a flight of grand stairs to another hall. Eventually, they halted before a set of grand oak doors guarded by a pair of scarlet-coated Scots Guards. At a silent nod from the secretary, one of the soldiers swung the doors wide to permit their entry into the room beyond.

It appeared to be a waiting room or antechamber of sorts, elegantly appointed with leather and heavy oak furniture. Floor-to-ceiling bookshelves lined two of the walls. A small fireplace, flanked by two tall windows, permitted a narrow view of the spire of St Giles silhouetted against a bleak gray sky.

The secretary indicated that they should take a seat by the fire before he disappeared behind another door at the far end of the chamber. Heart slamming against her ribs, Jessie lowered herself onto one of the leather wingchairs, hoping they wouldn't have to wait too long for Lord Arniston to make an appearance. The suspense was playing havoc with her exhausted nerves.

Lord Strathburn mopped his brow with a silk kerchief. "A cup of tea right about now wouldn't go astray would it, my dear?"

Jessie nodded absently but seriously doubted if her stomach was in any fit state to partake of anything. Aside from being a wee bit puffed, Lord Strathburn showed no other sign of being ill at ease. She was more than a little envious of his self-possession.

Jessie had begun to count the Scottish thistle motifs in the molded plaster ceiling above her head when the sudden click of a latch made her jump. Her mouth dry, her palms damp, she rose in a rush of skirts just as a distinguished looking gentleman attired in an elegantly coiffed wig and robes of office entered the room.

It was undoubtedly the Lord Advocate himself, Robert Dundas, Lord Arniston.

Although her legs shook, she swept into a low curtsy. This man was King George's representative in Scotland. *And he held Robert's life in his hands.*

"William Grant," Lord Arniston intoned in a resonating baritone as he strode toward them. "It's been far too long since we've seen each other." He grasped Lord Strathburn's hand firmly and pumped it in a hearty shake before turning his penetrating gaze to Jessie. "Ah, and if I'm not mistaken, you must be Lord Strathburn's soon-to-be daughter-in-law, Miss Munroe."

"Aye... Aye, I am, milord." Astonished that Lord Arniston clearly knew who she was, *and* that she was betrothed to Robert, Jessie somehow managed to gather her composure enough to smile as Lord Arniston bowed over her hand. But how on earth did the Lord Advocate know such particular things about her when they'd never met before. Perhaps the earl had mentioned her name when trading messages with the Lord Advocate to arrange this appointment...

But the earl looked equally confused by Lord Arniston's uncanny intelligence. "Yes, this is indeed Miss Jessie Munroe. But if you don't mind my asking, how did you know?"

The Advocate turned to look at his friend, keen amusement lighting his eyes. "Believe me, there is very little that occurs around here that escapes my attention, Strathburn." Jessie's heart leapt at the wily Lord Advocate's next comment. "Now, my friend, I suppose we had better release your wayward son into your custody, so he can settle down and wed this bonnie lass."

Lord Strathburn looked even more dumbfounded. "But—but I was expecting—"

"To plead Robert's case for his past transgressions against King and country?" Lord Arniston patted his friend on the shoulder while continuing to smile, his manner jovial. "When I heard Robert Grant, Viscount Lochrose and the Master of Strathburn, the eldest son of one of my oldest friends had been installed in the Tolbooth, I arranged to have an interview with him. I'd already sighted your handwritten appeal for clemency, and I must say, Lord Lochrose pled his own case very well. I was very impressed by his honesty when confessing his part in the Rebellion. It was obvious he deeply regrets his involvement. And of course, now he's made a pledge to be a loyal subject to His Majesty the King, I see no reason to hold him to account for the rash misdeeds of a decade ago when he was barely a man."

Jessie could hardly believe what the Lord Advocate was saying. *Robert was to be released.* The decision had already been made to grant him clemency.

His life was to be spared.

A heady combination of relief and nervous excitement bubbled through Jessie as swiftly as the swirling torrent of a Highland burn. This meant she and Robert were undoubtedly going to be married. Her gaze darted to Lord Strathburn, seeking his reaction to this astounding good news.

There were tears in the earl's dark blue eyes as he grasped Lord Arniston's hand. "I cannot thank you enough for your tolerance and understanding, my friend. You have made an old man, who'd given up hope of ever seeing his son again, so very happy."

Lord Arniston beamed his pleasure and summoned his secretary to bring the required custody documents for Lord Strathburn to sign immediately. They all sat in the leather chairs before the fire while the earl perused the papers.

"Now, Strathburn, you will see when you read this document that your son is being released into your custody. He is, in fact, on probation for the next year and a day." Lord Arniston's tone was now all business. Despite his previously affable manner, Jessie could now see the authority that befit his former position of Solicitor General of Scotland and current position of Advocate.

"You must ensure Lord Lochrose remains a loyal subject to His Majesty, King George, and law-abiding at *all* times forthwith," he continued. "After the required probationary time has passed, he will be granted a full pardon by His Majesty. And I must say, the fact Lord Lochrose will soon wed this delightful young lady goes a long way to helping his bid for freedom." Lord Arniston threw Jessie a benevolent smile. "There's nothing like the love of a good woman to make a man settle down and reform his wild ways. I trust you find the terms satisfactory, Strathburn?"

"Indeed, I do." Lord Strathburn smiled warmly at his friend then signed the documents with a flourish. "Rest assured, my son will not put a foot wrong from now on."

And as easy as that, Robert's release was secured.

Jessie could hardly believe it. It had all been so quick, so simple. Whilst overwhelming relief and joy that Robert was to be set free still washed through her, an underlying current of uncertainty tugged at her like an undertow. Try as she might, she couldn't suppress the doubts Lady Strathburn had stirred up. If she were truly honest with herself, the same doubts had been on her mind from the very start: that Robert did not really wish to be married and was being forced into this handfasting—first by his father and now, perhaps, even the Lord Advocate.

More than anything, she wanted to learn how Robert really felt about her. Were there any feelings beyond physical attraction and a degree of protectiveness? Did he love her as she loved him? How would it feel to have gained your liberty, only to be trapped in an unwanted marriage?

She didn't want Robert to feel that way. *Trapped.*

After counter-signing the release papers and stamping them with his personal seal in red wax, Lord Arniston rose from his seat and rubbed his hands together in obvious anticipation of what was to come next. "Now we've reached the part of the afternoon that I've been looking forward to the most," he declared and nodded at his secretary who promptly disappeared into the adjoining chamber.

Moments later, the door swung open to reveal Robert.

Jessie's breath caught. For one long moment, her beloved *fiancé* simply stood in the doorway, his expression inscrutable until his deep blue eyes locked with hers. All at once, his features were transformed by a heart-stopping grin and Jessie's pulse took flight. She rose shakily from her seat, wanting with all her heart to rush over and throw her arms about Robert, but conscious of the presence of others, in this most formal of places, she restrained herself.

Instead, she smoothed her skirts and waited, trying in vain to prevent Lady Strathburn's poisonous observations from infecting her thoughts again.

Even so, she couldn't entirely push away the troubling question: did Robert really want her for his wife?

For if he didn't want her, as much as it would disappoint Lord Strathburn and perhaps even her own father—as much as it would pain her—she would walk away. Rather that, than stay and watch Robert tire of her just as Lady Strathburn had predicted.

Jessie resolved that as soon as the opportunity arose for her and Robert to be alone, she would ask him how he really felt.

I'm free.

A wave of pure elation hit Robert when he laid eyes on his father and Jessie. The life he'd missed so much, the future he'd always longed for, was back in his grasp. Swallowing back a surge of joyful tears, he strode across the room toward his father and hugged him warmly before turning to Jessie.

My betrothed. He swept his gaze over her, taking every beloved detail of her in. For a moment he considered throwing caution to the wind— his desire to take Jessie in his arms and kiss her soundly was incredibly strong. But propriety won out. He hardly wanted to create a scene in front of the Lord Advocate and cause Jessie any embarrassment. So he simply caught her hand and placed a soft kiss on her fingertips. There would be plenty of time, indeed all the time in the world, to kiss and take pleasure with his soon-to-be wife.

When he lifted his head and met Jessie's eyes again, he noted a fleeting look—was it diffidence or apprehension?—cross her features, before she smiled uncertainly back at him.

God, he hoped she wasn't having second thoughts about their betrothal—especially now he knew beyond a shadow of a doubt that he was in love with her.

Love?

Yes, he was in love with Jessie Munroe. The realization struck him like a lightning bolt from above. Grinning like an idiot, he shook hands with Lord Arniston then conversed with his father. All the while he was secretly reveling in the potent joy flowing through his veins, swelling his heart.

Jessie may be a little subdued right now, perhaps even a wee bit unsure of him, but it wouldn't be long before they were alone. Then he would chase all her doubts away. He had to. Gaining Jessie's love in return was one campaign Robert definitely wanted to win.

CHAPTER 22

The short carriage ride back to Auldgate Close was exquisite torture for Jessie. Ensconced in the far corner of the leather bench seat, opposite Lord Strathburn, she was in equal measures thrilled and dismayed to find Robert sitting close beside her.

His large masculine frame filled the confined space in a most disconcerting way. Whenever the carriage rounded a sharp corner, his muscular thigh pressed against her leg and she found herself blushing. Indeed, the physical contact brought to mind other lean, hard parts of Robert's naked body, and Jessie had to fight the urge to squirm against the tight ache between her own thighs. It seemed her wanton self had swiftly returned and demanded to be satisfied.

Thank God, both Robert and Lord Strathburn were deeply engaged in conversation about plans for a celebratory dinner that very evening at Strathburn House, so they did not seem to notice her flustered state. Heavens, she needed to harness some semblance of control around Robert. They weren't in an isolated cave or out-of-the-way inn anymore—they were in polite society. She needed to behave with decorum, especially as she was suddenly unsure of his commitment to her.

She willed herself not to dwell on the countess's pronouncements about Robert. The odious woman clearly had her own agenda and would like nothing more than to see them part ways.

But truth to tell, Robert's actions when he'd entered the Lord Advocate's antechamber had confused her. He'd looked happy to see her, and at first, she was certain he would embrace her as he had his father. But in the end, all he'd done was simply kiss her hand as any gentleman of passing acquaintance would. Whilst she could hardly have expected him to greet her with a passionate kiss in the Lord Advocate's office, she wondered why he hadn't displayed a little more affection than that cool perfunctory gesture.

Perhaps Robert *was* having second thoughts about marrying her. *And that's perfectly understandable and it's better to know now,* she told herself, trying to ignore the heavy feeling in her heart. Blinking away the prick of unexpected tears, she looked out the carriage window and tried to think about something, anything else.

But that was proving to be very difficult when Jessie was acutely aware of Robert's every movement and every glance her way. She risked her own peek at him. *If only he wasn't so handsome.* That was part of the problem. Even in a crumpled shirt and mud splattered buckskin breeks, with a three-day growth of whiskers, he looked darkly attractive. Her eyes lingered on his jawline, recalling how his bristles had felt beneath her fingertips and against her cheek when he'd kissed her this very morning—when he'd called her "*my love.*"

And that was the other problem—her memories of being in his arms, his caresses were all too vivid. Her eyes strayed to Robert's lips, wide and firm, curved now in that crooked grin of his that never failed to make her breath catch.

Dear Lord, she must speak with him. She needed to know if she really was his love, or had he just uttered the endearment in a moment of desperate passion when he believed he was going to be executed. It was too difficult to be this close to him, feeling the way she did, and to not know if he really, truly felt the same way.

"Jessie, we're at Strathburn House." Robert's voice broke through her musings and she started. She noticed with some surprise that Lord Strathburn had already started to climb out of the carriage with the assistance of one of the footmen.

"Oh... Ah yes...Thank you," she murmured, finding it difficult to meet Robert's gaze. Instead, she busied herself with gathering her skirts in preparation for alighting from the carriage, hoping Robert wouldn't notice how desperately self-conscious she suddenly felt.

The sooner they spoke in private, the better.

~

Robert frowned. Jessie seemed unusually quiet and distracted. Again, he wondered if she'd begun to be assailed by doubts about their betrothal. Was it too confronting a reality for her now that he'd been released?

Perhaps his desire to wed her—and take her to his bed—was greater than what she felt for him. He would have to be more careful with her, to court her as a gentleman should rather than continue to chase her like a rutting stag.

Mindful of his new resolve, Robert gently curled his hand around Jessie's elbow and helped her negotiate the carriage steps. She was still limping slightly, but he resisted the impulse to sweep her into his arms and carry her inside. Although, once they gained the entrance hall, he paused and caught one of Jessie's hands between his. He couldn't bear this awkward silence. Why, she wouldn't even look at him.

"Jessie lass," he prompted softly. "Is everything all right?"

She lifted her chin and met his gaze with what seemed to be some effort. There were purple shadows like bruises beneath her eyes, and her smile seemed brittle. "Aye, milord," she replied, her tone too formal for his liking. "I am verra tired, that is all."

"I see." Perhaps everything that had transpired over the last few days was just catching up with Jessie—her injuries, the long journey, the constant threat of danger. She must be exhausted. Nevertheless, Robert was still torn between the urge to kiss away her reserve and the need to take care with her. "I am aware that I must appear quite the ruffian at present," he said in a low voice meant only for her. "Perhaps we can agree to meet later, after you've rested and I've had a chance to make myself look more...civilized. Then we can discuss how we both wish to proceed...with our situation. Do you agree?"

Jessie nodded and, to Robert's relief, she smiled up at him.

There was little chance to say more because all at once there was a swarm of people gathering in the entrance hall to greet them—his father and stepmother and a line of the Strathburn House staff.

All, besides Lady Strathburn, were beaming with undisguised pleasure at him and Jessie.

Robert greeted his stepmother smoothly, briefly bowing over her extended hand. "My lady, it has been far too long. You are looking well."

"As charming as ever I see," she replied archly, her gaze flicking past him to settle on Jessie.

It was a narrow, menacing look.

An intimidating look.

Wariness pinpricked its way along Robert's spine. What the devil was his stepmother playing at? He tried to catch Jessie's eye, but she'd cast her gaze downward to the toes of her shoes. Her hands twisted at her waist. Something was going on between the two of them, he was certain of it—and he suspected it might have something to do with Jessie's sudden reticence.

He returned his attention to Lady Strathburn. "I trust I will be installed in my old chambers, my lady?"

"As you wish," she replied coolly. "I shall send Gordon up to make it ready for you. Although, I'm afraid most of your possessions—and that includes all your clothes—were disposed of long ago." She ran her eyes over his disheveled state, her distaste openly apparent.

"No matter." Robert turned to his father. The sight of him standing so tall, his eyes alight with pride and joy, brought a lump to Robert's throat. "Father, perhaps I could presume on your generosity and borrow MacGowan and your carriage for a short while to rectify the sorry state of my appearance?" Although he was reluctant to leave both Jessie and his father, he had a number of matters he needed to attend to, including visiting Leith Docks where the *Phoenix* was moored. Whilst there, he would be able to collect several trunks of his possessions as well as invite Drummond to tonight's celebratory dinner.

His father patted him on the shoulder. "Of course, my son. Whatever you require, it will be made so. I shall see you when you return."

Once his father and stepmother had quit the vestibule—in opposite directions to each other—and the servants had begun to disperse to attend to their various duties, Robert turned to find that Jessie had started to climb the stairs.

Good God. Was she running away from him?

This just wouldn't do.

"Jessie," he called, striding toward her, unease twisting in his belly. He couldn't let her go, not when there was this strange undercurrent of tension vibrating between them. He didn't like this subdued version of Jessie, not one little bit. Something was *definitely* wrong.

The conversation he'd intended to have with her later, he needed to have right now. Despite his previous resolution to play the gentleman, he was determined to take whatever measures necessary to see the spark return to her eyes. The warm spark that flared just for him.

Jessie halted on the bottom step and turned, one elegant hand on the newel post. He approached her slowly as he might a frightened deer and stopped before her, close, but not touching. Instead, he trapped her gaze. He could have sworn she was holding her breath.

He began without preamble. "I wouldn't believe a word my spiteful witch of a stepmother says about anything, especially if it's to do with us."

Jessie's eyes widened as she released a breath. "I... How did you know?"

Robert's mouth quirked slightly. "My stepmother is renowned for her self-serving ways, *mo ghaoil*. I suspect she would go to great lengths to maintain her influence, and Simon's, in this family. That may include trying to sabotage our union. She views us both as threats. I have returned and replaced Simon as heir to the earldom—and you, you will be Lady Lochrose and in time, the next Countess of Strathburn. I imagine my stepmother has intimated that my interest in you is passing?"

Jessie nodded, flushing.

At last, a reaction from her. He'd been right.

"Aye." Uncertainty clouded his *fiancée's* usually clear brown eyes as she continued. "But truth be told, Robert, I wouldna blame ye if that were the case. It is no' like you've been given much choice in the matter of our handfasting. It was, as I recall, verra much a *fait accompli*. Now ye have gained yer freedom and I'm no longer in any danger, I would understand if ye wanted to take some time to reconsider...our situation."

There was no chance of that, not when Robert's heart beat solely for the woman before him. He slowly reached out and took her hand from the newel post then brought it to his chest. With his other hand, he gently brushed her cheek with the back of his fingers. "I know exactly how I feel about our situation, Jessie. But what I'd really like to know is, how do *you* feel?"

Jessie's breath caught and her gaze dropped to Robert's mouth. "I think... No, I know..." Her voice was edged with a delicious breathlessness. "I want ye... And I want ye to kiss me."

Thank God. At last Robert could claim Jessie in exactly the way he'd longed to since his release. Cradling her delicate face between his hands, he angled his mouth over hers and drank deeply of the honeyed warmth within.

Jessie's response was everything he'd dreamed of. She took everything he gave her, every caress of his lips, every stroke of his tongue, and teased and aroused him in return. She wanted him—there was no doubt in his mind she'd been waiting for this moment just as much as he had.

Yes, Jessie, you are mine. Robert felt it in every fiber of his being, to the very depths of his soul. *Yes.*

Desire flared, hot and intense, and without thinking, Robert pressed Jessie against the banister rail and cupped one of her breasts. She whimpered and wrapped her arms around his neck, pressing herself into his palm. Even through the layers of her clothing, he could feel the impudent peak of her nipple. When she instinctively pushed her hips against his own, his already half-aroused cock stiffened even more.

God, he wanted more. So much more. But now was not the time.

But later tonight...

Heart pounding, Robert broke the kiss. He smiled with satisfaction at the sight of Jessie, pliant in his arms, lips red, cheeks flushed. Her eyes, still drowsy with desire, were the warm amber of liquid honey. He had succeeded in chasing away the shadow of reserved distance between them. With that kiss they had both come to an understanding. They wanted each other, they were tied to each other. *Handfasted.*

"I must go, my love," he murmured, stroking his thumb lightly across Jessie's swollen bottom lip. "I have some things to take care of on board my ship, but I shall be back by this evening. Later, after dinner, perhaps we may continue this discussion, in private, to clarify our positions even further."

Jessie's eyes glowed. "I look forward to it, *mo chridhe.*"

Robert's face was still wreathed with a besotted grin when he left Strathburn House in his father's carriage a few minutes later. He rather thought he would be smiling for the rest of the afternoon.

The White Horse, Edinburgh's largest coaching inn, was but a short distance away from Auldgate Close. Robert didn't intend to stay long. He viewed the slight deviation from his intended path to Leith Docks as an unpleasant but necessary duty, akin to removing vermin from the hold of his ship.

He left MacGowan with the carriage in the coaching yard and within a few minutes—courtesy of an avaricious innkeeper with dubious loyalties to his patrons and a penchant for coin—he had the key to Simon's room. The innkeeper had also helpfully informed him that Mr. Grant's manservant, Baird, had just recently departed in a sedan chair for the Grassmarket to run some errands for his master.

Robert paused by Simon's door, listening for a moment before entering. All was silent within. Given Simon's past love for anything and everything that fit into the category of "debauched," he surmised that Simon was likely abed, sleeping off the effects of too much alcohol.

Although Robert knew Simon had also been fond of the company of prostitutes since at least the age of seventeen—and most likely still would be—he doubted his brother would be partaking of the company of one of the local harlots at this time of day. Whilst the innkeeper could be easily bribed into parting with a key, it was unlikely he would let Simon flagrantly reduce the reputation of the coaching inn during daylight hours. The White Horse had to keep up the appearance of having *some* standards.

When the door swung open it was to reveal, as Robert had suspected, Simon practically passed out, face down, in the rumpled bed.

The room stank of stale sweat, spilt ale, and the contents of a used chamber pot.

Simon did not so much as stir as Robert closed then locked the door, pocketing the key. The shutters were closed and there was nothing but cold ashes in the grate. In the weak light, Robert spied a wooden chair on the other side of the room by the window. With a determined stride, he crossed the clothes-strewn floor and flung open the shutters.

Simon groaned and rolled from his stomach onto his back, throwing his arm over his eyes to block out the light. "I told you, you stupid sow, I didn't want you to clean my room," he croaked.

"I'm afraid it's not the chamber maid, dear brother," drawled Robert with a grin.

Simon bolted upright. His puffy eyelids flew open to reveal bloodshot eyes that fixed on Robert in disbelief. When he opened his mouth to speak, nothing came out. Instead, he simply stared in horror, his bare chest rising and falling rapidly, his face gray.

Robert swung the chair around and straddled it in one fluid move, his arms resting on the back. He knew he looked like the worst kind of ruffian with his three-day growth and unkempt clothes. But if his rough appearance intimidated Simon, all the better.

Narrowing his gaze, he pinned his half-brother with a deliberately cold, uncompromising stare. "Yes, Simon, your worst nightmare has been realized," he said softly. "I've escaped the executioner's axe. And you, being struck dumb right at this moment, suits my purpose exactly. Now, all I want you to do is listen because I'm only going to say this once."

He then leaned forward over the back of the chair, intentionally flexing his biceps so they strained against the linen of his shirt. Simon immediately shrank back against the stained bedclothes, looking for all the world like he was going to be sick.

Undeterred, Robert continued in a silken, almost pleasant tone of voice that was completely at odds with his menacing physical stance. If it further rattled Simon, good. "Within a week, you will be taking up residence in lodgings that I will arrange for you here in Edinburgh, with an annual allowance that will be sufficient for you to maintain an adequate level of comfort while you complete a university degree. I really don't care what it is. What you study is entirely up to you. Thereafter, I expect you to find some sort of gainful and respectable employment. You will continue to be the recipient of my most generous offer, so long as you abide by my further stipulations—you will not set foot in Strathburn House, or Lochrose Castle, ever again."

"Oh, I say," spluttered Simon, finally finding his voice. "You can't do that. What has Father to say about this? My mother won't stand for it."

Robert's mouth twisted and he cocked an eyebrow. "From what I understand, Father has already banished you from Strathburn House. And I don't give a toss about what your mother will or won't stand for."

Simon's face grew an alarming shade of puce. "This is ridiculous! It's not like Father has died, making you king of the castle. You've got no right whatsoever."

"I have every right, Simon, because I'm the one who will be providing your funds," growled Robert. "*Not* Father. I also suspect that he's not planning on being particularly magnanimous where you're concerned, considering you've had me arrested—twice. You need to be accountable for your actions, especially those which have hurt others. You've lived a hedonistic, self-serving existence for far too long. It's definitely time you learned to live within your means and stopped leaching off our family's estate."

Robert stood abruptly and pushed the chair away, looming over Simon. He laced his voice with steel to deliver his final pronouncement. "And my final condition is this. It concerns Miss Munroe, who is soon to be my wife."

Simon sneered. "Surely you jest. That Jezebel is to become *Lady* Lochrose? Now there's a contradiction—"

Enough. Robert slammed his fist into his brother's face and Simon hit the pillows, groaning.

Shaking his hand and flexing his fingers, Robert continued speaking as though nothing had happened. "You will never set foot anywhere near Miss Munroe, the future Countess of Strathburn, *ever* again. She will never have to look upon you again. If I ever find out that you have breached this condition I assure you, you will face a lot worse from me than a mere punch. Do I make myself clear, *brother?*"

Simon nodded his assent, clutching his cheekbone where a second dark purple bruise had begun to flower.

"Good. I knew you'd see it my way." Robert moved to the door and unlocked it. "I'll have Father's man, MacGowan, advise you of the details of your new accommodation when it has been finalized. If I never see you again, it will be too soon."

~

It was not long after his brute of a brother's departure when another knock sounded at Simon's door. He groaned and sat up. He doubted it was Robert, given that his brother had somehow managed to purloin a key. It was probably the maid.

The knock came again, more insistent this time. "Simon, it's me. Open this door at once."

Mother. Simon cursed under his breath. What the hell did she want from him other than to inform him of Robert's release and the subsequent change in the status quo? As if that would fix anything.

Simon staggered from the bed and approached the door. "Mother, I'm not decent," he called.

"Well, that's nothing new," she hissed back at him. "I'll meet you in one of the private parlors downstairs, the Green Room. Don't tarry. It's urgent."

Ten minutes later, Simon joined his mother in the parlor she'd hired. A pot of tea and an assortment of scones and cakes were laid out on a small table before the fire.

Simon thought he would be ill when his mother offered him a cup as he sat down. "No, thank you," he said.

Lady Strathburn cast a critical eye over him. "Simon, you look shocking. You really should curb your drinking somewhat." She frowned at his freshly injured cheek then continued, "And how on earth did you get that awful bruising? Not brawling in some cheap tavern, I hope. You look like a common criminal."

Simon grimaced and probed the tender, swollen crest of his cheekbone. "Bloody Robert paid me a visit, not less than twenty minutes ago," he grumbled.

Lady Strathburn sucked in a sharp breath. "The rogue."

"I suspect that's what you've come about, to warn me my brother has escaped the lion's den and that Father's agreed to his ludicrous stipulations to have me all but banished."

Lady Strathburn's mouth twisted with a malicious smile. "Yes, in part. But I also have a plan in mind, my dear Simon, to get rid of your brother and his upstart of a *fiancée*. But to succeed in this venture, you will need to maintain your sobriety for at least the rest of this day and the next—and to find some backbone when the occasion calls for it. Do you think you can do that for me, and for yourself?"

Despite the painful twinge in his cheek and jaw, Simon smiled back. "Yes, Mother, I think I can."

CHAPTER 23

Jessie found it difficult to settle to anything for the remainder of the afternoon. Even though she was exhausted, her mind was too restless for sleep, yet she was unable to concentrate on any activity for more than a few minutes. Several books were selected from Lord Strathburn's small library downstairs then discarded. She attempted to repair a tear in the hem of her black wool cloak, but soon tired of the task.

Eventually she deposited herself in the gray damask shepherdess chair in her bedchamber and simply stared into the fire, her mind lingering on Robert. Exquisite anticipation curled through her as she allowed herself to think about tonight when she and Robert met privately to discuss their future...and what that might look like when they were husband and wife.

And if they just happened to kiss, and kiss again, and then they made love...

Jessie's heart fluttered with excitement. Closing her eyes, she leaned back against the headrest of her chair, imagining what could be...

"Miss Munroe, it's time for ye to get ready for dinner."

Heavens, she'd fallen asleep. Jessie stirred and stretched before attempting to focus her drowsy gaze on Alison. "What time is it?" she asked on a yawn.

"Five o'clock, miss," replied the maid, lighting the candles on the mantel. "And dinner is at seven."

"Oh." Jessie frowned, her stomach suddenly aswarm with nerves. She'd slept for over an hour and had much to do to get ready for Robert's celebratory dinner. Which brought her to her next concern. What on earth was she to wear?

A stained traveling dress or simple woolen day gown would not suit at all. She was betrothed to a viscount and would be dining with an earl. She so didn't want to disappoint Robert.

Rising stiffly from her seat, her gaze drifted to the bed—and her breath caught. There, upon the gray brocade counterpane, was the most beautiful gown she'd ever seen. The garment's amber-gold silk bodice and full skirts were offset with a rich, cream silk stomacher adorned with delicate bows and tiny ribbon rosettes, and a profusion of cream lace cascaded from the ends of the sleeves.

"Who...? How...? Where did this come from?" Jessie stammered as she crossed to the bed and gently touched the exquisite garment with a trembling finger.

"I canna be sure miss, but perhaps it was the same someone who delivered the matching shoes and undergarments." Alison pointed to a pair of cream silk slippers embroidered with tiny seed pearls sitting on a nearby footstool. A pair of almost sheer, ivory silk stockings and a fine lawn chemise had been draped across the armchair beside the bed. There was even a pair of satin gloves.

Jessie smiled, grateful tears brimming as she clasped her hands together beneath her chin. Robert *must* have purchased all this for her. No doubt from a *very* expensive modiste. She would never be able to thank him enough.

Within an hour, Jessie had bathed and with Alison's help, had changed into her new evening attire. Everything fit perfectly. Well, everything except for the bodice perhaps...

Regarding herself in the dressing table mirror as Alison arranged her hair, Jessie could see a good deal of the tops of her breasts as they swelled above the gown's low neckline. Never in her life had she worn anything quite so revealing. She was certain she'd be blushing all night.

Alison, on the other hand, did not seem to notice that there was anything amiss with her mistress's appearance. She tamed Jessie's curls into an elaborate yet artfully arranged pile on top of her head, with a few longer tendrils cascading over one shoulder. The effect was indeed eye-catching, perhaps even elegant. Jessie smiled at her reflection. Perhaps she would look the part of a viscount's *fiancée*, even though inside she was as jumpy as a mountain hare.

When she was ready at last, Jessie moved to the full-length looking glass by the washstand, and turned slowly this way and that, admiring the swish of the fine silk and the way the light caught the dark golden honey tones. The color of the dress was the perfect foil to her red-gold hair.

"Oh miss, you look verra beautiful," sighed Alison, looking on.

"Indeed, she does," agreed a deep, decidedly masculine voice.

Jessie whirled around to face Robert.

Oh, my Lord. The sight of him lounging against the doorframe took her breath away. He'd shaved, revealing the strong, tanned planes of his face and she instantly longed to feel his smooth jaw beneath her palm. His brown-black hair was simply tied back as usual but with a black velvet ribbon instead of a leather strip. She was pleased he resisted the fashion of wearing powder, or a periwig. With hair so thick and darkly rich, it would be a crime to hide it.

Jessie's gaze drifted further downward over Robert's superbly tailored evening attire. A black velvet frock coat that seemed to be molded to his broad shoulders was worn over an ivory silk shirt and torso-hugging waistcoat of cobalt-blue brocade. A sapphire pin, the same deep blue as his eyes, winked at her from the depths of a snowy lace jabot at his throat. And how sinfully tight were his black, satin knee-length breeches and ivory silk stockings? Why, they clung, almost indecently to the long, well-defined muscles of his thighs and calves.

There was no trace of the Jacobite rebel left. Lord Lochrose, devastatingly handsome rake, had indeed returned.

And he's all mine. Jessie swallowed, stunned by the realization. So much so, she barely registered the fact that Robert's gaze drifted over her with blatant appreciation in turn, a smile tugging at one corner of his mouth.

He pushed away from the door and stepped into the room, glancing at Alison. "Thank you for so ably assisting Miss Munroe. That will be all for now."

The maid bobbed a curtsy. "Thank ye, milord," she murmured, blushing prettily before quitting the room.

Jessie somehow found her voice. "It was ye, wasn't it, Robert"—she gestured at her attire—"who arranged all this for me? I dinna ken how ye managed it, but I want to thank ye. Never in my life have I worn anything so divine."

As Robert moved toward her, his admiring gaze stroked over her again. "The clothes only look beautiful because of the divine creature wearing them, *mo chridhe*," he said huskily. He gently placed his hands on her shoulders and turned her around so she was facing the looking glass, her back pressed against the hardness of his lean torso, her bottom resting against his hips.

Transfixed by their reflection in the mirror, Jessie watched as Robert bent his dark head and placed a light kiss on the sensitive flesh where her neck met her shoulder, before trailing a long finger along her collarbone, raising gooseflesh.

"You know, as beautiful as you are," he murmured, his breath a caress against her skin, "there is still something missing from this ensemble." As his eyes met hers in the looking glass, his mouth quirked into a smile.

Jessie shook her head in awed bewilderment. "I dinna need anything else, Robert. Truly," she whispered. What else could he possibly have to give her?

"Ah, I beg to differ, *mo ghaoil*." Robert, continuing to smile, reached into the inside of his evening jacket and withdrew a long, slim sandalwood box, fastened with a silver clasp. He reached his arm around her and placed the box in her hands. "For you, Jessie, my love."

With trembling fingers, Jessie undid the clasp and lifted the lid. Inside, nestled against a bed of midnight blue satin, lay a string of lustrous, creamy pearls and a matching pair of pearl drop earrings. She gasped, overwhelmed. She raised her gaze to Robert's reflection and noticed he was grinning broadly.

"Robert... I... This is too much," she breathed.

He responded by placing another feather-light kiss behind her ear.

"It's not nearly enough," he said, reaching for the necklace before placing it carefully around her neck and fastening the ear bobs to her ears. The pearls glowed warmly against her skin.

Never before had Jessie felt so beautiful. Or adored. The way Robert's deep blue eyes glowed, she could almost believe he really did love her. Her heart capered beneath her breast. *Could it be true?*

"Now, my lady"—he reached for her hand and placed a soft kiss on her fingertips, making her quiver anew—"let me escort you to dinner. I believe some of our guests have already arrived."

Jessie placed her gloved hand on his sleeve and together they descended to the drawing room.

All heads turned as Gordon, the butler, announced their arrival. "The Viscount Lochrose, the Master of Strathburn, and Miss Jessie Munroe."

Jessie could see Lord and Lady Strathburn by the fireplace, the earl beaming proudly and the countess, unsurprisingly, glowering at her and Robert. To Jessie's pleasant surprise they had been chatting with Lord Arniston and an attractive, dark-haired woman who appeared to Jessie to be of similar age to the countess. Lord Strathburn introduced her as Jean, Lady Arniston.

Jessie was also intrigued to learn that the Lord Advocate had wed Jean, his second wife, a mere month ago. She wondered if Lord Arniston's recent re-marriage had contributed to his magnanimous attitude toward Robert. Perhaps the romanticism of a handfasting influenced his decision to grant a pardon as it strengthened the impression that Robert was over his wild ways. Jessie had a feeling that Lord Strathburn had known the engagement would work in Robert's favor all along.

Robert led Jessie around the room, introducing her to the rest of the assembled guests—the minister of the nearby Canongate Kirk and his lovely wife, as well as long-time friends of Lord Strathburn, Baron Brose, his wife, and their daughter, Agnes. The last guest Robert introduced Jessie to was an interesting character indeed—Kenneth Drummond, the captain of Robert's merchant ship the *Phoenix*.

Jessie warmed to the barrel-chested and bluff seaman immediately. There was an obvious close friendship between him and Robert. She liked the way Captain Drummond's dark eyes crinkled at the corners when he smiled at her, which was often. She suspected he had a trove of amusing stories about his travels around the world and, no doubt, Robert's exploits. She certainly looked forward to hearing them.

Following the round of introductions, Gordon and Alison served French champagne—courtesy of Captain Drummond—to everyone. Glass in hand, Lord Strathburn led his guests in a heartfelt toast to Robert's return home.

"And now, ladies and gentlemen," he continued, scanning the room, carefully catching everyone's eye. "I have one more pleasant duty to perform before dinner." He gestured toward Jessie and Robert, smiling broadly. "It is with the greatest joy that I officially announce the betrothal of my dear son, Robert, to the delightful young lady you've all just had the pleasure of meeting, Miss Jessie Munroe. Please, raise your glasses and let us drink a toast to the hand-fasted couple."

The spontaneous applause and immediate good wishes bestowed by all—with the notable exception of Lady Strathburn—lifted Jessie's spirits so much, she couldn't help but smile at the assembled group. When everyone turned to their own conversations, she sipped her champagne and over the rim of her glass, noticed Robert watching her.

He leaned close and taking advantage of the cover the folds of her skirts provided, reached for her hand. His voice was low in her ear. "It warms my heart to see you smiling so much. May it always be so, my love."

Jessie gently squeezed his fingers. Her own heart, indeed her entire body, felt suffused with warmth. But beneath the quiet pleasure of knowing Robert cared for her, she also felt a trifle melancholy. Everything was perfect, but for one thing.

The guests began dispersing to the dining room, but Robert kept her by his side. He brought her captured hand to his lips. "What is it?"

"I canna hide anything from ye, can I?" she said, summoning a wry smile. She let out a small sigh. "I'm just a wee bit sad that my father is no' here this evening to share these special moments."

Robert's thumb lightly caressed the bare skin of her wrist. "I understand completely. Tomorrow, Father and I will send word to him at

Lochrose. In a few days, after I've arranged my affairs here, we will return to see him. Will that ease your mind?"

Jessie nodded and smiled her gratitude. "Aye."

"Excellent." Robert tucked her hand into his arm, then escorted her into the dining room.

The next few hours passed pleasantly over a dinner Jessie suspected was fit for the King himself. By the end of the four-course meal, she felt quite sated and relaxed, warmed by the convivial conversation and the wine she'd sipped during dinner. All the stresses and worries of the past few days had slipped away from her like a dissipating mist. She slanted a glance at Robert beside her, still quite bemused by the fact she was engaged to someone like him. Perhaps sensing her gaze, he turned and through the cool silk of her skirts she felt his large hand on her knee.

"Remember we both agreed to finish our stairway conversation about our *situation*, sweet Jessie," he murmured, his breath caressing her ear. "Will you wait for me in your bedchamber after our guests depart?"

A tremor of delicious anticipation slid down Jessie's spine. "I look forward to it, milord," she whispered back, all trace of contented drowsiness gone, replaced instead with a feeling of heady expectation. She couldn't wait.

She took another small sip of her wine and let her attention drift to the far end of the table where Lord and Lady Strathburn sat...and her breathing faltered. The countess was watching her. The woman's lips twisted in a strange smile as she arched a brow and raised her glass to Jessie, making a mock toast.

Jessie's nape prickled with unease as her gaze skittered back to Robert.

Both Robert and Lord Strathburn might care for her, but how was she to live here, or at Lochrose, with that vindictive woman breathing down her neck? Wishing her ill at every turn? Lord Strathburn had banished Simon from the house, and she was certain Robert would take further measures to ensure his half-brother never crossed paths with her again. But unless Robert arranged an alternative situation for them once they were wed, it was likely that she would be living under the same roof as the countess.

How was she to endure that?

As if attuned to her disquiet, Robert reached for her hand and entwined his fingers with hers beneath the cover of the table. Jessie squeezed his hand in return and he smiled. The warm light in his eyes made her heart flip and she crushed down the foreboding inside her.

Everything will be all right with Robert by my side. Come what may, Jessie was certain they could build a happy life together. She wouldn't have it any other way.

CHAPTER 24

Robert was quietly pleased that the gentlemen of the party did not want to linger over whisky and port after dinner. Indeed, within half an hour, the entire company had repaired to the drawing room. Jessie and his stepmother dispensed tea to all the ladies while Gordon poured coffee for the gentlemen.

Stationed by the fireplace with Drummond, Robert watched Jessie ably filling Lady Arniston's fine bone china teacup, fully aware his mouth was curved in a besotted smile. His *fiancée* had played the role of secondary hostess to perfection tonight. For someone who'd not yet had the opportunity to be formally introduced into polite society, he was quietly impressed. Jessie's manners were impeccable, and she displayed a natural, canny ability to converse easily about a wide range of topics with all of the assembled guests. Without a doubt, his Highland lass would suit him exactly as a wife.

Drummond smiled knowingly. "So it looks as though ye've been lured and verra much snared by a veritable siren. I always thought that ye would fall hard for some bonnie lass one day. I just didna think it would happen so quickly after ye arrived home."

Robert grinned. It was useless to try and hide his feelings. "Neither did I, my friend, and I have been well and truly ensnared by Jessie.

Although, I'm ashamed to admit, our first encounter was a near disaster —entirely my fault—and I'm amazed she appears to reciprocate my feelings, considering the inopportune circumstances."

Drummond raised a bushy eyebrow in query. "So ye came upon her *dishabille*? Ye trod on her toes? Ye spilt yer whisky on her dress?" When Robert shook his head at each of these suggestions, Drummond gave him a good-natured poke in the ribs. "Come on. Out with it, man."

Robert grimaced at him over the rim of his whisky tumbler. "I shot her. In the arm. Thought she was a deer."

Drummond's hearty guffaws drew bemused looks from all of the ladies and gentlemen, including Jessie. She caught Robert's eye and raised a delicate eyebrow in query. He shrugged a shoulder before shooting Drummond a pained look.

Heedless of his discomfort and the questioning stares, Drummond slapped Robert on the shoulder. "Ye truly have been away from the Highlands too long when ye mistake a lass for a hind. I'm astounded Miss Munroe would even speak to ye, let alone wed ye!"

"So am I, Drummond," returned Robert jovially. "It must be fate that drew us together, that's all I can say. It certainly wasn't because of the charming court I paid her."

Drummond swallowed the last of his whisky and placed the empty glass on the mantelpiece. "I willna stay for tea with the gentlefolk, Robert, but I'll expect ye on the morrow at the docks to farewell the *Phoenix*. She's verra much packed to the gunwales and ready to sail on the first high tide."

Robert clapped his friend on the back in a gesture of farewell. "Aye. It's about time she was on her way back home to the Caribbean. But don't look for me at the crack of dawn. I think I shall be keeping gentlemen's hours tomorrow."

Drummond winked at him. "Quite rightly so. I'll expect ye'll be needing to regain yer strength after tonight."

It took all of Robert's strength to resist the urge to cuff Drummond behind the ear as he walked his friend around the drawing room to say his farewells.

～

"Would you like me to help ye undress, miss?"

Jessie started at Alison's question, nearly dropping her unread book, *Pamela*, onto the hearthrug in her bedroom. She sighed. Lost in delicious thought ever since Robert had bid her goodnight in the vestibule not five minutes ago, she'd been unable to concentrate on the story about the plight of the young maidservant who in many respects, reminded her of herself and her own situation...until she'd met Robert.

Giving herself a mental shake, she turned to face the young maid. "No, I think I shall stay up a wee while and continue reading," she said, brandishing the ignored novel in the air. "I really canna put it down. If you dinna mind lighting a few more candles, and turning down the bedcovers, that's all I need. I'm quite used to looking after myself."

Even to her own ears, her excuses for denying Alison's help sounded weak. Jessie blushed, knowing her real reason for staying awake must be patently obvious; that she was waiting for Robert to visit her room. Could Alison tell how hopelessly distracted she was? And why?

But Alison, discreet as ever, did not even blink. "Aye, of course, miss." The maid bobbed a curtsy and, after quickly fulfilling Jessie's few requests, took her leave.

Left alone, Jessie dropped poor *Pamela* onto a nearby table before sinking into the soft armchair by the fire. Kicking off her new brocade shoes, she elevated her recovering sprained ankle onto a small ottoman. No, reading was definitely not on her mind as she stared into the bright flames licking the fresh logs in the grate.

She smiled as she pressed her hand to her hot cheek. She could have sworn the flesh still tingled from where Robert had placed a tender goodnight kiss. The memory of his intensely blue eyes—the way they'd also caressed her face and figure, promising so much more—made her shiver with desire all over again.

How long would it be before Robert came to her? Although he evidently wanted her to be his wife, part of her still wanted, *needed* him to tell her he truly cared for her. He'd called her his love, *mo ghaoil* and *mo chridhe*—my heart. But could he say he loved her? An experienced, worldly man like him? They'd met a week ago, after all.

Jessie closed her eyes against the light of the flames and smiled, recalling all their encounters, the intimate moments they'd shared since they'd met. She suspected it would not be long before she found out the answer to her question...

A sound—her bedchamber door clicking shut—made her jump. She was not sure how long it had been since she'd drifted asleep, but she suspected only a short space of time had passed. The fire still burned brightly in the grate and the candles on the mantelpiece had not burned down at all. The flames guttered slightly in the slight draft that had come in through the door, making the shadows dance.

Her pulse thrumming in anticipation, Jessie sat up straight and turned her head toward the door, expecting to see Robert. But no one was there. Frowning in confusion, she rose from her chair...and was immediately grappled from behind by a man she knew instantly.

Simon.

Oh God, no! The smell of brandy and his cologne assailed her senses as he roughly hauled her against his chest, his arm like a band of steel about her neck, crushing the breath from her.

A scream rose in her throat, but Simon's hand smothered her mouth and nose, stifling all sound.

"Ah, sweet Jezebel." Simon's breath was hot and foul in her ear. "I've been waiting too long for this moment."

Blazing, white-hot anger speared through Jessie, lending her strength. She struggled, legs kicking, hands grasping at the arm across her neck, but it was all for naught. The brute dragged her inexorably backward toward the bed as if she were only a rag doll. A strangled sob caught in her throat as her bodice ripped and a rain of pearls pattered across the floor. With renewed vigor, she twisted wildly and clawed at the hand covering her face.

Simon hissed as she drew blood. "Bitch," he cursed as he flung her face down on the end of the bed, roughly pushing her head down into the coverlet whilst his other hand gripped her throat. "I was prepared to be gentle with you, but it seems you like it rough."

Jessie couldn't breathe. This could *not* be happening. Any minute now, Robert would come in the door and stop this. But now Simon was pushing up her skirts...

No, no, no. She had to free herself. She *had* to. Jessie thrashed again and managed to turn her head to the side. And screamed.

"Shut your mouth." Simon clamped his hand over her face again, abruptly cutting off her cry. She jerked and when his hand slipped, she bit into his flesh as hard as she could. She'd do anything to make him stop what he was trying to do.

Simon released her, shouting a string of oaths. As his weight shifted, Jessie rolled to the side and instinctively reached for something to use as a weapon. Her hand came into contact with the pitcher on the nearby washstand. She grabbed it and swung...

CHAPTER 25

It was a quarter to midnight when Robert finally bid his father a warm goodnight. After the rest of the guests had departed and Jessie and his stepmother had retired, the earl had suggested the two of them share a wee dram for old time's sake in his study before turning in.

Impatient as Robert was to join Jessie in her room, he couldn't deny his father this one simple request, not after all he'd done for him since his return. Besides, to ensure a degree of discretion, he calculated the time it would take to share a whisky and some quiet conversation would be a sufficient interval for Jessie's maid to have finished attending her mistress before he too ventured upstairs.

All was silent in the house apart from the crackling of the logs in the grate as Robert bided his time before the study fire, watching another ten minutes tick by on the mantel clock. He'd just finished off the last of his whisky—the same rich golden brown as Jessie's eyes—when a scream rent the air.

Jessie's scream.

Christ. Robert dropped his glass and sprinted from the library toward the stairs. What in God's name could be happening? Panic searing through his chest, he took the stairs two at a time. He could have sworn her scream had come from the first floor, quite possibly her bedchamber. As he reached her door, he heard a man cursing violently, and then a crash.

"Jessie," Robert cried, then cursed when he discovered her bedchamber door was locked. He took a step back and aimed an explosive kick just below the handle. The door burst open to reveal a scene of nightmarish pandemonium.

Her hair a disheveled mess, her gown torn, Jessie stood by the bed clutching the handle of a broken pitcher. At her feet sprawled Simon, wig askew, his face and one hand bleeding, shards of china and pearls from Jessie's broken necklace strewn about him.

"The bitch bit me then bashed me with the bloody pitcher," he moaned.

With a roar, Robert lunged at Simon, hauled him to his feet, then threw him up against the wall so hard his brother's teeth rattled. It took every ounce of Robert's restraint to stop himself from pounding Simon to pieces right then and there. "How dare you! How the hell did you get in here?" he demanded through clenched teeth.

Simon, bastard that he was, smirked. "Through the front door, of course. I thought I was invited to the party."

"You will pay for this," Robert ground out. "This is unforgiveable. I demand satisfaction."

Simon sneered. "My pleasure. Shall we say short swords, tomorrow at first light in Holyrood Park, at the common between Dunsapie Hill and Arthur's Seat?"

"Agreed." Robert stepped back abruptly and thrust Simon away from him, toward the splintered door. "Now get out, before I slay you like a dog right here and now."

Simon stumbled back into the hall just as MacGowan and Gordon appeared.

Wiping blood from a long shallow cut across his brow, his damned half-brother bowed to Robert, a derisive smile twisting his features. "Until tomorrow then, dear brother. Seven sharp, if you'll pardon the pun. I look forward to the opportunity to skewer you with my sword."

"See that my brother leaves, gentlemen. Take his keys, then lock and bolt all the doors," ordered Robert.

MacGowan and Gordon, both white-faced and grim, nodded their assent and escorted Simon away.

Robert turned his attention to Jessie who'd remained motionless by the end of the bed, her fingers still clutching the pitcher handle. She stared at the floor, trembling.

He approached her slowly, carefully. "Jessie lass," he murmured gently.

She raised her ashen face to his. Tears misted her eyes. "He...he broke your pearl necklace, Robert," she whispered. She took a great shuddering breath and seemed to realize she was still holding the pitcher handle. With a grimace, she tossed it onto the floor with the other shards, then half-stepped, half-staggered toward him.

Robert's arms immediately came up around her, cradling her as she buried her face in his chest, her shoulders shaking as she gave herself up to tears. Running his hand up and down her slender back, he murmured soothing words into her hair. All the while, anger shook him to his very bones. He'd already noticed bruises about Jessie's neck. He dreaded to think what other injuries had been inflicted.

Oh yes, Simon would pay dearly for this outrage.

When Jessie at last raised her head, he gently brushed away the remaining tears from her cheeks with his thumbs. "Jessie, *mo ghaoil*, it doesn't matter about the necklace," he whispered, holding her gaze, mentally preparing himself for the worst with his next question. His precious, precious lass. "What I need to know is—as difficult as it may be for you to tell me—how...how much did Simon hurt you?"

Jessie's eyes grew wide when she realized what he was asking, and cold dread froze his blood. But then, thank the Lord, she smiled shakily. "Aside from a few bruises, I'm all right, Robert. Unlike yer brother, I'm verra pleased to say. It's true that I bit his hand and hit him with the pitcher, though. It was the only way I could get him off me—"

"Thank God, Jessie." Robert drew her into his arms again and kissed her forehead. "You fought bravely, my love."

Inwardly he vowed, *And I promise you that come tomorrow, you will never have to worry about my cur of a brother again.*

As if hearing Robert's thoughts, the hall clock portentously began to herald the hour of midnight. The duel was no longer tomorrow. It was today.

As the last of the chimes ceased, Gordon appeared in the doorway again. A wide-eyed Alison and grim-faced Mrs. Bowie hovered behind him, the cook bearing a tray of tea and scones.

"Forgive my presumption, milord," Gordon began, his gaze fixed discreetly on a point somewhere on the other side of the room. "I thought perhaps Miss Munroe would like some...assistance."

Robert reluctantly released Jessie from his embrace, but continued to hold her close, his arm about her waist. "You are quite right, Gordon." He turned to the female servants and addressed them in turn. "Alison, please find some suitable night attire for Miss Munroe and take it to my suite, along with a basin of warm water and some linen bandages. Mrs. Bowie, I thank you—please take the tray to my sitting room." He didn't much care what the servants thought about the fact Jessie would be installed in his rooms. The whole evening had ended in disaster. The servants' sensibilities were the least of his concerns.

He returned his attention to the butler. "How fares the rest of the household, Gordon?" No doubt others—including his father—had heard Jessie's scream and the ensuing commotion.

Gordon was succinct in his appraisal. "All is secure downstairs, milord. MacGowan has explained the situation to his lordship. Lord Strathburn kindly requests that you speak to him when ye have the opportunity. Her ladyship hasna stirred from her rooms. The other servants havena been told anything, other than to mind their own business."

"Well done, Gordon. I'd also like a horse to be readied and brought round to the front of the house." Robert needed to visit Leith Docks to ask Drummond to be his second for the duel.

"Verra well, milord. I'll send word to the stables in the mews."

Once Gordon had departed, Robert drew Jessie closer and gently tilted her chin upward so he could gain her attention. During his exchange with the servants, she'd remained mute and strangely still. She was clearly in shock.

"Jessie lass," he said softly, nothing but relieved when she met his gaze. "I'm going to carry you upstairs to my sitting room." He'd noticed that her feet were covered only with silk stockings when she'd stepped toward him, and he didn't want her cutting her feet on all the shards of broken china.

Without hesitation, Jessie reached for him, and he swung her up into his arms. He kissed her temple, swallowing past a sudden lump in his throat. Her complete trust in him meant so much.

His suite lay on the second floor, occupying the north-eastern corner of the house. As Robert carried her into his sitting room, he was pleased to see a fire burning brightly in the grate and that Mrs. Bowie had laid out the tea and scones on a low table on the hearthrug. Robert gently eased Jessie into a leather chair by the fire, then, ignoring the well-intentioned pot of tea, went to a sideboard and poured a tumbler of whisky. Returning to the fireside, he pulled up a low footstool and sat in front of her, offering her the glass. "This will ease the trembling, my love."

Jessie dutifully took a few sips of the strong liquor, coughing a little, but it seemed to revive her. Almost straightaway she seemed less disconnected from her surroundings...and from him. She gave him a small smile, a glimmer of golden warmth returning to her brown eyes. "This is no' how I envisaged our evening would end."

Relieved to see her spirit returning, Robert smiled back. "No. It certainly hasn't progressed the way I had anticipated either." He reached out slowly, and tenderly pushed a tangled lock of hair away from her face. "Jessie, would you mind if I let the rest of your hair down?" he asked, praying she wouldn't reject his touch. If she did, he would understand. "I must confess I have been dying to do just that, all evening."

"Of course," she said softly, then blushed as she put a hand to the collapsed arrangement of curls. "I know I must look a fright."

"Never. You could never look anything but beautiful to me." Robert leaned forward so he could more easily loosen the remaining pins, and in no time at all, her red-gold curls were cascading about her shoulders. He sat back again on the stool and forced his hands to stillness. His fingers were itching to ease the ruined dress from her shoulders so she could don something else—even one of his robes—but he would not push her for further intimacies after what she'd been through.

Besides, he had other matters to take care of.

He smiled ruefully. "As much as I would like to stay with you a while longer, unfortunately, I am going to have to leave you. I need to tell my father about what has happened and... and I need to make some arrangements for first thing in the morning."

~

Jessie frowned in confusion. *Arrangements?*

With a sense of mounting horror, she suddenly recalled Robert's exchange with Simon before he'd been forcibly ousted from her room. The memory returned to her in full force, as if a veil had been ripped away from her eyes.

Her heart seizing, she reached forward and gripped Robert's hands. "Ye're making arrangements for the duel," she breathed. "Please do no' do this, Robert. I ken what Simon did was wrong, unforgiveable. But dinna risk yer life or yer freedom, defending my honor. After all ye've been through, I dinna want ye to throw it all away because of me."

Although it was customary for gentlemen to resolve disputes of honor in this way, Jessie also knew that dueling was heavily frowned upon by the law. If Robert were caught engaging in an essentially illegal act whilst on probation—and indeed, if Simon were killed—there was no doubt in her mind that the consequences for him would be dire. There would be no escaping an execution this time.

Robert raised her hands to his lips and gently kissed her fingertips, his blue eyes dark with emotion. "You are worth immeasurably more to me than my own life, *mo chridhe*. Defending your honor is definitely worth the risk. Besides"—the expression in his eyes suddenly changed, grew bleak, and he ran a hand down his face—"I feel partly responsible for what Simon has done."

Jessie's eyebrows shot up in disbelief. "Whatever do ye mean? Ye ken Simon has been looking for an opportunity to have me, ever since I met him. Ye canna blame yerself for what that *monster* tried to do tonight."

Robert stood abruptly and paced to the sideboard. He poured himself a whisky and took a swig before he turned back to face her. The pull of his skin across his cheekbones and the rigid lines bracketing his mouth clearly marked his anguish. "Earlier this afternoon, I paid Simon a visit at his lodgings, and made it clear he would not be able to continue to leach off the family's fortune. I also warned him not to go anywhere near you again. I think I goaded him into taking rash action. If I had known that he would go so far...to hurt you to get back at me—"

He broke off and ran a hand through his dark hair. A stark look of self-recrimination clouded his eyes.

Jessie rose from her seat and approached him. "Do no' dare blame yerself, Robert Grant," she chided gently. "The only ones to blame for what happened tonight are yer brother...and Lady Strathburn."

Robert raised an eyebrow. "Why do you think my stepmother is involved in tonight's events?" he asked. "I know I said earlier that she would possibly go to great lengths to maintain the upper hand in this family. But to orchestrate a direct attack upon you?" He shook his head. "Surely she wouldn't sink so low."

Jessie frowned. "I dinna know exactly, it's just a suspicion I have." She crossed to the fireplace, head bent, chin resting on her clasped hands as she contemplated how best to put her thoughts into words. The fire crackled and a log fell, shooting sparks toward the hem of her gown, but she didn't care. Turning back to Robert, she began to explain. "Earlier this afternoon, Lady Strathburn made it abundantly clear that she does no' want me to become her daughter-in-law. I have no proof, but I strongly suspect this attack was designed, in part, to get rid of me. Perhaps she thought if Simon...if Simon 'ruined' me, so to speak, ye would no' wish to marry me."

Robert put down his glass and strode over to her. He tilted her chin up, capturing her gaze. "That would never be the case," he said in a velvet-soft voice. "Nothing could stop me from marrying you." He trailed a fingertip along her jaw and tucked a loose curl behind her ear. "If that was my stepmother's plan," he continued, his voice developing an edge of steel to it, "she has not planned well. All she's done is guaranteed that her son will be run through with my sword."

Before Jessie could even draw a breath to reply, Robert pulled her into his arms. With a shaky sigh, she gave into the impulse to rest her head against his broad chest, to breathe in the now familiar scent of his soap and the heady essence of the man himself. She could hear his strong and steady heartbeat thudding beneath her ear, feel the rise and fall of his ribcage as he drew breath. *What a wonderful, wonderful man he is.*

She closed her eyes, wishing she could stay like this forever, but even though her body began to relax, her thoughts were still awhirl. There was something about this whole turn of events that made her extremely uneasy. This was not just about her. It was almost as if the attack on her tonight had been engineered to provoke Robert.

She sensed treachery.

Aye. That was it. *Treachery.* Icy tendrils of fear curled around Jessie's spine.

She straightened and gripped Robert's arm. She had to make him see that he was in danger. "I verra much think that all this business has more to do with getting rid of ye, Robert, rather than me. The more I consider everything that's happened, the more I'm convinced that ye're being manipulated into doing something that will bring about yer own downfall."

Sharp interest sparked in Robert's eyes. "I'm listening."

Jessie took a deep breath and prayed Robert would believe her. His very life might depend upon it. "We know yer stepmother has always wished Simon to be the next Earl of Strathburn," she said carefully. "This afternoon, I rather got the impression that she was counting on ye being executed...but then ye were released, foiling her grand plans."

"I agree," said Robert. "But go on. I interrupted you."

Jessie nodded, relieved he was prepared to hear her out. "I may be wrong, but I think yer stepmother had a hand in arranging Simon's attack, knowing that you would undoubtedly challenge yer brother to a duel. She would know the conditions of your parole. That ye need to stay out of trouble. If you violate those conditions—and ye're caught dueling—ye could be arrested and imprisoned again. Or worse. Aside from that, I also find it more than a wee bit passing strange that Simon seemed so ready to agree to a duel in the first place. I suspect that half the Scots Guard stationed in Edinburgh Castle will be waiting for ye in Holyrood Park come dawn. Although I dinna possess the slightest bit of evidence, I think yer stepmother and brother have set a neat trap to get rid of at least one of us, if not both, in one fell swoop."

Robert ran a hand down his face. Jessie was right. There was a ring of truth to what she'd just suggested. Indeed, the more he thought about it, he really couldn't fault her logic.

It was true that his stepmother had always wanted to supplant him in favor of Simon becoming the next earl. Caroline was more than capable of plotting tonight's attack, and Simon would be more than willing to participate in a plan that involved ruining both him and Jessie at the same time.

It also made perfect sense that Simon would only agree to a duel if he thought there was no real chance he would get hurt—which would undoubtedly be the case, if there were soldiers lying in wait.

Simon was a bully and a coward at heart. He was more likely to turn tail and run than face a swordfight he had no chance of winning. Yet Simon had been the one to suggest the time and place for the duel without hesitation.

It was more than passing strange as Jessie had suggested.

But his brother must face the consequences of his actions. Of that there was no doubt.

Robert let out a long sigh. "Jessie, I think you might be right. But I can't let this go, despite the danger. After what Simon has done, he needs to be taught a lesson."

Jessie shook her head, her eyes wide with fear. "Please do no' do this. I couldna forgive myself if something happened."

Her bottom lip trembled and as tears welled, Robert knew without a shadow of a doubt that Jessie cared for him; perhaps even loved him. While his heart clenched to see her so desperate with worry, his blood sang.

"I will be all right, my love," he whispered, brushing her tears away with gentle fingers. "Trust me. I have a plan."

"But—"

She got no further. Why use words when he could show Jessie how much he cared for her?

Capturing Jessie's beautiful face in his hands, Robert kissed her with sincere and tender reverence, his mouth gently claiming her. *Loving her.*

She sank into him, immediately pressing her soft curves against his body, reaching up to clasp her hands around his neck to draw him yet closer. His mouth firmed against hers, his tongue teasing the full curve of her lower lip, seeking access to the velvet sweetness within.

Parting her lips on a sigh, she surrendered completely as Robert slowly deepened the kiss. Her tongue danced with his, tasting and teasing and exploring him just as thoroughly as he tasted her.

God in heaven, his Jessie was as ardent as she was fearless. Her encounter with Simon obviously hadn't reduced her enjoyment of kissing. As for her enjoyment of anything else of an intimate physical nature, when the time came, Robert vowed he would be patience itself. She would dictate the pace of their loving. He would follow her lead.

But now was not the right moment to take things further. He had a matter of honor to attend to.

With a groan of frustration, Robert broke the kiss, reluctantly dragging his mouth away. He looked down at Jessie, watching her eyes flutter open before her gaze reconnected with his. A slight smile curved her lips. "I know you must be exhausted, and will no doubt want to retire for the night, but would you mind if I wake you on my return?" he asked, relieved some of her calm had been restored. "I still need to see my father. And I need to pay a quick visit to Drummond at the docks...to put a few things in place for the coming morning. But then... At least I was hoping..." He drew a breath and stroked her cheek. "I'd very much like to continue this particular conversation... But only if you want that too..."

"Of course," Jessie murmured. "I would like that verra much. I would do anything for you."

Robert's mouth slanted into a smile. "Hopefully I won't be longer than an hour or so. I'll ring for Alison to assist you while I'm gone." As he took his leave, he consoled himself with the thought that the sooner he made the necessary arrangements for dealing with Simon, the sooner he would be back to show Jessie exactly how much she meant to him.

How much he loved her.

CHAPTER 26

Alison arrived soon after Robert departed. Jessie was thankful that the young girl was all business when it came to helping her change out of her ruined gown. There were no curious questions or comments about Simon's attack or the various bruises starting to bloom on her arms and neck. Nor were there any censorious looks about the fact that she would be installed in Lord Lochrose's rooms for the night. Jessie was grateful for the girl's matter-of-fact attitude. She rather thought Alison *would* make an excellent lady's maid.

Jessie gasped and blushed however when Alison produced her new night apparel—an exquisite night rail of saffron silk and lace with a matching *robe à la française* and slippers. They were obviously additional purchases that Robert had made that afternoon at the modiste's. She adored how much he was spoiling her with these luxurious gifts. It made her feel special and cherished. Truly desired. And dare she think it...loved?

The fine, almost transparent fabric whispered over Jessie's skin as she donned the garments. They were certainly not the practical flannel or cambric night rails she was used to wearing to bed. She wondered what Alison would make of the daring, even scandalous attire, but thankfully the girl continued to be the epitome of discretion.

The ormolu clock on the mantel was close to striking the half hour after midnight when Alison finally departed, but Jessie was curiously wide awake, despite the late hour. She poured a cup of tea, but was too agitated to drink it. Her emotions leapt wildly from anger at Simon's assault to trepidation about the potential danger Robert was in, to nervous anticipation of what would happen when Robert returned.

Unable to sit still, she eventually discarded her cup and explored Robert's suite of rooms. He had invited her in here, after all. She trusted he wouldn't mind.

The sitting room was elegantly furnished. A pair of leather wingchairs and a striped damask settee were arranged around a richly patterned Aubusson hearthrug by the fireside. A sideboard, desk, and bookcase in heavy oak stood at intervals between windows hung with curtains of burgundy velvet. Above the sideboard, Jessie noticed a framed painting of a distinguished and very handsome couple. The earl at a much younger age, perhaps in his thirties, posed beside a very beautiful young woman with an abundance of light brown curls and large solemn, blue eyes. She was presumably the late Countess of Strathburn, Robert's mother. Jessie imagined Robert must feel her absence terribly, just as she missed her own mother.

Through a communicating door she discovered a dressing room, largely empty save for a few items of Robert's clothing and a wooden traveling trunk. Another door at the end of the dressing room led into Robert's bedchamber. The soft glow of candles and the firelight revealed an enormous four-poster bed, hung with curtains of dark golden damask. The bed was covered with a rich gold and cream brocade counterpane and an abundance of fat ivory silk pillows lay against the ornately carved headboard. It looked sumptuous.

And tempting.

Someone, perhaps Alison, had also turned down the covers to reveal fine cotton sheets. Jessie had the sudden, overwhelming urge to crawl between them. Her pulse raced to think she might very well be sleeping beside Robert tonight.

But would they only be sleeping? She smiled. If she had her own wicked way, they certainly wouldn't.

But if Robert were to face Simon on the dueling field at dawn...

Jessie's stomach plummeted to the plush rug at her feet. No, she didn't want to think about that. She had to believe Robert's assertion that he had a plan to foil Simon and that everything would be all right. That *he* would be all right.

Her exploration complete, Jessie returned to the sitting room to wait for Robert's return. After kicking off her new saffron silk slippers, she settled into one of the chairs in front of the fire, sipping the whisky Robert had poured for her earlier, hoping the fiery liquid would calm her thoughts and skittering pulse. She'd just tossed back the last of the dram when the door creaked open, revealing her *fiancé*.

Robert. Thank God. Her impulse was to run to him and throw her arms about his neck but as she began to stand, Robert motioned with his hand. "Jessie, my love, don't get up on my account."

As she subsided back onto her chair, he shrugged off his velvet evening jacket and removed his lace jabot. "I must apologize for taking so long," he continued, tossing the garments onto a nearby settee. "But with the benefit of your canny reasoning, I needed to...adjust my plans surrounding the duel. It took a little longer than I expected to set the stage, but"—his mouth tipped into a wicked grin—"you can be rest assured that with the help of Captain Drummond, Tobias, and my father, I will not be waylaid by any of the King's men. With minimal risk to myself, Simon is about to be taught a valuable life lesson." With his shirt now open at the neck, Robert pulled up the footstool and sat in front of Jessie. He leaned forward, his arms resting on his muscular, satin-clad thighs. There was a smile in his eyes. "Does that ease your mind, my love?"

"To be honest, no' entirely," she replied in a voice breathless with both nerves and maddening desire. She shouldn't be distracted by Robert's physicality right now, but she was.

Dragging her gaze away from the tantalizing sight of her *fiancé's* strong throat and the tanned patch of chest below, she forced herself to consider his words. His plan seemed too hazy and vague for her liking. "I canna help but be worried about ye being involved in any sort of risky endeavor given the conditions of yer release. I dinna suppose ye were intending to share yer plan with me?"

Robert's smile widened. "Suffice it to say, I think Simon will be most surprised to find that he's about to embark on a character-building journey—of sorts. But most importantly, *I* will not be attending any duel."

"I'm most relieved to hear it," said Jessie, at last returning her *fiancé's* smile. She would also trust Robert's assertion that one way or another, Simon would be dealt with.

"Now, enough about duels and my half-brother's overdue comeuppance." Robert's gaze softened. "I believe we have unfinished business to attend to."

Jessie's pulse quickened. *Could he mean...? Were they about to make love?*

Robert was rolling up his shirt sleeves, revealing tanned, well-muscled forearms. "Let's dispense with this robe so I can see this graze of yours," he said, gesturing toward her left arm. "I passed Alison in the hall earlier, and she informed me that your bandage was a wee bit blood stained. I'm worried your stitches have been torn."

Oh. Jessie bit her lip. *That* wasn't the unfinished business she'd had in mind. All the same, she was suddenly acutely aware that she was only wearing flimsy night attire. "I'm sure the wound is fine," she murmured, her cheeks heating. "It doesna hurt. Really."

As she self-consciously checked the ribbons securing the front of her robe, she inwardly chided herself for being so shy and contrary. She and Robert had been through so much together. They'd already been intimate. And she *wanted* to take things further—to share her body completely with this wonderful man—so very much. But now the moment was upon her to do something as simple as shedding her robe, she'd become as diffident as a maid who'd never even been kissed.

Perhaps Simon's attack had rattled her more than she'd thought. *Curse him.* She really didn't want to think about that vile creature. She only wanted to be consumed with thoughts of Robert.

Perhaps sensing the reason for her reticence, Robert's lips curved into a soft, reassuring smile. "I'll only be looking at your arm, I promise."

Jessie nodded, her body suddenly too warm, her skin tingling beneath Robert's intent gaze. She wondered at the potent effect this man had on her every time he looked at her or touched her. But she knew it was more than desire. In the space of only seven days, she'd fallen irrevocably, hopelessly in love with him.

More than anything, she trusted him. Her eyes locked with Robert's, Jessie cast aside the last of her doubts, untied the robe's ribbons and let the saffron silk slide off her shoulders.

~

Despite his good intentions, Robert's gaze slipped inexorably downward to the fine lace décolletage of Jessie's night rail—the one he'd chosen himself when he'd visited the High Street modiste earlier in the day. Sweet Lord, Jessie was beautiful. The enticing sight of her breasts as they rose and fell with her uneven breathing had his cock jerking with awareness.

His lips firmed into a hard line, however, when he noticed the evidence of Simon's attack. The purple marks around Jessie's neck and on her arms stood out like obscene circlets against her perfect alabaster skin. With considerable effort, he dragged his mind away from the great pleasure he was going to derive from making Simon pay tenfold for what he'd done to Jessie. Somehow, he refocused his attention on attending to Jessie's bullet wound.

As he began to gently unwind the bloodied linen, he was abruptly transported back in time to another evening, when he'd first stitched her bullet graze before the light of another fire. That was only seven nights ago, yet he felt he'd known Jessie forever. Now he couldn't imagine being without her.

Robert slanted a glance upward and noticed Jessie was watching him. Her lips were slightly parted, her pulse beating rapidly in her throat. He bit his lip to suppress both a groan and the urge to bury his face in her neck. *Dear God.* Did she have any idea what she did to him?

Reining in his desire by focusing on the task at hand, he pulled the last of the bandage away to reveal the wound. A small amount of blood had seeped around the stitches, but otherwise, his handiwork remained intact.

He looked up and smiled encouragingly. "It's fine, *mo ghaoil*. I'll bathe it and redress it."

Jessie nodded and offered a small, tremulous smile. "Thank you."

She's still nervous around me. Which was completely understandable under the circumstances. Jessie was a canny woman; she could probably sense he wanted her.

When Robert had finished rebinding her arm, he gently slid her robe back into place. Then, with what felt like an enormous effort, he removed his hand from her smooth-as-silk shoulder.

Dear God, he was shaking.

Now at long last was the time for them to clarify their positions on being handfasted to each other. But Robert couldn't concentrate if he touched her.

And he had to get this right.

He felt as skittish as a lad about to kiss a girl for the first time. Tongue-tied and hopelessly daft with desire. But then, he'd never told any woman what he was about to tell Jessie.

His pulse racing, Robert looked her directly in the eye. "Jessie…" He dragged in another breath and somehow marshalled his thoughts and his courage. "Earlier today, we both agreed we needed to come to some understanding about our betrothal. Fate has clearly thrown us together, but the real question is: what do each of us want? Now that we are both free to choose."

Jessie continued to regard him steadily. "Aye… That's true," she said, her voice slightly breathless, betraying her own nervous state. She ran her tongue over her bottom lip, leaving a moist sheen across the luscious fullness.

Robert nearly groaned aloud. On an impulse, he reached forward and gently clasped her hands, fighting for the control to say what he needed to before he gave in to the desire pounding through him. "I know exactly how I feel about you, *mo chridhe,*" he murmured. "In fact, I think I've felt this way from the moment I first saw you by the loch at Lochrose. You stole my breath away. And my heart…" Inhaling another bracing breath, he continued, "Jessie Munroe, I'm in love with you and I can't imagine my life without you."

Dropping to one knee, Robert raised her hands to his lips, brushing the lightest of kisses over her elegant fingers. All the while, he held her eyes with his. "I have something to ask you, not because I have to, but

because I want to." He swallowed and firmed his voice. "Jessie Munroe...
will you marry me?"

~

Jessie's breath caught in her throat. Her heart soared. She couldn't
believe what she was hearing. *Robert loves me.*

He truly wanted her to be his wife.

She searched his face. His deep blue eyes were expectant, his
breathing shallow. Was he...nervous? Yes, Lord Lochrose, the Master of
Strathburn, was hanging by a thread, waiting for her answer. *Silly man.*
Didn't he realize her heart beat only for him? Nevertheless, his uncertainty leant a poignant sweetness to the moment and brought a smile to
her lips.

"Aye, I will marry you, Robert," she replied, her own voice shaky
with emotion. "No' because I have to, but because I want to, so verra
much."

Robert's lips curved in a smile, and he angled his head forward to
kiss her, but Jessie stopped him with a hand to his chest. Surprised, he
raised questioning eyes to hers.

Even though she was breathless with desire, she had to tell Robert
how she truly felt as well. "Wait. I havena finished clarifying my position
yet," she murmured huskily. Sliding off the chair, she sank to her knees
and raised one of Robert's hands to her chest where her own heart lay. It
pounded so wildly with abandoned joy, she wondered if he felt it.
"Robert Grant, I love you completely, with my entire heart. And
tonight, I want us no' just to be promised to each other, but truly handfasted, as husband and wife."

~

Robert drew in a steadying breath as he tried to control the potent mix
of emotions surging through him. Unadulterated happiness at Jessie's
confession of love blended with a heady wave of desire. She wanted to be
with him, be one with him, as his wife.

"Are you sure, Jessie?" he asked, his voice thick with emotion, his eyes searching hers.

"I've never been more certain of anything in my life." Jessie gathered his hands between hers and held them against her breasts. "I, Jessie Elizabeth Munroe, take you, Robert James Alexander Grant, the Viscount Lochrose and Master of Strathburn, to be my husband as of this moment and forevermore," she whispered, her eyes shining with love.

Robert smiled back at her like a besotted fool, but he didn't care. "And I, Robert James Alexander Grant, the Viscount Lochrose and Master of Strathburn, take you, Jessie Elizabeth Munroe, to be my wife as of this moment and forevermore." His gaze dropped to her lips and, praise heaven, this time Jessie did not stop him from lowering his mouth to hers.

He kissed her deeply, his mouth urgently moving over hers, the desire he'd kept in check for so long suddenly pulsing through his veins without restraint. He buried his hands in her cascading locks drawing her closer, taking everything she offered. Her lips. Her tongue. Her mouth responded to his every demand.

He felt Jessie fumbling with the buttons of his waistcoat, pulling his silk shirt out of his breeches and within moments, her hands slid beneath the fabric. A hiss of pleasure escaped his lips. He let her play, thrilled at the feel of her gentle hands caressing his heated flesh. When she broke their kiss and lowered her mouth to taste the sensitive hollow between his collarbones, he groaned aloud at the erotic sensation. Her lips and tongue branded his skin like fire.

However, when she reached for the fall front of his black satin breeches he stilled her hand. "Not yet, my love," he murmured, his voice rough with lust. Although his cock was harder than an iron poker, he wanted to take his time. Jessie deserved more than a rushed, rough coupling.

He wanted this to be perfect for her.

Robert captured her face in his hands and worshipped her mouth again until they were both breathless. Brushing her curls aside, her feminine scent—redolent of flowers and Jessie's own essence—swirled about him, intoxicated him as he traced a line of fiery, open-mouthed kisses along her delicate jaw and down her neck. She released a low whimper, a sound of deep pleasure echoing in her throat. God he wanted her. More than anything else in this world.

And it seemed she desired him just as much. Jessie restlessly kneaded his shoulders until he helped her to peel off his waistcoat and pull off his silk shirt. His upper torso now naked, she caressed and nibbled and licked. Her untutored yet uninhibited exploration of his chest and shoulders quickly drove his own arousal to such a fever pitch, he thought he might combust.

To distract her—indeed to stop himself from spending too soon—Robert gently eased away her saffron-hued robe. The silk whispered to the floor around her knees, but she didn't seem to mind he was now undressing her. Far from it. The firelight cast a golden glow over her bare arms and shoulders, rendering the flimsy confection of silk and lace that made up her night rail all but transparent. He could clearly see the outline of Jessie's full breasts and the hard points of her nipples as she arched her body toward him. His cock throbbed.

He had to see more, taste more. Have all of her.

"Perhaps we should retire to my bedchamber," he groaned against her temple, using his breath to caress her ear. "I want you in my bed, Jessie. Now and forever."

She responded by rising to her feet, pulling him with her. It appeared she was as eager as he was. Robert was determined to do this properly. He swept her into his arms and carried her through to the bed, laying her gently against the pillows. But he didn't join her immediately. The fire had burned low in the grate and greedy man that he was, he wanted to look his fill of Jessie's heavenly body.

Plus, the momentary distraction might stop him coming in his breeches.

He bent to the wood pile and threw a few additional logs into the fireplace. Light flared as bright and hot as his passion for Jessie. *His wife.*

~

As Robert threw logs into the fire and brought it back to life, Jessie swallowed and licked her lips, the agony of her wanting almost too much to bear. The sight of taut muscles flexing across Robert's broad shoulders and back made her tremble with desperation, made the folds between her thighs slick with moisture.

"Come to bed," she urged restlessly, rising to her knees. She clenched and unclenched her hands in the silk of her night rail. She couldn't wait for her handfasted husband to make her his wife in truth.

When Robert straightened and turned back to her, his gaze fixed unerringly on hers. Without so much as a blink or a blush, he swiftly shucked off his shoes, then stripped off his silk stockings and satin breeches, at last revealing his own blatant desire for her. His cock was long and hard—ready for her—the head glistening with moisture.

Oh my. Jessie bit her lip to stifle a purely wanton moan. Although she'd already seen Robert in an almost completely naked state at the inn at Invercauld, she was struck anew by how magnificent, how powerfully made he was. He had the frame of a warrior—all long limbs and lean sculpted muscle. Even though he was battle-scarred, it didn't matter. In her eyes, he was perfect.

"Look what you do to me, *mo chridhe*," he groaned, gripping his cock as if in pain. "God, I want you so much."

Despite the nervous excitement fluttering in her belly, a deep thrill shot through Jessie, clear to her toes. Her lips curved in a small smile, and she held out her hand. "You are no' alone, Robert. I want ye quite desperately too. Make love to me, husband of my heart."

With a low growl, Robert climbed onto the bed, every movement sinuous and graceful. "Aye, I intend to, my darling wife." His mouth took hers again in a hard, passionate kiss as he pushed her down onto the pillows. His long hard length pressed hotly against her belly, and she clutched his upper arms, arching into him, urging him to take more.

Pausing for breath, Robert raised his head and cradled her jaw with one hand, his gaze heated and heavy. "I have to see you, Jessie."

Without a word, she adjusted her position so Robert could help to ease off the silk and lace frippery. She then lay back on the pillows, burning with need, watching Robert through half-closed eyes as his midnight-blue gaze wandered over her. Instead of feeling self-conscious —she was still a virgin after all—she felt worshipped, cherished.

Desired.

But most of all, she felt loved.

~

Robert swallowed hard at the sight of Jessie's beautiful body.

"You are...perfect," he managed to rasp, his eyes devouring her full breasts, her small waist and flat belly, the gingery curls at the apex of her thighs, her long, slender legs. Cupping one of her breasts, he lowered his mouth and suckled her rosy nipple whilst he rolled and tugged the other distended bud between thumb and forefinger. Moaning, she speared her fingers into his hair, pulling it free from the velvet ribbon. He loved that he was driving her wild, making her lose control...and he'd only just begun.

Slowly, deliberately, one of his hands stroked down the flat plane of her stomach toward her inner thighs, and she immediately parted her legs to allow him access. With sure strokes, he teased her slick cleft and pulsating center, before easing one finger, then another inside her tight, hot sheath. She gasped at the invasion, her body tensing at first, but she didn't pull away. When Robert began to gently slide his fingers in and out of her, all the while circling his thumb over the swollen nub of her clitoris, she instinctively matched his thrusting rhythm, her hips arching and circling. Her mewls of pleasure were the sweetest sounds he'd ever heard.

But Robert wanted more than to just touch her. His own ravening lust urged him to taste and possess all of her.

Dragging himself away from her delicious breasts, he ran a trail of sucking kisses down her body until his mouth hovered just above her soft ginger curls. She might be a virgin, but she was passionate and adventurous. It couldn't hurt to ask...

Perhaps confused by his inaction, Jessie raised her head slightly and slanted him a glance from beneath her lashes.

Robert offered her the tilted smile he knew she loved. "Jessie, I want to kiss you, all of you. Will you let me?"

God, he hoped she said yes.

~

Jessie gasped. "Down...down there? Really?"

Robert smiled, his beautiful rakehell's smile. The one she could never resist. "Yes. *Really.*"

Wicked man. She couldn't hide her shock. She trusted Robert with all her heart, but the idea of him placing his mouth on her most secret parts...it was almost too much.

But then, she'd tasted *him* once before...and she knew she wanted to again.

Perhaps Robert's request wasn't so outlandish.

Curiosity won out. "Verra well," she whispered.

Her heart beating a wild rhythm, Jessie dropped her head back onto the pillows and closed her eyes. Robert's hair brushed her inner thighs, his fingers gently parting her wet folds.

Oh God, she couldn't believe she was letting him...

All thought scattered as his wicked tongue slid along her wet cleft then flicked against her throbbing center. Intense, hot pleasure, shot through her. Writhing mindlessly, she gripped Robert's head and cried his name, but he gave her no quarter. His powerful hands held her hips firmly as he suckled and licked her ruthlessly, relentlessly worshipping her body until the rising tension within her was almost unbearable. When he thrust his fingers deep inside her and simultaneously suckled hard on her throbbing core, it was too much.

Her grip on reality slipped and bright stars exploded behind Jessie's eyes. On an agonized cry, she came, blazing rapture sweeping her up, throwing her heavenward.

As the rippling waves of pleasure slowly subsided, she felt Robert returning to her side. Gathering her into his arms, he nuzzled her neck and ear, murmuring Gaelic endearments against her heated skin.

Jessie snuggled into him, pressing herself against his hard body, eyelids so heavy with sated desire, she could barely open them. "I didna have any idea... It never occurred to me that ye could kiss me...that way," she murmured against his bare shoulder.

She felt, rather than saw Robert's smile against her temple. "So I take it you particularly enjoyed that, *mo chridhe?*" he teased, his hands caressing her breasts once more, rekindling the slick warmth between her legs. She raised her head and answered him with a kiss. His lips and tongue were salty with the taste of her, but she didn't mind. In fact, she found it strangely pleasurable. *Deliciously erotic.*

Robert groaned her name and rolled her onto her back, gently parting her thighs with one of his knees. "Are you ready for us to be joined as man and wife, my love? I'm afraid it might hurt at first, but I will be as gentle as I can." His body hovered over hers, his straining manhood resting heavily against the sensitive flesh of her belly.

"Dinna mind me. I willna break." Boldly, Jessie encircled his pulsating, rigid length with her fingers, urging him to make them one. "Make love to me, husband of my heart."

Robert groaned and closed his eyes, pushing into her hand. "Aye. I will, my love. I will."

Briefly, Jessie wondered *how* Robert would fit inside her, but she so wanted to please him. He clearly wanted to be joined with her, so very badly. Moisture was already leaking from him onto her fingers.

Robert took his weight on his forearms, then pushed his hips forward, the head of his manhood nudging her entrance. Jessie whimpered as the pressure intensified, and she gripped Robert's shoulders. The burning pain was almost too much.

"Tell me if you want me to stop," he gritted out, shudders wracking his body.

Jessie realized that the restraint he exercised for her was causing him pain too. "Dinna stop. Take me, Robert," she whispered, reaching up to caress his tense jaw with trembling fingers. "Make me yours. Yours alone."

~

With an agonized groan, Robert surged forward and with one swift stroke, entered Jessie's hot, wet sheath. Dear God, she was tight. Despite her readiness, Jessie cried out and buried her face in his shoulder, panting.

Robert immediately ceased all movement. He'd hurt her. Guilt knifed through him.

"My sweet Jessie, I'm sorry," he whispered into her hair. "But trust me, it will get better."

Jessie nodded and kissed his neck. "I-I know. Remember, I want this too."

So brave. As much as his balls ached, as much as his cock throbbed, Robert vowed he wouldn't move until she was ready. Ignoring his own acute urge to pound into her, he took his weight on his elbows and rained feather-light kisses across Jessie's eyelids, cheeks, and forehead, waiting until she'd adjusted to the feel of him inside her.

Her eyes soon fluttered open, and she smoothed his hair away from his brow. "I'm all right now," she murmured huskily, and drew his head down for a slow, deep, languorous kiss. Then she tilted her hips. Welcomed him in.

Thank God. She still wanted him. Following Jessie's lead, Robert slowly withdrew, then glided into her again, deeper than before. Jessie released a delicious moan and her hands slid to his buttocks, as though urging him to keep going. Heartened, he repeated the action and this time Jessie sighed with pleasure. Joy flared like the incandescent heat of the Caribbean sun.

Gaining confidence that she was beginning to enjoy their coupling, Robert began to slide back and forth with slow sure strokes, powerful yet controlled, watching Jessie's changing expressions, gauging her reaction, making sure she continued to enjoy this as much as he was enjoying her.

Panting beneath him, Jessie matched his rhythm, her hands gripping his sweat slickened shoulders. Her inner passage started to quiver, and he gritted his teeth against his own compelling need to let go. He would make sure she came first, even if it killed him.

Adjusting his angle to give her everything, Robert pounded, faster, harder until he knew she was on the edge of bliss. When she cried his name, when her sheath clenched and rippled around him, he rejoiced.

But he could no longer control the rising tide of his own passion. With a final driving thrust, Robert too succumbed to the all-consuming rush of release. His body shuddered again and again as great waves of pleasure claimed him. Pleasure like nothing he'd ever experienced before. He buried his face in the curve of Jessie's neck, groaning her name.

Spent at last, Robert rolled sideways, gathering Jessie into his arms, still joined with her. He softly traced the outline of her kiss-swollen lips with his thumb and then brushed back a tangled lock of hair from her face. "I love you, my wife," he whispered, a smile of pure happiness curving his mouth.

Jessie smiled back with drowsy-eyed contentment. "And I love you, my husband," she murmured, then curled herself into him.

With her languid limbs still entwined with his, Jessie soon floated into sleep. The quiet rhythm of her breathing soothed Robert's soul like nothing else possibly could. He stroked her soft hair, gloried in the feel of her warm, silken skin pressed against his, and at last, he let the awe and profound satisfaction of knowing this beautiful woman was really, truly his, sink into his very bones.

Everything he did from now on would be for her: her, and the children they would make together. The morning and the days ahead would undoubtedly bring challenges to their door. But Robert vowed that no one—not Simon or his stepmother or the devil himself—would stand in the way of his happiness and Jessie's. Not ever.

CHAPTER 27

Simon sat on the edge of his bed at the White Horse Inn, clutching his pounding head in his hands, waiting for the world to stop spinning. Why the hell hadn't he listened to his mother and kept away from the demon drink like she'd ordered? A hangover was the last thing he needed on top of a bruised and scratched face, cut forehead, and bitten hand—all of which still pained him.

Devil take him, he was a mess.

He doubted he could stand, let alone fight a duel with his bloody brother. His only consolation was that if all went according to his mother's plan, it was unlikely he would have to lift a finger, let alone a sword.

He had no idea what the time was, but judged it was close to dawn. Baird, his valet, had woken him a short time ago before disappearing into the adjoining room to fetch his clothes and short sword.

Passed out in the chair before the spent fire snored his fair-weather friend and reluctant second for the duel, Sir Archibald Ramsay. Simple bribery had secured his services. The promise of covering Archie's substantial gambling debts for the evening as well as the inducement of visiting a brothel in the Grassmarket had eventually done the trick.

Thanks to the considerable amount of wine and brandy he'd imbibed, Simon had only vague recollections of the red-headed prostitute he and Archie had both used before they were tossed out into the street by the madam of the establishment and her henchman. Apparently he and Archie had been too rough with the wench. In Simon's mind, she hadn't been accommodating enough.

Just like Jessie.

A smirk quirked the corner of Simon's mouth as he envisaged how he'd treat Jessie when he finally had her all to himself.

It wouldn't be long now. If all went according to plan, his bloody brother would be locked up again in the Tolbooth before the sun even appeared over the Firth of Forth.

Baird's return roused him from his musings. Rising from the bed so he could begin to get dressed, Simon noticed his manservant was soaked to the skin.

"What the hell happened to you?" he demanded, clipping Baird around the ear with his uninjured hand. "And mind my clothes, you fool. You're getting them all wet."

"I'm verra sorry, Master, but it's been rainin' fit to drown the fishes in the Firth. I havena had the chance to change, seeing as I've only just returned from watching the main gate into Holyrood Park."

"Well?" Simon's voice was edged with impatience as Baird pulled up his master's buckskin breeches and laced them for him. "Don't dilly-dally about with the details. Was there any sign of the Scots Guard?"

The involvement of the Scots Guard was part of his mother's ingenious plan to entrap Robert. Last night, Baird had conveyed a message from the Countess of Strathburn to the dragoon regiment stationed at Edinburgh Castle about the impending duel. Simon was counting on the fact that the Guard would be in place to arrest Robert before the rogue even had a chance to draw his sword. He was not foolish enough to believe he could best his older brother in a physical confrontation, but he was certain that he and his mother could outwit Robert, hands down.

"Aye, Master," replied Baird, as he handed Simon a fresh cambric shirt. "I saw a Redcoat officer with six soldiers ride past not ten minutes ago, headin' toward Arthur's Seat."

"Good. Damned inconvenient this weather though." Simon grimaced as he shrugged into a heavy redingote jacket of broadcloth.

"The bloody lobster backs had better be there, or I'll have your guts for garters, Baird. I don't want to brave these elements for nothing."

Baird simply handed him his belt and short sword. He was accustomed to his master's foul moods. "Shall I wake Sir Archibald?" he asked woodenly. "It's already half-past six."

Simon glanced over at his all but unconscious companion. "Don't bother," he snorted, throwing on the oilskin cloak Baird passed to him. "He'll only slow us down and you can stand in for my second just as well. Besides, there'll be no duel if the Scots Guard time their interruption at the right moment." Just then, a squall of rain hit the window-pane. "Bloody hell, what are the chances of rooting out a carriage at short notice, Baird? I don't fancy riding in this downpour."

"I'll see what I can do, sir. I believe there's a small hackney carriage in the mews runnin' beside the inn that can be hired. I saw it when I came back from the Park."

"Good. I'll meet you on the front stairs when you bring it round. And you had better be damned quick."

After Baird left, Simon splashed cold water onto his face to help clear his head. His hands were shaking as he dried his face with a towel— a pointless exercise, given he was about to get soaked through. He could hear rain drumming steadily against the window now. When he opened one of the shutters and peered down to the courtyard below, he could barely see a thing. It was as black as Hades.

A dark carriage appeared at the entrance of White Horse Close. Baird had been successful. At least the devil's own luck seemed to be working for him at the moment.

Simon trusted it would continue.

The entrance of the inn was deserted when Simon entered the vestibule and pushed through the front door onto the rain slicked portico. The carriage waited for him at the foot of the short flight of stairs, the door closed against the rain.

Where in Lucifer's name was Baird? Simon scowled. Had the cocky bastard taken the liberty of sitting inside the carriage, out of the rain? He certainly wasn't standing at the back of the carriage or hastening forward to open the hackney's door for his master.

Simon squinted through the rain and darkness at the driver, but he was shrouded in a hooded oilskin and wasn't making a move to assist Simon either.

With a low growl, Simon rushed down the stairs. He'd kick Baird's arse later for not doing his duty. He flung himself into the pit of the cab and slammed the door—

Only to be met by the touch of something metallic and cold between his eyes. Then there was an unmistakable click.

Fuck. It was the sound of a pistol being cocked.

"Now then, *Mister* Simon Grant," came an unfamiliar, rumbling bass baritone from the dark recesses of the cabin. "Welcome to Purgatory."

As much as Robert would have loved to stay abed with Jessie until at least the middle of the next day, he lay with her in his arms for only a few hours. He didn't dare fall asleep and miss these sweet moments—and of course, he didn't want to miss the opportunity to serve Simon his long-overdue just deserts.

The ormolu clock on the mantel in the sitting room was chiming half past six when he at last gently disengaged himself from Jessie's warm embrace. She barely stirred as he moved the sleep tousled curls from her face and placed a tender kiss on her brow. As soon as he'd dealt with his brother, he swore he would return to her side. His wife.

His love and his life.

Careful not to disturb her, Robert moved into the adjacent dressing room and threw on a linen shirt that he left untucked and open at the neck, black broadcloth breeches, a silk brocade banyan, and black leather boots. He didn't bother to shave or even comb his hair. The greater his *dishabille* when the King's troops inevitably arrived on the doorstep of Strathburn House, the better.

He moved into his sitting room and rang for tea. Within a short space of time, the fire was restoked, the candles lit, and a tray of warm baps and a pot of tea was brought up from the kitchen by one of the footmen.

As Robert mulled over the plan he and his father had devised to expose Caroline's and Simon's treachery, he noticed the increasing intensity of the rain drumming on the casement windows. The gutters and cobbled streets would undoubtedly be awash and the common below Arthur's Seat in Holyrood Park would be a quagmire. It was definitely not the kind of weather in which to be fighting hand-to-hand combat with short swords. He *almost* felt sorry for the poor sodden Scots Guards who would be lying in wait for him and Simon to arrive— but not quite. How long would they stay in position before they realized the duel would not be taking place?

With cup in hand, he wandered to the window and flicked the curtains to the side. The square below was deserted for now. Over the looming bulk of the Salisbury Crags, he fancied that the heavy pall of dark gray clouds was beginning to lighten a fraction. He estimated that within the hour, there would be a mightily annoyed and bedraggled officer pounding on the door of Strathburn House.

Robert wasn't far off the mark. The clock was heralding half past seven when he heard the clatter of horses' hooves on the cobbles outside. He put down his second cup of tea and waited patiently for Gordon to summon him.

Sure enough, within a few minutes, the butler appeared. "Beg pardon, milord, but Captain MacBryde from the Scots Guard kindly requests yer presence."

"Indeed. I believe my father would like a word with the captain as well, Gordon. If you would be so kind as to send word to MacGowan to wake his lordship."

The butler's lips twitched with a smile as he bowed. "Of course, milord."

Robert ran his hands through his hair, ruffling it. Deciding he still looked suitably sleep rumpled, he descended to the vestibule.

Captain MacBryde stood in the middle of the entrance hall, looking both sodden and disgruntled in equal measure. Water streamed from his greatcoat onto the parquetry floor, and his boots were caked in mud. The front door was still ajar and Robert could see at least a half-dozen other Redcoats shivering on the portico outside. The rain was coming down in sheets.

Robert bit the inside of his cheek to suppress a smile as he greeted the officer. "Captain MacBryde," he said with an incline of his head. "What can I do for you at this early hour?"

MacBryde bowed but not before he had looked Robert up and down, noting his obvious state of dry *dishabille*. It was clear Lord Lochrose hadn't been out in the rain, looking for a fight in a muddy park. A look of resignation replaced the expression of annoyance on the officer's face. "My apologies, Lord Lochrose, for having roused ye from yer bed. It seems I've been led a merry dance by someone."

Robert feigned a look of confusion. "I don't follow you, Captain."

MacBryde sighed and swiped at a trickle of water running off his nose. "At ten o'clock last night, my commanding officer received a missive—written on paper bearing the Strathburn coat of arms—stating that ye'd instigated a duel with yer brother, a Mister Simon Grant. Said duel was supposed to have taken place half an hour ago in Holyrood Park. Given that ye'd only been released from the Tolbooth yesterday and ye're on probation—Lord Arniston's office informed the Guards of the terms of yer release yesterday—we were duty bound to investigate. But as neither ye nor yer brother arrived, I can only conclude that one of ye, or both, thought better of it and forfeited."

Robert looked at the captain squarely. "It is true that my brother and I had a disagreement last night over a somewhat...private matter. Harsh words were exchanged and in the heat of the moment, my brother did propose that we settle the grievance at sword point at first light in the Park. But to go against him in a duel...that would be fool-hardy to say the least, considering my current situation. I decided it was not worth it, as my forfeiture clearly demonstrates."

Just then his father appeared on the landing. "What is the meaning of this?" Lord Strathburn demanded before MacGowan assisted him down the stairs to stand beside Robert. It was obvious he'd only just emerged from his bed as well—he wore a velvet banyan over his night-clothes and his periwig was slightly askew.

A masterful touch, thought Robert.

Anger fairly radiated from the earl as he skewered the captain with a gimlet stare.

Captain MacBryde gave a creditable bow in the face of such noble ire and again explained the situation.

"What rubbish," declared his father. "And before my morning coffee, too. Show me this letter purporting there was to be a duel between my sons."

The captain pulled a somewhat soggy piece of parchment from the folds of his greatcoat and handed it over. Lord Strathburn ran his gaze over the missive quickly before glancing up at Robert.

"What is it?" Robert asked with what he hoped was deceptive mildness. He was already certain what it was his father was about to announce, but it wouldn't hurt to feign ignorance.

His father cleared his throat and looked at the captain, a suitably embarrassed expression on his face. "Well... As much as I hate to say it, I believe my wife, Lady Strathburn, penned this. This is her personal stationery complete with wax seal. I would recognize her handwriting anywhere."

Robert had difficulty suppressing a wry smile. His clever Jessie had been right about who had masterminded the plot against both of them. He addressed the officer. "But then... What I find strange, Captain MacBryde, is the fact that my stepmother sent this letter to the Guard well before Simon and I had even had our altercation. It was close to midnight when the duel was called. I wonder how Lady Strathburn knew it was going to happen."

MacBryde looked thoughtful for a moment. "Lord Strathburn, would ye mind if yer wife was summoned so that I might have a word?"

"Of course, Captain. I completely understand. In fact, I insist," replied the earl with a heavy sigh. "Gordon, please wake her ladyship and make it clear that I expect her in the library in ten minutes. If she isn't, tell her I will send several of the Scots Guards upstairs to assist her."

Gordon bowed, his mouth twitching as he said, "Aye, milord."

~

A short time later, a visibly pale and shaken Lady Strathburn appeared in the library. She was wearing a crumpled morning gown *a la polonaise* and her hair had been pushed roughly beneath a lace mob cap.

Robert watched her from the darkened corner of the room where he had installed himself in a brown leather wingback chair. She was so flustered, she had barely acknowledged his presence, other than to cast him an uncharacteristic nervous glance.

This interview would be interesting indeed.

His father directed her to a chair before the fire. A stony-faced Captain MacBryde stood by the hearth, hands behind his back. In his full officer's regalia with a sword at his hip, he was a truly imposing presence.

Lady Strathburn looked wildly from her husband to the glowering Scots Guard. "Wh-What is it? Why isn't Simon here with this...soldier? Has something happened to him?" she asked, voice quavering.

"Now why would you think that, my dear?" asked Lord Strathburn, leveling his steely, dark blue gaze upon her.

"B-Because of the duel..."

"And how would you know anything about that?" queried the earl in a studied tone. "I believe you were abed when it was called last night."

Lady Strathburn swallowed and wrung her hands, her gaze darting between her husband and the captain. "The servants... You know how they gossip—"

His father thrust the letter toward her. "Balderdash. You detailed the event in this letter you addressed to the Commanding Officer of the Scots Guard. Do you deny that this is your stationery and handwriting?"

Lady Strathburn barely even glanced at the page. "All right then, yes. Yes, I did write it," she admitted with defiance. She raised her chin, a hint of her usual acerbic manner reemerging. "A crime was going to be committed by your traitorous, good-for-nothing son." She then turned in her seat to face the captain. "I hope you are going to arrest Lord Lochrose after his recklessness at Holyrood Park. If he's injured my poor Simon—"

His father waved the page at her. "How did you know about the specifics of the duel, my lady? A duel I might add, that has turned out to be a non-event."

Lady Strathburn's mask of belligerent confidence slipped a little. "What...what do you mean?"

Captain MacBryde spoke at last. He eyed the countess with

obvious disapproval. "Neither Simon Grant nor Lord Lochrose were in Holyrood Park at the designated time or place ye described. It seems ye have sent me and my men on a wild goose chase, milady. In the rain."

Lady Strathburn was twisting her hands again. "I don't understand. Perhaps the weather prevented Simon from attending..." Her next words were uttered with considerable venom. "I was so sure Robert"—she turned her head to his corner and sent him a pointed look—"would have made a show to defend his strumpet's honor."

"I take it ye mean me, Lady Strathburn?"

Dear God, it was Jessie. Robert whipped his head around to the doorway as did everyone else in the library. *What on earth was she doing here?* This hadn't been part of the plan. Robert couldn't bear the idea that she would be exposed to further trials. Had she not endured enough already?

And yet Jessie took his breath away. She looked nothing like the strumpet his stepmother had just declared her to be. She stood just inside the door, looking as fresh and lovely as a summer's day in a silk gown of periwinkle blue. It was another of the creations which he'd persuaded the modiste to sell to him yesterday. With her red-gold hair arranged in a becoming, loosely bound style that cascaded down one shoulder, Jessie was undeniably the Viscountess Lochrose, his wife. At least in his eyes.

Robert stood, and across the room, his gaze met Jessie's. He hesitated to introduce her for a moment, trying to gauge what she would be thinking. They had pledged themselves to each other, become man and wife last night, but did Jessie want him to announce that fact to the whole room? Even though they'd exchanged legitimate vows and consummated their union in accordance with the common-law practice of Highland handfasting, he had no doubt that Alasdair Munroe would prefer that his daughter was wedded before God in a kirk. As would his own father.

As if sensing the reason for his indecision, Jessie gave him a brief but knowing smile before she turned her attention back to Captain MacBryde. "I am Jessie Munroe, Lord Lochrose's betrothed," she said clearly.

MacBryde introduced himself then addressed Robert. "So...is that what this is all about, milord? Defense of this young lady's honor?"

Concern furrowed Robert's brow as he looked back at Jessie. He wanted to spare her from whatever public humiliation he could. But how could he do that, yet make it clear that his stepmother and Simon had instigated the heinous attack on her?

"It's all right, milord," Jessie said, returning Robert's gaze steadily as she stepped farther into the room. Even though the library was only dimly lit by firelight and the weak morning light filtering in through the windows, it was enough to reveal the shocking bruises around her throat. She'd tucked a fichu of a fine diaphanous fabric into the low-scooped neckline of her gown; no doubt she was attempting to hide the evidence of Simon's assault. Nevertheless, Robert saw Captain MacBryde's gaze flicker to the telltale marks. "It is true that Lord Lochrose sought to defend my honor," she continued, "but he was sorely provoked by his brother."

"I would appreciate it if you could describe exactly what happened, Miss Munroe?"

Both admiration and a sharp pang of sympathy penetrated Robert's chest when his brave Jessie did not blush or look away from the captain. "Shortly before midnight, after the household had retired for the evening," she said, "Simon entered my bedchamber uninvited and attempted to force himself on me."

Caroline snorted. "A likely story. This hussy of a servant's daughter has been throwing herself at Simon ever since she first darkened our doorstep."

"Enough!" her husband commanded. "Don't you dare utter another lie against this lovely young woman."

Lady Strathburn paled but the remonstrance did not prevent her from throwing Jessie a baleful glare.

Captain MacBryde inclined his head. "Please continue, Miss Munroe. If you can."

Jessie drew a steadying breath before she resumed her account. Meeting the captain's gaze again, she succinctly recounted each harrowing detail of her ordeal. Robert couldn't help but admire her bravery.

"Thankfully, Lord Lochrose heard my scream and came to my aid," she concluded, casting Robert a grateful glance. "If...if it hadna been for him..." Her hand rose to her bruised throat and she closed her eyes for a moment before looking back at MacBryde.

MacBryde nodded, understanding and compassion in his eyes. "I can see how difficult this is for ye to talk about, Miss Munroe. Ye do yerself credit with yer forthright explanation." The captain turned to Robert. "I can also see why ye would have been compelled to defend yer betrothed's honor, Lord Lochrose. But ye obviously thought better of acting so rashly come the cold light of day. I commend ye for that."

"Indeed," Robert replied with a sardonic lift of one eyebrow. "Believe me, Captain, it was not easy to pass up the opportunity to make my brother pay for his transgressions. But in the end, I realized my desire to be free to wed Miss Munroe was stronger than my desire to exact revenge. The Tolbooth or the gallows are hardly the places to begin married life, wouldn't you agree?"

MacBryde nodded once, a slight smile cracking his seemingly implacable facade.

Robert crossed the room until he was standing before his stepmother. Now was the time for her to be made accountable for her perfidy. She visibly shrank back into the wingback chair, her hands plucking at the sleeves of her robe. It was satisfying, after all this trouble, to see her squirm.

"Now, *dearest stepmother*, would you care to explain how you came by such detailed knowledge of the duel well in advance of it actually being called? Simon didn't propose the time and place until close to midnight. He was then forcibly ousted, for the second time this week, from Strathburn House. As you clearly weren't present during the confrontation, how is it that you were able to inform Captain MacBryde's commanding officer about the precise terms of the duel at least two hours before the challenge was actually made, madam?"

Caroline gawped like a fish out of water. "I... Captain MacBryde must have been mistaken about the time he received the letter."

MacBryde cocked an eyebrow. "Indeed, I am no', Lady Strathburn. It was precisely five past ten last night when I was handed the letter by my commanding officer. There can be no mistake."

"Well, it hardly matters about the timing," scoffed Lady Strathburn. "Lord Lochrose has clearly broken the terms of his probation by challenging his brother to a duel. Duels are against the law, are they not? He should be arrested for attempting to murder my son! He was going to commit an act of out-and-out violence!"

Lord Strathburn stepped forward. "That is not the case. Robert has forfeited the duel, therefore no crime has been committed. But *you*, madam, and Simon seem to have been party to a conspiracy against both Robert and Miss Munroe. I should have the good captain here arrest you for the crimes of conspiracy and incitement to commit violence. You instigated, aided, and abetted Simon's attack on Miss Munroe, a scheme clearly designed to provoke Robert into committing a crime of passion for which he would be arrested. I'm sorry to say so, but you disgust me, madam." Robert's father turned to Captain MacBryde. "What do you think we should do from here, Captain?"

MacBryde frowned. "There is certainly enough evidence to warrant further investigation into both Mr. Grant's and Lady Strathburn's involvement in the attack upon Miss Munroe. There definitely appears to be an element of premeditation on both their parts. Would ye like me to refer the matter onto the Lord Advocate's office, Lord Strathburn?"

Ignoring the horrified gasp of his wife, Lord Strathburn looked to Robert and Jessie. "How would you feel about this being taken further? Especially you, my dear Miss Munroe."

Jessie's brow pleated as she considered the question. "I rather think that you and Robert have had to deal with enough scrutiny and hardship, milord. I dinna feel the need to take things any further."

Robert crossed to Jessie's side and reached for her hand, raising it to his lips. *His brave, brave woman.* "Are you certain, my love?"

Jessie nodded, a faint flush brightening her cheeks. "You and I are safe. That's all that matters," she said softly, her eyes glowing.

Robert tucked her hand into the crook of his arm and addressed MacBryde. "As much as I would personally enjoy seeing my stepmother and half-brother charged for their crimes, my wife-to-be and I have no wish to add to the infamy already associated with our family's name." He glanced at his stepmother; her face was now a sickly shade of green. "And by the looks of *Lady* Strathburn, perhaps the threat of prosecution has been punishment enough for the time being. Wouldn't you agree, Father?"

His father's gaze was decidedly cool as it came to rest upon his wife. "Perhaps. I will think on it. At this point in time, I will say that I'm decidedly less inclined to be as magnanimous as I have been when it comes to the allowance I bestow upon her. As for our younger son, I have a mind to disown him completely."

Lady Strathburn's jaw dropped. "You—you've already banished Simon from this house," she gasped. "Surely you wouldn't cut off his only source of income. He would be ruined. Think of the scandal, William!"

"Perhaps you should have thought of that before you and Simon both embarked on this foul scheme to ruin my eldest son and his future wife," snapped the earl. "I've had quite enough of your carping presence for one morning. I suggest you retire to your room."

Lady Strathburn rose unsteadily to her feet and turned to leave. However, by the time she reached the door, she'd managed to dredge up enough anger to fling one final barb Robert's way. "You play the innocent, but I don't trust you at all," she hissed. "You wouldn't let Simon get away with this. There must be a reason he didn't arrive for the duel. What have you done with my son?"

Robert kept his expression perfectly neutral. "I've done absolutely nothing, my lady. I have no idea where Simon is. If he isn't passed out drunk in his room at the White Horse Inn, he's probably holed up in a house of ill-repute somewhere. You know as well as I that the rain would be enough to put him off setting foot outside. I'm sure he'll turn up."

CHAPTER 28

When Robert descended into the hold of the *Phoenix* with Drummond an hour later, it was to find his half-brother shackled in irons in the stronghold below the cargo deck.

In the wavering light of the cargo lanterns, he could see that his brother's eyes were closed—whether he was asleep, unconscious, or just plain foxing, he couldn't be certain. Although he derived some grim satisfaction from the sight—after ten years, the tables *had* finally turned—Robert knew it was not nearly enough to appease his thirst for retribution. Simon needed to pay for what he'd done to Jessie.

Justice would be served, one way or another.

"As soon as he knew I had a pistol, he fainted dead away," explained Drummond with a chuckle. "He knocked his head on the handle of the carriage door on the way down. There's only a wee bump mind. Would you like me to call Tobias to fetch a bucket of bilge water to throw over him? That should startle him out of whatever fug he's in."

Just picturing the look of outrage on his despicable brother's face as filthy water dripped from his nose made Robert smile. "An appealing idea, but I don't think we need to go quite that far yet." He peered down at Simon through the latticed bars. "Time to wake up," he called. "You've languished down there long enough."

Simon cracked an eyelid and groaned. "You bastard. You won't get away with this."

Robert smiled. "Oh, I think I will, especially after you write your mother a farewell letter I will be dictating."

"Go to hell."

"From where I stand, I rather think that's where *you* are, dear brother."

The bosun's mate and Tobias were summoned and within a few minutes, they had hauled a still shackled Simon out of the stronghold and up to Drummond's cabin where he was unceremoniously deposited onto a chair before the captain's desk. Tobias and the bosun's mate took up positions by the door whilst Drummond slouched negligently in his own seat, a darkly amused expression on his bearded face; he played the role of an hirsute, menacing pirate very well.

Robert leaned against the desk, his arms folded across his chest, staring down at his brother. In the gray light filtering through the cabin's windows, he noticed that beneath the various cuts, scratches and bruises, Simon's face had also developed the greenish pallor of one who was decidedly seasick. He smiled inwardly at the thought.

"You can't do this," Simon ground out, resting his forehead in his hands. Below his brother's grubby lace cuffs, Robert could see that the shackles had already left raw, reddened areas on his wrists. "It's kidnapping."

Sardonic amusement twisted Robert's mouth. "Oh, but I can. And I think kidnapping is too harsh a word. Think of it more as...gainful employment. You're about to discover what it's like to be an able seaman. Once the ship's underway, you'll be expected to work like anyone else on board."

Simon dropped his hands and shot Robert a look of pure hatred. "Over my dead body."

Any trace of amusement left Robert's voice. "Believe me. That can easily be arranged."

His brother snorted. "You don't have the guts. You didn't even show for the duel."

Drummond stood abruptly and leaned forward over the desk. "I'd take him at his word, laddie," he growled. "Yer brother used to be a mercenary, ye ken. There's verra little he wouldna do."

Simon paled. "I...I'm going to be sick."

Drummond sighed heavily and nodded at the bosun's mate. "Och, give the puling pup a bucket." By the time Simon had finished emptying the contents of his stomach, Robert had a quill, ink, and parchment at the ready.

Simon wiped his mouth on his sleeve. "I'm not going to write a bloody thing," he muttered with less conviction than before.

Robert sighed. "I thought you might say that. But you will." He doubted he would need to actually administer any type of physical coercion to make Simon comply. Like most bullying cowards, his halfbrother would likely accede to his demands at the mere hint of anything that was even remotely painful.

Making a show of it, Robert shrugged off his greatcoat and riding jacket and began to roll up his shirtsleeves, flexing the taut muscles of his forearms. He glanced back at Simon and noticed him biting his lip. He was nervous.

Good.

"Now we can do this the easy way or the hard way, Simon. It's entirely up to you," Robert continued smoothly. He turned to Drummond, trying not to grin. "What do you think we should start with as motivation?"

Drummond narrowed his dark eyes on Simon and scratched his beard, playing along. "I personally think a nice hot branding iron applied to the nether regions works verra well. But then, ye canna really go past a good flaying. Shall I send Mr. Kennedy, the bosun's mate here, to fetch his cat o'nine tails, milord? It's been a long time since he's had the chance to administer a decent flogging."

Robert considered his brother's pasty face. He was already looking decidedly green around the gills again. It wouldn't be long until he gave in. "Hmm, tempting. But I was thinking of something more immediate, and if you'll pardon the pun, ready to hand. Do you still have that set of thumbscrews?"

Drummond grinned. "A verra good idea, milord." He reached for one of his desk drawers. "I have 'em right here—"

Simon lifted his chin in a last-ditch attempt at bravado. "You wouldn't dare—"

Robert gripped his brother's shoulder and said in a voice imbued with soft, barely controlled menace, "Oh yes, I would. You can't even imagine what I'd do to hold you to account for what you did last night, what you've tried to do before, and what you've undoubtedly done to other poor innocent women. Do you really want to push me to find out?"

Simon leaned back in his chair. "All right," he croaked. "I'll write the bloody letter."

"Excellent. I knew you'd see it my way." Robert smiled and pushed the writing implements toward Simon. "You can release his hands from the irons, Mr. Kennedy."

With shaking fingers, Simon reached out and picked up the quill. He was about to dip the nib into the ink when he paused, the quill suspended over the pot. His pale gray eyes lifted to Robert. "Exactly just how long will my *penance* last?" he asked in an uncharacteristically subdued tone.

Robert's lips thinned. "That entirely depends upon you, Simon, and how well you fulfill your duties aboard this ship. I shall leave Drummond to attend to the day-to-day details. But suffice it to say, all going well—including a demonstration of sufficient contrition—I envisage your tenure will end after a year and a day—much as my probation will."

Simon's face was the color of whey, but he nodded and bent to his task.

Robert rubbed his chin. "Now, how shall you begin? *Dearest Mother...*"

~

Dearest Mother,

After much soul-searching I realize that because of my transgressions against my family, and in particular Miss Munroe, I am

*not fit to remain within the sphere of polite society. I have brought
untold dishonor to our family's name, and for that I am sincerely
sorry. Please convey my heartfelt apologies to all I have wronged,
especially Miss Munroe.*

*However, as it is clear to me that I will never be able to adequately
atone for my misdeeds, I believe the only reasonable course of
action is to remove myself from the family fold. I have decided to
look upon this as an opportunity to explore new horizons and look
for a better purpose in life.*

*Robert has been very supportive and is assisting me with my quest
for self-improvement. Never fear, I shall write to you periodically
about my adventures.*

Your devoted son,
Simon

Caroline, Lady Strathburn, threw the letter down in front of her
husband as he finished his tea and scones. "What utter rubbish,
William," she snapped, sharp irritation and hot anger spiking through
her. "You know as well as I that Robert has forced him into this. Simon
would never leave of his own accord."

The letter, which had been addressed to her, had been delivered just
after ten o'clock by a young street urchin, and she had opened it immediately.

Lord Strathburn sighed and picked up the paper. He perused it
briefly before casting it back onto the table between them. "Caroline, I
think it would be best for all concerned if you let this drop. It is about
time our son got to experience more of life than this sheltered corner of
the world has to offer. If Robert is prepared to support him in that
endeavor, who am I to interfere?"

Caroline glared at her husband. She knew something terrible had
happened to Simon and that her bloody stepson was behind it. "What
rot! Our son has been kidnapped, I'm certain of it. Yet you won't lift a

finger to help him. Unless..." Her eyes narrowed with suspicion. "You know exactly where Simon is right now, don't you? I'd wager my soul that you and that Robert of yours planned his abduction together."

Lord Strathburn stood and coolly met her gaze. "All you need to know is that Simon is learning a life lesson. One long overdue."

Caroline snorted as she snatched up the letter. "I'll find out where he's gone and get him back. And then there'll be hell to pay, mark my words."

She stormed over to the bellpull and rang for Gordon, who responded almost immediately. She suspected that the butler had probably been listening outside the door, but she couldn't afford the time to berate him. "Tell my maid to fetch my cloak and have my sedan chair brought round. And make sure you hire some decent chairmen, I'm in a hurry," she snapped.

The butler bowed. "Yes, milady. But I think I should warn you that it is still raining."

Lord Strathburn frowned. "Perhaps it would be best if you used the carriage, Caroline."

"I don't have time to wait for it," she retorted as she snatched a cloak of black velvet from her maid, who'd been hovering in the vestibule. She threw it over her day gown of rich purple silk and shot her husband another furious look. "If anything has happened to Simon, I'll hold not only Robert, but you to account as well."

The sedan chair arrived promptly and within a short space of time, Caroline was hammering on the door to Simon's room at the White Horse Inn.

Baird, his valet, cracked the door open, but on seeing whom it was, swept it wide and bowed. "Milady?"

Caroline pushed past him into the stale, empty room. "Where is your master?" she demanded.

Baird, a tall, sallow-skinned man of middle age, stared at the floor. "I'm verra sorry, milady. I-I dinna ken... I havena seen him since early this morning..."

Quelling a wave of rising panic, Caroline glanced about the room. As far as she could see, there were no signs of foul play here. "Tell me what happened. Did he prepare for the duel? Where is his second?"

Baird swallowed and looked up at her as if lost for words. She noticed for the first time that the valet was looking decidedly worse for wear himself. In fact, he looked like he'd been dragged through a filthy puddle.

"Don't stand there gaping, you fool," she snapped. "Out with it."

Baird shook his head, lank brown hair hanging in his eyes. "That's the problem, milady. I dinna ken exactly what happened. I woke my master and helped him to ready for the duel at ha'-past six as planned. His second—Sir Archibald Ramsay—was asleep, but the master didna want me to wake him. He thought he wouldna be needed on account of the fact I had seen the Scots Guard entering the Park. It was raining verra heavily, so the master asked me to hire a carriage for him. I ken the inn keeps one in the mews. But when I went down to ask for it...weel, I think I was struck on the head from behind." He gingerly prodded the back of his skull and winced.

"And?" Caroline demanded, gesturing impatiently. "I do not want to hear about your incompetence, you dolt. What happened to your master? Where is this fellow, Sir Archibald?"

Baird grimaced. "Weel, the thing is, milady, I was clean knocked out and didna come to for a wee while. And when I came back here, the master was gone. Sir Archibald was still here, but he didna ken anything about what had happened. He only left about an hour ago himself. I think he was headed back to his lodgings in the Lawnmarket if ye wish to speak with him—"

Caroline flicked her hand in a gesture of dismissal. "Enough, you idiot. You're supposed to look out for your master. With a skull as thick as yours obviously is, I can't believe you were laid out by some common footpad. Unless..." Her eyes narrowed. "You say you didn't see who it was who struck you?"

"No, milady. It was verra dark in the mews, and pouring rain. I'm so sorry, milady—"

"Oh, shut your mouth, Baird. I need to think on this."

Caroline crossed to the room's only window and looked down onto the cobbled courtyard below where her sedan chair and hired chairmen waited. One or more of Robert's lackeys had obviously knocked out Baird and had then taken Simon.

But two could play at this kidnapping game.

She smiled slowly, then glanced over her shoulder at the valet. "Did Simon leave his dueling pistols anywhere about?"

Although the morning was dismal with rain, Jessie was light of spirit when she decided to venture forth from Robert's rooms and seek the company of Lord Strathburn. After the interview in the library, Robert had departed for Leith Docks to say farewell to the *Phoenix* before it embarked on its return journey to Jamaica.

And to farewell his brother.

Robert had shared his ingenious plan of recruiting Simon as a crew member of his ship with her. She very much hoped that after a year of such employment, Simon would be a reformed man. To her abiding relief, it meant she wouldn't have to see him for some time. No more looking over her shoulder, jumping at the sound of a door opening— just happiness, with her new husband.

Traversing the hall which led to the stairs, Jessie smiled softly as she also recalled how Robert had kissed her thoroughly before he'd left Strathburn House. She touched her fingers to her lips and let her mind wander to thoughts of how she and her handfasted husband would spend the afternoon when he returned.

He'd sworn he'd be back as soon as he was able.

The click of a door unlatching and the rustling of silk directly behind Jessie caught her attention.

"Don't make a sound or I'll pull the trigger."

Jessie started at the sound of Lady Strathburn's voice close to her ear. Then she felt something hard being pushed between her shoulder blades.

The muzzle of a pistol.

Oh God. Jessie froze and her lungs seized as ice-cold terror gripped her heart. The countess was obviously launching a counter offensive because Robert had taken her son. But what, in heaven's name, did Lady Strathburn have planned? Revenge of some sort was clearly her agenda, but how exactly was she intending to exact it?

Dragging in a breath, Jessie attempted to turn around. "This willna help, milady. What could you possibly hope to—"

"I told you to shut it, you little bitch." Lady Strathburn grabbed Jessie by the arm then pulled her roughly back so that she was pressed up against the countess's body. The pistol was now pushed into the left side of her ribcage. Jessie stilled instantly. A shot discharged into her chest would be fatal.

"Now, here's what we are going to do," Lady Strathburn continued, her voice low, her words hot and hissing. "You and I are going to walk quietly downstairs and climb into my sedan chair. If you attempt to warn anyone or try to get away from me, I won't hesitate to shoot you. Do I make myself clear?"

Jessie nodded, attempting to tamp down her fear. *The woman must be mad.* But she dared not risk escape, not with a pistol cocked ready to kill her.

"Move!"

She did as the countess demanded, praying someone would appear and notice that she was being coerced into leaving. Surely Robert would be back soon. But the stairwell and vestibule were completely deserted as they made their descent. Even Gordon was nowhere to be seen.

The rather luxurious sedan chair and its two stoic bearers stood in the square directly outside Strathburn House. Sheets of rain teemed down upon Jessie as she emerged from the covered portico. She struggled not to slip on the wet stairs leading to the cobblestoned pavement. Within moments she was almost soaked through. Her damp hair hung in her eyes and her silk skirts clung to her legs, making it hard for her to climb into the cramped enclosure of the sedan. She hoped Lady Strathburn might lose her footing, but not once did the pistol's muzzle lose contact with her body.

Once inside, Lady Strathburn slammed the door and took a seat beside Jessie, the pistol now pushed directly into her side. Even though the countess's sedan was significantly more commodious than the hired one Jessie had taken a ride in the day before, she found herself pushed uncomfortably sideways against the Moroccan leather panel and curtain covered window on one side whilst Lady Strathburn's hip and leg were pressed hard against her on the other.

"I've heard gut shots are a particularly slow and painful way to die so I wouldn't be planning anything if I were you," threatened the countess. With her free hand, she knocked on the ceiling of the sedan, and despite the rain and the added weight of an additional person, the chairmen took off at a steady jog.

A small amount of light filtered into the enclosed cabin through a narrow crack in the curtains covering the door opposite the bench seat. In the dim interior, Jessie could just discern the unflinching hardness in the countess's eyes. Her heart plummeted like a stone. It would be difficult to reason with the woman, but she must try.

Jessie drew a shallow breath, her throat tight with fear. "Why are ye doin' this?"

An unnerving smile slowly spread across Lady Strathburn's face. "I think you know why. In case your silly little mind hasn't worked it out, your *fiancé* took Simon, so now I'm taking you. Simple."

Jessie raised her chin, a flash of anger giving her strength. "Ye willna succeed."

"Of course I will. Why should Robert be the only one who is allowed to get away with breaking the rules? Drastic circumstances call for drastic measures. When I have my son back, Robert can have you."

But will I be returned to Robert dead or alive?

Terror twisted Jessie's belly into tight knots. The cold, uncompromising expression in Lady Strathburn's eyes belied the notion that she was going to escape from this situation unscathed.

She looked away from the countess toward the window. Where were they going? With the velvet curtains drawn, it was impossible to see anything other than passing shadows. Icy spurts of fear prickled beneath her skin. She was shivering. Dare she ask what the countess intended? Perhaps if she knew more, she could think ahead and formulate a plan of some sort. Although there was little she could do at the moment, she would not give up on the idea of escape. She had too much to live for. She'd found love, and she knew that love was returned in full. She would take any chance she could to make her way back to Robert.

The sedan chair suddenly slowed. Jessie glanced out of the crack in the curtains, but could see little more than the back of the chairman and a splinter of dark gray sky. The sedan veered slightly as if negotiating an obstacle in the road, and then between the crowded rooftops, she caught a brief glimpse of the turrets of Holyrood Palace and its gate house.

"Wh-Where are we going?" Jessie's voice cracked with despair. Robert would never find her so far afield from Strathburn House. They could easily disappear down any one of the maze-like wynds or closes. Or worse still, venture into one of the more disreputable and desolate areas of Holyrood Park. The former royal hunting ground, complete with towering cliffs, gorse covered commons and boggy marshes covered a huge area of over six hundred acres. The area to the east around the Salisbury Crags would be largely deserted, especially on a day like today.

Lady Strathburn sighed. "Never you mind," she said with bored disdain. "Knowledge of your immediate destination will not help you in any way, if that's what you are thinking."

It suddenly occurred to Jessie that they could not be going too much farther in the sedan chair. If they were to leave the city's environs, Lady Strathburn must have some other conveyance waiting close by. She would have to act soon to free herself if that were the case. Her mind worked furiously: there must be someone else involved in the countess's scheme...

Somehow, Jessie found her voice again. "Who have ye enlisted to help ye? Ye canna think to carry out my kidnappin' all on yer own."

Lady Strathburn smirked. "Baird. You remember him, don't you? He was more than willing to help, especially when I offered him free use of you during your confinement. He's quite used to taking care of Simon's leavings."

Oh God, no. Bile rose to Jessie's throat and spots danced before her eyes. Horror like nothing she'd ever felt before threatened to overwhelm her. She dug her fingernails into her palms and willed herself not to pass out. If she did, there was no chance of escape.

She sucked in a breath and forced herself to look the countess directly in the eye. Was there any chance she could appeal to the woman's better self? "How can a high-born woman such as ye behave so unscrupulously and condone such depravity?" she demanded, her voice shaking with both fear and outrage. "Do ye no' have any sense of moral decency, Lady Strathburn? Please, I beg ye to reconsider—"

The countess suddenly thrust the pistol against Jessie's temple and leaned forward until their noses were almost touching. Her breath was sickly sweet against Jessie's mouth. "Now listen here, you conniving little slut—"

At that moment, the sedan chair lurched wildly to the side and hit the road with bone-jarring force. Jessie screamed and clutched frantically at the leather hand-strap by her head to stop herself from falling off the seat. Lady Strathburn tumbled into her, and Jessie felt the pistol's cold, hard muzzle push sharply into her temple. *Oh God, please don't let it go off.* One slip of the countess's finger and she'd be dead.

Through the haze of her fear, Jessie became aware of the great cacophony of noise outside—a horse's startled whickering followed by the crack of splintering wood and the sound of something crashing onto the cobbles, voices shouting and swearing.

Within seconds, the sedan's front door was thrown wide open and one of the chairmen looked in. "Are ye all right, milady? Mistress? I'm verra sorry, but there's been an accident. My partner slipped and has done himself a wee bit o' mischief. And a cart has overturned."

"Yes, of course we're all right. Out of my way, you stupid man." The countess shifted, gripping Jessie tightly around the shoulder with one hand as she hissed in her ear, "Climb out. Don't say a word, or I swear I will kill you."

Jessie nodded weakly, too paralyzed by fear to speak. Why hadn't the chairman noticed that the countess had a gun pressed to her head? Perhaps the muzzle was obscured by the damp, tangled mass of her hair. She whimpered but the man had already disappeared from view.

With no recourse other than to obey, Jessie somehow made her shaking limbs work and clambered out of the sedan chair. The countess continued to grip her shoulder as they both emerged, the pistol now pushed into Jessie's back. They were at the bottom of the Mile, in the very middle of the road where the Canongate, Water Gate, and the Abbey Strand intersected. The gate house to Holyrood Park stood right in front of them. And somewhere nearby, Baird must be waiting with a carriage.

No.

Jessie blinked against the needles of heavy rain lashing against her face as she frantically glanced about, unsure of what to do or which way to turn. All around her was chaos. The chairman who'd fallen was lying on the road, moaning horribly as he clutched his leg. His ankle was bent at the strangest angle. And there was blood. A protruding bone—

Oh God. Nausea swelled within Jessie at the gruesome sight. An overturned cart lying directly in front of her had lost its load. Apples, onions, cabbages, and heaven knew what else lay scattered across the streaming cobbles. A wild-eyed horse reared and whinnied. People were everywhere but they seemed focused on the chairman's plight, or were diverting approaching traffic. Someone was ringing a warning bell and several men tried to control the panicking horse.

I should break free now and run.

The pistol bit into Jessie's back again and the vice-like grip of the countess's hand about her shoulder increased.

Lady Strathburn would not be foiled so easily. "Keep walking. Move."

Jessie staggered around the cart and crossed the road, toward Holyrood's gates. Hope flickered at the thought the constable at the gate house might notice her plight, but the countess forced her to turn a sharp left toward the Leith Road, away from the melee. Away from any prospect of help.

Oh Lord save me. This can't be happening.

But it was. Jessie stumbled along the edge of the road, beneath the Water Gate, past the public well and the Back of the Canongate until the countess forced her to stop at the entrance to a filthy laneway. A row of tightly packed, dubious looking tenement houses, stables and warehouses stood on one side. A stretch of boggy plotted ground lay on the other.

"I-I don't know which way to go." Jessie's voice was thick with tears and desperation. She hadn't realized she was crying.

"Baird is waiting down there. Hurry up."

Lady Strathburn pushed her again and Jessie started forward, her legs stiff, her feet like lead weights. This couldn't be the end. She couldn't let Lady Strathburn get away with this.

I have to get back to Robert.

But how?

A deserted common yawned at the very end of the lane and just to the right, slightly obscured by a small copse of trees, was a plain black hackney carriage and a man... *Baird*. His dark hair was plastered over one side of his sallow, weasel-like face. As they drew closer, his mouth spread into a strange, lascivious smile.

No. Jessie halted and the countess crashed into her. "Lady Strathburn, I willna go with you."

CHAPTER 29

Where, in God's name, was Jessie?

Robert paused, his horse on the edge of Auldgate Close, looking frantically up and down the Royal Mile for any sign of his stepmother's sedan chair. Although the traffic was relatively sparse for this time of the day, his vision was hindered by the bucketing rain.

A torrent of fear coursed through his veins. His stepmother had kidnapped Jessie, he was certain of it. He castigated himself for having sent on Simon's letter to Strathburn House before he'd returned from seeing off the *Phoenix*. He should have anticipated that Caroline was capable of acting both rashly and callously, that she would not hesitate to take an eye for an eye. The woman had already demonstrated that she was corrupt to the very core.

Yet again his lack of foresight and judicious planning—brought about by his own arrogant overconfidence—had placed his beautiful young wife, the light who warmed his own dark soul, in imminent danger.

If anything happened to her, he would never forgive himself.

Fortunately, Gordon had seen Jessie and his stepmother climb into the countess's sedan chair less than ten minutes ago. They couldn't have gone far in this weather. But where would they be headed?

Robert narrowed his eyes against the icy splinters of driving rain and glanced down toward the end of the Canongate. The White Horse Inn and Holyrood Park lay that way. If Caroline was going to spirit Jessie away—or worse—he guessed she might head in that direction, rather than up the hill toward Edinburgh Castle where the Scots Guard regiment was stationed. Of course, there could be any number of obscure wynds or closes she could have directed her sedan down. If that were the case, it would be near on impossible to locate Jessie swiftly.

Robert angled his horse out into the main thoroughfare. The gutters and cobblestones were aflood—the conditions were indeed treacherous underfoot. The urge to travel faster than a steady trot was strong, but he kept his impatience tightly reined in. It would be easy for anyone, pedestrian or horse alike, to slip over on the road in this weather. He pushed down another surge of fear for Jessie; she must be terrified. And the idea of her being hurt, or worse... Robert's breath all but froze in his lungs. No, he must not panic. He needed to focus on locating the sedan, not on wild imaginings.

He'd traveled perhaps only a hundred yards down the Canongate when he noticed a commotion ahead not far from the gates of Holyrood. Voices shouting, a warning bell clanging, the distinctive neigh of a terrified horse.

What the hell had happened? Instinct told him it had something to do with Jessie.

Ignoring the risk, he kicked his horse forward toward the chaos in the street...and stopped short of what could possibly be a tableau from his worst nightmare. Between the wheel shafts of a splintered cart and the legs of the gathering crowd, he caught the fleeting glimpse of someone on the ground moaning horribly and writhing.

Oh no, no, no. His heart hurtling against his ribs, Robert leapt from his horse and pushed through the shocked bystanders.

Not Jessie. Thank God. It was a man—a sedan chair bearer by the looks of him—with a shocking ankle fracture. He winced in sympathy before scanning the faces around him.

Still no sign of his wife.

Then he saw it. Close by, beside the toppled cart stood his stepmother's sedan chair, the door hanging open. *Hell, was Jessie inside? Injured?*

Fear knifing through him again, Robert forced his way through the crowd and rushed over to the sedan.

There was no one inside.

Holy hell. Robert didn't know whether to curse God or thank him.

He straightened and turned around, scouring the dark openings to all of the nearby closes and wynds, then beyond the scene of the accident to the Abbey Close and Holyrood Park. Down Horse Wynd? Toward the busy road to Abbey Hill and Leith? Jessie must be close by. It was almost as if he could sense her presence.

There. Farther along, well past the Water Gate. He could just make out two female figures—one slender and redheaded, he'd wager—rounding a corner into another street.

Caroline was surely armed. Jessie would never have gone with his stepmother unless she had been compelled to. Thank Christ he'd thought to bring his own weapon—a pistol. Tucked into the waistband of his breeches at the small of his back, Robert's greatcoat hid it from view. Being seen with a proscribed weapon certainly wouldn't do him any favors if the Town or Scots Guard were about...or the High Constable stationed at the main gate into Holyrood. His probation could be revoked for even the most minor of transgressions, and that could not happen.

Not now he had a life worth living.

After finding and mounting his horse, Robert maneuvered the gelding through the crush of onlookers, then spurred him into a fast trot down Leith Road to the side street.

Yes. There they were at the end of the lane, heading toward a stand of trees and the edge of the wild common leading up to Calton Hill. Not wanting to waste time, but keenly aware that a silent approach was in order, Robert slid from his horse halfway along the narrow thoroughfare and handed the reins and a crown to an urchin boy lurking in the shadows between two boarding houses. He would follow on foot. Observe, then take action as required.

The sheeting rain continued unabated. It obscured Robert's gaze, but it also masked the splash of his footfalls as he traversed the muddy lane. Although his heart thundered in his chest and his belly twisted with anxiety, he couldn't afford to give into thought-robbing panic. He needed to keep a clear head. For Jessie.

On reaching the copse he halted and took cover, listening hard.

"Lady Strathburn, I willna go with you."

Jessie. His gut instincts had been right.

His stepmother spoke, her voice dripping with malice. "Ah, so you obviously want a bullet in you right now then—"

"You bluff, Lady Strathburn. You will no' have a hope of ever seeing yer son again if ye kill me. Robert will see to that, ye can be sure."

Good lass. Stall. Robert chanced a glance around the trees. There was a carriage. A tall, gaunt-faced, slightly built man seemed to be in the process of unlatching the carriage door and putting down the steps.

Caroline's next utterance reached Robert's ears and his blood raced, hot and angry through his veins. "Well, perhaps Baird can provide you with some incentive to cooperate. You'll get in the carriage, or I'll get him to fuck you right here, right now while I watch."

Robert ground his teeth together. *Over my dead body. Dispose of Baird, then deal with Caroline.* They wouldn't be going anywhere if there was no one to drive the carriage.

Taking advantage of the fact that everyone currently had their backs turned to him, Robert bent low and dashed over to a bedraggled clump of gorse bushes and a broken wooden fence to his left.

Hang on, my love, I'm close. Indeed, Jessie was less than a few yards away now. He caught a glimpse of Caroline's weapon—a heavy dueling pistol, by the looks of it—pressed into Jessie's back as the countess roughly pushed his handfasted wife toward the carriage.

Shit. He prayed his stepmother didn't have itchy fingers.

Baird stood to the side, near the traces, smirking as he stroked his groin with one hand, his attention on Jessie as she began to lift her skirts to climb into the carriage. *Bastard.*

Robert pulled his pistol out from the back of his breeches and focused his concentration, preparing to strike. A nice, clean hit to the back of the cur's head with the butt of his weapon would do.

Five fast paces, a short cracking blow and Baird was down. "Step away from Jessie, Caroline," Robert growled as he trained his pistol straight at his stepmother's head, "or you'll be dead before you know what's hit you."

Caroline shrieked and hauled Jessie up against her own body. The bitch might be trying to use Jessie as a shield, but at least her pistol was now aimed at him. "What have you done with my son?" she screeched, her aim wavering wildly as she spat out each word. Her face was white except for two ugly blotches of red, high on her cheekbones.

Jessie whimpered. Her eyes were wide, terrified. "Robert—"

Caroline yanked cruelly on Jessie's hair with her free hand. "Shut your mouth," she screamed.

Hell, the woman was more unstable than Robert had ever realized. He swallowed past the tight ball of fear suddenly jamming his throat. *God knew what his stepmother would do.* "Put the pistol down, Caroline, and I'll take you to Simon. I assure you, he's fine."

"Liar," cried the countess. "I don't believe you." There was a click— the distinct sound of a weapon being cocked.

Christ.

"No!" Jessie twisted in Caroline's grip, attempting to wrest away the pistol.

"Let go, you bitch." Caroline's face had contorted into an ugly, hate-filled mask. For the space of a heartbeat, the two women grappled with each other to gain control over the weapon.

Sweet Jesus Christ, no. If anything happened to Jessie... Robert lurched forward just as the women slipped in the mud and toppled to the ground, Jessie on top of Caroline.

A shot rang out.

No, no, no. "Jessie!" Terror ripping through him as surely as the bullet that had just been discharged, Robert lurched forward and eased Jessie away from his stepmother. *Blood. On both of them. No.* "Jessie, love?"

"I'm all right, Robert." Jessie reached for him and he fell into the mud holding her, rocking her in his arms as she sobbed against his neck. "I-I dinna ken what happened. I didna mean for the pistol to go off, but I thought she would kill you. It...it was an accident. Thank God, ye are all right too."

Yes. Thank God. As head-spinning relief swept through him, Robert stroked Jessie's dripping, tangled hair and her shuddering back. *Safe. His beautiful wife was safe.* He could scarcely fathom it. Not wanting to, but knowing that he had to, he then glanced down at his stepmother. She'd been shot in the chest. Left side. Stone dead.

We need to get away from here. "Jessie, lass. We must move. If anyone finds us with Lady Strathburn..."

Jessie sucked in a sharp breath and pulled back from his tight embrace. "Oh, my Lord, ye're right. Ye especially. Ye canna be seen here."

As they both clambered to their feet, Jessie's legs buckled momentarily. Robert swore and pulled her against him. After he'd pushed his pistol into the waistband at the front of his breeches, he shrugged off his greatcoat and wrapped it around her shaking body. He then swept her into his arms. "Hopefully my horse is still where I left him."

Thank heavens the young boy he'd entrusted was reliable. The lad accepted another handful of coins without a word, flashed Robert a gap-toothed grin, then scurried off into the murky shadows of one of the tenement houses. After placing Jessie on his mount, Robert swung up behind her and turned his horse in the direction of the Canongate again.

"Are we g-going home?" asked Jessie through chattering teeth.

Robert pulled her close against him as they trotted down the lane. "I'm afraid we're going to return to the scene of the accident, *mo chridhe*. There will be the Scots Guard, or at the very least the Town Guard looking about the place by now. They won't fail to notice the Strathburn coat of arms on the side of Caroline's sedan chair, and when questioned—and we undoubtedly will be—we will both attest that you've been there the whole time, and that I came upon you by chance after I'd farewelled the *Phoenix*. I'm counting on the fact that confusion is still reigning, and no one will have noticed our comings and goings. That no one will suspect that we've had anything to do with my stepmother's demise."

Jessie nodded. "I pray that ye are right. But...but what if the authorities arrest someone who's not to blame for what happened to Lady Strathburn?"

"Hopefully, that won't happen," Robert said grimly. "But I'll cross that particular bridge if it comes to it. Rest assured, I will not let an innocent take the blame for Caroline's death. However, my main objective at present is to protect you."

As they approached the foot of the Canongate, Robert could see a huge flurry of activity still around the sedan chair accident site. He estimated they must have only been gone ten minutes. With any luck, no one would have looked for Jessie or the countess yet.

He dismounted, then helped Jessie to alight. He took her hand. "Do you think you can walk from here?"

She nodded and gave him a tremulous smile "Aye."

Within half a minute, they'd reached the Royal Mile again. Robert secured his mount and then drew Jessie into the dark entrance of a nearby close so he could gather her into his arms. He could still barely believe she'd survived this nightmare unharmed. Crushing her body against his, he breathed in the sweet scent of her hair. Tears escaped from his eyes and mingled with the rain on his face and hers as he showered light kisses across her forehead and eyelids and cheeks. "Are you sure you're not hurt, my love?"

"I'm fine," Jessie murmured breathlessly, reaching up to push his wet hair away from his face. Her eyes locked with his, but he could see their expression was more solemn than relieved. She couldn't hide from him. The shadows of her ordeal still lingered in their depths and most probably would for some time to come. "Ye probably gathered yer stepmother was trying to kidnap me—to ransom me for Simon's return. I dinna know how ye found me."

"Gordon saw you leaving with my stepmother. Then the accident caught my attention. It's unfortunate, but if it hadn't been for that... I'll make sure the poor chairman and any family he has are well compensated."

Jessie nodded, then closed her eyes briefly before she focused her gaze back on him. "What about Baird, yer brother's valet?"

The muscles of Robert's jaw bunched tightly. "I'm sure that he's already come to, and if he has any brain at all, he'll beat a hasty retreat. He can go to hell, along with Simon and my stepmother. It's no less than they all deserve." As much as it grated, he was inclined to let Baird skulk away. And as Simon was now gone, he doubted he'd ever see the servant's face again. Baird was just damned lucky the terms of his probation tied his hands in meting out any form of real justice.

The clanging of another bell drew Robert's attention to the street. Reluctantly letting Jessie go, he turned around. An ambulance cart had at last arrived and the injured chairman was being moved onto a stretcher. A pair of Scots Guard soldiers and a few of the Town Guards could also be seen in amongst the other members of the crowd. In fact, the uninjured sedan chair attendant speaking with one of the dragoons suddenly pointed Jessie's way. Robert's heart rate kicked up a notch. It wouldn't be long before someone would want to question her. They would most certainly ask about the whereabouts of Lady Strathburn.

"Despite everything yer stepmother did...I'm verra sorry that things have ended this way," Jessie murmured. Emotion had thickened her voice. "For yer father's sake, at least. He must have loved her once."

Robert turned back, amazed at Jessie's capacity for compassion and forgiveness. She truly was a beautiful soul. He drew her into his arms again to not only offer her comfort but to reassure himself she really was safe...and that was when he felt the butt of his pistol pressing sharply into his hip bone.

Damn, bloody damn. If the Scots Guard or the Town Guards saw it, he was done for.

As surreptitiously as he could, Robert slid the pistol behind his back and tucked it into his breeches, praying his woolen riding jacket would be enough to conceal the suspicious bulge. He had nowhere better to hide it. His greatcoat was still draped around Jessie's shoulders and she clearly needed it; not only for warmth but to cover the blood stains on the front of her drenched blue gown.

To think he'd nearly lost her...

"I don't care about anything else except for the fact that you are safe, and with me," Robert murmured, gently pushing strands of damp hair away from Jessie's eyes. He cradled her lovely face in his hands, brushing his thumbs lightly along her cheekbones where traces of her tears and the rain still lingered. His attention dipped to her mouth. He shouldn't steal a kiss out here in the street, but—

It seemed Jessie's thoughts were in concert with his. "Kiss me," she breathed, and Robert suddenly found himself drowning in the warm glow of her whisky-brown eyes.

Dear Lord, how could he resist? "Whatever my lady-wife desires," he whispered.

He meant the kiss to be soft and lingering, a gentle homage to everything Jessie meant to him, but it soon became apparent that his passionate wife had other ideas. When she grasped the back of his head and moved her mouth urgently against his, he lost control of all the pent-up emotion within him and returned her kiss with equal ardor. And the mad world behind them disappeared.

Robert pushed her against the brick wall of the close and devoured all she offered. His tongue and lips explored her mouth thoroughly, savoring her heady sweetness. Jessie's hands slid beneath his jacket and frantically clutched at the wet linen clinging to his chest and back; her hands were everywhere, as if she wanted to rip his shirt away. He, too, was impatient to touch Jessie's skin. The wet silk of her gown was suddenly a barrier he couldn't tolerate. His hunger for her, all of her, was growing steadily with each passing moment. He pushed his hand under the folds of the greatcoat, seeking her breast ...

"Now, now, Lord Lochrose. Dinna make me arrest ye for engaging in inappropriate displays of affection and harassment of a lady in a public place."

Robert dragged his head up and looked over his shoulder. Captain MacBryde, atop a fine cavalry steed, was right behind them. *Damn the man to hell.*

Panic spiked. Robert prayed the soldier's keen eyes hadn't noticed the outline of the pistol butt beneath his jacket. He pulled Jessie closer to his body to hide the telling blood stains on her gown.

Despite the officer's outwardly stern expression though, Robert thought he detected a glint of amusement in the man's eyes. Clearing his throat, he said smoothly enough, "I'm just taking care of my wife, Captain. She was in the sedan chair with Lady Strathburn, you know."

Captain MacBryde raised an eyebrow. "I see." To his credit, the man did not baulk in the slightest at Robert's use of the word *wife* when he'd referred to Jessie. He glanced behind Robert to Jessie. "Do you know where Lady Strathburn is then, milady?"

The question was inevitable. Robert felt Jessie stiffen in his arms, but she held the captain's gaze steadily. "I'm afraid no', Captain. Ye see, I took a wee bump to the head and in all the confusion I'm no' sure what happened."

Robert smiled inwardly. He was nothing but impressed with Jessie's quick thinking and display of *sangfroid*.

MacBryde was frowning. "Are ye sure ye're all right?"

"I'm quite well, Captain," Jessie replied with apparent calmness. Her mouth lifted into a shy smile as she added, "Especially now my Lord Lochrose is here to look after me."

Perhaps still sensing something was amiss, the captain's gaze darted to Robert, before returning to Jessie. Given the incident this morning, and the peculiarity of Jessie accompanying the countess in a sedan chair meant for one, it was no wonder he was suspicious. Nevertheless, he merely smiled back and inclined his head. "Perhaps I could call on you later this afternoon at Strathburn House to take yer statement about the accident."

"That would be quite all right," said Jessie with an elegant tilt of her head. "We shall expect you."

MacBryde's brow suddenly creased with mock sternness. "And are ye sure this man isna bothering ye, Lady Lochrose? I can still have him arrested if he is, ye ken."

Her smile widened. "I can assure you, Captain, that I'm being verra well taken care of."

MacBryde grinned as he caught Robert's eye. "Well, as you were then, milord." He turned his horse away.

Robert gathered Jessie close again and cast her the lopsided smile meant only for her—the woman he loved more than anything, his wife. "Who am I to disobey the law?"

EPILOGUE

Lochrose Castle, Strathspey, Scotland
April 1758
Almost two years later...

The mirror-like waters of Loch Kilburn reflected the clear blue sky and the spring green foliage of the surrounding woods when Robert and Jessie chose a place to share their picnic. A weeping willow tree seemed as good a place as any to spread their blanket amidst the clusters of daffodils and purple crocuses. To Jessie, it seemed like their own private paradise.

It had been some weeks since they'd managed to steal some time alone together during the day. Their infant son, William Robert Alasdair Grant—or Will, as Jessie was wont to call him—had only recently settled down for a proper sleep after a few fractious days and nights of teething. Although Annie Shaw, Tobias's cousin, had made an excellent nursemaid, it was not until this morning that Jessie had felt comfortable enough to leave their precious seven-month-old son for more than a few hours. Dark-haired like Robert, brown-eyed like herself, he was a beautiful boy, healthy and strong, with generally—teething aside—a happy disposition and ready smile.

Just like his father, Jessie thought as she glanced at Robert. He was unpacking the bread, cheese, and French Chablis from the basket Mrs. MacMillan had packed. A lock of his dark hair had fallen across his brow, hiding his deep blue eyes from view. He'd removed his jacket and top boots, and was now dressed only in a linen shirt—open at the neck —and buckskin breeches, thanks to the warm weather. She was suddenly hungry, but not for what was being spread before her on the blanket.

Jessie smiled to herself, contemplating how they would spend the next few hours. Yes, today she was determined to enjoy every single moment she had alone with her handsome husband. She knew they could count on complete privacy here by the loch. There was no one else at Lochrose, save for their son, who could have any reason to claim their time. After all, Lord Strathburn and her father were currently in Inverness on estate business and were not likely to return for another few days.

Even though she was now a viscountess, her father had chosen to continue on as factor. He'd reasoned that the estate would need to have the best of managers to ensure his grandchildren would be inheriting the healthiest of legacies, after a decade of neglect by Simon. And Robert and Lord Strathburn had been happy for him to do so.

Robert had seen that in a very short space of time, her father had made a real difference to the estate's profitability. In fact, it had taken only six months for the estate, under her father's careful stewardship, to generate enough income for the reacquisition of the land which had been sold off to pay the mountainous debts of Lady Strathburn and Simon.

With the restoration of Clan Grant lands and rapid replenishment of the family coffers—helped, in part, by the sale of Robert's ships the *Phoenix* to Captain Drummond, and the *Griffon*, to a friend by the name of Alexander MacIvor—Robert was able to offer what he considered suitable compensation to all the clan families who'd lost someone at Culloden. Jessie suspected that Robert's guilt would never be completely assuaged, but she knew he was less troubled than he had been before.

Of course, her father had been initially confounded—and perhaps secretly, more than a wee bit troubled—at the unseemly haste with which she'd become handfasted to Lord Lochrose. Jessie, out of a desire to spare her father unnecessary disquiet, had provided him with a highly edited tale of the events which had taken place over the tumultuous seven days that had brought her and Robert together. She did not like to lie to her father, but detailing all of her near misses —particularly at the hands of Simon and Lady Strathburn—would only cause him stress and would not do a thing to alter what had occurred.

Naturally, her father had also been deeply concerned that she was marrying a reprobate of the first order, even though Lord Lochrose was now a pardoned Jacobite. But Jessie had soon convinced him that Robert genuinely cared for her and she for him, and that she did indeed wish to be his wife. And so it was on a clear, snow-powdered day in November of 1756 that her father had happily walked her down the aisle of Kilburn Kirk to be officially wed to her reformed gentleman Jacobite. It had been one of the most joyous days of Jessie's life.

Lord Strathburn continued to be the most gracious of fathers-in-law, despite Jessie's humble background. He always made her feel like she was Robert's perfect match, and for that she was most grateful. Even after a year-and-a-half of marriage to a peer of the realm, Jessie still found it difficult to believe she would be the next Countess of Strathburn, and that her bonnie wee babe would one day take his father's place as the earl. She felt truly blessed for all that she'd been given, not the least of which was her most beloved and loving husband.

Lord Strathburn had quietly mourned the untimely death of his wife. After the countess's body had been discovered with Simon's dueling pistol in a deserted laneway near Calton Hill, there had of course, been an investigation. Fortunately, Captain MacBryde had believed both her own and Robert's stories—that she had been dazed after the sedan chair accident, and that Robert had come upon her as he'd been returning from Leith Docks. As for Baird, he was never seen or heard from again.

Given the lack of evidence to explain the untimely end of Lady Strathburn, the coroner had ultimately made a finding of "death by misadventure" rather than suicide, much to the relief of the scandal-mired Strathburns. Jessie thanked God every day that she and Robert had both somehow managed to escape unscathed.

Jessie suspected Lord Strathburn felt both the sorrow of losing a woman he'd once loved as well as the disappointment of realizing how bitter and vengeful she'd become. But he'd slowly adapted to the life of a widower. Indeed, it was evident to both Jessie and Robert that the earl's recently recovered *joie de vivre* and vigor had directly coincided with the birth of young Will. Lord Strathburn was very much the doting grandfather—though he had stringent competition—and could often be found in the nursery or the garden, dandling his laughing grandson on his knee.

Jessie also firmly believed that Robert's return home, together with the arrival of a healthy grandson, were the only reasons her father-in-law was able to cope with another loss in his life—the unexpected death of Simon.

Word of Simon's demise had come to Lochrose a little over a year ago. After the *Phoenix* had departed for the Caribbean, Robert had sent word of Lady Strathburn's death to Drummond via another merchant ship bound for Jamaica. According to Drummond, Simon had not taken the news well. He had, by all accounts, gotten horrendously drunk in a tavern in a highly disreputable part of Kingston, and had been killed in a taproom brawl.

Jessie knew that Robert had fully intended to release Simon from his tenure aboard the *Phoenix* once a year and a day had passed. Drummond had reported that prior to putting into port in Kingston, Simon had actually started to show some acceptance of his lot and had begun to willingly participate as an active crewmember aboard the ship. This news had comforted Lord Strathburn a little. The idea that his youngest son had demonstrated some strength of character indicated that perhaps at last, Simon had seen the error of his ways and was actively attempting to reform himself.

As for Robert, Jessie knew in her heart that the deep scars he'd borne for so long were beginning to heal. He'd embraced his life here at Lochrose. Reveled in it. She could see it every day in his easy smiles and the laughter frequently alight in his blue eyes...or oftentimes it was desire. Indeed, the eyes regarding her now contained a decidedly heated, speculative look as he handed her a glass of wine.

Jessie accepted the cool, pale Chablis and gave her husband a deliberately provocative smile. Keeping her eyes locked with Robert's, she took a sip, then she carefully placed the glass to the side of the blanket. She wondered if he'd already guessed what her plan was. Although they'd been married nearly eighteen months, they'd never once visited the loch to make love. It was definitely time for her and Robert to create a new and lasting memory of their own in this beautiful place.

Robert raised a dark eyebrow. "The wine is not to your taste, my love?"

Jessie smiled again and began to fiddle with the ribbons lacing the front of her gown's bodice. "It's lovely, but...I rather think I hunger for the taste of something else right now."

She noticed the immediate flare of reciprocal hunger in Robert's eyes as she continued to loosen the ribbons, slowly revealing her fine lawn chemise. She'd deliberately chosen this dress—a gorgeous albeit frivolous creation of pale lemon and ivory striped silk with a low scooped neckline and trailing ivory lace sleeves—for its combination of prettiness and ease of removal.

Since seduction of her husband had been foremost in her mind as she'd readied for the picnic, she'd also dispensed with wearing stays. Jessie let her gown slip off her shoulders before she proceeded to slowly undo the three pearl buttons fastening the front of her chemise, one by one. All the while, Robert was watching her with eager and avid attention.

He leaned back on one elbow, his long legs and naked feet extending out across the dark blue wool rug, the wine glass he held in his fingers all but forgotten. When she dropped her eyes to the telling swell within his breeches, she felt the force of her own arousal begin to pulse deep within her. Her breathing quickened and her nipples hardened to tight, aching points.

What was more arousing? How he looked, or how he looked at her?

Her breasts now free of the constraining fabric of her bodice and chemise, Jessie set about the task of slowly unpinning her hair from the carefully styled arrangement on top of her head, letting the long curls tumble about her bare shoulders. She knew Robert loved it when she wore her hair unbound, and her husband's eyes didn't leave her once. She was thrilled to see that the pace of his breathing had increased as well.

"I think it's a wee bit warm today, milord, and ye're wearing decidedly too many clothes, dinna you agree?" Jessie asked, her voice husky with want. She leaned forward and set aside his wine glass before loosening the cuffs on his sleeves and pulling the shirt from the waistband of his breeches.

She was about to lift the garment over his head when Robert sat forward and pulled the shirt off himself, throwing it onto the grass unheeded. Her eyes dropped briefly to take in the sheer beauty of his lean, well-muscled torso. His mouth was now a mere breath away from hers. She licked her lips and his mouth tipped into a wolfish smile.

"Still hungry?" her husband asked, his lips brushing against hers as he spoke. He sought to tease her too, but she was not finished with him, not by any means.

Jessie kissed him lightly on the mouth before drawing back. "Verra much so. But I think I'm in the mood for something a wee bit more full-bodied than a kiss."

After eighteen months of wedded bliss to a passionate, loving man, she was shy no more when it came to giving and receiving physical pleasure. Not that she ever really *had* been when it came to Robert.

Robert let her push him back onto the rug and she ran her fingers over the hard planes of his chest and ridged abdomen until she reached his breeches, delighting in the way he was holding his breath, waiting.

Jessie flicked the buttons of his fall front open with tantalizing slowness, deliberately building his anticipation until at last, his engorged member sprang free. An intensely hot thrill shivered through her.

He was all hers to do with as she liked.

Smiling, she caught his heavy-lidded gaze and brushed one of her peaked nipples across the head of his cock, noting with satisfaction his sharp intake of breath. She lazily ran her fingers down the long, rock-hard shaft until she grasped him firmly around the base, the better to hold him steady as she feasted.

No longer able to resist the temptation he offered, she bent her head and swirled her tongue around the ruddy head, glorying in the silky texture and musky taste of his sex.

Delicious.

He groaned and she felt his hands twist into her hair. She took as much as she could of his rigid length into her mouth, sucking rhythmically up and down with hot sliding suction, knowing just how much aching pleasure she was imparting.

Jessie reveled in the power she had over him, thrilled to hear him pant and groan her name as he began to lose control and swell even more in her mouth...until he exploded and she drank willingly of his warm, salty seed. Raising her head, Jessie licked her lips and smiled down at her husband as he lay sprawled before her, spent and gasping. There was no sight in the world she could ever possibly enjoy more.

When Robert opened his eyes at last, they were dark, almost black with desire. He reached up and pulled her head down to claim her mouth, his tongue stroking and teasing her thoroughly whilst he gently tugged and rolled one of her nipples with the fingers of his other hand. Jessie moaned and he released her mouth.

"My turn now," he growled before rolling her underneath him. "You're not the only one who's starving, *mo chridhe.*"

Robert looked down at the beautiful woman beneath him and tipped his mouth into a slow, crooked smile. The divine creature that was his wife had taken her fill. Now it was definitely his turn to taste and tease until she shuddered and cried out his name.

He'd already suspected that she had more than a picnic in mind when she'd asked Mrs. MacMillan to pack a basket for luncheon. Will, their joyful, healthy son, had been all smiles in the nursery earlier so he knew Jessie would be happy to leave the babe in the care of his nurse for most of the afternoon.

Which meant he'd been looking forward to this time alone with Jessie all morning.

No, that wasn't quite true. If Robert were brutally honest with himself, he knew he'd longed to make love to Jessie by the loch from the moment he'd first laid eyes on her, right here, all that time ago. For the life of him he didn't know why he hadn't thought to organize a lakeside tryst sooner.

But his wife had, and he was about to thank her.

He claimed her sweet siren's mouth and caressed the sensitive undersides of her full breasts with feather-light touches that provoked her rose-pink nipples into tight succulent buds. She shifted so that his fingers grazed over the furled points.

He smiled against her lips as he gave one of her nipples a gentle pinch. "Do you want me to taste you here, *mo ghaoil*?"

"Aye," Jessie murmured, burying her hands in his hair and pushing his head down as she arched up. "Ye torture me with wantin'."

"Hmm. Well, let me see if I can ease the pain." Robert dipped his head and began to suckle and lave each breast in turn until she was panting and squirming, her legs and hips pushing against his, making his cock throb all over again.

He rose up onto his knees and lifted her skirts, running his hands up her stocking-clad calves, then over her bare slender thighs until he reached the tight ginger curls that hid her sex. She parted her legs willingly, and he smiled with lazy satisfaction when he saw how she glistened with moisture. He was going to enjoy this.

Robert slid this thumbs along her folds, parting them gently until he had exposed the hard nub of her clitoris. Hot lust pounded through him at the sight, making him dizzy. Bending forward, he delicately flicked her quivering center with his tongue. Jessie gasped and her hands twisted into the blanket beneath her.

"More?" he murmured, glancing up along her body to meet her gaze. He was pleased to see desire had darkened her eyes to the color of molten honey.

"Much more," his wanton wife panted as she spread herself wider.

This time when Robert lowered his mouth, it was to sup with reckless abandon until he'd sampled every part of his wife's delicious sex. Her musk-scented dew was like manna from heaven on his lips and tongue. He couldn't get enough, especially when she writhed beneath him, arching her hips and pulling his hair. The thing he relished most of all was hearing her increasingly frenzied gasps and moans until she neared, then reached her peak. Bringing his wife to a spectacular, quaking, cataclysmic finish was one of his principal joys in life. It always would be.

Robert looked up from between Jessie's thighs as her soft cries of ecstasy began to fade. Even though she appeared thoroughly sated, he wasn't done yet. His cock was definitely ready again. "I'm afraid I'm still ravenous, my lady."

Her eyes flew open, and she laughed, a sensual throaty sound. "You are a greedy man, Lord Lochrose."

"Always when it comes to you, *mo ghaoil*."

He gently drew Jessie upright so that she was kneeling. Her fiery hair was tangled all about her bare shoulders, but the sleeves of her gown still managed to cling to her upper arms. The scar where his bullet had grazed her had long since faded. He placed a soft kiss on the faint mark, then eased her sleeves and chemise down until her upper body was completely bare except for her wildly tumbling locks.

He swallowed, drinking her in. Jessie was indeed a goddess. And she was all his.

Robert lay down, then lifted his wife upward and forward until she was straddling him, her warm slick folds teasing the head of his cock. She smiled, gold heat flaring in her eyes as she reached down to grasp the base of him before sinking down gracefully, almost languidly, taking his throbbing shaft deep inside her. The moist heat and clenching muscles of her body were almost Robert's undoing. Dear God, he was suspended between agony and ecstasy.

He gritted his teeth, willing himself not to give into the urge to spend straightaway like a green youth. As if sensing the tenuous grip he had on his control, Jessie stilled. She didn't rock or bob or pulse. Instead, she bent down and kissed him gently, easing his tension a fraction.

When he'd regained sufficient mastery over his urges, Robert locked his gaze with hers.

"Ride me, my love," he all but growled, gripping her hips and encouraging her to set the rhythm of their coupling. "Ride me however you like."

Jessie took his cue and rose slowly up then down, up then down, establishing a deliciously unhurried pace. The sliding friction of her tight wet passage, the way she clasped his engorged flesh, all of it—everything she did to him—was the most exquisite of tortures.

Of course, it wasn't long before they were both overwhelmed by the need to find ecstasy. Jessie's breath started to come in short, ragged gasps as Robert bucked his hips harder and faster, perfectly matching the tempo of her wild plunging. When she leaned forward, bracing her weight on the ground by his shoulders, he cupped her breasts and plundered her mouth, pushing his tongue deep inside. He couldn't get enough of her.

And then at last, Robert felt Jessie spasm convulsively around his pumping length. She threw her head back and cried out with pleasure. As her body rippled around him in greedy climax, his own release was immediately triggered. With a long guttural groan, Robert lost himself in Jessie, his seed erupting into her clenching womb. Replete, sated at last, he buried his face in her neck and breathed in the sweet, intoxicating scent that was so essentially her, glorying in the knowledge of their shared bliss.

And love.

Jessie raised her head and stroked the tangled, damp hair from his brow. Her eyes glowed with deep emotion. "I love you, Robert Grant," she whispered. "Ye're the master of my heart and body and soul. Do no' ever doubt it."

Robert framed his wife's beloved face with his hands, holding her warm gaze with his. This woman, his Jessie, she'd captured his heart and soul from the first moment he'd seen her, his lady of the loch. She made him feel whole again. Healed.

"And I am yours, Jessie Grant, completely. Now and always," he stated with absolute sincerity.

Her answering smile, soft and languid, was all the invitation Robert needed to claim her mouth again. He pushed his fingers gently into her hair and kissed her deeply yet with tender reverence, wanting her to know not just through words, but his touch, that his whole world began and ended with her.

And he would never stop loving her. Ever

AUTHOR'S NOTE

Dear Reader, you've no doubt noticed that the hero of *The Master of Strathburn*, Robert Grant, has not one, but two courtesy titles. While this isn't common, I believe it isn't unheard of. The seventh Earl of Glencairn (a title that is now extinct) was apparently known as Lord Kilmaur *and* the Master of Glencairn when he was the heir apparent. So, my Robert Grant is both the Master of Strathburn and Viscount Lochrose. (And of course, this is a work of fiction.)

I will admit, I used a little poetic license with regard to the Inverness to Edinburgh public coach Jessie Munroe attempts to catch. At the time *The Master of Strathburn* is set, 1756, there appears to have been a public coach that ran from Glasgow to Edinburgh once a week from around 1678 and twice per week from 1749. However, a regular public coach service did not operate between Inverness and the township of Perth (en route to Edinburgh) until 1806. As I needed a coach for my heroine, I have deliberately tweaked this historical detail to suit my story.

Robert's release from the Tolbooth by the Lord Advocate into his father's custody appears swift, but releases of this nature were not without precedent. There are numerous accounts of how Aeneas Mackintosh—Chief of Clan Mackintosh and a supporter of King George—was captured at the Battle of Prestonpans during the "45," but was then released into the custody of his Jacobite sympathizer wife, Anne Farquharson-Mackintosh or "Colonel Anne" by Prince Charles Edward Stuart, the "Bonnie Prince." Following the Battle of Culloden, "Colonel Anne" was arrested by government troops, but after six weeks, she was apparently released into the custody of her husband. For the purposes of my story, I chose to have Robert paroled in a similar fashion.

There are several historical figures that appear in *The Master of Strathburn*. Robert Dundas of Arniston, the younger (1713–1787) served as Lord Advocate—the chief legal advisor to the Crown and British government for both civil and criminal matters—from 1754 to 1760. In 1756, Lord Arniston was indeed a newly wedded man—he married his second wife, Jean Grant, daughter of William Grant, Lord Prestongrange in September of that year. It is purely poetic license on my part that Lord Arniston is depicted as being particularly lenient when dealing with my entirely fictional character, Robert Grant.

Governor George Haldane, who makes a brief appearance at the beginning of the story, was a general who fought in the 2nd Jacobite Rebellion. In 1756, at the age of thirty-four, he was appointed to the office of Governor of Jamaica.

The Tolbooth that Robert is imprisoned in is not the same building one can visit today along the Canongate in Edinburgh. The Old Tolbooth, which no longer stands, was located in the middle of Edinburgh's High Street, at the northwest corner of St Giles Cathedral. Constructed in the 14th century, over the years it functioned as a toll collection booth, a council chamber, and courthouse. The Tolbooth was used as jail from the late fifteenth century. It was demolished in 1817.

Although the name of the popular English pudding "Spotted Dick" is attested from 1849 when it first appeared in the cookbook *The Modern Housewife, or Ménagère* by Alexis Soyer, it appears to have been a popular dessert in Britain for some time prior to this. The origins of the pudding's unique name are unclear.

And lastly, while Grantown—now Grantown-on-Spey—appears to have been established in 1765, there was apparently an older village in the area prior to this. And of course, Dunraven Hall, Lochrose Castle, Loch Kilburn, and Auldgate Close are my inventions too.

THANK YOU FROM THE AUTHOR

Thank you so much for reading **The Master of Strathburn**, Book 1 in my Highland Rogue series! If you have the time and inclination, please do consider sharing a review. I would greatly appreciate it!

Amy Rose Bennett

~

WANT TO READ MORE IN THE HIGHLAND ROGUE SERIES?
THE LAIRD OF BLACKLOCH
HIGHLAND ROGUE, BOOK 2

Revenge might be sweet, but love is far sweeter…

Following the Battle of Culloden, Alexander MacIvor returns to his ancestral home, Blackloch Castle, only to find the Earl of Tay, the chief of a rival clan, has laid waste to everything he holds dear. Alex seems doomed to live the life of a fugitive Jacobite...until a stroke of luck allows him to escape the Highlands and begin again. Years later, styling himself as a wealthy Englishman, Alex reclaims his forfeited estate, becoming the new Laird of Blackloch. But it's not nearly enough to quell his thirst for vengeance. Hell-bent on destroying Lord Tay, he single-mindedly sets about driving his nemesis to bankruptcy. When Alex learns Tay intends to wed the English heiress, Miss Sarah Lambert, he devises a devious plan: kidnap Sarah and ransom her to hasten Tay's ruin.

Abducted and whisked away into the wild Highlands by a wicked rogue she knows only as Alexander Black, Sarah Lambert refuses to be a pawn in the man's diabolical schemes. Even though she discovers her fiancé, Lord Tay, is faithless and not the man she thought he was, she determines that somehow, some way, she will regain her freedom. If only she could unlock the secrets of her darkly handsome, enigmatic captor...

Living in such close quarters, Alex and the spirited Sarah soon find that even the best laid plans can go awry when passion flares and perhaps even love sparks. When the shadows of the past begin to gather, will this Jacobite rogue and English rose find their way forward together...or will the threatening darkness destroy them both?

DON'T MISS AMY ROSE BENNETT'S OTHER ROMANCES...

Visit Amy Rose Bennett's website at **www.amyrosebennett.com** to find out more about her books...

SCANDALOUS REGENCY WIDOWS

Lady Beauchamp's Proposal, Book 1
The Ice Duchess, Book 2
A Most Unsuitable Countess, Book 3

IMPROPER LIAISONS

An Improper Proposition, Book 1
An Improper Governess, Book 2
An Improper Christmas, Book 3
An Improper Duke, Book 4

About the Author

Amy Rose Bennett is an award-winning Australian author who has a passion for penning emotion-packed historical romances and more recently, historical rom-coms with a dash of fantasy. A former speech pathologist, Amy is happily married to her very own romantic hero and has two lovely, exceedingly accomplished adult daughters. When she's not creating stories, Amy loves to cook up a storm in the kitchen, lose herself in a good book, and when she can afford it, travel to all the places she writes about.

Visit Amy's website at **www.amyrosebennett.com** to find out more.